Morgan Gallagher is in her late 40s, spending her writing life with vampires. they refuse to go away and leave her a Borders, with her husband and their six for her husband who is severely disabled, Morgan also works as a volunteer for several charities and is passionate about the rights of babies, children and mothers. She has campaigned vigorously against child detention during immigration procedures. She and her husband home educate their son and attempt to keep a never ending stream of cats under control. The North Sea pounds their fishing village every winter, and every major storm, the entire family are to be found in the car parked on the headland admiring the view. Apart from the cats, that is, who are at home dreaming of summer.

Changeling

Book one in the Dreyfuss Trilogy

Morgan Gallagher

Ethics Trading

CHANGELING
By Morgan Gallagher
Published by Ethics Trading
© Copyright 2011 by Morgan Gallagher
ISBN: 978-0-9556887-3-7

Discover other titles by Morgan Gallagher through
www.ethicstrading.com.

Contact Morgan Gallagher:

http://thedreyfusstrilogy.blogspot.com/
Twitter: @DreyfussTrilogy
http://www.facebook.com/TheDreyfussTrilogy

Cover design by Morwenna Rakestraw.
Editing by Toni Rakestraw at unbridlededitor.com

This book is dedicated to the work of

Women Against Rape

and the

Black Women's Rape Action Project

who have been fighting to keep women and children safe, since 1976 and 1991, respectively.

Please donate to them, via the button found on
http://www.womenagainstrape.net/women-against-rape

or send monies to them via
Crossroads Women's Centre
230a Kentish Town Rd
London NW5 2AB

"It took me two sittings to read it. Why two, because I started reading in at 8pm. If I had started earlier, this would have been one of those books you don't put down until the last page and you read that twice not wanting the adventure to be over. Morgan has mastered the emotional ride... a new talent to be discovered."

Betty Carlton

"It was impossible to put down, disturbing and intriguing at the same time."

Alison Sauer

"...brutal and visceral -- so well written that it was almost physically painful to read. [*it does*]... a very good job of depicting physical and psychological torture – people either crack into catatonia or fight with every scrap of their being. Even when fighting means taking it passively. "

Dr Christine Whitley

"This is a very smart, well-written novel. It delves deep into the psychology of both the abuser and the abused. It contains graphic scenes of physical, psychological and sexual abuse that will upset those made queasy by portrayals of torture. But... this isn't splatterpunk. It's purposeful. So if you can handle that, you won't find a much better vampire tale than *Changeling*. ... I think that fiction should both entertain and make you think. It's surprisingly difficult to find novels that do both. *Changeling* does."

Alan Ryker

CHAPTER ONE

The door slammed shut with the deadened finality that comes with the emptying of a living space. Silence filled in behind her, flooding the rooms with despair. The air in her bedroom, thick with deodorant, hairspray, floral shower gel and perfume, settled into scented layers around the debris of her work clothes. The cat, nonchalant about her absence now it had been fed, climbed onto the front room window sill, looking out on its domain of kebab shops and off licences. Endless traffic piled the corners, hooting and groaning as it snuffed along, pouring stink into the already sickly late afternoon air. It felt more like the middle of September, than that of April. The cat preferred the view over the back windows, endless roofs, tantalising birds and other cats to snarl at. It would wait until the acrid chemical smells in the other room faded, before proceeding to settle in its usual spot, angled out to the inner square of the backs of the houses. It would mewl and scratch fruitlessly on the glass at the outside wild life: desperate to be free to attack, to chase. Or so it thought. Once, a pigeon had settled on an open window sill in the summer's heat, and the poor cat, comfortable and safe in its window glass world, had hissed in fright. It was so big, so aggressive, compared to the small fluttering victims of its day dreams, tiny and fragile on the roof spars opposite. The bird had eyed him coldly, without fear. The cat had hissed and growled its warning, but it had had no effect. It was a stand off until the bird flew away, unruffled. Since then, the cat went into a frenzy any time a bird landed on the other side of the window. The other side of the closed window.

Had she known it was the last time she'd abandon both the cat, and her flat, she might have washed the dishes. As it was, she had rushed around the flat, ignoring the smell from the sink. That morning, as she'd fallen out of bed to find that only her best suit was wearable, she'd planned to come in tonight and clean, ridding her life of the guilt the week had scattered around her. The resolution had been spurred on by the blissful thought of a Saturday morning lie in. A pristine flat all around her, requiring no effort on her behalf. Her change of plans, however, had left her with less than twenty minutes to bathe and change: she had once more ignored the chaos. Stopping only to throw some biscuits in the bowl (tinned food stank the place out) she vowed her allegiance to the hum drum of living; tomorrow. She'd do it all tomorrow. Clean out the cat litter, empty the bins, do the laundrette run and find her bedroom carpet under the skin of peeled off clothes that she kicked out of her way to find a matching shoe. Tomorrow would be good enough, and Sunday morning would be the sweet spot, as she lay in bed wondering how to fill a lazy day. She grabbed her keys and ran, heading off down the stairs at full pelt.

After four days unexplained absence, during which all answer phone messages had been ignored, her boss finally called the mother of her erstwhile assistant. Mrs Maitland, to the embarrassment of all concerned, exploded into tears at the thought of her only child's fate. A day later, after some hemming and hawing, the police were called, forcing open the flat in absence of anyone with a spare key. They found the dishes partially in the sink, partially on the floor, courtesy of an exceptionally hungry cat. The cat took its revenge on the probationary policewoman, leaving a trail of claw marks across her cheek. The sergeant, who had cautioned against such inappropriate action, handed a clean handkerchief over and called in the RSPCA. Their elbow length leather gauntlets would handle the animal, which had conveniently hidden itself inside the fold down couch in the living room cum kitchenette. He had never had any truck with people who took free ranging creatures and locked them into tiny fourth floor flatlets, or patted them as if human sentimentality could mitigate a completely empty stomach. He left his charge dabbing at the blood and had a good look round.

There was a strong whiff of cat in the air. Cat sick, and well developed litter tray. Having scoured both rooms of what little food there was, the cat had evidently chewed through the motley crew of long suffering pot plants scattered awkwardly around, subsequently throwing up with abandon. Splotches on the carpet and furnishings tracked its comings and goings, mostly goings. It was a very annoyed cat, he had no doubt of that. The smell was one that the sergeant could easily stomach, was greatly relieved by, given what else there might have been in evidence, both of the girl's disappearance and the cat's subsequent hunger. As it was, there was no sign of the girl. The usual clutter of single living met his eyes; the fridge testament to the overall lack of care, or comfort, this young woman had afforded herself. Diet drinks, weeks' dead salad, a dehydrated lump of cheese, rancid low fat spread and half a mouldy loaf. Two bottles of white wine and half a carton of milk, long turned to cheese. The bin, before it had been dragged around the floor, had been stuffed with various take away containers and two empty bottles of wine. She preferred Chinese, apparently, as the Chinese was six doors down, after the chip shop and the kebab house. On the other hand, the Chinese was first if you were walking back from the tube. The cupboard had several packets of fat free powdered soups, all well past their sell by date. The usual collection of tins and half a bottle of cheap vodka. The vodka had dust on the edges: no clues there then. The bread bin was stuffed with chocolate biscuits and crisps. The cramped and musty shower room gave evidence of the usual obsessions with creams and lotions, all feminine in nature. Nothing in the cabinet to suggest any other bad habits, not even the pill. The toilet bowl itself was clean and shiny, which confirmed his opinion. Make up was scattered out over the tiny table that served for a make shift dressing area, but that could have been the cat. The bed was single, unmade and rented out old. The sheets looked clean and the duvet was brightly coloured and newish looking. The clothes spread out on the floor were the formal side of business casual, the shoes impeccably heeled and well cared for. All the used knickers were in a laundry basket, but the bras were spread around. She used panty liners.

An ironing board filled up the tiny space on the other side of the bed, with an expensive iron on the floor beside it. Not the cat this time, as it had been carefully placed to cool out of harm's way. For all the chaos in the room, an expensive jacket in dark blue hung impeccably on the back of the door. A matching skirt had been hanging in the shower room, obviously left to steam out its wrinkles. The tiny fragrance bottle by the bed was pricey but affordable enough to have been a present to herself. A secretary, the report had said. The flat screeched up and coming PA at him; with three daughters of his own, he was wise enough to know the difference. The probationer sniffed around after him as he called in the details, heeding his warning to touch nothing. She crumpled her nose in disdain at the mess, and smell. She'd learn. She'd learn bloody fast. A double duty of nights in the riot months of summer and her no doubt currently pristine room back at the police house would look the same. He logged the time and complete lack of evidence in any direction. Her suitcases were on top of the wardrobe, and the drawers filled with underwear, clothing and two sex toys. A vibrating egg and slim finger sized vibrator. This made it extremely unlikely she'd just walked away. He finished his report and sighed: this didn't feel a good one, not at all.

A week of searching saw Joanne Maitland's neatly typed details logged and filed, the case unofficially closed. She was lost somewhere in the mystery that the city became at these times, her disappearance overshadowed by a sensational libel case and another marital dispute over at the House of Windsor. Mrs Maitland, crumpled and creased from the jostled and chaotic trip South, shed her tears for the camera, wailing a little at Fleet Street's seeming indifference. Had a paparazzo photograph of a distraught Princess of Wales not stolen the morning headlines, a little more might have been made of her one shot appearance on the evening news. As it was, London lifted its head in grief for a split second, returning to business as usual by close of trading. Jo, oblivious to the future of her good name, left behind a less than fitting epitaph in the form of her last confirmed sighting. Breathless, half in her jacket, red from the run, she had stood and watched the tube she had just missed hurtle down into the depths of Archway station.

'Shit!' is what she had said, loudly, as she stalked up and down the platform. 'Shit!'

It had been another vile day. Too much work, not enough time. Fridays were always her worst day, not the usual Blue Monday of office worker fame. Friday was the day she'd be in such a rush that she would skip breakfast completely, her Monday good intentions on sensible eating abandoned sometime around Wednesday. Friday breakfast usually joined Thursday dinner as a non-event. Friday break would find her stuffing chocolate biscuits down her throat as quickly as she could, her now up and running body desperate for anything that looked and acted remotely like a calorie. If she was lucky, and this Friday she hadn't been, lunch was a sandwich and a doughnut, washed down with lukewarm coffee. Every Monday she began a perfect routine of fruit for breakfast and break, with peppermint tea to wash her virtue down. She would smile sweetly at the others as they moaned about the coffee machine being broken again, as she waited for her tea bag to infuse. By Wednesday she was beginning to think maybe she should phone through for a new machine herself, as she waited for the damn thing to gurgle out more tepid caffeine. Friday always found her deciding that she'd damn well put the order through as urgent as soon as she had a minute on Monday, as she sent out an order for a massive triple mocha from the coffee shop on the high street.

Minutes were Friday's real problem: there were not enough of them. Work that had not seemed too important and could be put back for a day or two, suddenly had to be cleared and logged out of the office before the weekend. Logged and cleared by her, for she'd learnt, as had her boss, that if she didn't do it personally, it sometimes wasn't done. Friday nights usually saw her pegged on the couch, having missed the soaps again, picking the topping off an extra large pizza, a bottle of plonk for company and a tub of ice cream melting in the sink, awaiting her pleasure. Fridays she was fit for nothing but collapse and retreat.
This Friday had been a Friday from hell. The end of financial year accounts about to be closed and set. She hadn't even got to the chocolate biscuits 'til after 2. The phone never stopped, the fax machine had over

spilled twice and her boss had looked at her with one of those looks. The 'I know you are so very busy and you are so very competent, but can I please have the report on my desk *now*' looks. Yes, she loved the bustle. Yes, she was good enough to do everything well, no matter how busy it got. Yes, it was great fun. Sometimes. But it wasn't really her job to do all of it and it was about time someone recognised that. They'd almost had words, Jo backing down at the last moment when the phone had rung once more, embroiling her in another minor crisis in the photocopying room. She had sent out for coffee and a sandwich, but either they had never arrived, or she hadn't noticed them in the mêlée.

She had felt defeated when it was all sorted out, not exultant so, when the usual shout had gone up about where and when the office was congregating for party mode, she'd listened. She rarely joined in with the Friday night extravaganza that the bosses actively encouraged the staff into. She was always late, always tired, and found getting it down and boogying with the others a waste of time. Today, however, had been different. All she wanted to do was go out and get absolutely smashed out of her skull. Forget it all and start the weekend in bed, too past it to care about anything. She may even get laid, or try to. The safety of getting drunk in the company of her fellow workers stood against her managing a little horizontal jogging. Embarrassed encounters over work areas on Monday mornings were not her idea of fun. Not that she'd ever had such an encounter, but it might happen yet. There was a Northern chill to her backbone that usually saw to it that nothing squidgy happened, despite her fantasies. Perhaps tonight, she'd shuck off the puritanical streak she hadn't realised was part of her until she moved to London.

Unprepared for a night out, she'd made the decision to leave some of the work undone and rush back home to change. With luck and the right connections, she would meet up with the others as they made their way across London to catch a boat that was going to let them drink themselves sick as it drifted along the Thames. Experience had shown that this was very convenient, both for throwing up discreetly, and for controlling who had access to you in a 'fragile' state. With the train now hurtling away from her into the darkness, there was a good chance she was going to be late. Thankfully, the next train popped up quickly, although she was going to have to change at Leicester Square, which suited her well enough as she didn't have that much cash on her. Her temper had cooled as she stopped off to pick up money from the hole in the wall. Folding the notes into her purse, she allowed the chiming of the nearby Swiss Centre to register the time with her, bursting the bubble of her self-delusion. It was too late. She had missed the launch, they'd be heading downstream by the time she got there. She didn't have one jot of a clue as to where it was picking up along the route, should have listened better as they all chattered about who was wearing what, who was gunning for whom.

She fought back the irrational prick of tears that threatened to engulf her, concentrating on what she wanted to do now. She was dressed for fun, she was in the right part of town. She had money in her purse and the night, if not the evening, was still young. She couldn't face returning to her flat so soon after rushing out of it, all caught up with the idea that she had somewhere to go. Unnoticed by the crowds she slipped into the first decent looking pub she found. A quick glass of wine, some time to calm down. A meal, maybe a movie. Something of the evening would be salvaged. Besides, she'd be so much safer on her own.

Restlessness had brought him out onto the streets earlier than usual. The day had been hot; sticky and close. There was a fine drawing of his nerves building; a faint twitch. He cruised the bars from Soho down to the Square, scanning the eager young faces he passed. It was too early for the true desperates to be abroad. He wondered where they went in the city centre bustle between the hours of the commuter's rush and the emptying of the bars. The young and helpless, tricking the night away to fill their bellies and their veins. The air was grey and stale, not heavy enough to call with it rain. Deep and dark enough that it lay in layers around him. The scents caught by each step forward drummed the sense of city into his bones. Sweat, concrete, cheap perfume. The sharp and noxious odour of urine, splashed carelessly behind bins and crates. Dark alleyways completely overlooked by the tourists. Rotting vegetables and rubbish caught in the trap of the gutter, wind brushing all to the corners of the streets. Noise assailed him from the edges of Chinatown, ancient spices and herbs drifted out to him from the apothecary's shelves. Tonight was not a night for easy prey, swift endings. Tonight, he was in the mood for fun.

The pub was packed and she'd found her way to both the bar, and an empty table, with a lot of pushing and jostling. The table was crowded with bottles and had an overflowing ashtray. She edged it away, wrinkling her nose in distaste. The table was tiny, a fake hardboard top over a fake beer barrel. There was only one stool but she'd be nearer the door where there was a sense of fresher air to be found. Squeezing into a gap in the heaving bodies around her she settled into the seat, ruefully reflecting that the fresher air from outside was just as cloying, if somewhat drier than the sweat and lager laden fug around her. She scanned her somewhat sketchy memory of the area for rememberings of a good restaurant. One with air conditioning.

The street was a small one, lined with pubs and wine bars. The prices in each varied greatly. He'd learnt that such a range offered interesting possibilities. He took his time, savouring the appearance and demeanour of everyone around him. There was a tow-headed young man, a boy really, sitting on one of the cheap plastic seats outside a cafe. He looked as if he'd just been jilted, his eyes staring intently at the label of the bottle he held. He almost didn't fit the new jeans he was wearing, his shoes scuffed and rather more worn than looked cool. Promising. Next door, a wine bar with pretensions of glamour. The woman taking advantage of the dim light of an alcove was in her late forties. High quality make up sought to cover the lines and wrinkles of excess, powder clogging her pores, eye shadow making pretence of much younger looks. Good clothing, bag and matching shoes. Expensive perfume barely masking stale body odour. Dark roots just peeping into view. There was a harshness, a nervousness about her. Eyes constantly roaming, searching, eager. Her hands were never still, the rings surrounding her fingers twisted and turned this way and that. She brought her hand up to her face regularly, hiding, entreating. He savoured her plight, how easily she would be caught. He shook his head, not for this evening, although he may return at a later date, not doubting that this was a favourite haunt.

The boy had gone when he returned to the street, his place taken by three giggling girls, their almost skirts not quite matching their almost tops. Make up applied with more enthusiasm than skill, their flesh tones lost in a jumble of clashing shades and colours. Long gangling limbs embraced in cheap bangles and bracelets, shoes all bought in a sale. A vestige of some shared shopping spree no doubt. He smiled at them as he passed, evoking shrieks of delight and raucous comment on his intentions. The smile was genuine as he savoured the raw scents they spread around him. Musk, heat, and the fresh tang of just washed flesh exerting its own perfume over that of soap and deodorant. He mellowed into the chase, thoroughly enjoying the pace and selection the evening had so far offered. He tipped them a wink and moved on, relishing the sounds as he passed them by.

Jo found her glass of wine soothing. It had a sour taste, kept overlong in a bottle behind the bar, but the alcohol warmed her blood. It was a stupid thing to do, get so frazzled, just for another pointless office party. She studied those around her, making guesses at who they were and what they did for a living. The main performer in a tightly woven pack of young men looked over at her and winked. She smiled, dropping her head to look at her glass. When she looked up he was engaged in another tall tale, his mates well on the road to joining him in a night of excess. A small part of her was disappointed that she'd been dismissed so easily, laughing the slight off with a quick toss of her head. A gesture for a mythical companion who was at the bar buying the next round, or weaving his way back from the Gents. A clear signal for the one who'd passed her over so quickly. It didn't make her feel better; it made her feel worse, more aware of how vulnerable she was feeling. It was stupid to take it to heart, she was alone after all. No matter the attraction, the guy who had winked would have only broken ranks to approach her if she had been surrounded by her mates. Something for them all to get their teeth into. Shares for everyone, that was the pack rule. As she drained the glass her stomach announced its immediate rebellion. She must eat, must fill the void. Collecting her jacket and bag, she rose to leave.

The glimpse of white caught his eyes as he scanned the packed pub from outside. Too many people was as dangerous as too few. He preferred to analyse the opportunities from the large display windows theme pubs were beginning to build into their decor. She was in her early twenties, fading tan bought from a machine. Hair an untidy mop of curls, a better perm than it looked, dried with less care than the style demanded. She'd had it trapped up all day, released it without washing, the ridges from the clasps still evident. Her hair and eyes were the same warm colour of earth. Nothing too exciting, but a nice complement to her facial skin, which was paler than the rest of her. She read the magazines, this one. Knew to keep sun away from her face, even as she allowed it domain over her body. Make up had been hastily applied, the dress showed signs of a recent hanging in a crowded wardrobe. The single ring on her right hand was no more than a cheap silver memento of a Greek package tour. There was a drowsiness around her: fatigue. Her head came up and eyes made contact with someone else in the crowd, her smile warm and inviting. The movement of dropping her head to coyly study her glass entranced him. She was both naive and aware, testing her way along the path of the evening. Her face hardened as she realised she'd been overlooked, her head shaking away the slight. Look what you've missed, she was saying, look what you passed up. He smiled.

The air was slightly clearer as she left the bar, although it was still too warm, too old. As if it had been used too much that day, been dragged in and out of many sets of lungs. The greying light was losing its unequal battle with the electric lights all around, the street leached of its colour. It left a chill on her, made her feel transient, transparent. She really had to get some food. She perused a series of windows, ostensibly checking prices, really having a good look inside to see who was sitting down, what sort of feel the place had. Too many places were packed, overflowing with good cheer and heated bodies. Almost in desperation she headed for the Steak House on the other side of the Square. It was a tourist place, overpriced and stuffy. It would not be cool to have admitted eating there from choice but the green velvet booths would give her some space, the air conditioning respite from the now expected early summer. There was a small queue, which she didn't mind. Other places had far larger queues and she quite enjoyed the wait, watching the life and colour return to the Square as natural light retreated and the neon took over. As she reached the head of the queue the maitre'd raised his head and smiled to the right of her.

'For two, sir?'

Startled, she turned to find a man standing slightly to one side. His face registered his own confusion at the question. Flustered, he looked first to Joanne, then back to the maitre'd.

'The lady is not with me.' He caught her gaze again and smiled at her. 'Unfortunately.'

She grinned back at him in thanks for the compliment. He raised his arm, to allow her full access to the head of the queue and the now impatient staff.

'A single, madam?'

The voice betrayed his feelings on one of his precious tables being given over to a single occupant on a Friday night. She nodded. He looked past her again, to the gentleman whom he'd mistaken for her companion.

'And you, sir, a single also?'

The second nod of the head sent him in a scurry of disdain as he searched through the room for evidence of two small tables about to come free.

'It may be some time... unless...?'

The maitre'd allowed the word to hang in the air, hoping the two dim and sad people cast upon his restaurant on a busy evening would come to their senses. Joanne started to fidget, unprepared to deal with such complications. The man stepped into the breach, silencing the sighs of exasperation that were beginning to make their way up the ever lengthening queue. He stood forward, side by side with her, acting as if both the maitre'd and the queue had disappeared.

'I would be honoured if you would join me for dinner.'

His smile won her, the touch of self deprecation in his humour, the secret he was sharing with her that anything was worth getting out from under the eyes of the officious man whose evening they were disrupting. Even so, she hesitated.

'I promise I will not bite,' he whispered to her, as she looked around for good reason to turn him down, 'not unless you ask me to.'

The humour in his voice reached her again. She looked at the crowding room, the maitre'd, the queue. She was hardly at risk. Smiling what she hoped was gracious acceptance, she allowed them to be seated together. Where was the harm?

She soon came to see that harm might have been preferable to the uncomfortable feeling of embarrassment that settled between them as they sat opposite each other. The sensible solution that appeared so practical in front of the maitre'd soon gave way to confused silence. They each studied their menus in mock concentration. Joanne was aware that the man was probably more embarrassed than she, wishing he had not been so gallant. She racked her brains, trying to think of something witty and interesting to say.

'You live in London?'

God, what a trite thing to say! She swallowed hard, sweat breaking out on her palms.

'Yes, yes I do. And you?'

He had smiled in relief at her, obviously pleased she had opened up the communication. She felt a little better.

'Yes, oh yes.' She nodded too enthusiastically. 'For a few years now.'

She trailed off, out of even trite things to say in response. He smiled at her again, reassuringly. He had nice eyes she mused, a light brown, not dissimilar to her own.

'Uhm, pardon?'

She realised he had spoken to her and she had missed it.

'Drink. Would you like a drink?'

With a start she realised that the waiter was standing next to her, order book in hand. He was looking at her with the disdainful sufferance of one dealing with the doltish. Had he spoken?

'The lady would like a glass of white wine. No, bring a bottle, let me see...' He rifled through the wine list.

She was relieved he had spoken up, taken charge; it was nice to be taken care of for a change. The waiter wrote the order down with a sigh and hurried off.

'I hope you do not mind my presumption?'

He was looking at her again with those eyes, those beautiful dark brown eyes. She smiled back, shaking her head.

'No, no, not at all. I must... I must be more tired than I thought.'

She fumbled to unfurl her napkin to cover her confusion. Had they ordered yet?

Oh, it was going to be a fine night. He studied her with pleased indulgence. His original assessment of exhaustion had been wonderfully proven by how easy she had been to enthrall. After he had ordered the food, enjoying the opportunity of filling her up with all the enticing scents and aromas of alcohol, she had prattled away, filling up the table with her chatter and youth. She was a delight. Half little fox, working away cannily at her job, sorry, her career, half a total innocent, lost in the big wide world. Her loneliness intrigued him, made a joy of her catching. She was so utterly childlike, unable to guess that she could have had many of those around her if she had only played a better game at being chased, and caught. He even liked her voice, which was soft and rhythmical, a legacy no doubt of the voice lessons she had taken to rid her of her working class tones. It was going to be a fine night, a slow and even one. As she finished her dessert he asked for the bill.

'Oh no, of course not, I'd be delighted.' she stared into his eyes as he paid. 'Just don't expect me to be able to dance much.'

She laughed, entranced by the darkness in those eyes. It was so flattering, after all, for him to keep looking at her in that way. As they rose, collecting their things, she wondered if she'd ever seen eyes that dark, almost completely black. Yet they glimmered so, were so very seductive. She smiled as he opened the door to her, sweeping her out into the street, oblivious to the blast of heat that enveloped them.

CHAPTER TWO

She was aware of a vague feeling of disquiet as they walked across the Square. She wasn't quite sure where she was going, what time it was. Fumbling, she looked at her watch, to be met in turn with his smile and those eyes. She forgot why she had wanted to know the time, returning his smile and wondering if she was boring him with her chit chat. He seemed so relaxed in her company and she responded to his confidence. He hailed a taxi and she found herself staring at the West End as it passed. She felt warm, rested, secure. He smiled and nodded at her, patting her hand, caressing her shoulder. It was all so very wonderful, so very exciting. To find such a companion by sheer accident, to have such a relaxing evening in the face of the earlier disappointment. She studied the lights as they passed, wondering if perhaps she'd had a bit too much to drink. There was something niggling at the back of her mind, something uncomfortable. She tried to put it away from her as the cab stopped, she didn't want to lose him for lack of giving him her attention.

They were in the sudden quiet of a back street. She smiled as he opened the cab door, inviting her out with a dignified flourish. He was so *romantic*. She thrilled inside, a secret smile of pleasure at the thought. In the shadow of tall buildings the air was cooler, cleaner. As he paid the taxi driver and his face bent away from hers, she felt her mind once more straying. There was something she was worried about, what was it? It was lost as he smiled again, encouraging her to walk with him. He opened a door, ushered her in. There was the faintest scent of citrus, something tangy. Small, enclosed, yet neither intimate nor comfortable. Where was she? It was a lift, moving silently up. She giggled as she watched the lights on the panel flicker. Oh dear, she had better not have any more to drink. She didn't want to appear sozzled, leave a bad impression. The disquiet returned as she stood outside a heavy wooden door, her companion pressing buttons on a glittering steel panel. Something about what he was doing made her realise how expensive the door was. Expensive doors were heavy, solid: immovable. That door was expensive.

She turned, to look back for the lift, see if she could work out where she was. His hand reached down and touched her chin, pulled it gently towards him. He kissed her then, for the first time, and the ground swayed under her feet. Oh yes, this was it, this was it! He was the one, the one she had been waiting for, longing for. She smiled, leaned into him, felt his clothing against her. Smooth, sensual. The door opened and she was walking inwards, his hand gently covering the small of her back. She could feel his coolness through her dress, excitement flooding her. She took a step forward, hesitated, stopped. Something was wrong, something was very wrong. It was dark where they were heading. She turned, to move back, but his hand was on her shoulder, cool and demanding, what was it she wanted to say? She opened her mouth to speak, and he was there again, kissing her, swallowing her up. There really wasn't anything wrong; it was all rather exciting. She was as light as a feather, dancing, being carried through the air by his charm. Pale colours flowed around her, lights moving as they walked. The stars above her head were swirling, dancing with them as they moved. Dark green splashes of colour whizzed by. Her head lolled back, losing contact with his body. He tipped her forward again, and she snuggled onto his shoulder. This was so very fine, so very very fine.

The feel of the bed coming up from under her sent the warnings ringing out again. That was what was wrong, had been wrong since the restaurant; those damn bells. When were they going to stop that damned clanging? She tried to sit up. A mouth fastened over hers, drew out her breath, pulled at her, tugged something from her. What was she doing? All she could focus on was the cool mouth that was draining her of warmth. No, that wasn't right, she was enjoying this. His mouth on hers, drawing, sucking. Imagined so many times before, she knew it was to have been warm, comforting. Not cool. But this mouth was cool, almost cold. Her surprise at that thought almost surfaced, but at the same time a hand started a soft, circular caress on her right breast. Joanne found her senses slipping into the heat and drive of the man floating somewhere above her. There was that cool mouth again, his salty taste, his hands, rough but welcomed, so very welcomed. His mouth lifted away from her, leaving her empty. Disappointment shook her body, she moved to follow after him. A tongue rested lightly on her neck, teasing, a hand moving over her stomach, rubbing downwards, pushing her back on the bed. Her trembling intensified. She had never imagined it could be like this. Back car fumblings and quick passions in parents' beds, hurried to make sure they weren't caught, had never been like this. This was what she'd waited for, dreamed for. This is what she'd known was in her path, one day. No silly stationary cupboard humping for her: no office tensions had yet caused her to drop her standards. Her body caught fire, the sharp, contracting pain in her groin catching her by surprise. The pain was intense, as she curled around the thought of loving him, being breached by him. She groaned and arched her back, truly slipping beyond her own awareness. There was only that tight, cutting pain, the burning in her breasts, the need for more. Her legs opened.

Although it had been a long time since Dreyfuss had loved physically with a woman, he had not forgotten the art of seduction. On whimsy, he excited the young woman beneath him, pulling out from her responses she had not known were hidden within her. He could feel her awareness, her excitement; it was this that served to pleasure him. He stroked and petted her, kissed and caressed, till the fire that was upon her, was upon him. Her complete physical acceptance touched him, was pleasing to him. She was an open book, and he could read her language with ease. There was a vulnerability that teased at him, made him feel protective and paternalistic. He had wanted to play, and in her trust found a game of innocence and beguilement. An odd taste for the evening, but the palette responded well to change. He waited until she was almost sated, when the scent of her salt and musk flooded him: then he moved. Centring his mouth along the vein which coiled around the base of the neck, he kissed her hard, sucking, biting, bringing her blood up to meet him. The sharp piercing pain as he opened her was lost in her climax, in the sudden hot flush to his mouth. Salt and heat as he filled himself. The first rush of pleasure over, he drew slowly; swallowing: savouring. All ceased to exist apart from his mouth, its convulsions, the endless stream that he drew up into himself. Her blood was incredibly rich, loaded with the earlier meal. The alcohol he had pushed upon her coming back up to meet him, warming him. Soon, all that she was would be his, and it would be a fine moment for them both. She would die in ecstasy, a rare gift in this world, and he would live by her sacrifice, satisfied with what she had offered. He fell into her blood and drank.

Fire exploded all through her. There was nothing but heat and flame and the enveloping waves that pulsed from her groin. Everything was washed ahead in the wave of pleasure, so intense it was akin to pain, ripping through her. She felt herself cry out, her spine convulsing, her legs jerking, her throat tightening. There was nothing; nothing but the long, slow flow of blood pulsing through her. She throbbed in its wake, the heat subsiding. She longed for rest, for safety. Everything in her wished to relax and give herself up to that binding, to the warmth that filled her. To fall into the sleep offered her. That sated, resting sleep. To heal herself upon its joy. She sought the sleep, sought the rest. Reaching out with her mind, she tried desperately to pull it down with her, bring it with her into her dreams.

She shivered. Shivered again. Somewhere, somehow, she was cold. She could feel the cold. It fell upon her, swallowing her. Swallowing her heat, eating her dreams. She fought the cold, tried to move back to that feeling, that feeling of belonging and completion. It slipped away from her. She moaned, muttered, moved, protested. She wanted the feeling back, and she was not going to go until it came with her.

Movement jolted him, impinging upon the scent in his nostrils. Under him, the body had tensed, was trying to throw him off. How amusing; that had been the least expected of reactions. Remedy was swift and effective. He felt a surge of power as he further opened the wound, her essence flooding him, sending him flying into the night, soaring through the darkness. He could hear her heart falter as pressure dropped, veins beginning to slurry. There, teasing in the back of his mind, he could sense her death, waiting for him to finish his pleasure. He pulled her closer, eagerly awaiting her final gift. Then, from nowhere, as the life's flow was at its sweetest, he was without blood: without source. His vision cleared and the dreaming fell from him. He blinked, bringing the room back into focus. She was standing there, pale, beside the bed. Blood flowed freely from the gash that the leaving of him had torn across her neck. She was shaking, not from fear, from fury.

Her eyes blazed at him: how dare he, how dare he!

Dreyfuss sat up and stared at the being who had defied him when he was in full feed. He looked at the girl, her life flowing from her neck, oozing onto the floor. She was a pale and empty little thing, not even fully aware of her own needs. He smiled into her shaking eyes, lifted his hand to her, inviting their reunion. She took a step back, so fast she almost stumbled and fell. It was his turn to stare, to wonder. It was slow to build, lost as he had been in the feeding, but anger at her defiance entered the game. He shook his hand again, repeating the invitation, a warning about refusal openly given.

She stared at him, horror growing in her eyes: she was breaking the thrall. His eyes narrowed in annoyance. Open panic filled her features, she turned to flee.

His hand snaked out instinctively, grabbing her by the hair, yanking her back to the bed, back to his embrace. She whirled round and slapped him across the face. The tide of his own anger lit out from him, fast and bright. Releasing her hair he pulled back his arm, the blow sending her away, to land heavily against the wall. She crumpled and lay still. To defy him, at the moment of their shared ecstasy? To raise a hand to him? She would die in pain for reward.

Catching her up, he fastened again on her throat, intent on sucking her dry. His hands held her fast, fingers dug deeply into flesh too spent to bruise. The torn throat gave him easy purchase and he set to devour all she had, all she had ever been. Even then, almost dead, wrung like a cloth, she groaned, moving against him. He felt the bitterness of her rebellion on his tongue. He pulled back, spoiled for her. He reached for her neck, a quick snap and she would be gone forever. His hands enclosed her, seeking to find the right spot, where vertebrae would be easiest pushed apart from vertebrae. Still she protested, fought his actions. Her hand had risen to weakly push him off, fight him away. He grasped it and pulled it away, back under her own body. What strength was left in her was used to arch her back, giving off her message: fight, no matter how trapped you are; fight. He smiled and leaned down to kiss her. Somewhere, in the haze of her dying, she noticed him, and whispered up to him.

'Fuck you.'

The words barely made it out of her mouth such was her weakness. My, he thought, such language from an innocent! He let her loose, grinning at her stubbornness. Some things were eternal, after all. Spirit such as this was rarely found, never mind uncovered so surprisingly. A part of him was pleased to have found a little savage in a cheap white dress. Without much thought for it he picked her up and tossed her back on the bed, the action more to do with an innate sense of tidiness than anything else. In the roots of his mouth an ache was building. He had been roused by her, his instincts kindled. Nothing would substitute for a full life, not now. The thirst was upon him, and he would quench it. He changed quickly, abandoning her gore for cleaner clothing. She would probably bleed to death before he returned.

The catching was easy, there were many who walked the streets in search of love, or death. When he raised his head he realised that her anger was still upon him. There was no throat left to the boy who had courted him, thinking only to find food for the night. Well food was what had been found, if not to his precise liking. He dropped the empty flesh onto the rails of Earl's Court tube station. Another suicide, or fumbling mishap. London was used to that.

He returned home on foot, enjoying the night air and sense of freedom. The scents from the park beguiled him as he slipped past the shadow of the Albert Hall, disappearing out of the streets as effortlessly as he had emerged. After washing he retired, falling into a deep and dreamless sleep. When he rose in the middle afternoon he felt surprisingly rested. Light and alert. Active. As the coffee percolated, he went to check on his guest. To his surprise, she was still alive. The bruising on her jaw was minimal as there had been little blood within her to damage. She and the bed were splattered with dark brown splodges of dead blood; a shocking waste. What to do with her? Strangely, he had no instinct on the matter. Dreyfuss was mostly instinct. To survive as he survived, he had to be. He mused upon his own lack of immediate direction: a Dreyfuss without purpose was a strange and curious thing. He returned to his own bedroom and studied the matter.

As he showered, it occurred to him that the decision may be taken out of his hands. Returning to her room, which was a curious way for his mind to put it given how many had occupied it before her, he checked her pulse and blood pressure. A choice had to be made. To let her die, and end the matter, or allow her life? That was a nonsense, for she was meat as he looked at her. Dead was dead. The issue was when, not if. But something about that stubbornness had surprised him. Surprise in a life such as his was precious: unexpected bounty. Perhaps he'd kill her tomorrow? Regardless, she would die when he said so, not before.

He made a quick phone call. An hour later a courier delivered ten units of basic saline, plasma and sterile equipment. He set a drip, inserting the valve into the back of her hand quickly and cleanly. He refrained from polluting her with any drugs: if she'd been going to go under it would have happened before now. Wary of leaving her unconscious with a needle in her arm, he phoned his apologies through to the golf club; someone else would have to deliver the after dinner speech. Thinking that through, he contacted his second in command: things would have to run without him for a few days. He'd attend to any urgent mail that came into his study but apart from that, he was not to be disturbed. Well used to this, Gerald signed off in eager anticipation of a week in which he could call the shots.

Filling a bowl with tepid water and antiseptic, Dreyfuss attended to her neck. With all the gunge off, the tear was less than he had thought. Pressing the ragged edges together long enough to stop the fresh weeping, he carefully applied four paper stitches, sealing the mess with his own blood. Then he cut her dress and knickers off, sponging her down with cool water, remaking the bed around her. Rechecking her pulse and respiration he adjusted the flow of the drip and switched the light off as he went. He made a light snack of steak and eggs, settling down to watch a movie in peace.

Her dry coughing woke him from the rather pleasant slumber that he had slipped into. He had been dreaming of Eléan; which was unusual, for he had not dreamt of her in years. In the dream, she was calling to him, with that wicked half grin on her sly face. The call in the dream became the cough of his guest: he roused himself. She was half conscious, drifting in the way of those lost in the fight to waken. He gave her a few sips of water, checking her vital signs. She was fine, more or less, and he took out the drip. He needed to sleep, and she would be in the way, so he filled her veins with sedative. He went to bed and dreamed another dream of Eléan.

Looking in on her the next morning he was satisfied to see she had responded well to the enforced slumber. Her fatigued body was slowly recovering from the added stress of their encounter. Her mind wasn't happy with the arrangement, her twisting and turning had pulled the sheet out from under her, but her skin tone was improved greatly. He shot her through once more with enough sedative to keep her under for a few more hours. His body ached from lack of activity and he felt in need of more work out than could be achieved on his home equipment. It wouldn't do to have her up and around, screaming and pathetic when he returned from the gym. Without thought of it, his hands drifted over her body in more than a clinical assessment of injury. He hesitated over her breasts, slowly dragging his fingers over her left nipple. It sprung to life, reacting to his touch. He smiled, that sense of complete possession as sweet as ever. For whimsy, he brought the other to attention by the merest of touch of his breath. Sensing his invasion, she pulled away, a frightened moan escaping her lips. His smile deepened as he reached once more for the sedative. He pushed her so far under he heard her heart slow, her breathing hesitate, before settling into shallow swoops. He pinched her hard, on the fold under her arm: nothing. Lifting a lid he touched her eye: nothing. The smile that slipped from his lips as his hands travelled down to her groin was nothing short of a gloat: it was always so easy. The pleasure in digging his fingers deep inside her was not the pleasure of invasion, for that was a pleasure that palled all too quickly. It was the complete absence of awareness in her slack face, the total surrender of her limbs that enthralled him. She had no clue as to what was happening to her. He dug around, pushing the dry warm flesh this way and that, until it filled with moistness and expanded. He stabbed his rigid fingers into her cervix: nothing. All that was in her world, now, was his will. Even when she was unconscious, all she was, was his. Satisfied, he cleaned his fingers on the bedding and left.

He enjoyed the walk through the back streets to the gym he favoured for swimming. Most of the weights and running equipment was too light-weight, but the pool was almost perfect. He mulled the situation over as he pushed himself endlessly through the water, length after length ripped in two and left behind him. Which was the more sustained pleasure, the subtle yet silent power of the invisible, or the more immediate involvement of fear and struggle? It was an eternal question, one that he never truly managed to answer. For as he indulged in one, the other would entice his mind, beguiling him with the promise of more: a longer lasting satisfaction, a sharper and sweeter joy. It was a dilemma that shaped much of his life, that pushed and pulled at many layers of his living. Even now, as he changed back to the butterfly, it teased at him, took his mind off the rhythm of his stroke. For strength, he preferred to work out at home, where prying eyes could not react to the dead weights he could so easily conquer. He could pile the pressure onto his body, fighting his own limitations, testing out his mind's strength in complete secrecy: no awareness of watchful humans to slow his responses and advise caution. Stamina however was always a public sport. No pleasure there unless observed, no triumph unless the bested stood in front of him, wheezing and shaking in their defeat. Five of the gym's finest had slowly watched as he turned again and again, each length timed exactly to match the previous. In stamina he was only slightly more than they, each turn meting out as much punishment on him as it did them: yet he never lost. Three had taken his silent challenge today, and two were spent and useless, fighting for breath at the pool's edge. He gloried in their weakness, their lack. The one still struggling on and on with him, ploughing a now straggly furrow in his wake, was going to drop out soon: the switch to butterfly had seen to that.

He smiled as he tucked under once more, kicking softly against the edge, unwilling to allow his strength to gain him advantage. The victory would be his fairly; there was the joy. The only pain was that it would soon be time to move on, find new territory. Few accepted the silent challenge anymore, too much defeat etched in their faces. A new club with a well sheltered pool would have to be found. New meat to be taunted with his pale and slender body. New muscle bound fools to pitch against him, to be fired up by his feet kicking dust in their eyes as he passed. He mused on the pleasures in his life as he dried, aware that today's prize had been bought for him by his sleeping playmate. The joys had once more begun to drain out of his life, slowly, almost unnoticed. The taste of her defeat had awakened him, brought life back to a jaded palate. A few days off work to play, to sport: that was just what he needed. What a gift he would give her, letting her final days serve his greater needs.

CHAPTER THREE

The first thing she was truly aware of was a cramp, low in her back. She wasn't sure exactly when she became aware of it, how long she'd been listening to her body groan, but slowly, carefully, the awareness that this was real, her back was hurting, she was asleep, or had been, settled in her mind. It was dark, too dark; that wasn't helping. Where was it, that it was this dark? Not her own bedroom for sure. Not her lumpy bed and rickety windowsill, traffic noises seeping through with the streetlights. The bed beneath her was straight, even with her weight on it. The dark around her, absolute. She closed her eyes and tried to concentrate on waking up. Her mouth was dry and filthy, caked with gunge. As she struggled to push her body awake, to sit up, make sense of the confusion, she flitted her tongue round and round, desperately seeking moisture. The pain from her back was sharp and fresh as she pulled forward, making her wince. What on earth had happened that her back hurt so? The question sat in her mind, trying to make some sense to her. She fumbled around, feeling the soft bed that surrounded her. How big could a bed be? She leaned to the side, reaching for an unseen edge, trying to find an end to this smothering softness. Her head spun, dizziness almost overwhelming her. A nausea rose within her, she gagged. She wasn't going to throw up, she wasn't going to throw up. She certainly wasn't going to throw up until she had worked out where she was. She dropped back on the bed, closing her eyes. She'd moved too fast, the dizziness got worse not better. She groaned, which turned out to be a worse move than flopping back on the bed. Her throat felt awful, like she'd swallowed crushed glass. Hot and dry and raw all at the same time. As she lay there, trying to control her panic, her breathing, her dry mouth, her head began a wicked beating. Thrum, thrum, thrum. If this was a hangover, she didn't want to think about what she'd been drinking. Her back had eased slightly on lying back, but when she tried to move upwards, it screamed protest once more. Fear started to edge out panic: what had she been doing that had hurt her back? Whatever the answer was, she wasn't sure she wanted to know about it, not yet.

Gritting her teeth she forced herself to sit up, sitting straight up on the bed. The wave of nausea hit again, as did the dizziness. She rode it out, clutching a sheet to her face, concentrating on not throwing up, not passing out and not going back down into the bed. The thrumming threatened to split her head open, but she kept on in there. The feeling of sickness passed, as did the dizziness. Her back stayed raw and sharp, but got no worse. As the thrumming finally started to ease off, she became aware of a harsh rasping breath in the room beside her: laboured, dangerous. She almost screamed, clamping her hand over her own mouth, the noise stopped. Fear froze down her spine, blocking out all thoughts of her back, her pain, her headache. She clutched herself tightly, knees automatically raised to tuck under her chin. The rasping breath started again. She scrunched her eyes tight shut, tears squeezing out of the edges, and once more clamped her hand over her mouth, anything to make herself disappear. The noise stopped again. She held her breath, better to hear the darkness: nothing. The moment stretched and broke. She let the trapped air in her lungs out, the movement forcing more pain from her throat, her back, her head. The rasping started again. A whimper fled from her throat and was out into the darkness before she could help it. She again held her breath, this time her hands flying up to cover her head, her chin tucking down, seeking protection from her knees. The rasping stopped. As she lay there, tight and curled, awaiting whatever monster was in the room with her, she thought this through. An idea occurred to her. Lifting her head, she gasped in some air, once more releasing the bottled up feeling in her lungs. The rasping started once more. She held her breath. The rasping stopped. She breathed out. The rasping started up again. Relief flooded through her, limbs turning liquid; she crumpled once more back onto the bed. It was her! The noise she'd heard, that awful rasping breath, it was her own. The darkness, the silence in the room, it had fooled her.

She giggled, a strange and monstrous sound on its own, forced as it was through her aching throat, but she didn't care. The fear that had frozen her bones melted, leaving them molten and warm in its wake. She was drained, shaking a little, almost shivering with the relief. A laugh escaped her lips, god, she was a goose. What a stupid cow, to get herself into such a fright from listening to her own breathing. She flung her hands back, pulling air deeply into her lungs, listening to the sound of it all around her. Her back once more announced itself and she stretched, trying to persuade the aching to retreat, she was okay, it was just cramp from sleeping wrong. Her back wasn't convinced, but she kept it up, tightening and then flexing her spine, her legs, her arms. Her head hated it, the thrumming increasing, but she wasn't going to let herself get back into the state she'd just left. As she stretched her right hand and arm out, moving her shoulder this way, then that, her hand connected with something solid. She leaned back, tracing the line her hand found: the headboard. Great, with a little bit of luck, she'd find out where she was. Following the line of the padded board, she inched around to the edge of the bed. It seemed to be miles away, but she got there. Left hand still touching the headboard, right hand on the edge of the mattress. She lifted her right hand and gingerly stretched it out, into nothingness, fingers splayed, seeking. There was a bump, and she nearly screamed again, but she'd found what she was looking for. Her arm had connected with something soft, yet solid, movable. A lamp shade. Shifting over a little, both hands examined the shade, which was your normal round sorta-pyramid shape. The noise of her moving the cover blotted out her breathing. She found the wooden stem it sat on, and her fingers explored, seeking. There, under the bulb, where it should be, there was the switch. It was stiff, and she had to really push to get it on, something she should have thought through a little more, for as light suddenly flooded the room, she screamed and once more fell back onto the bed. *Her eyes, shit her eyes.* She threw her arms over them, to protect them from the light, but it was too late. Brightness danced in front of her, stabbing the backs of her eyes, hurting more than the headache. She dug her hands into them, rubbing hard, as if she could rub both pain and after images away. Shit, why hadn't she thought of that? She lay there, convinced she should feel the light through her skin, trying to get her breath back and her eyes back into their sockets. She turned over, ignoring the agony this caused her back and buried her face in a pillow. The stabbing lights slowly calmed down, although even with her eyelids closed tight, buried in the pillow, she could see ghostly images as she moved her head.

Anger began to chase out her panic. Anger at her own stupidity and whoever had gotten her here, to make such a fool of herself. She turned and sat up, once more ignoring both back and head, and shifted back till she was leaning on the head board, her hands protecting her eyes. She forced herself to calm down, to unwrinkle her eyes. Light was leaking through both her fingers, and her lids, turning everything red. The ghost of the lamp still danced in front of her. She held this pose for what seemed like forever, forcing her pupils to adjust, to get used to the partial light getting through to them. Gradually, she dropped her hands till only her lids protected her. She blinked, opening her eyes and closing them again, testing their responses. She turned her face away from the main source, away from the light, so she could look into the shadows on the left hand side of the bed. It wasn't comfortable, but it was bearable. She forced them to open, to adjust. Blinking away tears, she turned her head slowly, making it come into contact with more of the lamp, so she could see where she was. The scream that bounced around the walls pierced her, made her jump, made her throat contract with the pain and fear of it. She didn't recognise it as her own such was the shock.

Just by the lamp, there was a man sitting in a chair, looking straight at her.

He allowed himself a small smile then pulled his face back into emptiness. Would not do to give her too much to work with, would it?

The scream just kept echoing, on and on; she pulled back, scuttling as far away from him as she could. She stopped only when she knocked into the lamp on the other side of the bed, the crash as it flew back adding to her panic. Wedged in the corner, her body pushed as far as it could into the soft headboard on one side, the hard edge of a bedside table digging into her back. The scream just kept on going, filling the room, filling her. He stared at her, not moving, doing nothing but look. The voice stood between them, a solid, viscous barrier, carrying her shock and fear, but it couldn't hold up. The already bruised and swollen muscles in her throat gave out, the screams became less powerful, more broken, more hoarse. When they shattered into a wretched moaning, she realised they were hers, that she had been the one screaming, and that it wasn't achieving anything. She slowly wound down, a fractured organ running out of air. Silence crashed around them, her ears ringing with the force of it. Still, he did nothing but sit and look.

The initial shock was leaving, terror settling in its place. The silence between them became charged with it, alive with it. The pains all around her, her throat, her head, her back, became nothing in that awful stillness, as she watched him and he, her. His gaze upon her was terrible, frightening beyond words. She was caught between fear of not looking at him, in case he moved, and fear of being seen by him. In tiny, desperate movements, her eyes began to flit away from him, to and fro, attempting to build a picture, make sense of where she was. Behind him, in the shadows, there was the outline of a door. The bed she was on was massive, huge. He was easily six feet away from her, six feet of bed between them, then a few inches of space from the bed to the chair. The light from the lamp was actually quite low; there was no sense of colour in the room. There was only dark and light, although she was sure the sheets were white. She clutched them to her, they were soft, luxurious. The touch of them was comforting, reassuring. The reassurance fled as she thought on this, on the feel of it. For the first time her eyes dropped to look at herself, her own state. She was naked. She was totally naked and her right breast wasn't covered by the sheet. With a yelp, she cowered down more, making herself smaller, pulling the sheet up to her chin. Her hair swung into her eyes, plastering itself to her face. She pushed her right hand up from under the sheet, pulling her hair back. It was soaking, soaked through. Her hair was sodden. She looked at the hand that had touched it, it was wet, but clear. Water, not blood. She had suddenly been afraid that she was covered in blood. It was sweat, she was covered in her own sweat. Around her, the sheet was staining where it touched skin. All at once she could smell it - the stench of her own body. Sweat and fear, that's what she smelt of: sweat and fear.

Joanne Maitland hadn't known that it was possible to smell of fear.

The thought almost broke her, almost made her close her eyes and slip under the white sheet, not caring what happened as long as she couldn't see him, didn't have to admit what was happening. It was all so wrong, so very wrong. It was a nightmare, and something was trying to tell her that if she just closed her eyes and slipped under the sheet, all would be well. All she had to do was close her eyes and go back to sleep, then she'd wake, and the nightmare would be over. She ignored the voice, the tiny whispering in the back of her mind. The whispering could shut the fuck up, for nothing, nothing was going to get her to close her eyes with that man looking at her.

He watched the tiny spark in her eye, the glowing heat. He was entranced, delighted. Anger, such a very quick show of anger. This was turning out to be a much better evening's entertainment than he had hoped for. Anger at this stage boded very well, very well indeed.

Having decided she wasn't going to close her eyes, wasn't going to run away, she returned to checking out her surroundings. Her looks away from him gradually became more bold, sustained. A picture was starting to build. Over in the corner, by the door, ran some sort of unit. Dressing table perhaps, with a single shelf that ran the end of the room. Her vision ended where a second lot of drawers began. Carefully, she turned her head slightly, taking in the line as it grew to become a set of wardrobe doors. It was harder for her to sense their exact size and shape as she had to keep flitting her eyes back to check on Him. She couldn't follow the line all the way through, the angle was wrong. She returned to looking at what she could see, her captor, for that was undoubtedly what he was. Still he sat, still he stared. As if he was made of wax. She dragged her eyes off him, it was terrifying to keep him in her gaze. She stared again at the doorway behind him. The door. He was between her and it. Her and the door. The little voice whispered again. No way, no friggin' way. She wasn't going to go any closer to him, not even an inch, never mind run right past him. Her eyes moved off the door, she didn't even like to look at it, not while that traitorous thought was in her mind. She flicked back to Him: no change. She flicked away, once more examining the wall opposite the bed. On the wall, above the shelf of what might be a vanity unit, there was a drawing, a large one. She couldn't see what it was, it was too dark, murky. But she could see something, could see the glass which protected it. How hadn't she noticed it before? It reflected the room back at her. Dimly in places, but clear enough to her now adjusted eyes. In one corner, there was the lamp, his reflection. Then, a straggle of hair framed by a ghostly image of the headboard; herself. Next, in the nearest corner of the picture, showing part of the room she could not see, there was a dark rectangle. A tall dark rectangle that swallowed light utterly. Her eyes flicked between it, and Him. It and Him. The voice was back but this time she was listening. This time it was making sense. Sure, she didn't know where it led. Sure, it was a slim chance, but it was a chance. She looked back to him, checking. He hadn't moved, hadn't changed. She looked one final time at the reflection, sizing it up. The open doorway was on the same wall as she was, just a little over from the bed. Had to be, or it wouldn't be in the reflection. Seconds, that was all it would take, seconds. She decided.

'No.'

The sound of his voice went off beside her like a bomb. He hadn't shouted, hadn't spoken at more than a whisper, but it ruptured her illusion of safety, of the possibility of escape. She stared at him.

'Do not leave the bed.'

She saw the lips move, heard the words, but still he was so completely empty, so completely dead. For a moment she doubted herself, doubted he had spoken. What if it was her? What if she was making him up, had imagined his presence, never mind his voice? The thought scalded her, stole away what little composure she had. Without thought of it, she was up and off, heading for the doorway. Away, away, that was all she could think of. *Away.*

She tripped on the sheet that was wrapped round her, fell heavily onto the cool floor, found almost no purchase in it. A scrabble, a frantic scrabble, as she desperately tried to make the doorway just ahead of her. She kicked the sheet away, bare feet slipping and sliding on the surface of the bedroom. The darkness was really just ahead of her, the doorway was there, just there. With a push, she was over the threshold, scrabbling round on all fours, scooting through. The darkness was complete, she could see nothing once more, feel only the cold slickness underneath her. She tried to stand, found the door to her right, found the door handle. On her knees she rose and slammed the door shut, shutting out the light, shutting out Him. The silence crashed around her again, the darkness. The sound of rasping laboured breath. She put her thoughts away from her, to one side, and concentrated on the door. A door handle, maybe there was a lock, a key? In the dark she searched, her hands sodden with sweat once more. Nothing, she found nothing. Substituting her body for a lock, she turned around, slamming her back against the door, grimacing at the pain it caused. Sliding down, ignoring more pain, she landed on her bum and pushed. All she was she put into pushing against that door, feet barely gaining hold on the cold floor. She'd gone from a sheet between them, to a solid wooden door: she wasn't giving it up. As she pushed, feet endlessly slipping on the floor, a thought did occur to her. It was the little voice again, the tiny echo somewhere in the back of her mind, the one that kept making suggestions, good, bad, fucking dangerous. *You're not being chased,* it said. *Nothing has come after you.* She listened to it despite herself. All she wanted to do was concentrate on that wonderful solid door, and relish that she couldn't see Him. No, that he couldn't see her! She was this side, he was the other: it was going to stay that way. But the voice still niggled, still murmured, still sought to betray her jubilation. There was no one following her. There was no weight being pushed against the door. Nothing. It sank in, slowly, as the darkness around her did. She'd made the door because she hadn't been chased: no one was after her. This thought slithered in as she continued to press against the door, continued to fight and slip and slide and desperately scrabble for support, something to hold onto to help her block Him out. No one was after her. It was just her, and the dark, and her rasping, echoing breath, and not knowing where the hell she was. Again.

It didn't take long for tears to start. The feeling of complete helplessness, of humiliation. The dark around her once more became a physical thing that pressed down on her, swallowed her. She fancied she could taste it as it entered her mouth, beat against her eyes. She screamed, to force the dark away from her, to scare it out of her mouth, away from her eyes. The scream echoed, empty, hollow, fading. The sweat had started to pour from her again, rancid, slick; coating everything she touched. It became harder to stay against the door, to keep her folded legs under her. The more she tried, the more she slid around, the less hold she had. In a desperate movement to retain her position, she tried to stand a little, wedge her body harder into the cool frame. Her feet slid away and she fell, banging her head against the door. It didn't hurt that much, but the unexpected motion of meeting something so hard and unyielding, of slipping again and again, of getting nowhere: it all took its toll. Before she could stop herself, before the voice could tell her this wasn't a smart idea, she gave up. Lying on the floor, trying to ignore the wet sucking sounds of her own body, she put her hands over her face and folded herself in. She didn't care, she couldn't care: it was all too much. All there was were her tears, her terror and the dreadful stench of herself in the dark. She wasn't going to play anymore, she was going home. The crying took her over, her head bowed so her face touched her knees, her hair plastered over her. She rocked in the sobbing darkness.

He sat, waiting, listening. He made a bet with himself: an hour, no longer.

She discovered going away was problematic. She didn't know how long she had been rocking, how long she had been crying, but slowly, and as surely as when she had woken up, awareness started to reaffirm, force her to take notice of herself. Once more it started with her back. What had been a deep aching cramp was now a burning pain, spread up and around from the base of her spine. Her shoulders were bruised and aching too, adding their own tones to her back pain. Rocking, it had to be admitted, might have been comforting in some strange way, but it also hurt. The floor beneath her was no longer cold, but it was hard, hard and raw and pressing into her hip bone. Her head was filled with cotton wool, hard, impacted cotton wool that weighed her down and made her feel sick. Her face was just as sore, raw and open from the tears that stung their way endlessly over her skin. A gob of snot trailed from her nose down her cheek, sliding off into her hair. It was no good; as soon as she noticed one thing about her body another brought itself to her attention. She wiped her nose. Her hands ached, as did her wrists. Her knees felt raw and bruised, the soles of her feet tender and sore. Her lungs hurt and her throat felt as if it had been torn out. She was finding breathing difficult, a situation not helped by her being bent double. It was no good, the voice was saying, no good at all. She was just going to have to unfold, stretch out, breathe. She didn't want to, didn't want to admit she was awake, conscious, feeling. But the feeling part was not open to negotiation, she was feeling entirely too much.

It hurt to move but there was a great sense of relief, satisfaction, in turning on her back and stretching out. She realised she had been feeling stuffy and over hot, as moving back her head and letting in a great gulp of air, a sense of openness and coolness caressed her mouth and face. There was also a feeling of dizziness, but it soon passed. Lying there, spread out on the floor, heat and moisture evaporating off her body, she felt better, better than she had done. She sucked in the air, grateful for the release, grateful that there was something nice about the world. The room around her fell into perfect silence as her breathing slowed, calmed, became still. She concentrated on that for a moment, bringing her world down to the tiny regular movement of air going in, air going out. Air going in, air going out. The pains faded for a moment as she felt the air coming in, going out. The voice started up again. Started to think ahead, wonder what was going to happen, was she going to stand, was she going to sit? How had she gotten there? She pushed this question aside, it wasn't to be looked at. She didn't know why, but just thinking about it made her stomach clench, brought an iron band around her lungs making it difficult to breath. She searched around for another question, something easier. The voice accommodated: was she going to lie there for ever till she died of hunger and thirst? What a dramatic thought, she mused. To lie here and die of hunger and thirst. The voice laughed at her, began to talk through the odds of that, given what was on the other side of the door. This thought galvanised her, made her sit up too quickly, the dizziness almost overwhelming her. The other side of the door. He was on the other side of the door. Shit!

He loved to win bets. That had made three in a row this evening. He stood, silently moving towards the door. His hand reached for the switch. Soon, very soon.

CHAPTER FOUR

Her back was once more against the door, her legs, aching and cramped, brought round in front of her. How could she have let herself go all floppy, all silly and stupid, to lie down and cry, hoping she would die from the pain of it...? How could she? The anger burned in her mouth. She was a stupid cow. She was a complete fool and no matter what she was going to get out of this. The voice approved, told her that was a good thought, she should hold on to it. It wasn't all she needed to hold on to. Sitting up had released another sensation in her body. Her bladder was bursting. The dark was once more around her, her body once more wedged against the door, and the need to go was suddenly with her. Strong, insistent, as if she had been ignoring it for some time. Now what was she going to do?

His finger lightly stroked the switch, pulsing, sensing, judging. Stand up little bird, stand up for Daddy...

The more she thought on it, the worse it became. It soon blotted out all but the pain in her back, even her throat became less demanding than the pressure, the actual physical pain that was starting to build in her groin. It was absurd to her, totally surreal, that of all things to concern her, pinned as she was on the side of that door, she was being driven wild by the need to pee. Even the voice agreed that this was silly, stupid, ridiculous. What could they do? She and the voice thought it over. They both came to the same conclusion, the only sensible conclusion there was: she should pee. Let it out, get rid of the pain and concentrate on the door. Sitting up there, in her brain, full frontal: an idea. It wasn't an appealing idea. Sensible yes, appealing, no. She changed her mind, arguing with the voice: it was a terrible idea? The voice, she discovered, was somewhat of a fair weather friend: it didn't answer her back. It had gone away, gone in the now grinding pressure of holding herself in. It was no good, she was going to have to move, sitting here on the hard floor wasn't helping. She was going to have to stand up, leave the door alone, and try and work out where she was. She dimly realised that not wetting herself, crumpled on the floor, in the dark, was more important to her than holding onto the door. She didn't understand it, but there it was. She took a deep breath and scrambled awkwardly to her feet.

Flick.

She screamed, a small part of her aware that this was another pathetic action, but the pain once more blotted all rational thought out. Her eyes once more protested, her hands flung instinctively to protect them. She would have dropped back down, but the fear froze her, kept her stranded up there, standing, caught by the brightness that had pierced her through. Red flooded her eyes, ghost images once more dancing in front of her, keeping track as she shook her head to and fro. The crying started, a wail tearing itself free of her chest. Shit, he was there, he was there! It was no good. He was there. The smell hit her from underneath: sharp, acid, pungent. She felt a warm puddle build around her bare feet: she had wet herself.

The acrid scent flooded under the door. Urine filled to its limit with toxins. A delightful bonus in a game already filling him with glee. His hand reached for the handle.

She was stooped over, half way to the floor, half upright. Her hands were jabbed in her eyes, rubbing, trying to force them to adjust quickly. She couldn't be here, she couldn't be here, in the middle of nowhere, naked, wet. She just couldn't. She couldn't move; she knew that she needed sight, she needed some direction. She forced her hands away, forced herself to blink. She must conquer this, must take charge of her senses.

'I told you not to leave the bed.'

She startled, whirling round, trying to face where the voice was. A scream was caught fast in her throat; she would not let it out. She wasn't going to scream again, not ever. Her feet slipped in the puddle. As she opened her eyes and tried to bring her head up, she fell back, back onto the soaking wet floor, back onto the hardness and the pain. Her shoulder hit something half way down. Hit it hard. Stars danced around in her eyes, pain blossoming out from the joint, her head snapping forward. She slid down on her side, dazed. Too dazed to scrunch up, to hide. She lay there, sprawled, wedged between something. Something hard, cold, at her back, something hard and cold in front of her. Naked, apart from a coat of her own urine and sweat. The small, distant voice came back: it wasn't very helpful. She pushed the thoughts down with some effort. Shame was riding her, riding her harder than the fear. Her eyesight was clearing, helping her identify where she was. A toilet bowl was in front of her, a brilliant white sheen that showed the wreck of her all too clearly. Her arm was screeching, shouting that she had to move before something got mashed. She tried to sit up, found she couldn't. It was a narrow space, she was sore and slippery. She tried again, her elbow banging against the cold hard behind her. She slipped back down on to the floor, defeated.

There was a sharp intake of breath from somewhere above her, a sigh of impatience. She scrunched her eyes shut tight, turned her head to the floor, her fists clenching. She wouldn't look, she wouldn't look.

'Allow me to aid you.'

The words didn't make sense to her, couldn't make sense.

'I will not repeat myself. Allow me to help you.'

There was a tone in those words, an unmistakable air of menace. It was a threat clear and loud. 'Do as I ask,' his voice had said, 'and it will be okay. Fight me, it will not.' She heard it plainly. Her own inner voice heard it too. Her voice urged her to get up, to turn round, to do *anything* rather than just lie there. She followed the advice.

She couldn't see him clearly as she first turned round. The light in the ceiling was behind him, dazzling her. All she got a sense of was his shape leaning down to her, an arm clearly extended to her. She reached up for it. His grasp was strong and firm, pulling her to her feet in one sure movement. Her body screamed its dislike of the action, her mind screamed louder. No sound left her lips. She felt proud of that, if nothing else. He let go of her as soon as he was sure of her footing. She stood, clumsily, trying to hide herself from him, which was impossible. Defeated, her arms dropped to her sides, her head down. He had very shiny shoes. Very expensive shoes. They didn't look pleased, those shoes, standing in her piss. A hand reached for her, lifted her chin up, to stare at him. Their eyes were of almost equal height, which she found curious. A light brown, flecked with tiny shards of amber. Dark hair matched his eyes.

'You smell. You smell foul.'

His emphasis on the 'foul' made her flush red. She tried to drop her eyes, her head, away from his piercing gaze, her hands automatically coming back up, trying to hide, to cower. He held her firm, forcing her attention.

'Clean yourself and come back through to the bedroom.' He turned back to the door, opening it, leaving. Before he disappeared through it, he turned back, addressed her in that no nonsense voice. 'Do not be long.'

The door closed quietly. Tears coursed over her burning cheeks. As he left the bedroom, aiming for the kitchen, he started to hum to himself. *Gods, what a find.* She gave such great fear. He switched the kettle on and busied himself. He had plenty of time.

The bathroom was huge; black and white marble. The floor and walls matched perfectly. White marble flecked with black on the floor, black marble flecked with white on the walls. The toilet and bidet, between which she had so recently rested, were brilliant white. The double vanity unit was gleaming black stone with equally gleaming white stone sinks. The fixtures were silver and black. The shower stall alone was bigger than her bathroom at home. It took up about a quarter of the room, easily holding about six people. It had a series of shower fixtures up the walls and across the top. She'd seen the like in movies, never in real life, not even in hotels at business conventions. The bath was actually quite small, compared to the rest of the room, but it was oval rather than bath shaped, with vents along the sides which she guessed meant it was a jacuzzi. There was a floor to ceiling cupboard with louver doors in silver. It looked like they were real silver, at least to touch. The back of her head, the voice, was screaming that she had to stop looking at the frigging decor and *do* something. She ignored it. Looking was doing something, it was doing about the only thing she could cope with. She'd crumpled down onto the wet floor when he had left, shaking. When she realised what she was doing, she had jumped up like a scalded cat. 'Sides, she wasn't getting into no shower 'til she'd checked what was in the damned cupboard. The voice told her *he* wasn't in the cupboard. She knew that, she told the voice, she was just being cautious. The cupboard was filled with towels. Pure white, soft. Looking at them, touching them, the tears started again, the shaking. No, screamed the voice. *No! No! No!* No way. If she fell apart, he was coming back for her and she didn't want that. The thought did drive some of the dreamy feeling from her, did drive her into the shower. It took a few moments, but she finally got the water out of at least half the jets, first too hot, then too cold, then okay. There were plenty of gels and shampoos and such, on a fitted wire shelf right there in the shower. She stared at them, unthinking. The water ran off her, down the drain. The first thing she noticed, the only thing she really noticed, was that the smell was going. The smell of steam was replacing the smells of... let's not think about that. She'd never thought that steam had a smell, that it smelt clean, warm, friendly. Her hair was flattened down onto her scalp, the water running off it over her shoulders. She tried to run her hands through it, it was matted, sticky. The water was making it wetter, not cleaner. She reached for the shampoo.

The warning wasn't the stinging of her skin, it was the water beginning to run cold. She'd scrubbed and scrubbed, rinsed and then scrubbed again. All of her was red, raw looking. She hadn't noticed. So much of her was pain that it wasn't important. But the water running cold, that was important. That said something about time, about how long she'd been in there. The whole of the cubicle was fogged, cloudy. Opening the door, a blast of seemingly frigid air enveloped her. As did the stench of urine. She stepped carefully out of the cubicle, reaching for the towels warming on the heated bar. She placed them all on the floor, watching them soak up the fluid, watching the stain soak through them. When they were all down she walked round them, skirting them, and opened the cupboard. She brought out fresh towels and wrapped her body in one, then her hair. They were massive, covering most of her. She added a third across her shoulders, like a cape. All that showed was her shins, her ankles and her hands. And her face. She looked around. There wasn't a mirror. She sat down on the toilet seat, shaking. She wasn't sure if she could ever stand again. She looked at the door. It was white, with black running through it, as if it too was marble. There was no lock. No bolt. Nothing. The panic started up in her. She pushed it down, ruthlessly pushed it far away, away to the place the questions were. When she could afford it, then she'd bring it back. Not now. With a deep breath, she forced herself to stand, forced herself to open the door. The voice inside her was utterly silent, for which she was grateful.

He had to admit he was startled as the bathroom door opened: surprised. He had expected to have to go and fetch her. He had taken the stopping of the shower as his cue and was waiting long enough for her nerve to break before going in and getting her. He was undecided if he was pleased, or annoyed, at the change of plan. The going to get her plan had involved wondering if she would fight, or try to run? Run was fun, fighting was fine. Would give him a chance to lay down some rules. He had been running through both scenarios, deciding which pleasure he actively wanted her to present him with. She had done neither, forced him to recalculate: he was pleased. Good thing he had laid the table out all ready. It would not have done to be caught on the hop. He watched her edge nervously into the room. Great fun. Yes, this was better than having to go fetch her. He lifted the first pot.

'Tea?'

She jumped when he spoke, then froze, her exit from the bathroom interrupted. He stood by a table, a table laden with plates and cups and tea things. His raised hand held a silver tea pot. She stared.

'I find tea a most refreshing drink.' He picked up a plain white cup and saucer, deftly filling the cup. ' Also...,' placing the pot back onto the cloth, he picked up a silver jug. 'I find it an excellent activity in those awkward social moments.' He smiled at her. 'Milk?'

She stared. He ignored her.

'It is quite interesting you know, that today...,' he poured the milk and placed both cup and jug down. '... very few people take sugar in their tea. Once, it was almost unheard of not to put sugar in your tea. Now, no one I know puts sugar in their tea.'
He had moved round the table, till he was on the far side of it, and sat down. As he poured his own tea, he glanced up at her, smiling, then busied himself. He finished speaking as he dropped two white sugar lumps into his own cup. The noise of his stirring mesmerised her, transfixed her. Nothing she could think of, nothing she could imagine, explained what was happening. He finished stirring and placed the teaspoon delicately onto the edge of the saucer. As he lifted the cup to his lips, he inhaled deeply. He smiled, then sipped.

'Delicious. One of my favourite mixes. Most refreshing.' He indicated her own cup, sitting on the table. 'Will you not join me?'

The menace was thick, the message clear. It broke through to her. She moved forward slowly, awkwardly, not wanting to get closer to him. She wanted to look around the room, get her bearings back, but the need to keep looking at him overrode everything. The chair she was to sit on was pulled back and angled, making it easy for her to seat herself.

'Excellent. Do try the brew, see if it is to your liking. Biscuit?'

Again, as he offered her a plate of pale Madeleine's, his tone was unmistakable. She reached forward, hesitated, then picked one up. She cradled it in her lap as he prattled.

'It is an interesting blend, mostly Assam with some Darjeeling....' his voice droned on, somewhere above her.

She was staring fixedly at the white linen table cloth. The voice at the back of her mind was assessing it dispassionately. Had to be linen, such a large, yet fine, weave. It gleamed. The light bouncing off it with a shimmer. Her hand reached forward involuntarily, touching it. Damask, said the voice, definitely the finest Damask linen.

'It is Damask,' he said. 'Do you like it?'

She startled out of her reverie so suddenly she couldn't breathe, blood pounding in her temples. She looked over to him. The terror in her eyes was almost a force, a tangible sensation that flooded him. He took her gift eagerly, pressing for more.

'Do have some tea, it will make you feel better.'

He pushed the cup and saucer towards her. His hand reaching closer froze her for a moment, sent her blood pressure racing, her heart skipping beats. She was transfixed, unable to take her eyes from the smoothness of his hand. Pale smoothness, not unlike the cup. The contents swelled slightly, resettling. The dreaming quality returned, the cup shimmering, shifting in front of her. Her eyes hurt with the effort of looking at it, looking so hard she wondered that it didn't shatter. There was a slight noise, he cleared his throat: impatience. She lifted her hands, which were very heavy, unwieldy, one aiming for the cup, the other the saucer. Both landed roughly where they should, she grasped, pulling them back to her. The cup trembled slightly as it travelled, liquid swelling up, dribbling over her hand. The heat was warming, she cupped both hands around and raised it to her lips. She felt the heat rise and touch her skin, tickle her nose. The tea was very milky, not at all what a good Northern Lass should be drinking. She swallowed some down, closing her eyes as she tilted her head back, not wishing to see him. There was pain as it flooded down her throat. She found it hard to swallow, had to force the muscles to work. Yet it was also good, refreshing. Her thirst roared within her, demanding more. She clattered the empty cup back onto the saucer.

'There, I thought that might be just what the doctor ordered.'

She didn't look up as he drew the cup back, poured another cup, pushed it back to her. It was just as milky as the first. She reached for it shakily, her hand overshooting the mark. The cup, and its contents, spilled wildly across the table, soaking the perfect Damask. Her hand stayed where it was, over the now empty saucer, her eyes watching the spreading stain.

'Tut tut, what a pity. Here, allow me.'

He'd stood somehow, and was now beside her. White napkins, which she hadn't noticed, were being piled onto the tea stain in an attempt to soak up the mess. The tea blossomed through.

'What a nuisance, here, let me have this towel.'

The towel from around her head was whisked off before she'd reacted to his request, its thick pile more use than the napkins. He was so close to her, she could feel the air between them move as he leaned this way, then that. He pushed the pot, sugar bowl and Madeleine's back, mopping at the massive stain one small cup had made. When it was contained, he picked the Madeleine's up, wiping dry the bottom of the plate.

'What a mess. Dreadful of me, to over fill that cup.'

He carried on mopping, pushing dry towel onto wet cloth, drawing out the stain, carefully blotting round its edges. Satisfied, he turned to her.

'Here, run and get me a towel soaked in cold water, to stop it drying.'

He handed her back her towel, smiling. He motioned to the bathroom door, encouraging. She watched his back as he again turned to the table, moving things around. She stood, shakily, clutching the soiled towel to her middle, afraid the ones wrapped around her body might fall. She backed away, eyes never leaving his back, until she bumped into the edge of the bed. With a tiny yelp, she turning, fleeing into the bathroom, almost tripping on the towels she had left dealing with her other stain.

She dropped the one she held, pulled a fresh one from the cupboard, stuffing its bulk into a sink and turning on the cold tap. The water spouted up and over her but she barely noticed. Her mission was to get that towel as wet as possible, as fast as possible. She jammed the towel in one end of the sink, watching as it pushed out the other. This just wasn't working. The whole dammed thing was never going to fit in the sink! Panic started once more, and she picked the towel up and threw it into the bath, turning off the sink tap as she went. This time, as cold water flooded the towel, it started to soak quickly. The water pressure was immense, the bath rapidly filling. She switched it off, swirled the towel round, picking up one edge and wringing it out over the bath, working her way up the length as she pulled it clear of the water. It could only have been two, maybe three minutes before she was back in the bedroom, hurrying forward with her burden. He'd cleared the cloth out from the table and folded it neatly. He took the towel from her and wrapped it around the tablecloth, as if he were wrapping a gift.

'There, that should keep it from drying out until I can get it cleaned. I shall just go pop it into a plastic bag.'

He smiled once more, and quickly left the room via the door that she'd been not looking at. Silence crashed around her. Her legs felt weak and before she'd really noticed what she was doing, she'd sank down onto the edge of the bed. He'd left the door open, light spilled in, forming a long rectangle on the floor. She stared at it. A thought was just beginning to form, who knows what it might have been, when she saw his shadow precede him. She lifted her head. He was drying his hands on a small towel, no a tea towel. He used it to wipe clean the surface of the table. There had been a tray, somewhere on the floor on his side of the room, for he leaned down, lifting it up onto the table top. It took seconds to clear the clutter, all neatly piled up. He sighed, then leaned down to the floor, picking up the Madeleine she'd cradled.

'Clumsy.' He shook his head. 'Never mind, mess can always be cleaned up, *always*.'

His voice on the second 'always' was faded, distant. It sent a chill down her spine, the hairs on her neck prickling. She contained the shudder that went through her as he once more swept out of the room, this time with tray in hand. Her eyes returned to the light that blazed across the floor. The floor gleamed under its impact. She moved her feet, feeling the cool surface. The light continued to bounce up at her, bounce up from the smooth, seamless floor. The floor was covered in linoleum. Thick, dark coloured linoleum. Her hands rested back onto the bed cover as she puzzled this. As they sank onto the sheeting, she felt the slight crinkling underneath. The voice inside her head rang out with authority, with warning. She realised it had been trying to say something for some time. Her hands massaged the soft covering, investigating. The crinkling was way down, two or three layers. She pulled back the edge of the sheets. There, under three sheets, was a bed protector, sealing the mattress. Gleaming, exactly as the floor gleamed. The voice became louder, more insistent. Instinctively, she covered the bed back up as she tried to grapple with what it was saying, what her mind had noticed. The panic it brought set off her body, dizziness once more threatening to overwhelm her. Her hands began to shake, breathing more difficult. Sweat once more sprang out of every pore in her body. He came back to the room as the scream was fighting up through her chest, desperate to get out. She wouldn't let it and the effort was choking her. She would hold onto this, her mind was insisting: she had to get a grip. She didn't look at him, her eyes again studying the floor, the deadly, smooth, eminently *cleanable* floor. She was wrong, she just had to be wrong. He must have spoken, but she didn't hear the words, aware only that there were other sounds in the room apart from her heartbeat. The scream was still trying to get up, get outside her, make itself large over her thoughts; she couldn't risk looking up. She dropped her head lower, her chin dropping onto her chest: she would not scream. Her left wrist was yanked upwards, her head following naturally. He was standing over her, the light from the door once more making his face indistinct. His mouth was moving. She stared at his lips. Her arm was pulled sideways. The pain made her focus.

'I expect to be answered, do you hear me?'

His face was twisted up, his voice too. She nodded, unsure of what he'd said.

'Good, I am glad we have that settled. I did not speak for my own amusement.'

His voice had evened out, unkinked. He let go of her wrist. The pain immediately bloomed through her bones, shot up her arm. She grabbed the wrist with her other hand, rubbing. The pain lit out again, making her groan. He'd turned away from her, closing the door softly.

The light was shut out, returning them to the dimmer glow of the lamps. He was there again, beside her.

'Whilst we are on the subject...,' the pause had the desired effect. She raised her face to his. 'There is still a little outstanding business between us.' His voice was soft, tender; cajoling. 'I distinctly remember telling you not to leave the bed.'

Persuading her to do something. She took a deep breath, attempting to calm things: now, more than ever, it was important to look as if she was listening. She raised her face to him, composing it as best she could: she would listen. She didn't see him move, had no time to react, to tense. The force that slammed into the side of her face lifted her off the bed, throwing her sideways onto the floor. She screamed.

CHAPTER FIVE

Her body convulsed as she hit the floor with bone jarring force. Every pain she'd awoken with was doubled, trebled by the impact. Her temple slapped against the floor before she slid to an ungainly halt. The breath had been driven from her and she lay there too dazed to be afraid. The pain was beyond her body's endurance, her stomach wretched, bile filled tea surging up into her mouth, spraying around her, soaking onto her hair, combining with the sweat once more pouring out of her. For a moment she thought she would suffocate, desperately struggling to bring air into her lungs. She spluttered, coughed, got rid of the foul liquid. Above her, there was silence. Awareness of her circumstance somewhat recovered her from the daze, she felt around, trying to find her hands, her arms, to raise herself up.

'Stay where you are.'

The words were quiet, spoken softly. It didn't really impact on her what he'd said, that he was speaking: she continued to find some hold to help her up, get her back into a less agonising position. The blow came low in her back, directly over her kidneys. Immense, downwards, a kick that drove her flat onto the unyielding floor. A low, desperate moan escaped her clenched teeth. Her mind was dealing with its own blows: *this couldn't be happening.* Her hands began to flex, stretch, try and make sense of the surface she was impaled upon. Her right leg, trapped under her at an angle, felt broken, wrenched from the socket. Her left shoulder was end onto the hard floor; a burning, urgent agony.

'Stop moving.'

Once more, she wasn't really aware, couldn't make sense of the soft voice above her. Her hands continued to fidget.

'Stop.'

The voice was terribly low, soft, cajoling. The force that pinned her increased, continued to mash her downwards. She felt her lower back stretch, something tearing, other areas writhing within her. She shrieked, instinctively flexing against the pain, her hands clenching into fists. Her eyes streamed silent tears. A great battle was starting within her, if she didn't move, she would die: something awful was going to happen inside her.

'Stop moving.'

Impossibly, for his foot was still holding her to the ground, his voice was in her left ear, a seductive whisper. This reached her when nothing else had. She ceased struggling. Ceased moving. For a few seconds, ceased breathing. The moment stretched. She lay, waiting. Nothing happened. The fight began again; her body demanding something change, something move, something happen *now*.

The nothingness, the void, continued. Panic once more started up with her, demanding that, if nothing else, she have complete hysterics. She tried so hard not to let it happen, not to give in, but the control was slipping, any second now... the pressure eased, shifted. He had stepped off her. The instinct was to move, to curl into a little ball, hug herself. The part of her that was detached, listening, aware, told her to stop, to wait, to continue in the nothingness. Her body rebelled at the instruction, demanding movement. Into her mind flashed the image of the plastic covered mattress. *Mattress.* She became inert. Another few seconds, then his voice, still quiet, still gentle.

'Get up and sit on the bed.'

She listened.

Movement, for all that her body had been crying out for it, was a terrible thing. She had thought she had been in pain, had thought some limit had been reached, but as she tried to sit, tried to move limbs into more normal lines, huge demons woke and began devouring her body. Her back didn't want to work, she pushed her weight up with her arms. Her right hip, which had taken the landing on the floor, was sending shooting lines of needle sharp pains down her leg. The pain in her shoulder joint eased as she came semi upright, to be replaced by the sick pounding from her left temple: the whole line of her face feeling raw, burnt. She was conscious of roughly drawing the loosened towel to her as she turned to sit slightly, willing her back to keep with it, to help her sit up. The dizziness and shaking threatened her once more and she fought it down. Her breathing was ragged, shallow; dots beginning to form in her vision, dancing in front of the linoleum. *Hyperventilating.* The word was scary. Scarier was the thought of what would happen if she passed out. She swallowed hard, swallowing down bile and vomit, chasing it with her fear: *she was not going to faint.* Her head flopped onto her chest, hair a thick, wet screen. She forced her mind to calm her body, forced her breathing to slow down. Deep breath in, hold, *one two,* breath out. Deep breath in, hold, *one two three,* breath out. Wait. Deep breath in, hold, *one two three four,* breath out. Wait some more. Deep breath in, hold, *one two three four,* breath out. She could do this.

He was both annoyed, and mildly amused. On one hand, her pain threshold was miserably low. She had barely a mark on her, had hardly been touched. Her fear laden sweat was rancid in the air, as was her conviction that she was suffering some grievous injury. Her movements suggested that ligaments had been wounded at some point, in her lower right back, which irritated him. There must have been more damage from earlier, for them to behave like that. He did not like it when bodies did unexpected things, things not planned for, weighed and accounted. He studied her crab like movements, his eyes flicking this way and that, checking what was her own fear and what was actual damage. If the ligaments were torn, rather than just bruised, it would mean a week's rest before he could play. Or rather, it meant he would drain her dry now, and go find something else for his play. She was on her knees now, pulling herself along to the end of the bed, somewhat hampered by her continual clutching of the towel, her dogged refusal to look up. This, along with the breathing control, was somewhat pleasing. Whilst she was in tatters, completely illogical and unthinking in ninety per cent of what she was doing and feeling, she had brought that breath under control, had the sense not to look him in the eye. Possibilities for pleasure, for making her willingly look him straight in the eye, flooded his mind. He schooled his body to stay still, remain silent, allow events to evolve naturally: it was always best.

She made it to the bed's edge and discovered a seemingly unclimbable barrier. No matter how she tried, she couldn't get her body up off the floor. He became convinced he had been wrong about her back, wrong in his estimation that it was merely muscle shock, that there had, after all, been significant soft tissue damage, when she did something totally surprising: she allowed the towel to drop and clambered up. It had been the need for holding the towel to her that had hindered so. He smiled, despite himself. It did not matter, for she was still not looking at him with great determination. She was flat on the bed, face down. Now what? She slowly inched sideways, moving up to the head board end of the bed. *Clever girl.* Maybe she was going to be worth the effort after all. He took the opportunity presented to fully assess her back, watching the muscles, ligaments and tendons bunch and relax as she moved. As he'd thought, no significant problems. There wasn't even going to be a great deal of bruising, the swelling was minimal. It was her own ignorance of her body that made her think her back was damaged, made her protect against moving it. She had reached the far end of the bed, her hip resting against the headboard. Now, this was going to be interesting. He had said 'sit up', how smart was she?

She began by bunching her hands into the sheets, pulling them up to her face. Then, she rolled her hip into the headboard, her right knee digging into the bed to help raise her hips. That had hurt, as a spasm had ripped down through the hip to the thigh. She hesitated, then pushed up with her hands. Oh what joy! The sheet was in her teeth, which meant that as she rose, her body was somewhat covered. Cute. When her backside was up high enough, she tucked her knees under her and slipped backwards, into an upright position, her back resting against the corner of the sideboard. Eyes still hidden by hair, head pointing fixedly at the bed, she wriggled under the sheets she had brought with her, freeing her knees from under her. Finally, she was resting her left hand side roughly between bed and headboard, knees tucked to the other side. Her head remained down. He wondered if he should applaud.

'Well, that did take you long enough.'

She flinched from his voice, which was expected. That was always the problem, when he had persuaded himself that he needed to refresh himself, cleanse his palate: most of it was so dammed expected. The voice had also placed him in the room for her, so she turned slightly more into the headboard, perfectly aligned to his form, seated behind the table at his chair.

'Now, if we are sitting comfortably, I will begin.'

She trembled, her breathing speeding up. A heartbeat or two, the breathing was once more contained.

'I have only a few rules, I expect them to be observed.' As he spoke his mind had geared up, taking on board all the information she was giving him; breath-rate, heart-rate, sweat-rate, movement, scent. Testing her responses, estimating what would gain him maximum hold. 'First, and foremost...,' a pause, to allow that heart rate to speed up a little more. 'I expect total obedience.'

Another pause, this time to allow it to calm down after that pleasing little spurt on *obedience*. Good word. Great response. His own heartrate increased fractionally. He modified his tones to bring down his own level.

'This means, simply, that whatever I want you to do, you will do.'

His emphasis on *whatever* had sent her into panic, her breath was not coming under control, her head turned sideways away from him. Not so good. He was not going to lock himself into repeating himself if she was too frantic to actually listen; that would reduce his own authority. Inklings on how epic this struggle might be were beginning to tease his brain; his adrenaline level increasing dramatically. He savoured the moment, the rush of power it brought with it, weighing the options. He waited, allowing her the space to choose the response. It took a while, but she climbed back down; breath calming, heart rate reducing.

He realised, somewhat belatedly, that her fear of sexual attack was sustained and deeply founded. Perhaps she had already been abused, some dark secret which had not been hinted at when he had probed her during dinner. More likely, as he was all too aware, she was a child of her age. A pathetic and illogical fear lodged deep in her psyche by constant reference, constant exposure. Tedious, but, on balance, unsurprising. It may have been more surprising to find a female in this culture who did not react so. Still, that was what this was all about, fundamentally. She, like all the previous occupiers of her current position, would furnish him with the culture of the day: her reactions would outline the fashions of the moment. Already, in trying to lay down one simple line, a huge battle area had opened up. A learning curve, to serve him well. It may have been pleasing to him to have her reduced so by one word, but the knowledge it brought, the *awareness*, was more useful. He considered; mediated his tone, reinforcing the actual point he had been trying to make.

'It is so simple, so clear. Whatever I say, you will obey.'

The emphasis rested on *will*. That was where the battle was, no matter her fears. Her breathing continued on, as even as it could be. He rewarded her by taking his tone as far away from dark threats as he could. Light, measured, patient.

'In the first instance...,' that was good. Pedantic. Cultured. *Educated*. That would calm her. Ironic, given how often he'd had to shed *educated* throughout his life, how threatening *educated* was to most of the known world. 'You may not leave this room.'

She had relaxed slightly at this seemingly innocuous command. Her fear of what he might have said making what he did say less threatening. He took the opportunity to expand.

'By this, and I am being very specific here, you must never open that door.' He gestured behind, aware she wasn't looking.

He let the moment build, gauging how well she had heard by her reactions: she had heard: understood.

'You may, of course,' he continued, light and reasonable, 'use the bathroom to your right. All that is in this room, and that, is freely available to you at all times.'

His hand had risen up, sweeping the arc of the room as he had spoken. She had not seen it, of course. Oh, delicious dilemma! What did he want to do now, make her look, let her hide? Make her look, let her hide? Make her look...?

'Beyond this door however, you must not stray.'

Her head had lifted up slightly, she had responded to his natural lead, but not enough to reveal herself. Unless... a prickling began at the base of his neck. A thought, a delightful, if a little piqued, thought, occurred to him. What if she was looking at him? What if, and this was quite a thought for a snivelling low life like her, she was peeking out at him from under that matt of hair? What if the angle of her head was about giving show that she was not looking, whilst she was actually keeping him in view now that she was sitting up, somewhat safely, on the bed? Well, well, how interesting... he considered how best to catch her out, if she was actually being bold enough to stare at him.

'In addition, you may not look at me, may not make contact with my eyes, or my face, unless I instruct you to.'

There! A tiny move of the head, a flick away from him. Her heart beat picked up, her breath tightened in her chest. She had been looking! The tiny movement was repeated, her head moving slightly in reverse. She had returned her gaze to him. *You little bitch...*

He stood up; contained muscle and silent speed. She jumped back in the bed, grasping the sheets up to her, her head ducking down. Too late, little bird, too late.

He backhanded her across the right cheek, her head banging up into the headboard, that damn hair flying back. On the rebound, he caught the other side of her face with an open slap. Already bruised, the pain made her scream out. He caught the back of her head with his left hand, pulling her face and neck up to him. Her hands tried to fight him off, he slapped her face again, the blow more effective for her head being held still.

'Stop struggling. Stop. Or I *will* hurt you.'

Her back arched, but after a second, the hands fell. A moan escaped her lips, her eyes were now truly looking down.

He used his leverage at the nape of her neck to pull her face up, at the same time placing his left hand flat over her mouth. For an instant, their eyes met. She held his gaze, then, in response to his focussing of his eyes, his signalling that he was displeased, she closed her lids. The heat of her blood, rising up between them, evaporating off her body, was distracting. *Finish the lesson first. Always.* Golden Rule.

'Look at me.'

Hesitation, the lids faltering in their closure. He tightened the grip on the back of her head. The eyes flew open. She looked out at him. He leaned forward, his head dropping away, his eyes boring into her. He raised his hand.

'Never. Ever. Do. That. Again.'

Each word was followed by a slow hard edged slap. Her head caught in the vice of one hand, he'd been free to aim the blows to perfection. Blood flooded out from her lips, her left eye closed over rapidly.

'Ever.'

The final slap sent an ark of her blood across the back of the headboard. He had intended to stop there, but her snivelling annoyed him. He raised her head back up to him, careful to check for real signs of damage as he continued.

'Also...,' his voice filled with as much menace as he could summon, 'you should know I do not *like* screaming. I *hate* moaning. I cannot *abide* crying and I *loathe girly little yelps of pain!'*

At each emphasis he slapped her across the face and head, increasing the force. The hands had come up, finally, to be punched away, the head had tried to struggle free: futile. Blood covered her face. The left eye was totally closed. She was screeching.

'I *said*, I *do not* like *noise!*'

The last had been a straight fisted punch into her diaphragm. As all the air exited her body, so did the noise. He moved back, allowing her to fall forward. Face down, bent double, body arching into the pain, arms clutching her stomach, she remained silent, even after the air had been returned to her lungs. Tears fled across her cheeks, chasing the blood onto the bed linen, drool escaping her swollen lips. The only sounds were the desperate dragging of breathing taking place under difficult circumstances.

'Now, that is *much* better.' He made his way back to his seat.

She lay there, willing her body to unfold itself again, to unfold out of the pain, back away from it. She concentrated hard on her breathing, on the noise she made as air dragged in and out of here: she would be *silent*. A few moments' battle and she could sense silence once more taking over the room, her breathing only a little ragged, a little uneven, around the edges. His voice spoke into the quiet:

'Much more like it. In fact, so good, so very very good that you have obeyed me, a reward is at hand.' He stood up, walking towards the door, turning before he left. 'No running off now, I shall return in just a tick.'

His laughter was genuine as he exited the room.

She didn't know how long he had been gone. Wasn't even that bothered, truth be known. Something had gone 'click' inside her as she'd lurched forward onto the bed. Some part of her had closed down, emptied the shop, slammed down the shutters. The curious thing was that she was aware of it, understood it, could sense it as it was happening. *Shock.* The voice, which was very far away, very weak, exceptionally useless to her, kept muttering the word. *Shock.* Was she in shock? Did she care? Tired, tired was all she could think of. *Shattered.* She was still musing about the voice, about how tired she really was, when he came back. How long had he been gone? She didn't move, didn't react. After all, he hadn't said anything yet. There was a clattering behind her, something being put down on the table. She felt so tired. Maybe, if he left her alone, maybe she could get some sleep...

'All ready for you now, turn over.'

His voice was different. Light hearted, happy. Gay, in the old sense (she should be so lucky). The thought of turning over, of moving, made her feel physically sick. She turned slowly, trying to protect her head from too much movement. The room was spinning. How often had she read that, heard it? How often...? Didn't matter, didn't matter at all. The room was spinning and she wasn't going to dwell on the cliché, just try and keep her insides from turning over once more. If she started to wretch again: she'd lose it. She knew it, the voice knew it. One more retch, one more jabbing pain from her stomach, one more jar to the head and she'd go stark, staring mad.

That would annoy him.

She clenched her eyes closed, as she turned to the light that was on his side of the room. She lay there, obviously facing the noises from the table, keeping them tightly shut. There was an impatient tut from above her.

'Oh, sorry, you can look.'

She opened her right eye slowly, not trusting what she'd see, or how it would feel. Once more, with impeccable positioning, he was framed by the lamps, his face in semi darkness. She squinted against the stabbing agony that her left eye gave out as she tried to focus. Impossible, she couldn't open it, could only see from one side, the perspective skewed to hell. She closed the good eye, swallowing down more blood and tears. He was moving something on the table. She listened to the noises, using them as her focal point. The world centred on what she could hear, could she guess what was happening? His hands moved, she flinched, despite herself, despite the mantra building within her.

Don't do anything to annoy him, don't do anything to annoy him, don't do...

'Lean forward, into the light.' His voice was light, happy, contented.

She did what he said, needing to shuffle forward in the huge bed to reach him. Dimly, she was aware that things weren't hurting as much as she'd feared. There was a sound of water. He leaned over to her and placed a warm cloth against her chin. Despite everything, it felt reassuring, comforting. He carefully pushed back the matted tangle of sodden hair and slowly bathed her face.

'There, is that better? Does that feel good? I always find the smell of hot water and clean linen comforting.'

He wittered at her as he progressed around her face. She could smell the fabric conditioner on the cloth, she didn't recognise the brand, or at least, the scent. There was also a faint hint of expensive male cologne, she wondered if it was him, or his clothes? As he worked, he avoided her lips and her left eye, both of which felt about forty times larger than they should have been. He was very gentle. His voice was light, delicate, sing-song in its cadences. She felt reality slipping ever further away. He'd had to return to the bowl, sloshing and squeezing, two or three times before he deemed the job finished. It was only as he reached down to her hands, washing them clean, wiggling the cloth between her fingers, slowly drawing the heat across the palms, that she realised she had slowly slumped back, onto soft pillows. Pillows he had plumped up behind her. She felt drowsy, drugged.

It's the shock, it's taking you down.

He patted the back of her hand.

'Just one last thing, before I let you rest.' He was still wittering on. 'Always a good idea to do this.' He'd reached up for her head, sending his fingers under the tangled hair at her neck, the cloth cooling in his hands. 'My mother always did this for me, when bad things happened.'

This information *literally* sent shivers down her spine, sent the adrenaline pumping back out once more. If he'd noticed her tense, he didn't react, didn't acknowledge it.

'She always said that the back of the neck was the most sensitive area the human body had. She never missed it out.'

He sighed in exasperation: his progress was impeded by her hair, by the awfulness of the fetid sweat and sick caught in its wild tangles. He persevered for a moment, trying to draw the now cold cloth across the nape of her neck. She tried to assist him, terrified he would grow angry, but he resisted.

'No, no little one. You rest, I am here now, I shall take care of you.'

He withdrew, back to the table, as he had done previously to renew the cloth. She closed her eyes, grateful for the respite. Touching her neck, trying to move her head forward, had hurt, her pulse pounding a painbeat deep into her skull. He lifted her forward once more, the cloth, warmer now, resting on the nape of her neck. He left it in position and placed her gently back. He pushed her hair back out of her eyes, her face. A strand caught in the folds of her swollen eye, tugging painfully. She flinched, but did not cry out.

'Very good little one, excellent.' He gently pulled the strand free. 'Let us see what else we can do to make you feel comfortable.'

He'd gone, it took her a moment to realise that, but she was past caring. One mantra filled her mind as the oblivion she needed so desperately finally set her free.

dontannoyhimdontannoyhimdontannoyhimdontannoyhimdontann oyhimdont

She had fallen into shock by the time he returned, as he had suspected. He slipped the drip back into her vein, the sedative and pain killers flooding her once more. He delighted in making them heal so quickly, confusing them, confounding. As the drip did its work, he filled the bath tub with warm water. When she was completely under, he took out the needle and lifted her into the tub, washing off the sick and the blood. Laying a good two inches of towel down on the bedroom floor, he left her there to dry whilst he stripped and remade the bed. A long time ago he had discovered the power of identical accessories, and took great pride in making sure the bed looked exactly as it had. The headboard cleaned off easily, and he re-laid the table with another Damask cloth.

The drugs had brought the swelling down, and he towel dried her hair carefully, gently untangling the knots with his hands, before laying her on the soft down of the pillows. He wondered about the advisability of an ice pack on her lips, but wasn't convinced the cold would not impinge on her slumber. She was so completely relaxed, that he could test her body with ease. Her face was a mess, but that had been the point after all. Her stomach showed a slight swelling, but there was no damage to the tissue or organs underneath. His accuracy remained unchallenged. Her back was mottling interesting shades of blue and black but the tear on her neck was fully healed. He was slightly concerned about the eye, which remained swollen despite the level of anti-inflammatories that had been used. Placing a line of paper stitches along the swollen ridge, he let his blood soak into them, holding its power upon the worst of the bruising. He then reinserted the line and changed the rate of drug flow. He switched off the light as he went.

He drove many miles, many hours from London. Deep in feral countryside, far from any human habitation he stripped and fell into the dark; naked but for the soles of his feet: hungry. All scattered in front of him, and he chased down the wild things in his path. A hardy little pony, young and fast, fell into his radar, and he played at catching it with great abandon. It was easily chased but harder to snare. He delighted in letting it 'go' several times until he could smell the blood on its mouth in amongst the thick white foams of sweat. Lungs had finally ruptured, a heart was close to bursting. He caught it quickly and tore it limb from limb. The sound of the tearing, the snapping and the splintering, the feel of his own power, excited him. Nothing else could raise that pulse of power from his groin anymore: nothing but complete physical struggle. Plunging his face into the just pulsating heart, he felt the heat and life soak into his bones as he drained the blood into his mouth. By the time he had rubbed the cooling flesh all over himself, his penis was rock hard and swollen to its limit. He let out a roar, a challenge to the sky, and took off, flinging himself at the night, the countryside, the rocks and earth with all the strength of his soul. He ran. Pushing himself, testing, ignoring the fire that devoured his limbs, his bones and his sinews. There was nothing here to bother him, distract him, decoy him. He could be what he was: elemental. She had allowed him the grace to rediscover his true nature, and that was one of fire and death. He ran until his body could no longer move, no longer think. He fell exhausted, spent, on the coarse gorse, relishing this feeling of power: the sheer physical wonder of his existence. He slept briefly, a sleep of the dead, one with the soil, before rising to immerse himself in the freezing waters of a stream. Cleansed, he located his car and in the growing haze of light that was another dawn, began the long journey home.

CHAPTER SIX

Naturally, she was still under when he returned. His blood, held captive on her skin, had worked its magic, and her eye was greatly reduced, almost clear. Bruising ran the line of her face, down her cheek and jaw. It looked three to four days old, well on its way to recovery. She was restless, once more fighting the drugs. The stench of urine from the soiled bed was high, but no solid waste was in evidence. He would attend to the smell in turn. Slipping the line out, splattering the tiny wound with some blood, it healed over almost instantly. Running a lukewarm bath, he washed her down, and spent five minutes combing her hair through. The water had a faint stain of pink by the time he finished. Even as she began to stir, he moved her to and fro effortlessly, 'tho her skin goosepimpled as he lifted her clear. He placed her on a thick layer of towels on the bedroom floor as he tidied the bathroom back into place. He left the light on and the door wide open, to show her the pathway when she woke. He cleared the clutter of the drip and once more changed the bedding. . Settled back into bed, she was clean and her skin showed excellent colour and fluid retention. He withdrew to check his mail and faxes. It would be a couple of hours.

She awoke on the bed, hazy remembrances that fear and discomfort had become her existence. She knew where she was instantly; the pain told her that. If he was sitting in the shadows beside her, she didn't want to know. She fell as she tried to raise herself up off the bed, the pain buckling her knees. The floor came up hard and heavy, and she lay there, tears streaming down her face. Her eyes protested the glare from the bathroom and she kept them tightly shut until the stars faded. When she was sure she could see, she crawled forward on her hands and knees. It took about five minutes to rise up and straddle the bowl but she managed. A faint dribble was all she could manage. With rubbery legs she scrambled into the security of the shower stall, grateful once more for the blast of steam that soon enveloped her. She lay on the floor of the shower cubicle, shaking under the rain of heat and comfort.

When she finally emerged into the bedroom, the main light was on. Her bed was remade, pristine, fresh. The table held a tray: tea, orange juice, a tub of yoghurt, croissants, jam and butter. She wryly wondered if she'd ticked the box for 'extra large' on the oj. She tried to take a small sip but the smell alone made her retch. Faint from the heat and exertion, she lay down on the bed and closed her eyes.

When she opened them again he was sitting there, looking at her. She caught her breath, then quickly turned away, staring intently at the bedcover. It had been pulled up over her.

'You were sleeping.'

She didn't reply, tried not to move, to react. The towel she had wrapped around her head had slipped onto her shoulders, the damp had settled on her neck.

'You have not eaten, or had anything to drink.' She stared harder at the bedcover. It was white, soft, expensive. Linen, she was sure, although not Damask, not like the table cloth. She looked again at the table, with the glittering tray. No evidence there of her earlier clumsiness. Her head swam and she sighed, moving back on the pillows. *Just let it happen,* the voice said, *just let whatever, happen. No thinking, no thoughts, no doing...just go with it.*

He stood up, came towards her. Her head moved further to the side, away from him. She tried not to flinch. He leaned into her and something heavy was passed onto her lap. He retreated. It was the tray, magically settled on her lap on little stilts. She could see steam curl out of the teapot's spout.

'If you do not eat, more importantly, if you do not drink, I will be forced to take action.' His voice was patient, measured.

She tried to absorb this, tried to make her body move.

'Besides, there are painkillers in front of you. Painkillers that require they are administered with food.'

This caused her to search the tray more fully. She was convinced they hadn't been there earlier, but sure enough, by a glass of water, was one of those little plastic cups you get in hospital. It contained two tiny white tablets and two huge pink ones.

'The white ones go under your tongue. They will make the aches go away.'

Should she trust him? Did she have a choice? She knew the pink ones were anti-inflammatories, she'd taken them often enough. *No thinking... do as he says!* Her hand reached over for them.

'Not before you have eaten, and drunk the juice.' His voice was compelling, insistent.

She lifted the juice, forced it to her mouth. It tasted incredibly sweet. Once started, her mouth appeared to have difficulty stopping. Juice dribbled out the sides of her mouth.

'Not too quickly, you will cramp. Eat now.'

She transferred her attention to a croissant, the thought of gaining some respite from the pain, the aches, the terror of her body, driving her on. It flaked in her hand, tasted of dust in her mouth. She swallowed it down with the remainder of the juice. She reached for the drugs again.

'Pink first.'

There was a pulse of impatience in her mind, an irritation at the command. The voice was there, panicked and insistent: *do as he says...do as he says... do as he says...*

She fished the pink tablets out of the tub, careful to keep her eyes from straying up. It took four drinks of water before they were gone, the second one almost choking her. She picked the tub up again.

'Yoghurt first, before you get those.'

She sighed, despite the caution. *Do not annoy him.*

The yoghurt was sharp, clean. She almost enjoyed it, although the silence dragging out between them as she spooned it down began to strip her of the little composure she had. *Do nothing, do nothing, do nothing, do nothing.* Sweat was once more pooling around her. The last spoonful gone, she reached for the little white tablets. This time, he didn't stop her.

'Put them under your tongue. Do not crush or chew them. Just let them dissolve.'

It was fiddly, getting them under her tongue, her distended lips making her entire mouth feel wrong, out of shape. She finally popped them under with a finger. It was a bitter-sweet taste as they dissolved. She waited for something to happen, either with him, or herself. Was this was his way of killing her? Had she taken some poison? *No thoughts, no thinking, no doing.* He stood, moved towards her, picking up the tray. She only realised this had happened as the weight was taken off her legs. The world was blurred, dreamy. As she realised she was no longer in pain, or rather, that she no longer cared she was in pain, tears slid down her cheeks. Everything was receding: her back, her legs, her shoulder, the burning on the left hand side of her face. The voice.

The bed beneath her was slowly becoming more comfortable, softer, cosier. The sharp, vicious world of the bedroom was losing focus, leaving her. The tears cascaded down her face, silent, unheeded. There was no emotion attached, no feeling at all. She was mostly concerned with how marvellous it was that she could know each and every part of her that hurt, map out the pathway of injury across her body, yet feel no pain. Her right wrist had its familiar ache, the always present sensation that constant use of her mouse caused. She'd lost it in the barrage of other pains, how odd it should be there now, when the others had left? He moved in front of her vision and she shrank away slightly. The bed on her right hand side dipped as his weight was transferred to it. She should recoil, she knew, but she was so content, in her numbness that she could not muster the energy. An arm slipped behind her neck, pulling her closer. Panic pricked at her then, although it was a faint, formless thing. Nothing worth her attention. She drifted, emptied, floating, semi solid, like a jelly fish deep in the ocean, swirled and caressed by the currents around her; directionless.

There was shuffling and movement, her body being jogged a little this way, pulled along that way. None of it hurt at all, which was just fine. His arm pulled her up, into him. She could smell his fragrance, clean and light. His clothes warm and soft. Her head rested on his chest, his arms enfolding her. Her body moved into his without thought, her arm snaking across him, grasping, reaching for some sense of support. Something warm to grab a hold of. His left hand reached up and stroked her forehead gently. The silent flood of tears continued, staining his clothes. She could hear the air moving in and out of his lungs. A heartbeat against her ear, soothing somehow. She moved almost imperceptibly into him, a tiny, rocking motion flowed out along her entire body. She curled tighter against him, made herself smaller. His right hand stroked down the length of her spine, sure, soft. Again and again, he caressed her back, his body matching the rhythm of hers: they slowly rocked together. Her breath quickened, her throat tightened. Tears that had fallen silently began to carry noise: distress, meaning. The pain was building. Not the pain in her drifting, echoing body, the pain elsewhere: deeper, darker, more insistent. Sobs emerged from her throat, burning tears now being squeezed from tightly clamped eyes. Throughout it all, his rocking held her, his hands soothed her body. True crying was starting to emerge, broken breathing, ragged sobs; she felt the panic begin to rise within her. As she tensed, his body changed, grew softer, released her a little. She took in a gasping breath, trying to hold onto the dreaming, the peace. A vibration distracted her slightly, building against her cheek. There was a thrumming there, a humming. A rhythm building that didn't owe its existence to her body, to her pain. Sound carried through the drugs, slipping into her mind. There was a song, singing, somewhere beside her. Gradually, she allowed herself to hear the words.

'...gonna buy you a lookin' glass, and if that lookin' glass gets broke...'

He had a nice voice. Soft, warm, secure. She listened as his hands resumed their slow, gentle soothing. Delicate strokes down her spine, tiny caresses of her forehead and cheeks. The crying subsided, fell away with the rest of her. Her breathing slowed, became more regular, deeper. Her heartbeat calmed, her mind melting. She fell asleep, aware only of his warmth, his weight and the blessed absence of pain.

He held her for much longer than he had intended, until she was completely, utterly asleep. He had found himself a little enchanted by her complete surrender to him. As her muscles had relaxed and her blood pressure dropped, her pulse calmed and her breath deepened, there had been pleasure in her ease. The fleeting glimpse of her as child had returned. His intent had been to do no more than hold her, calm her down, relax her with the warmth of his contact. The stroking, the singing, had surprised him. He rarely sang his loves to sleep. Not at this stage. He pulled his arm free, settling her back into the bed in a more comfortable position. It would have been useful to have examined her, checked for any serious injury, but the pain killers were giving her respite; it was a natural sleep, unlike the one induced by the sedative. A healing sleep. She might awaken and he wanted rest for her more than he needed to check her condition. Besides, that she was asleep naturally so quickly, suggested all was well.

He climbed off the bed carefully, pulling up the covers to protect her. It took moments to clean and refresh the bathroom. He tiptoed past her with towels and supplies. He took the tray back to the kitchen, returning with an insulated jug of iced water and a large bowl of fruit, which were carefully placed on the round table in plain view. The final touch was a plain white towelling dressing gown, which he hung up on the back of the bedroom door.

He made himself steak and eggs, filled a glass with water and settled himself in the TV room. He flicked here and there as he ate, never settling on one thing. His body was exhausted, in need of epic sleep. The run over the moors had used all his energy, he needed to rest, restore, build up his cells again. There was, however, no sleep in him and he knew it. Besides, in order to sleep for the three or four days he needed, he'd have to make plans for her. She was not at that stage yet. More ground rules needed to be laid, less panic and more submission, otherwise she might destroy herself in a frenzy, when left that long. He mused upon the possibilities. So far, there had been no time for her to think, everything had been about reaction and survival. She had not had time to register much and had, he knew, thought little of what the reality of her situation was: he had seen to that. To continue the disorientation, or allow her time to fester in her own mind? Whilst there was no room in him for doubt in his own strengths in the matter, there was knowledge that different approaches had, on occasion, resulted in different ends.

Pride kept him from the thought that it had ever gone wrong: it was merely a case of building up a database deep enough to be able to predict with greater accuracy. Regardless of how long it took her to die, or for him lose patience and kill her, she would be useful: at the end of the day there was no matter as to how he got there. There was that unsettled part though, that itch, that indefinable niggle that he sometimes felt... He treated it the way he always had: discarded, ignored, denied. The only issue was the path he chose to take, not which one was best. After all, it was not as if there was any aim other than his own rejuvenation within the culture. That, and pleasure.

As he tidied dishes and pans into the dish washer, listening to Radio 4, he decided, that given her stubbornness, he'd let the next few days run on her own energy. Build on her own confusion and doubts. No violence or overt interference from him. He was pleased to hear, via the news, that her disappearance had, at this early stage, disappeared. He had, as always, judged it perfectly. Apart from the drawn, miserable and colourless spectre of her mother, who had been as bewildered by the news conference as she might have been by a Martian dropping in on her for tea, there was no one to look for her. No one to worry and fret, make trouble, build campaigns and whisk the media into a frenzy. No one to keep her memory alive. The police, as always, could not have cared less: with no evidence of any foul play, she would be mentally logged with the disappeared, not the murdered. No one ever cared very much for the disappeared: on this simple fact much of his existence depended.

He took his aching body to a hot bath, music gently filling the room, a good book in his hands. There would be no need to feed now for several days, and sleep could wait until he had set the routines more clearly. As he drifted in the warm water and scented air, he thrilled, just a little, at the thought of what the next few days might bring...

CHAPTER SEVEN

It being important to control the flow of her next few hours, he made sure he was in the room when she started to wake. Her sleep was not going to last for much longer and he settled down with his book in a chair by the table. Not the most comfortable chair, to be sure, but then, that was why it was there. As her body started to rise out of sleep he slipped soundlessly away.

Her back, once more, was the first thing she became aware of; was the first thing she felt. She also felt heavy, fuzzy and half formed, her mouth had a sour taste and her head throbbed: all this came to her after she noticed her back. Pain. All was pain. The melodrama of the thought was lost on her, as she wasn't really conscious yet. She was lost in that half state, neither awake, nor asleep, but beginning to piece together the difference between the two. The voice, as of yet, was silent. The slow cramping of her limbs, signalling that they needed to move, to stretch, drove her upwards, up towards wakefulness, up towards thought. There was a caution there, a cry: *better to stay asleep, better to stay away*. Her mind hesitated, caught midway, wondering. The wonder was a step too far: why was she wondering? Was it Saturday, and her mind was telling her to go back to sleep as her body fought to wake at its usual hour? Was it actually Monday, and her mind had told her it was late and she must get up, whilst her body fought for more rest? Why shouldn't she wake up, why must she wake up? The questioning drove wakefulness upon her: it was too late. Tears leaked out between her tightly closed lids. She remembered. Remembered why she shouldn't wake up, shouldn't open her eyes, shouldn't look.

The fear caught her body in a fist, tightening every muscle, every sinew. Her back protested, her side, her face: everything. She felt a gasp, a smothered cry, tear from her throat. *No, she shouldn't make a noise!* The voice, her voice, was there, pleading: *don't annoy him*. The thought of him drove into her like a spike. She felt impaled upon the image of him, the fear of him. What should she do? Should she open her eyes, see if he was there? Should she stay like this, closed down, pretend she was still asleep? Thoughts and questions tumbled through her, confusing, contradicting. She rolled onto her side, drew her legs up under her, tucked her head down, began rocking: all without noticing what she was doing. The tears were flooding now, sobs beginning to build. Oh shit, what was she going to do?

What she did, again, with no awareness of it, was to burst into endless, wailing sobs. A pillow was pulled down, into her arms, and she wrapped herself around it as she rocked and cried. The cries grew in volume and desperation, her body tightening as it rocked faster and faster. Her blood pressure rose as her heartbeat and breathing raced. Her temperature began to climb as each breath came faster, pushing itself through pressured lungs. Dots began to appear in the darkness beneath her shuttered eyes, red and black dancing along her retinas. When her mind had taken her body close to passing out, her body exerted some control, pushing her back from the edge. She was aware of her legs straightening out, her body unfolding: her head came up and the gasping for air slowed. She felt the heat and the sweat upon her face, her forehead, and unconsciously drew her arm up to wipe them away.

It was no good. Try as she might, she couldn't avoid her situation, or her body. Basic physical needs once more exerted themselves, just as they had done in the bathroom, when she had been trapped on the floor, locked into her panic. She lay there for some time, her body calming down as her tears and sobs lessened.

There was simple truth here, one that wasn't to occur to her for some time: she couldn't escape into tears, into panic. Other things, more primal things, got in the way.

As the flow of tears lessened, became once more a slow and unconscious dribble from her eyes, she blinked, opening them reflexively. Her vision was blurred and she blinked furiously, rubbing them hard. She sat up slightly, fighting off the dizziness that had swept through her. The light was on: she wasn't in the dark. Somewhere, of course, she had to have known that, but it was a shock nonetheless. She looked frantically at the table and chairs on her left. He wasn't there. He wasn't there! She swung her head round, checking the rest of the room. No sign of him, thank God, thank all the heavens: *he wasn't there*. Or was he? Doubt crept across her mind, sweeping reason in its path. Her pulse and respiration once more began to rise: where was he?

She frantically searched the room with her eyes. There were two main possibilities, no three. The thought of the third chilled her, froze her limbs and her mind, if only for a second. Whilst she could see both sets of wardrobe doors on her far right, and the bathroom door on the wall to her right... she couldn't see under the bed. Was there an 'under the bed'? Was he there now, lying, waiting, ready to grab her? *Don't be so sodding stupid*, said the voice, ridiculing her no doubt infantile imaginings. But was it such a stupid thought? She was dealing with a madman here, wasn't she? This thought was so unpleasant she banished it from her mind. Concentration was going to be put on the problem of the bed, nothing more. She puzzled at her options as she wiggled into the middle of the bed, pulling the sheets and duvet up to her chin. This made her aware of her nakedness, which set off another shiver of fear. Tears once more flowed openly and a sob began to rise.

Silly cow! Stop it, nothing is happening to you. She pulled the tears back making a conscious effort to slow her breathing. *If she was going to get out of this she needed to stay in control...*

An excellent thought: two excellent points. Staying in control and *getting out of here.* Until now this simply hadn't occurred to her. Her eyes darted to the door on her left, in the far corner of the room. The door he had used to come and go. *What if...?* She flew out of the bed, ignoring the jerky stiffness of her body, flinging herself at the door. The handle came down and she pulled back: nothing, the door was locked. She wouldn't give up, put both her hands on the handle and pulled with all her weight. The door didn't budge. She tried again, and again, finally punching and pummelling at the door, screaming her frustration: *let me out!* She dissolved in tears, in a heap at the base of the door, bundled up around herself. The tears were no comfort, however, and she soon stopped. Her nakedness was intruding, making her feel vulnerable in a way that she hadn't when on the bed, tucked under the sheets. She was aware of fabric dangling around her face, and realised it was a dressing gown, hanging on the back of the door: she hadn't noticed it. How could that happen? How could she look at the door, pull at the door, punch the door, and not notice the dressing gown hanging from it?
She tried to pull it down to her, couldn't; the hook refusing to give it up. She stood, rather too quickly, the dizziness making her sag against the door. She didn't give a shit: that gown was all that mattered. It took a few frantic moments, fighting with arms and belt, feeling the panic rise and rise... but then it was done: she was clothed, no longer naked. She turned to face the room, tears of relief coursing down her cheeks. That felt so much better. She dragged the sleeve across her face, wiping away snot, sweat and tears. Her hair was thick and wet and matted, she pushed it back from her face and surveyed the room. Somehow, standing here, not cowering in the bed; the thought that he was in the wardrobe was very, very silly. What would be sillier, however, would be to not check it and then find he had been in it all along. There was, she assured herself, absolutely no chance he was in the wardrobe. She took a deep breath and marched across the room, to

the opposing wall. Two double doored wardrobe units faced her. There were no handles. Damn. What to do?

She stood for a moment, thinking. The wardrobes were part of a fitted unit set. On her left, on the wall opposite the bed, was a long run of unit top. It started about a third of the way into the wall, from the door, about level with the edge of the bed. There was a line of drawers underneath it from the start, then a gap, then two lines of drawers, another gap. Then it met the corner and the wardrobe units. The first gap was obviously for sitting down at; there was a small moulded stool tucked under it. Above, she noticed that the top unit had two fine seams that matched the gap. She moved to look more closely. The top was seamless, moulded, the edge facing her rounded. It was a nondescript beige colour. She placed her hand under the rounded edge in the middle of the gap and pulled up. The lid lifted back easily. It revealed a compartmented tray. It was, indeed, a vanity unit. The tray held little: a wide toothed comb and two hair brushes, one plastic, one bristle. She put the top back down and faced the wardrobe doors again. The second gap on the unit top met them at the corner. The gap was small, more or less matching the width of the door set at right angles to it. We don't want drawers and door to bang into each other, do we? Decided, she stood directly in front of the left hand set of doors. She raised her hand, rested it on the door where a handle should be, and pushed. As her hand came back, so did the door. They had magnetic catches. The door didn't open very much, she hadn't pushed hard. Terror was starting to prick at her, sweat once more rimming her face.

Nonsense.

This wasn't going to happen. She pulled the door fully open, nothing but a dark cavern. She pushed into the companion door, allowing it to swing back. The wardrobe was completely empty, perfectly empty: nothing. Not even coat hangers. Something had led her to expect it would contain hotel hangers. She closed both doors and moved to the next set. They too were empty.

Phew.

She turned back into the room, looking more critically than she had. The overhead light was on, as well as both of the bedside lamps. Even so, the light was soft, low. She realised there was a dimmer switch on the far wall, by the door. The table held stuff, stuff she hadn't noticed. She went over, kicking the solid base of the bed as she went.

Kicking it in temper: it made her feel better even as it hurt her bare foot. The table held some sort of stainless steel jug, she examined it: water. The lid became a cup. There was also a plate of fruit. Apples, oranges, bananas. She lifted an apple to her face, smelled its sweetness, feeling its texture. It was just an apple... and yet, the scent was so normal, so ordinary... Tears started to prick at her, the panic clawing its way back out of her stomach, where she had it viciously pushed down. She replaced the fruit and backed away from the table. Unbidden, her eyes went to the next challenge, the really scary one: the bathroom door.

The door was the same beige globby nothing that the rest of the room was. A different beige than the units, which were lighter, but still a nothing colour. The trim on the doorframe was identical. She looked down. There were no skirting boards. The smooth expanse of the gleaming dark brown of the linoleum flooring flowed up the walls a good five inches. It stopped under a tiny sill, before the painted walls began. Part of her mind was beginning a panic, piecing together an awful picture from the clues around her. Like the sealed plastic under the bed sheets, like the smooth floor, so much was so easy to clean... but the sill, the sill of linoleum up the walls... so easy to wash, to swish water around... She twisted back to look at the units, her eyes boring on their bases. There were none. The drawers ended abruptly, a good four inches off the ground. You could sweep, clean under the entire unit without meeting a leg. They were fixed to the wall somehow. The wardrobes did meet the floor, but they were the smooth moulded seamless material of the unit top. She stared at them, the other part of her mind, the one concentrating on survival, on *getting out of here,* instructing her to get to the real matter, the real threat: the bathroom. She couldn't do it. Couldn't throw the panic, the images, out of her mind. She was transfixed with a thought of blood. Red blood, wet blood, sticky blood: blood everywhere. She could smell blood, taste blood, see blood. Her right hand rose to absentmindedly rub the side of her neck. There was a soreness there, a rawness. She rubbed at it, unsure of what she was feeling, her own reactions. Something was wrong, something was trying to tell her something...

Nothing came but the insistent pleading of her other voice, the part of her mind telling her to desperately get off this thought and *check out the bathroom.* The image of blood wouldn't leave her mind. She sat on the edge of the bed, feeling like she was going to lose it again. Her breath was speeding up, her back aching and her mouth dry. She felt the panic slip loose and start to race around her body.

No. No, this wasn't going to happen. She couldn't afford it. Getting out of here came first, came above all else.

She took hold of her breath, forcing it to calm, to slow. It took several minutes but her body came back under control. When she was sure she could, she stood up. She faced the bathroom door for a few seconds: he wasn't in there either, no way! She pushed open the door.

A dark hole opened up to her. Staring into the blackness, she could see nothing. Was that someone standing there? Her heart sped up.

Nope, not this time: she was staying in control.

She wasn't putting her hand in there, in search of a light, however, that was for sure. She glanced at the wall around the door. Hadn't she been in there when *he* had put on the light? Sure enough, on the left hand side of the sill was a small light switch, almost invisibly beige upon beige. She flicked it and bright white light, far stronger than the lighting of the room, flooded her face. She walked into the bathroom. It was neat, clean and empty. She felt the tautness within her, give in, relax. A deep sigh left her and she sat with weak knees and shaking hands on the edge of the toilet. Her head dropped and hot tears splashed onto the tiles on the floor.

He wasn't there.

He truly wasn't there. It was another few moments before she could stand again, to find her bladder was bursting. She only just managed to raise the toilet lid and fumble the robe aside in time. She was sitting directly in front of the open door, which froze her in mid stream for just a second. She pushed the door over with her foot and finished. The smell was powerful: concentrated and pungent. She flushed it away and washed her shaking hands. All the towels had been replaced on the rail, they were warm, clean and comforting. She firmly closed the bathroom door, it had the same type of magnetic catches of the wardrobe, and explored. There must be something in here to help her.

The large silver louvered cupboard held what it had before: lots of towels. There was also a bottom shelf of white bathrobes that she hadn't noticed as not being towels when she'd last looked. The top shelf was hand towels and face flannels. Then a shelf of midsized towels, then a thick pile of bath sheets. All white. There was a separate cupboard high up which she could only just see into. It looked full of pillows. There were two bathroom cabinets, each centred over the dual sinks.

They were recessed and it had taken a few moments to notice them: their doors of marble matched the walls exactly. Again, magnetic catches opened them. They contained nothing. They were about six inches deep and had two shelves in each: nothing else. After much examining, the recessed cupboards under the sink units also opened. These contained a variety of bathroom cleaners. All of them were eco-friendly and promised not to harm the dolphins. There was a supply of expensive toilet paper and a plastic toilet brush. There were two silver covered wire baskets on the floor. One tiny, for rubbish, one large and with a lid, for laundry. Empty. The marble wall above the oval bath contained several wire racks that should have contained soap and sponges, bubble bath and creams. Empty. Apart from the toilet cleaners, the entire bathroom was empty. She didn't count the inside of the shower cubicle, for, in her head, that was another room. Or at very least, another door to close between her and... she pushed that thought away.

There were no windows in the room. There were two vents both quite small. One was in the corner of the wall above the bath, the other in the ceiling above the sinks. They hummed very quietly and she wondered how she hadn't noticed them before. Looking back up at the cupboard she couldn't see into very well, she set her mind at making sure there was nothing up there she was over looking. She was surprised at how anxious she was at re-opening the door back into the bedroom: she found the bathroom more comforting somehow. She peered into the room: nothing. It took a moment to grab the vanity stool out from under the unit and take in back in to the bathroom. She firmly shut the door again. She raked through the cupboard, ignoring the protests from her body, her back and shoulder. Nothing but pillows. Very expensive pillows.

Back in the bedroom, she searched the drawers in the unit. All were empty apart from the third set along, nearest the wardrobes. These contained sheets, pillow cases and duvet covers. All linen, all the same creamy beige as the bed spread. The bed itself had a huge, plush headboard in a darker brown colour that matched the lamp shades and the heavy bed cover. The side tables were part of this unit, protruding out from the headboard itself. They contained one small drawer each. The drawers did not contain a Gideon bible. There was a small waste bin in the corner by the table. The table itself was round and made from the same beige moulded plastic as the units. The two chairs were also moulded and nothing very special. There was a vague 60's feel about the set: one central leg and a rounded base. The chairs didn't have arms. The framed picture above the unit was a swirl of indiscriminate browns and beiges, as if it had been painted just for the room. It was firmly fixed to the wall, not one corner giving one inch.

There were no windows. There were four vents in the ceiling, just like the ones in the bathroom. She couldn't hear them hum. The bed itself was massive: wider than she was tall and she was five foot eleven. The mattress, with its ominous plastic wrapping, sat on a thick base which ran almost to the floor. There were huge castors on the bottom, but she couldn't budge the heavy weight. There were no drawers in the base. The last thing to examine was the central light fitting. It was pancake shaped and clear glass. There were three light bulbs inside it, in a sort of triangle. She could see them clearly when she turned the dimmer up full. Even using the chair she couldn't reach it. The ceilings were very high.

Her search and explore over, she sat on the bed, exhausted. It had seemed like hours since she had begun and she was covered once more in sweat. There had been three, maybe four, panic attacks that had driven her to rest and bring her breathing and thoughts back under control. When she realised that there were no windows, her subsequent panic had almost made it a good thing: she felt that if there had been one, she would have thrown herself through it. There was nothing left in the room but her, and everything ached. Her head ached, her back, her side, her hip, her jaw. She kept rubbing her neck, creating a raw line of pain she couldn't fathom. She wished there was a mirror. She knew her face was swollen and bruised but the black marble didn't show much except her general outline. There were bruises on her hip and legs, but they didn't represent much of what really hurt. She had felt progressively worse as she searched but the thought that she was going to find something to help her had driven her on. Now, deflated, purposeless, the physical crashed in. Her mouth was dry and throbbing and she felt sick. She lay on the bed, pulling a pillow into her and cried. They were quiet sobs; emptiness and despair rather than panic, and she slowly fell into sleep.

Her dream space was safe and comfortable. She was in her bed, at home, her cat asleep on the pillow by her head. The cat was purring in her ear and she was as warm as toast, snuggled under the duvet. Her hand reached up and stroked the cat's ears, doubling the volume of the purr. She turned over, fumbling to find its belly, and give it a good rub before getting up to feed it. It must still be night, or he'd be on her head, insistent about her getting up to feed him. He stretched and coiled and rolled under her expert scratching, and she slipped back into deep sleep. There was a heavy rumbling of traffic – screeching cars and a siren off in the distance, trying to break into her dream, to disturb her. She concentrated on the cat's purr and pushed all other sounds out of her mind.

CHAPTER EIGHT

Her actual emerging from sleep was just as it had been earlier. The pain in her back came first, woke the rest of her, and dragged her back into the nightmare. This was a much rougher awakening, far more abrasive around the edges. Her blood pounded through her skull with a relentless, tearing beat. Her mouth was bone dry and coated in foulness. Her body ached and moaned from end to end and her neck was stiff and sore on moving. She lay for a few moments, trying to coax her mouth to dampness, before she could move into the bathroom, on extremely unsteady legs, to pee and then slurp water from the tap. Her pee had been even stronger smelling, and stung slightly. She must drink, and as she was cupping more fluids into her hand, remembered the jug on the table.

It tasted warm after the fresh water from the tap, and she went back into the bathroom, emptied it, and refilled. Seated back at the table, munching through an apple, it occurred to her that the water in the jug might have been drugged, so throwing it for fresh had been a good idea. Her chewing stopped midway: *what about the fruit?* She stared at the white flesh of the apple in her hand.

Poisoned? Poisoned apple?

She gagged involuntarily, and fled once more back to the bathroom, to half cough, half vomit the fruit up. The water she had swallowed followed; bitter and vile. By the time she'd finished dry heaving, there were spots exploding in the back of her eyes and her head was fit to split. She lay down on the cool marble floor and sank once more into moans and tears. The tears stung her cheeks, her throat was wrecked, her head ached, her body was one massive pain. Again, she wanted to just simply drop away from it all. To faint, or pass out, or even die! Why the hell couldn't she just die and get out of this? Her right hand clenched into a fist and she pounded the floor for a few moments of complete fury: *this was just the most terrible thing in the entire world. It needed to stop!* It was actually quite difficult to stay down there, huddled on the floor, trying to wrap herself round the toilet base, when she was shaking in anger: she felt ridiculous. Her head tossed her hair back and damn the pain, when she scrambled back up onto the toilet seat. She fumed as she sat, feeling all the pains in her body, rubbing that sore point on her neck incessantly. She felt sweaty and stained and sullen, and by hell someone was going to pay for it. The thought of *someone* halted her little internal tirade. She hadn't wanted to think on anyone, least of all *him*. The bravado dropped as her body started to shake: a fine trembling that swept through her. Feeling like she was going to suffocate, be squeezed out of existence, if this awfulness took her over any further, she jumped to her feet. The black and white bathroom swam grey and she fell into the darkness, oblivious to the agony as her head slammed onto the edge of the washbasin.

He was not amused. This was not part of his planning and he felt she had called the shots here, for him to have to go in and rescue her like this. The injury was actually quite bad, he was certain she was concussed. Difficult call to make, with the dehydration, but if he wanted to play further, he was going to have to be careful. This angered him, and as the anger flared, he foolishly slapped her face a couple of times. Well, she was damn well concussed now!

He re-inserted the drip and also gave her a good dose of anti-inflammatories. He felt around her head, sure there was no actual fracture, and gave her some morphine. He pierced his wrist and dripped a good amount of his blood onto her forehead, which greatly reduced the swelling and bruising that had formed there. He looked at the swollen lips and cheeks and smeared them over too: may as well make a good job all round. When her fluid levels had recovered, he inserted a tube into her stomach and fed her a tiny dribble of semisolids. He did not wish for any complications, or rather, he would not tolerate any more complications. Then, in a complete fury, he went through the entire flat like a dervish. It was gleaming like a new pin, spotless to the point of sterile, by the time she woke.

He had enough warning before she came to, so that the line was out and all the medical equipment put out of sight. He again blooded himself, smearing it over the puncture from the canella. Thus, there was no evidence of it at all, as even the slight swelling caused by removing it had disappeared. He was sitting by her side when she surfaced, holding her hand.

She was on a beach, in Majorca. The breeze that flowed over her body carried that warm musky smell, the strange spicy flower smell that hit you as you emerged from the plane at Palma. Strange only because she was sure the scent came from the thick, low growing succulent plants that abounded, not any actual flower. The scent of Spain, is how she thought of it; yet she had never been on the mainland. The scent of escape, of rest and relaxation. The scent of rest from troubles and of no other bugger to annoy you. She always travelled alone, always booked herself a double room, and gladly paid the single supplement. She had learned that precious holiday time was not to be wasted with those her own age, and especially not in a shared room. She'd also learned that the now creaking holiday hotels from the Island's heyday of British package tours were a cheap and cheerful way to spend her precious time on the Island without any real expense. So she could then indulge on extras. *Was she booked in for a massage anywhere?* There was a kink in her neck and an ache in her back and... the breeze also carried sharper sea tones; a bit of salt, a sense of water, and the chemical overlays of sun tan lotion: her sun tan lotion. Piz Buin, with its distinctive aroma, and the smell of her sweat intermingled. Her head pounded and her mouth was dry.

Had she fallen asleep on the beach, under a sun brolly?

Was the sun drying her out and causing that sick throbbing, that deadly pulse beat? Was she in trouble? Had she drunk too much and fallen asleep on the beach? She tried to stretch, to relieve the kinks in her body, but nothing seemed to be working right. Had she been at a party? Was it a really bad sign that she didn't remember? The scents of the beach slowly faded, or rather, melded, into one: a strong, masculine smell. Aftershave and ironed cotton. She began to move about, something about the scent was alarming. The beach fell away, the surf disappeared, the pain and headache and nausea exerted itself. She emerged.

Under the pain, under the awful, jaw-wrenching awareness of pain, there was a strong hand holding hers. She clasped it tightly, holding it as her anchor, hauling herself out of the dreaming by the strength it offered. There was something so wrong, so alien about what was going on, but the pain she felt *inside*, the raw sense of terror and the sharp, tearing fear. What was wrong, had she been in a crash? Has the plane crashed? The hand holding hers responded to her clutching, and drew her up. Another hand gently stroked her arm. Had she been in a plane? Had it been the hotel? Has there been a collapse? Tears slid out of her eyes, she felt them move down her baking face. She had definitely had too much sun, too much heat. Her skin stung her in their wake, and she raised her hand to wipe her face. Or tried too: one was lost in the gentle embrace of the other hand, and the other felt too weak to make it. She cried a little, exhausted, exasperated: *what was wrong with her?*

A tender touch was at her eyes, and she felt her tears being wiped away. *Soft, soft, soft.* Such a soft, yet sure touch. The caress continued to her forehead, and she felt a damp cloth laid there. Oh yes, that was so very good, that was just what she needed, just right. She sank down a little, still holding on to that hand, and its cool touch, the gentle pressure and the comfort. Whatever was wrong, everything was going to be all right. Everything was fine. She clearly had a bad dream, and it was all right, and she was just going to carry on sleeping this off.

A thumb was slowly stroking the back of her hand, sending gentle waves of reassurance into her. She sighed and settled back, was that the sea she could hear, was the surf breaking on the beach? She tried to breathe in the spicy flowery smell of Spain, tried to find her suntan lotion and the salt of the sea…

'…if that mockingbird don't sing, Papa's gonna buy you a diamond ring.. and if that diamond ring…'

Her hand went rigid. Her spine froze as the sensations from her hand moved up to her brain. The sun disappeared and ice formed along her body. His singing continued, unaffected by her change; her heartbeat shot up. She could taste the fear on her tongue, and hear the terror pounding in her ears. Dizzy spots once more exploded along the backs of her eyes. A sharp tearing sound fell across her mind, and the voice was there, sudden, insistent and totally demanding:

Don't fucking move.

She did not move.

He was savouring the scents pouring from her body, as a fine diner examines the wine list. Her fear was written on the air, and each breath of his brought her deeper into him. He rolled the taste around his mouth, judging, weighing, sensing. That sudden all convulsing shift from dream to terror, had wrought the most wondrous changes upon her body, and he drank them all in. Curiously, there was a scent of musk, and he knew her inner folds were oozing moisture. That was curious, and unexpected and oh, such fun! Such such fun!

He carried on stroking the back of her hand, and gently tailed off the song, and silence descended upon them. She held steady for a few moments, then tears began to slide down her cheeks, pushed out from closed lids, no doubt from the pressure of all the other tears hiding there, awaiting their own release. He'd be a generous owner, and allow them all out, in their own good time. Whilst she had not moved, or spoken, or acknowledged him in any way, there was a trembling beginning in her muscles, faint seismic shocks that heralded much more to come, if this moment continued much longer.

He patted her hand in a brisk no nonsense way.

'Now little one, I am glad you are awake. You need feeding up! You are all skin and bone.'

Her hand shuddered, just a little. He moved up off the bed, and went to the table, collecting clutter as he talked her along her instructions.

'Now,' he began in a jaunty sing song voice, the beloved uncle favouring his almost no-longer-a-child, niece 'I am going to fetch you some nice hot soup, and perhaps some milk and some bread? I expect you to be out of bed and cleaned up for me, do you hear? What is the point of all that shower stuff if you do not use it? I shall not be long – do be quick.'

His tone stayed light and he refused to check for her attention as he left the room with the fruit bowl and the jug. He busied himself for a few moments, then selected a light golden broth, some good quality wholemeal bread, a yoghurt and a cool glass of milk for her. He nipped back to her room whilst she showered and laid out quite a fancy place setting for two. He chose a thicker lentil soup – almost a stew – for himself, with iced water. She was still in the bathroom when he laid out her feast, but was sitting on the bed when he came back with his own meal. He smiled, and lay down his tray, setting his own food swiftly in place. Her hair had been combed through roughly. This was pleasing. He signalled her to sit opposite him as he laid the linen napkin on his own lap. She rose from the bed and trotted over to the chair, sitting quickly and quietly. She didn't use her napkin, however, but sat staring at the food.

'Now, I am sure you are not aware of it, but you have not eaten for a few days.'

Little jolt of shock there, all down her spine. Wonderful.

'So I want you to be careful. You may have all the broth, but go carefully with the bread. Chew each morsel well, and do not eat more than half of it.' His tone was still light, but he was being clear. 'You may start with the milk if you wish.'

Her hand shot up and grasped the glass. Yes, she'd gotten the message, the true message. Eat what you are told. Do only as you are told. It took a few minutes, but she did slowly raise the glass to her lips, sipped a little, replaced it. He filled in the spaces with inane chatter, total drivel, about this or that, what sort of day he'd had, what had been in the Financial Times about completely anonymous business dealings. The sort of nonsense long married couples used to fill up the silences between them. She sat, silently, slowly and no doubt painfully, chewing and swallowing to his precise instructions. The bread was the hardest part – quite literally, as her throat was so raw, but she tore it into little shreds and bobbed them in the broth. By the time she got to them at the bottom of her bowl, they were sops, and easily swallowed. With little exception, just enough head movement to keep on track with the meal, she kept her gaze fixed on the soup bowl. He would not have been surprised if she had not actually seen him at all.

The milk was the most difficult part of the task. He had not said how much she could have of it. She had reached half way down the glass, when she hesitated, drawing her hands away. Several times, as she fought to swallow down all the soup and half the bread, her hand went to the glass, once or twice even raising it to her lips. But she never took a sip, returning in to its place and once more letting go. Finally, a good two hours after they had started, she struggled the last sop and broth morsel down. He was most impressed that she had not vomited back her ordeal, although there had been a few tell tale gags. He carried on prattling and ignored it, confident she would manage. Hoping she could manage, actually, as he did not wish his mood spoiled.

Finally, he let her off the hook about the milk.

'Well, I can see you were hungry. Now will that milk fill you all up, or would you prefer yoghurt?'

She had to look at him, of course. Worse, she had a decision to make. It usually fell apart a bit about now, giving them a choice. It went to their heads, and they would often slip into total panic. He waited for her to answer him, wondering what sort of voice she was capable of finding. Whilst her eyes were in his general direction – well, in the general direction of the yoghurt, she didn't actually acknowledge him. Rather, she raised her hand and returned her attention to the glass of milk, sipping it slowly and surely. He kept the silence up, determined to undermine that little show of independence. Sure enough, the tears started to slip out, and trembling began. Again, he left it just long enough to unsettle her badly, but not long enough for a total collapse.

'Oh good, glad to see your fluids are up. Oh, that reminds me, I will just be a moment...'

He was out the room before she could register his movement, out the room and with the door left open behind him. He wasn't really testing her on that, actually, as he was sure she would not have moved by his return. Which she hadn't. The milk, however, had not gone down anymore, and the tears and trembling were quite acute. He ignored everything.

'I have something for you to take, if you will. It is not an unpleasant taste, but not nice either. But you must take it all.'

He ripped open four little sachets and dropped the powder into the large glass of water he'd brought back. He used a clean spoon to stir it round until the powder was dissolved and the liquid clear again. He stood and placed the glass in front of her, using the clearing of the other plates to cover the confusion and panic this had caused. When he was finished piling up crockery, onto the tray, no sip had been taken. He sat down and stared straight at her.

'I really must insist.'

The silence was broken then, by a small sob. Her hand went and grasped the glass, but did not move. He coughed very lightly, and the glass was jerked up and brought to her lips. The silence began to stretch again. He snapped it in two, by standing up very swiftly, so swiftly she could not have seen him move just be aware of him suddenly being beside her. As he leaned in, to whisper in her ear, she took the first sip.

'Very good, little one. Most excellent. Now finish the glass, most surely, most slowly. Do not hurry, do not... spill... a...drop.'

The last three words were spoken so softly, that he almost didn't hear them himself. He stayed where he was, leaning into her body, as she started to drink the glass dry. By the time it was empty, she was shaking and crying and sobbing fit to explode. But she did not explode, she kept what calm she could, and no matter the shaking of her hand, not one drop was spilled. He was most disappointed... but also pleased.

Would life never be simple for him, would he always want more than he could have, especially when he wanted different outcomes for the same situation?

He backed off and let her collapse a little into herself. He suspected her bladder must be requiring aid, no matter how much cold sweat she was pouring out. He told her to go to the bathroom and 'freshen up' for him, and listened carefully whilst she peed, washed her face, and re-combed her now badly dishevelled hair. She did not throw up. Either by accident or design.

She returned to the bedroom, to find him lying on the bed, awaiting her. He signalled her to lie beside him, and drew her into his arms. She was a large, sweating rock, but she did as he bid.

Wonderful.

Pulling her into him, he lay and carried on his drivel, keeping her on edge, and awake, for another hour or so, until he was sure she had absorbed all the food with no problem. Then, when her composure was just about to break utterly, he excused himself, and left, bidding her a good night's sleep. After all, how was she to know it was almost noon.

She had begun to believe in the existence of God part way through the meal. She had prayed fervently, devoutly, constantly, through the rest of her ordeal at the table. By the time he had left the room, leaving her shaken and exhausted upon the bed, she had rejected God's existence and returned to stoic acceptance that she was alone, and all was lost. She had poison within her and there was nothing she could do about it.

For form's sake, she rushed to the toilet, and stuck her fingers done her throat as hard as she could. Very little was gained by this, as she had suspected, for it had been quite some time since she'd swallowed the vile, salty sweet foulness in that glass.

Why would he do this? That was all that had been in her mind, the entire time she'd lain on the bed, expecting to pass out lying next to him. Why would he kill her by poison, when there were so many other... she skipped that thought.

She was sure she could feel her breathing start to go, her pulse rise, her temperature plummet, or whatever it was going to do. But then, she'd been sure of that every second she'd lain there, and nothing much had happened. Her breathing had threatened to go many times, but she'd brought it back down every time. How long had she been counting her breaths in and out, keeping a rhythm? She'd drifted off somewhere in the 500s, and had to start again.

She paced the room angrily. She paced the room in defeat. She paced the room in pain and discomfort. She lay on the bed. She paced some more. Her eyes were at the door constantly. She'd laid her head up against it a few times, and discovered she could hear nothing through it. But throughout her frantic, desperate, agitated pacing, her eyes would be drawn back to it.

Finally, in exhaustion, she lay down on the bed and dozed.

The sensation was one of tearing, devouring, eating. She startled awake, already doubled over in agony. The pain deep in her groin, in her bowels, was indescribable. She was so overcome by the strength of it, the persistence of it, it took a few moments for her to remember where she was, and what this pain was. The poison was finally working. She tried to move off the bed, fell over in agony, and lay on the floor, writhing. This pain was low down, and moving, and terrible. She crawled to the door, and banged on it hard, tears flooding her face. She would not die like this, alone and helpless. He would bloody well come and pay attention to her! She needed a hospital, she needed help.

Her hand fell back, bruised and almost bleeding from banging and punching the bottom of the door. Nothing. She convulsed again, and felt the incredibly strong urge to get up, to move. Bad things were happening with this pain, and she wasn't sure what. But something drove her to her feet, and she headed back once more to the bathroom, the pain caused by her walking almost unbearable. She had an inkling what was about to happen half way there, and she ran forward, and actually screamed out loud. This so wasn't going to happen to her, not her, not now, she didn't care if she did die ten minutes later.

She almost made it, almost, but the action of trying to lift the dressing robe was one too many, and her bowels erupted before she was seated properly. She did scream, and cry, and rage, for it was a painful and humiliating experience, to soil herself in such a vulnerable circumstance, but her overriding thought was her fear that this was part of the dying, part of the poison. If it was, it was a strange part, for once the initial evacuation was over, nothing else happened. She sat on her soiled seat, and cried, and waited for death. The pains had gone.

Again, nothing very much happened, and she eventually had to attend to her circumstances in a plain and matter of fact way. Either that, or sit here forever and her backside was already numb. Disgusted, she cleaned off what she could of herself with toilet paper. This was hard, as the soiled robe was caught under her. There was the bidet beside her, and she filled it with warm water, and slid off her robe, and tried to hop over onto it without making more of a mess. She was partially successful, and managed a good cleaning in the water, all the time sobbing and horrified at the shame of it all. From there, she made her way to the shower, and once more scrubbed herself raw.

The water was cooling, and her dizziness threatening to overwhelm her once more. She was on the floor of the shower, her back on the wall, tucked into herself, water streaming around her. Her head ached and her throat hurt. She could feel that other parts of her hurt, but she wasn't going to think on that, on what had happened on the toilet, and how much it hurt there.

She walked her hands up the slick tiles, unbending legs and aching joints. The stench slammed into her on opening the shower door. Not only had soiled dressing gown been sitting there, she had by no means thoroughly cleaned either the toilet, or the bidet.

Anxious, paranoid, terrified and disgusted all at the same time, or at least with those feelings running through her and alternating so swiftly, they felt as one massive congesting emotion, she set herself the task of cleaning up properly. The dressing gown went into the bath, and she ran water through the stains until they became faint stains as opposed to humiliating smears of her own shit. Another thought to skip. Taking clean hand towels and flannels from the cupboard, she wiped and cleaned all traces from the toilet bowl, the seat and the surrounding tiles. Several times she had to stop to continue the emptying of her burning bowels. Whatever that stuff in the glass had been, it was effective. Finally, she cleaned the surfaces, including the bidet, with the dolphin friendly solutions under the sink. She'd wished she'd thought of that sooner, as the antiseptic cleaning smell made her feel better.

The bath was now half full of wet towels and the dressing gown. She left them there while she returned to the shower cubicle and scrubbed herself over in the luke warm water. On emerging, she took all the wet towelling and wrapped it in dry towels, placing the balled up mess into the metallic laundry basket. She could do no more.

Hesitating at the door, shivering and shaking, in pain and somewhat numb in her mind, she listened. Was he on the other side, was he there? Had he been there the entire time? Tears slid unnoticed along her face, as she pulled the door open, and peered round. Nothing, the room was empty.

She crawled into the bed, under the sheets, ignoring her wet hair, and burrowed down. She sobbed; hot and sticky, her breath caught under the duvet. She was oblivious to the slight rocking motion her body had adopted as she lay under the bedding. The pounding headache kept her awake for longer than she could ever have thought possible. Sleep eluded her, and finally she fell into chanting it under her breath: sleep, sleep, sleep, sleep, sleep…escape. The sounds of water lapping the sands caught her, pulling her down.

He slipped into the room and stuck a needle into the back of her hand when he was sure she was in deep sleep. She reacted with a groan, but the sedative acted faster than she could wake up, and he listened very carefully to her heart as it slowed. She had a very strong heart, with an excellent rhythm, and a good tone in all her internal muscles. It was a marvel, this world, with peasants such as she, so healthy and unmarred by either disease or starvation. There was a hesitation, and he thought he'd given her too much, and it might stop, but it rallied, and carried on its dance: slowly but surely keeping her going for him.

He was very pleased with the bathroom – for he hated cleaning up muck. The problems of no food and lots of sedation on the system had once lost him a playmate early on. As with everything, experience had taught him how to maximise his pleasure, even if some parts of the task were unpleasant. He simply took the laundry basket out and disposed of it whole, replacing it with an identical one. Likewise, dressing gown and towels were refreshed.

Bringing the IV back in and slipping it into her, he filled her veins with more rehydrating fluids and medicines. Her head wound, which had faded to yellow and green stains on her skin, he once more bathed in his own healing blood. By the time he had removed the drip and allowed the sedative to wear off, there was no evidence to the eye of the injury. Her back was also coming along nicely, although torn muscles would need to mend properly: there was a limit to what pain killers and anti-inflammatories could do there. As usual, his judgement was perfect: she fell back into a natural sleep as the sedative waned. Good! Fun for all when she woke.

CHAPTER NINE

Joanne sat on the edge of the bed wondering when he would come in to her. She was as ready as she would ever be, her hair neatly dried and fixed in a sophisticated chignon. He liked her hair like that, and had taught her how to do it by touch. When she'd said she would need a mirror to do it properly, he'd asked her how blind women cope, and assured her she would manage.

After all, it wasn't as if she didn't have lots of time on her hands for practice.

The comment about being blind had struck home, and she had not mentioned a mirror since. Her hands fiddled with the fixings in her hair. She could feel the flow of the hair with fingertips: it was perfect. Practice does, after all, make everything so.

She was dressed neatly in the skirt from the standard dress suit that she was allowed – plain knee length and tailored well. Classic. She did not wear the jacket, had never worn the jacket, as the room was always quite warm. There were several of this cut of suit in the wardrobe, ranging from dark brown through to light tan. She had on the one that had a slight green tone in the dark brown and she fancied that might go with her eyes better. She wondered if her eyes were the same colour as they used to be.

On her legs were the thick dark tights he allowed her, and she had finally been allowed soft black pumps for her feet. Her knickers were white cotton and utilitarian, and she hated them. It was of no comfort to her that she only ever wore new ones, their wrappings removed before they were placed into the drawers in the unit. She hated them so much, although she was grateful she was allowed them. The white silk blouse she had was full sleeved, generously cut yet neat on her frame. V necked, with a line of mother of pearl buttons, it had some cleavage but was not daring. It lay on the delicate mounds of her breasts, with her nipples always just on show beneath the thin fabric. She was not allowed to wear a bra. It was the first thing she'd asked twice about, and after he'd beaten her soundly for punishment, he'd kept her naked for several sleep cycles. That's how she thought of them: sleep cycles. She'd found that thinking of them as *day* and *night*, was too dangerous. When she thought of them as night and then day, she counted them. Sleep cycles, she just moved into and out of, with no thought of how many there had been.

There were no labels on anything. She thought that everything was at least two sizes smaller than she had worn *before*, as she had lost so much weight. So she was now the size she had always wanted to be. Her breasts were smaller too, of course, but somehow they looked just perfect under the blouse. Of course, she had more than one blouse, she had several of them, all identical. Some had been laundered once or twice as part of one of his games but she knew that most, like all her clothes, were just opened from their wrappings and placed in the units in an endless expensive stream.

Although they always appeared perfectly ironed, so she was confused as to who did that, or how that was achieved?

When waiting for him, as she was now, she preferred to sit on the end of the bed, as opposed to the chair. The chair was hard on her back, and her bum, if she was waiting for hours. The bed was softer, and gave her a better view of the picture. She knew every splodge and smudge and smear of paint in the picture, but could still manage to stare at it for several hours before feeling herself starting to go mad. Then she'd pace; but that could backfire, as he would be annoyed if he came in and she was breathless and sweaty from careening up and down and round the room. When she wasn't actively waiting, she would often spend a lot of time in the bathroom, doing the same sort of looking at the marbled tile swirls, as she did with the picture's paint. Although the picture was actually saying something, so it was more constructive looking at that.

She realised she'd fallen into the picture a little too hard, and brought herself back up. Being in a trance when he came in was so not a good idea. There were a lot of bad ideas to be had around *him*, but few more painful than failing to notice he was there. She shivered. She had successfully managed to avoid any *training sessions* for some time, hence today's excitement. However, no matter how deeply the fear was kept within her, this was going to be a perilous day. She was pretty sure she would be punished for something before it was through, but she was of the opinion that it would be worth it.

Although she had been wrong before.

The door opened inward quietly, and she perked up her spine and placed a calm and even smile upon her face. He came in, and beamed at her. He was wearing dark slacks and a casual grey knit sweater. He was barefoot and his hair was damp, as it curled round his shoulders. His brown eyes were deep and loving, so she knew he was in a good mood. It frightened her how his eyes could be different colours according to his mood, but she let it pass, as to dwell on it was madness.

Let it pass.

Those three words were now her mantra and her shield. Let it pass. It worked too, for she was still alive.

...if this could be called living...

'Are you ready?' His voice was light and cheerful. Santa Claus just before handing out the presents.

'Yes, Jonathan.' She nodded to emphasise her acceptance.

He beamed once more, and stood back, moving into the little hall, his hand extended to her.

'Then come join me, little one…'

She reached forward and took his hand, her touch light. But the rush of fear that spread through her as she walked the couple of steps to the threshold, was written large on her body. She purposefully tried to calm as she approached the point of no return. There, in the doorway, was the step down between the linoleum covered floor of her cell, and the… wooden flooring of the hallway. She had seen the wooden flooring before. She'd even walked on it, for about 3 seconds, before she'd literally been thrown back into her prison. That had been a bad one. He'd warned her not to leave the room, even if he left the door unlocked. She'd been so sure there was no one there. Hours she'd waited, frantic frantic hours, listening, waiting, sure there was no one there. Sure he'd just forgotten to lock it. Sure he was gone, away, not there. When she'd finally stepped over the threshold, the one she was staring at now, he'd been on her like a rabid dog. She didn't remember landing back in the room, just that the force with which he'd slammed into her, had lifted her up off her feet, and air was below her as she swung back.

She swallowed hard, pushing the memories of her screams out of her mind. Let it pass! She realised that was funny, and laughed a little… let it pass! Well she was certainly going to pass now… in fact… her foot hesitated, fearful. This was such a huge thing, and she was so unsure of it. Was he actually going to let her go through that doorway?

He felt her reluctance, smiled within, and encouraged her on with his hand.

What a power rush.

He felt almost as excited as she did, although no trace of that escaped *his* body.

She stepped onto the floor of the narrow hall. The other foot followed. They were crammed into each other, and she was sweating, her breath a little ragged, her heart pounding, but it was done. She was outside the room. He'd let her outside the room.

Giddy, breathless, the blood rushing in her ears, they stood framed in the darkened hallway. The walls were pale green, with a light coloured wood in repeating patterns on the floor. That she knew. Her prison doorway behind her, and with *him* still lightly holding her hand, she looked around. Light, natural light, lit both ends of the narrow hallway that held them, one side brighter than the other. Her eyes wanted to follow the brighter patch, to her left, but she warned herself against being too eager, too obvious, and turned to look the other way, to her right. A short corridor ran down to a corner that turned left into the natural light. She could see no doorways in the smooth walls, just the corner bend, the green walls and some artwork. She couldn't see the art work from this angle.

On this side of the corridor, the side she had never seen, the walls had two shades of green, with a sort of rail on the wall at about hip height. Above was the pale green she knew from the wall opposing her door, underneath the rail was a darker green. She stared at the rail, and the two colours, as if to touch, then pulled herself back and turned to look the other way. He caught her eye as her face turned, and he smiled at her. Careful to notice him, she acknowledged his concern with a tiny smile of her own, before her gaze carried on to drink in the other side.

On her left, the corridor stretched further, with doors off on either side and seemed to end in a wall, for there was a large painting of some sort of garden hanging there. There was a wide doorway, clearly open, on the right hand side of the corridor, a few feet from where they stood. The bright swath of light that shone through it made the wooden floor gleam and dance in front of her. She was hypnotised by the light. How long had it been since she'd seen daylight? How long? How long since...?

Let it pass.

But I was wondering how long it had been since I was ...?

Let it pass.

Her inner self was correct: this was not the moment to dwell on anything unpleasant. With practised ease, she slid all the bothersome thoughts to one side, concentrating instead on the daylight in front of her. She felt his pressure on her hand, as her body started to move forward, and her eyes looked to him for consent. He gave permission with a tiny nod and a smile, and dropped his hand from hers. She moved forward, feet silent on the smooth floor. In a moment, she was standing in an open doorway, looking into a large and spacious living room, with... windows. Huge tall windows, filled with light and air. Daylight streamed in, through thick and flowing nets. Light! As she moved forward she was sure she could feel the light being pulled into her lungs, and flowing through her body. There were three huge windows, really high, and she realised with a shock that the ceilings were higher than in the cell. She looked up. Way above her, feet and feet and feet away, was an ornate plaster ceiling, with a huge central rose that held a chandelier of crystal and brass. Richly sculpted cornices filled the corners. Her eye line dropped to the three elegant cord and sash windows that rose up from the level of the rail in the corridor, to a perfectly rounded arch. Her breath caught as her sense of place and time jolted: she was in an old building. All this time... she had been in this really old house? Was she still in London?

Her face drained of all colour, and he caught her before she fell. It was no more than a simple swoon... *how old fashioned*... and he led her to the couch, and once seated, pressed her head firmly down between her knees. When she started to protest, by pushing up with her head, he gently lifted up from her forehead and settled her back into the enveloping cushions. Her colour started to return, and he went and fetched a glass of water. She sipped it with biddable subservience. He let the silence grow.

As she took down each mouthful, she tried to swallow down the panic. Her mind had opened up into a maelstrom of questions and fears and terrors. She squashed them all firmly. Many a beating had resulted in her acting first and thinking later, and she was not going to end this day lying on the linoleum, bleeding and bruised. She was not! It had taken months... there it was an unwelcome admission but it was finally out... *months*... to get to this stage, to be allowed out of that stinking cell, and she was not going back into it yet. Not happening. So she sat and waited, squashing and squishing, until her mind was focused once more.

She did not look at the windows.

He adored doing this. Sitting with her, reading her, filling himself with her will and her obedience as she calmed herself. Others had tried this over the years. Others had tried to grab hold of themselves at this point in their shared journey, take control of their terror and fear of him. Calm themselves down after being allowed out for the first time. Some had managed it to some extent. None quite like her. Few had ever mastered themselves so completely, in his service. None had even given him this delicious sense of utter ownership... had they? Few had managed to school themselves utterly: to hold to nothing but his commands. Only she had appeared to do it with such lightness, such normality. Was that a sign of her age? All that reading, all those films and television programmes? Had it schooled her in so many more ways of thinking of the world, of what he might be to her? Had such things taught her to walk in nightmares with an even breath? Or was it something about her?

All had tried, of course. All had feigned calm and obedience: their bodies had betrayed them. Sweat would still ooze, stinking of fright. Heart would trammel, breath claw at the throat. So far, nothing of that here. Every time she had threatened to lose herself, she took her body with her: brought it under the mind, controlled it. It was such a ... *what was the word... buzz... such a rush.*

Not one of the few who had made it out of the room had brought this much pleasure. He was almost hesitant to carry on the training out here. He knew she would slip up – that was the point after all, and his hands and back *ached* from the need to escalate sometimes. But the current triumph was such a subtle flavour and he would lose it for some time, probably for ever, when he stepped up the training. It was not as if he was not looking forward to bringing her out of the room; he had wanted to move on before now. It had taken extreme self control to only use fists and bare feet in the room.

Extreme.

For when she did give way under his pummelling, when she did abandon herself to her own panic, she gave great battle. When she tried to fight back, it was awe some. The frenzy from her attempts to escape him was total, and his beast responded wholeheartedly. It was like drinking the sun. He swallowed up all the energy and all the power of the fear, and it swept molten through his body. When she had finally found somewhere inside herself to hide from his assaults, to escape him, to not react... he had forced himself to throttle back. Forced himself to resist the impulse to keep smashing into her until she responded physically. Allowed her time to feel she had a refuge. It had been a difficult journey, learning this lesson – many had been lost before, before he had found that the key was to accept these retreats. To accept them, move with them, and allow a false sense of security to form. They needed respite, now and then, before the true testing. They needed the space to be formed, before he conquered it.

When she had finally begun to accept the pain, to give into it, without fighting, without struggle... he had warred within himself. Fought the great battle that required him to do less, in order to gain more. Fought down his beast and fed instead on other pleasures. Fed on the knowledge that the compliant and seemingly dead body that he carried on punishing was *aware*, was thinking, was *conscious*. Was schooling her own body and mind to be perfectly still for him. She was laying there, taking a beating, and awaiting his will.

It was the opposite of escape. Everything was about him, and what he was doing, and her letting it happen. Take the pain, take the punishment, take his *training* and just lie there accepting. In these moments, one had to be very careful. For the ragged instincts of rage would want to challenge her stillness with the lash, and move them onwards in the dance. Move everything up a level and really see what her mettle was, reveal her true self. They were dangerous thoughts, however, and he had schooled himself against a premature move. There had been his own experience at Eléan's hands, his own awareness of how delicate the timing was. How often others had given out false signs. Signs that said they were ready. False prophesies revealed only when their minds had broken in pieces in his hands. *Weak: they were all so weak.* He turned from the thoughts of such fools and their weakness and their failure, and returned to the joys offered by her so far. Reflecting on the strength required of him, to retain this much control. That self control had brought him much joy, as witnessed now, by his pleasure on sitting next to her, watching her control her body, her only thought to keep everything calm *for him*. He basked in it, her stillness, her acceptance.

She had time to take a lot in, as she stilled her mind and body. The room was really quite large, by far the biggest living room she'd ever been in. Hollywood movie large. Sitting on the couch, with the large windows *she wasn't looking* at on her right, she faced across a massive expanse of soft rug over pale wood. Another huge sofa, the match of the one she was on, cream, and large enough to sit 6 or 7 people comfortably, formed a rough square, with two little tables in between them. Behind the sofa, after a gap, there was a wall of built-in cabinets.

Shelves and speakers and stuff. Stuff she'd look at later. On the left, was the wall that was this side of the corridor. I was not a real wall, she observed, it was a partition, for there was no doorway at the top end of the room where it opened into the corridor, it was just a gap. A large gap. The real wall started on the far wall of the cabinets. It had the two tone panelling where there was actual wall. Not a lot, as it was mostly the units. They were the pale green colour of the other side, or rather, the cabinets she was looking at were the same colour. The whole partition on this side was sectioned and had defined edges criss-crossing it in various sized squares. But it was smooth and featureless. She knew this was called *concealed storage* but she had never seen it in real life before, just in magazines. Just as she had never seen a wooden floor like this in a house, only in hotels and posh offices.

There was more daylight in that corner of the room but she couldn't see how the partition ended or if there was a door, as he was in the way. On her right, where the things she wasn't to look at were, the couch she was on curved into a corner, and carried on down part of the room. The sofa was all one piece, and she'd never dreamed that you could buy such a large piece of furniture in one piece, to fit a room this size. The whole room looked as if it was ready for a photo shoot. It was light and modern and calm and pastels, without being any one colour. Cool greens and creams and paleness.

A memory of dark green flashes troubled at her mind. She put it away.

She contemplated that it was time to give up noticing how expensive everything was. She'd obsessed about this in the cell. Did he only bring her expensive things, and dress expensively with her whilst he was actually a normal bloke trying to pretend, with huge credit card bills and a bailiff about to come knocking on the door? Had he built her cell with an inheritance, and was about to run out of money and give up? She doubted he had a job… although when she'd been left alone for days, as punishment, and she'd been convinced he was leaving her to starve to death she'd… *let it pass.*

Yes, let it pass. Looking round, faced with this expanse and the ceiling and chandelier, she gave up to it. He was rich. Stinking rich and no wonder he didn't need a job.

No wonder no one had ever found her.

She was as calm as she was going to get. Ignoring the windows even more, she took a deep breath and determined to carry on. She was going to see more before going back into the cell, no matter the cost.

CHAPTER TEN

Her placing the glass down on the occasional table in front of them was the signal to recommence.

He stood and held out his hand to her.

'Ready for more?'

The smile was soft and gentle, the eyes brimming with care and concern.

What had put him in such a good mood?

'Yes please Jonathan.'

She bit back the desire to apologise for feeling faint. The rules had been formed in her mind from pretty effective physical lessons. No doubt it would have demeaned him to actually speak them: much more fun to let her work it out herself. Of course, it always brought with it the option that she'd got it slightly wrong.

There were always more lessons to be had.

Currently, the operating mode that got her into least trouble was quite simple. Speak only when spoken to. Say the minimum. Use his name often. Defer to his gaze whenever doing anything. Do not ask questions unless offered the opportunity clearly. Today kinda mucked that up. So many unknowns.

He led her back into the narrow corridor, out the way she had come in. He moved them down to the end point, under the picture of the garden. On the right, backing onto the living room wall, was the kitchen. Large and long, with an odd layout. Like the living room, there were no doors into the kitchen, just a gap. There was a wall of appliances and units, on the left hand wall facing inwards. Then a breakfast bar cut it in half, and on the other side, what she would call an actual kitchen: sink, cooker, etc. The room was odd, and didn't have enough windows, just some on the very far corner, on the right. It was also an odd mix of dark colours – black and slate – and light wood. The unit tops were mirror polished, and had the look of stone.

Directly across from the kitchen, was a dining room. It held an oval table with four chairs, and various cabinets with china in. It was hard to see any detail as the tall windows in there had thick curtains pulled across. Next to that, and obviously on the other side of her cell, was a study cum home office. Very modern office furniture competed with massive wooden bookcases crammed with books and papers and various objects. It was slightly cluttered and untidy compared to everything else she had seen. As if he actually worked in this space for real. He let her look briefly, and then brought her back out. Her heart was beating as she'd seen the computer on the desk... The huge windows had not been shut out in there, but they did have the same thick obscuring nets featured in the living room.

Going past the door to her own cell made her feel sick and she had to swallow rapidly a couple of time. There were no doors on that side past her room, and on round the corner. As they turned the corner, she noticed two things. One, the bottom end of the living room, where they now stood, was also opened by a large gap, not a door, and two, the hall space in front of them was a really odd shape. Directly in front, the hall went forward to end with another picture after some windows on the left side, and a door on the other. But on her right, the wall ended just after a doorway, and turned another corner. Into an odd sort of 'dead' space. Odd, as it was somewhat out of proportion with everything else, being much wider than the corridors off it, and at the end there was another partition closing it off, not a wall. In this partition, was a door. She stared at it curiously. Noticing, he walked her right up to it. She looked from the doorway in the middle of the partition, and then back to him.

'Never open this door.'

He said it lightly enough. She nodded, her face draining of colour.

'Yes, Jonathan, I mean no Jonathan, of course I won't if that's what you wish.'

He nodded, and took her back to the small cross point. The door they had passed on the jut out from the original corner turned out to be a large bathroom. Ornate and in keeping with the old world splendour of the place – roll topped, curl footed bath, gleaming tiles, a walk in shower cubicle, quite small, and a toilet with an old fashioned water closet on high up. The luxury feel was still there however, and it was warm and inviting. The bath looked deep enough to swim in. There was no natural light, and the room was quite shallow. Again, an odd shape for the hall, and positioned weirdly in terms of the other rooms.

The final room, on the end of the corridor by the window, was actually a utility room, with washing machine and tumble dryers and ironing stuff and huge built in cabinets taking up one entire wall. It looked impeccable, as if it had never been used. It was a large room, and had the feel that it had once been a bedroom even though it too had no natural light. It was terribly mundane and out of place with the splendour of the rest of it.

A deep sense of sadness welled up within her as they left the room. The tour was over. So much of her world had been about getting out of that room. So much for so long. Now, she was going back to the room. There was nothing very hopeful about what she had seen, nothing to help her out of this. Now she would be going back in there. Did it help her, that she knew what was outside? Had anything changed from her being out of the cell?

Chemical changes alerted him to her changing emotional state. A foot or so in front of her, walking away, he could not physically see what was happening behind him. Her scent however, suggested panic was not far off. He kept on walking.

Turning the corner into the narrow hallway, he heard her sob quietly behind him. He ignored it, moving on slowly, but with senses heightened. As he passed the doorway into the lounge area, he heard her footfalls stop. If he judged it right, she was standing at the doorway of her room. He carried on, moving into the kitchen, looking up in a surprised motion as if he had only just noticed she was not obediently behind him.

She was shaking from head to foot. Silent tears coursed down her cheeks. Frozen, in pain, totally transfixed. Wonderful! His hand flinched, a pulse across the muscles. He flexed it, careful to keep it out of her view.

'Joanne?'

His voice cut through her... *shit shit shit shit shit...* she had to move, had to move, had to move. Nothing worked. Legs gone, brain gone, self preservation gone. *Shit shit shit shit shit shit.* Tears cascaded out of her eyes, blurring her vision. She tried hard to stop it, but a tiny whimper escaped her lips. She slammed her hands up over her mouth...

oh no no no! Maybe he didn't hear it... maybe she only imagined she had let it out? Maybe...

Delighted, he strode down to her, his best Face of Wrath fixed firmly. She buckled under the pressure, and fell to her knees, openly sobbing, her hands raised up to protect her head.

Leaving her for a moment, he turned into the lounge, and sprung the main unit door on the wall. It opened silently, as it should, and he surveyed his treasures. He really wanted to start with a thin lash, but that was the voice of pleasure speaking, not that of training and instruction. He reached in and brought out a one inch thick belt, supple and not too dense. He relished in the feel of it as he wrapped the buckle into his hand, and wound round a layer. His breathing had sped up, his heart rate and his blood pressure was rising. This was *magnificent.* Well worth the waiting, the discipline.

When he stepped back into the hallway, he found she had started to crawl back into the room, back to what she knew. One blow to her back, and that journey was over. She screamed, more in shock than pain, he was sure, and tried to scrabble back into the room. He caught her left ankle up, and strode down the hallway with her writhing behind, and twisted her forward into the wider more open space of the bottom hallway. His blood sang as he laid into her.

Completely shocked by the sudden onslaught of a belt, when she had never felt anything but flesh, she abandoned herself to panic utterly. All her careful lessons about keeping her face out of his way, about only offering her back to his blows, where possible: lost, gone in the first moments of this sudden and violent change. He worked her relentlessly, aiming for her back, buttock and upper thighs. There were many opportunities for her front, her head, her lower legs, as she screamed and moaned and strived to escape, but he kept to the more productive patterns this early on. She ended up in the corner, foetal, trying hard to make herself smaller and smaller... he grabbed her out by her hair, and threw her back down to start afresh. Gratifyingly, she never once got anywhere near going into passive acceptance. That tasted just fine. He'd been a very good master for a very long time, and now he would get his reward. He allowed her to escape him for quite long enough: there could be no pretend indifference with leather!

When blood began to seep through the remnants of the silk blouse, he stopped. Grabbing her by her hair once more, he brought her ravished face up to his: the pain and shock written large upon the swollen flesh. His aim had missed once, at least, for there was a welt upon her cheekbone. Oh well.

'I do not like crying, have you forgotten?'

He was just being cruel for the sake of it, for he knew nothing could stop her shrieking like the banshee as she was doing now. She was too far gone in the pain and terror of trying to escape the belt. Keeping a firm grip on her hair, he dragged her back up the corridor, not so easy this time, as she had, by now, a lot of bare skin to catch on the smooth wooden floor. With little ceremony he tossed her back into the room, keeping to the new rules. He pulled the door shut and was happy when silence descended. My, that girl could scream in an extremely satisfying manner. He replaced the belt, went to the kitchen and poured himself a glass of water. Thirsty work.

True hunger ascended, and he went and changed before going out to sate a more rewarding thirst. He felt sure he would kill, so he was careful on who he trapped and where. As he disposed of the rubbish, into a deep borehole on a building site on the other side of the river, he felt pleased: deeply content and enervated. True, there had been a stirring in him, he was sure, at the moment he took the life. A faint suggestion of an erection, which was annoying, troublesome to his equilibrium. It was a tiny shade against the joys from earlier, and to come, so he pressed the feeling, and the thoughts, down. He walked home with a merry step.

After having checked on her – she had crawled into bed and from what he could see, had taken off her soiled clothing and put them in the laundry basket – he retired himself. He needed his beauty sleep after all, and his rest. An exciting few days awaited him, and he fell asleep relaxed and at peace.

The peace was short lived, however. His dreams were not pleasant. Scent always arrived first, and the stench of a fetid body, unwashed for weeks, mingled with mud, blood and excrement, alerted him to the scene. Pungent, acrid, urine soaked cloths lay about him, as he felt the fire on his back, buttocks and legs. He knew where he was, and he fought it. Fought hard to surface before *she* arrived, fought to be free before she came to gloat. As he swam up through the layers, up through the dark and into the soft nightlight around him, he heard *her* laughing softly in his wake. His body dripped with blood tinged sweat. The sheets under him stained. He rose, showered, and stripped the bed, throwing all in the waste. After he had remade everything, he showered again. Totally alert, he checked on her before going to do some work in the study.

She was deeply asleep, lost in her only refuge. For now at least. He would gain dominion over her sleep too, before long. He settled into work with an easy will, the dream forgotten. Like all other pains in his life, it was wiped out of all knowing.

She wasn't aware of waking, for she wasn't actually sure she'd slept. She was still sprawled face down in the bed and it felt as if she'd dozed for a moment, maybe two. She blocked off the signals from her body as best she could, with some success, as she had no desire to make it worse by thinking on how it hurt. It was, in its own way, an easy trick: just think of something else. Today, the topic of 'something else to think of' was a slight challenge. Eventually, she decided the something to think of was that she needed a hot shower. That always helped. With immense effort, and taking huge amounts of time, she slid her feet out of the bed, over the edge, and straddled with her stomach on the bed, pushed up with her arms. She screamed. It caught her short, the sharpness. She'd think on that more.

Pulling her thoughts back down and concentrating on the thought of a hot shower running over her ... *aching*... her aching body, managed to get her moving. Moving caused immense... *discomfort, that's the word, stick with it*... discomfort in the back of her legs and her buttocks, and she decided she'd pee in the shower. Sitting down didn't seem an option. The heat controls were always left at where she wanted them, so she ran the water for a moment, checking the pressure, and stepped in. She moved back out of the water stream so quickly she smacked into the stall, and the little whimpering screams he detested were out before she could prevent them. The thought of the pain she was in... *yes, it was pain*... was her mind before she could block it. *Pain*... worming its way in and undermining her. Weakening her resolve, eating at her like cancer.

Confusion fought a round inside her, with her tears, as she tried to grapple with everything and thrust the pain away, before it threatened her precious sanity. Tears won for the moment, and she burst into hysterical sobs: as the tears ran down her left cheek – it stung badly. She was instinctively curling into what she thought of as her recovery position – curled foetal in the corner of the shower, with warm water coursing over her – when she understood what he had done. She could not curl down in that favoured position, for to do so, pulled on her back: muscles and skin both. It was out of the question that she curl up. Just as it was out of the question that she sit on the toilet seat, stand under running water, or lie in a hot bath. She was shaking with equal parts rage and despair by the time she'd thought through the implications. It was not just that her entire back, her shoulder, her backside and the backs of her legs were on fire – it was that she couldn't go through any of her routines. She couldn't do any of the things she did to get by. She staggered back to the bed, and flopped down on it, face down, trying uselessly to escape the agony on her back. There was no escape, no sense of control to get her through. She couldn't ignore things while she soaped and scrubbed. She couldn't pretend they weren't happening whilst she prissed and preened with her hair. She couldn't sit and stare at the picture. She couldn't even get dressed without a huge struggle. The tears were uncontrollable: she was naked and alone once more.

How the fuck was she going to get through the day like this?

He kept to the routine he'd established before he'd allowed her out of her room. Food was brought at appropriate times, he expected her to be clean, civil and capable of discussion on a variety of topics, should he choose to speak to her. She was allowed to take breakfast in night attire, but had to be decently clothed with cared for hair at all other times.

Regardless of any training that had been handed out.

That had been quite satisfying to watch. For whilst she managed to get a robe on for her for breakfast, preparing herself for lunch had taken much more effort. Dressing was clearly painful and difficult, and her fear of getting it wrong and being caught had made her fumble all the more. She did manage it, eventually, and he made no mention of appearance or her discomfort when he took in the lunch tray. He did not speak to her, in fact, for about a week, when the welts were faded and most of the bruising well healed. He had sat with her a couple of times, whilst she chewed and swallowed, to highlight the lack of communication. She began her curious custom of sitting slightly off centre in her chair, a sign she was needy and emotional, on day three of the silence. By the time he did break it, her face had fallen into that pinched and starved look, no matter how hard she tried to hide it. As he started to discuss the weather with her, and how bothersome the rain had been, tears spilled down her face, and her face flushed with the glow of gratitude she had, whenever he gave her something she really needed. He enjoyed seeing that little flush, as she so hated herself when she displayed it.

When he returned with the evening meal, she had perked up, and the starved look was diminished; well hidden. Now he was talking to her, she was eager to both keep the conversation flowing, and pretend she was indifferent to it. Not that she dared pretend this to him, but he always knew by the pattern of her swallowing, when she was at her most rejecting of her need for him. He had signalled that need to her clearly, when he had brought in two trays, and they had eaten together.

It took a few false starts for the new routine to be established. For one thing, she took much longer to understand that avoiding punishment was simply impossible, now she was allowed out of the cell. When it finally occurred to her that the entire point *was* the belts, she gave into to it all much easier than she would have ever thought. Unlike inside the cell, when she still had some semblance of the order of his madness in her head, and could avoid punishment, outside, in the larger flat, his behaviour, and handing out *lessons* was simply random. As was her complete inability to avoid what was happening to her. In addition, there was just no room for passive acceptance in her body, when leather was biting her flesh.

Certainly, he'd started by following the old rules, but on the afternoon she'd been sitting on the couch, looking at her hands, when he'd swept her on to the floor and drawn blood in several extremely creative and very painful ways... with a variety of the differently shaped belts he kept in the cupboard... she'd come to realise that he just simply liked what he was doing. There was no method, for she was as well trained as it was possible to be. So she gave up hoping that what she did, or didn't do, would guarantee she wouldn't get punished. It took longer for her to try and stop moving, reacting. The passive acceptance of fists had been a comfort, and that comfort was torn from her. Nothing she tried, stopped her trying to claw herself away from the lash. She'd revisited several major Hollywood films that had featured in her growing up, with stoic and slightly ruffled heroes clenching their teeth, and looking slightly strained as they'd endured 40 lashes, as if they were constipated. How funny was that, when the battle was to keep her bowels closed?

She had managed to close down, eventually, but only her voice. She had to claim something for herself, she knew, and that was all she could find. She didn't make any noise anymore, no matter what he did. Silence had been achieved under the onslaught, and that was something. It worried at her though, for she was acutely aware, as she replayed those black and white scenes of pirate justice and derring do, crinolined beauties looking on with a tearful eye... that he had never actually used a whip. Only belts. Would he move onto that? Could she keep quiet, with an actual whip? She doubted it, and the thought made her sick. He seemed to get worse, when she cried out. She did move and squirm, and try to escape. It was not possible to ignore her body, the pain, once a certain amount of damage had been inflicted. Survival instincts cut in, and no matter her need to keep still... there was a point when hands would start to try and find traction on the smooth wooden floor, and her body would try and crawl away.

Traitor.

Otherwise, she was as perfect as it was possible to be. She was always dressed, and at the dining table for meals, when told too. All shared meals now took place in the dining room, or on the small breakfast bar. She was always clean and tidy, when not covered in aching bruises, welts, tears and blood. Her hair always up and neat, although its increasing length was making that challenging. She never argued back, never angered him. She was docile, polite and awaited his prompt on everything. She learned very quickly that once she'd left her cell for breakfast, that she was not allowed to go back to her retreat until he told her she was free to do so.

Retreat.

That was what her cell was sometimes... a *retreat*. And the much fought for, much desired, much yearned for… outside... was now just a much bigger cell.

Except for one thing, that made it different to being inside her cell, no matter what. One small thing that somehow served to keep her going. The windows. There was sunlight, coming in from those windows, windows she was not allowed to approach. But there was light: natural light.

She'd sit, for hours, silent, still, staring at the sunlight. Watching the pattern of shadow and sparkle move across the floor and furniture. She knew every moment of every day, mapped out in the change in tone, colour and texture, of the sun's path through the obscuring nets. The windows brought her two elements that she had sorely missed: day and night, and the changing seasons. It was coming into winter, that much she knew from the short days and the grey light that changed darker then lighter in swift, rain soaked bursts. The cooler air in the flat. She could hear the rain, sometimes, on the window panes, but not very often. Just like she could catch bus noises and horns blaring on the other side of the flat, the outside side of the flat. But the sound proofing was too good for more than the awareness that traffic was endlessly present... but distant.

The other windows, on the other side of the flat, the living area, the kitchen, the strangely shaped hall. She'd realised they were inner windows. They turned a square on themselves, after all. The kitchen window turned the corner on the long run of the living area, and turned back in the corner window of the lower hall. Like a very large bay window; that's why both hall and kitchen were an odd shape. The sunlight was more diffused through them however, than the other side of the flat. Rain very rarely drove into them, the way it did on the dining room window. There were no traffic noises on that side, and very few bird wings flashed by. Daylight was shorter, and darker, and there were shadows of buildings very close. It was a puzzle. As was the door she wasn't allowed to open. He obviously went through it, if only to find his own bedroom. She never saw him go near it. She never approached it, even in her mind: she simply couldn't afford it space in her brain. It was. End of. Move on.

She wasn't allowed near the actual windows, of course. She'd never seen anything out of them. Well, not quite. There was blue sky, and greenery, outside the dining room one. But it was just blurs. She wasn't allowed within five feet of those windows, and the testing of that boundary had caused her much pain, mostly as she yearned to see it so much, that the emotional pain of longing, had made her careless to the physical pain of approaching them. She gave up the longing rather than have her body, and heart, broken too completely.

Often, when left to heal alone in her cell, she'd decided she would never go back outside to the flat again. It was easier in the cell. Less complicated, certainly a lot less painful. In some ways, the added pain of the belts had actually reduced her terror, once she'd given up to it. The beltings were so intense, so savage, the damage on her body so long lasting, in terms of being able to turn, to sit, to lie down... that she'd found a hole in herself that was very comforting. Unable to use the routine in the bathroom to soothe herself, her physical routine, she'd found one in her mind. Sometimes, when she was falling into that well of pain, she'd find her mind flying up over her body, up and out, into the blue sky she knew was somewhere above her.

Not always, of course. Not always. Sometimes, it was just bleak and hell and a wish for death. But sometimes… just enough times… she could fly away from the pain, even as her body writhed.

The outside also gave her more of his company, when he was in a good mood. She was required to sit quietly, and just be, all day long. She was forbidden from doing any housework, or cooking, or helping in the domestic in any way. After the cell, and the swirly picture, and the bathroom tiles, it was still much more interesting. She could see more, and chat more, when he was in a mood for talking. She was allowed to sit and watch, as he chopped and stirred and cooked, or loaded the dishwasher after they'd eaten. He was a very good cook but he never cooked enough. Portions were tiny, and she spent most of the day feeling hungry, even as she watched him tip food into the bin.

If he went to his office, which she'd never seen inside of again, she would feel more lonely, stuck on the outside. She yearned for things to do, to occupy her mind, but nothing was allowed to her. There was nothing to read, not even cereal packets, as everything in the cupboards was decanted into plastic or glass tubs and serving dishes. She'd asked if she could have food from the fridge, and been belted for it. She'd asked if she could have something to read, and been belted for it. She ceased asking, or thinking of things to ask for. Simply passively accepted what was offered to her. Her every plate of food was emptied no matter what it contained. She'd once left something foreign and alien looking, and had been punished by not being fed for several days. She took what she was given and was grateful.

She thought through everything about her containment, and used her mind to read the clues. There was a large viewing screen in the living room, she knew, he'd talked about it. But she'd never been allowed to see it. Music must happen when she wasn't there; the stereo system was expensive and no doubt impeccable. It was never on when she was out. The music itself was no doubt in the concealed storage she was not allowed to explore. In the early days, once she'd know what was outside the door, she'd sit for hours, trying to hear him move on the other side, straining to hear a note of music, or a tinny television voice. She never heard anything. Hardly surprising, as allowed through it regularly, she'd realised the door itself was almost four inches thick. The step down into the hall was about three inches. And there was the fake roof of her cell, and the recessed walls. The cell, was at least four feet shorter in length than the dining room. The ceiling in the cell a good foot, maybe two, lower than the rest of the flat. The flooring higher. The central drain in the floor, and in her bathroom, must drop into the 'real' floor somehow. There had to be a window, back there, behind the wardrobe units. Had to be, if the flat's architecture was followed through. She'd given up obsessing about it. Given up trying to find cracks, evidence, fake panels. She just accepted that the stuffy, oppressive and silent atmosphere of the room, was down to the epic amounts of insulation, and sound proofing, and let it go.

Another reason to enjoy being outside, no matter the pains of the belts and the random manner in which she incurred them. She could breathe freely, literally, on the outside. Not feel like she lived in a lift shaft, which was how she felt when she was locked into the cell, and abandoned.

No matter how awful being with him was, not being with him, being left alone in that cell, with little or no food, for days... that was much, much worse. Terrified she'd starve to death in there, or suffocate if the tiny whirs from the air vents ever ceased. Losing her mind to loneliness and dread.

But still, *outside*... outside was hard work. Sometimes, she prayed for the moment she was told she could retire for the evening. Prayed for release. Just as she often prayed for release back to the outside, from the cell.

Thus her prayers, at the moment her world expanded to the larger prison of the flat, reduced. Focussed upon the internal: how she should be allowed to move from one side of her prison, to the other.

It did not occur to her that she had stopped praying for freedom.

CHAPTER ELEVEN

The afternoon sunlight was painting the book spines a warm red, highlighting the gold leaf and patterned leather. He liked this time of the day, in his study, and enjoyed the light as it moved on the great bookcase that took up the entirety of the wall on that side. Chiaroscuro patterns formed as the light fell into the deeper shadow of the smaller, lighter, more modern books. Flaming reds, golds, browns, contrasted the pools of shadow. Some of the spines were getting rather faded; time to move them around. Part of the pleasure was that no one could have guessed that the wall with the heaviest of the books was the false one. Hence why the great books were stored there. The subterfuge was considerably more enjoyable than the books. Not that all the spines were books.

He knew that she was sitting on the floor outside, in the hall way. Cross-legged, back to the partition, staring at the study door. He had been in here a couple of hours, and it was her habit, of late, to slowly drift to the corridor, and sit on the floor, and study... the study door. It was amusing... study the study door. It was one reason he had allowed her slightly more variety in clothing, and had added in a fuller cut, but shorter, black skirt, complemented with thick tights and soft leather slippers. She had looked so waif like, sitting there on the floor with them, he had added a thin casual wrap around sweater, in a soft green cashmere. She would hike up the sleeves, pulling them over her hands, as she sat. He had wondered about releasing the dress code for her hair, to see if she then left it hanging in those moments, and completed the street urchin look. She was not quite ready for that: it could wait.

They were faced directly towards each other, with the door blocking their view of each other. Not that she knew that. Nor did she know he could see as well as hear her. It was his habit to close his eyes as she moved from one room to the other, and use his other senses to track her pathways, only using the images from the cameras to confirm what he had already perceived. It was also his habit to never leave the study, whilst she sat there. She would be moving soon and he did have a little more work to be sorted. He stared at the door, imagining her face looking back at him.

He was quite content. In that contentment, he permitted her to thrive, somewhat. She had a knack of being pleasing company. Her general understanding of the world around her, both in terms of history and design, was so woeful, that he enjoyed talking with her, and filling her up with *more*.   More knowledge, more understanding, more viewpoint. She did not have the awareness to uncover what lies he chose to tease her with, and she was so grateful for attention... she was a sponge, to absorb his every word.

Certainly, she feigned some of her attentions, but in general... in general... she was a willing and apt pupil. He had even talked business matters with her, at points, and had been somewhat impressed on her well founded opinions.   Good secretaries always knew more of a business than a mediocre manager, something he had made many a fortune upon. She was good, in her own way, and he allowed her to flourish a little there.

She was well trained, considerate and house broken: she was silent when it mattered most. Silent, unless spoken to. Just as now, she was silent in the corridor, not breaking into his afternoon. He had almost finished the tedious paperwork sent over by the lawyers, and stretched the kinks out of his back, relaxing back into the soft leather of his bespoke office chair as he busied with feeding everything through the fax.

He knew that in her silence, was her life. He too had found the silence she had now. He too had found space to remain dumb to Eléan, and her blood taking. He too, had escaped being torn further, deeper, by leaving his cries unheard. Cries enticed so. They goaded. They called. They called to blood, they called, and answered, rage. They called out strength, power. Her silence brought benediction. In that quietness, her breathing was permitted to continue. In the deepest of his dreams, when nightmare had melted to needful desires, he remembered the feel of *her* body, on his, as he had offered *her* only more silence, more peace, more silent blood.

When he did hear tears, it was never his own, never hers... only the mewlings of the daughters before they died...

Awake, his memories never troubled him, were never allowed exit from the dark. He would wake grumbled, or refreshed, or empty, or... whatever... in its own separate state of being. There was never any connection with the night, and his sleep, to his living and his awakening. Only when he drank of heart's blood, or tore limb from limb, in memory of *his daughters* was there any hint of past, of memory. And then, it was all too fleeting, all too swiftly suppressed and denied. Death washed all in its wake. Death cleansed.

He was content.

He was in pain.

He studied the study door.

He was in pain, and it was her duty to receive it from him, to allow him to be relieved of the burden of it. He transferred the pain to her: she took it and kept it. In many ways, he watched its path upon her, and felt sated, eased. In other ways, this created more pain. The cycle had begun to build. All the little ways, that keeping her, caused him pain...

His diversion business; that which had been a delightful distraction, had begun to pall, quite early on. Spending so much time with her, and then with hunting to fill the needs she caused to rise. He had had to sign over advertising accounts, find others to take his workload. He spent less time there, more here. His mind was distracted by her, his mind spent less time hunting down new clients, servicing their needs and banking their grateful thanks.

Gerard now ran the business day to day. He was not even sure of who had been reassigned the accounts. He just sat in this room, and signed things for the ad agency, and the rest of the portfolio, all of whom did not have one jot of a clue who he was – he was a series of bank accounts and management companies.

Which was one of the things most annoying him: he was a stranger in his own company offices. Someone who came in, occasionally, and was feted. He had already lost his own PA, who had refused to see her career go down with his. He had not replaced her. He had begun to eye the company status on the stock market, with a view to selling. Yes, he would always be busy with his overall portfolio, but he hated losing a hard fought for actual living construction. It would be years before he could pick up a similar company in London and show his face. It would have to wait until all those who knew him in this one, had moved or died, and in advertising the skills he had now, would be useless, so why bother? His income did not require him to labour, but it galled, that a pleasing diversion, hard won and fought for tenaciously, had been so easily given up.

He continued to stare at the door. Stare through the door.

His social life... almost completely gone. Business required contacts. It was one reason he always ran at least one company at any one time, although modern communications were fast making it that you could only operate one in total. Contacts had to be made, and maintained, in any business stratum. Golf played, theatre engagements offered, expensive dining shared. His diary was now empty. Some of those contacts could not be rebuilt, and a completely different type of occupation would have to be found, with a new set of contacts. Again, something increasingly difficult in the face of the growth of communication technology. Very soon, in business, there would be no hiding place. Realistically, once he severed his connection with this company, he would only have the option of beginning again outside the UK. That was incredibly inconvenient as he hated leaving London.

He forced himself to meet Gerard at least once a week. Even then, he was thinking about getting back to her.

There she sat, on the other side of the door.

Hunting. Vastly increased. Therefore, vastly more difficult and time consuming. Freshly spilt blood built blood lust. In the quiet moments of death he visited upon her flesh, lust for more, much more, grew. Lust that had to be sated as appetite increased. He never took a drop from her, but gave plenty. Her back, in particular, often needed some healing if she was to recover in a timely manner. He did not muse on this, as it was an unpleasant thought, with undesirable memories. But it was also factual, and thus required he attend to it. He had always favoured young and easy flesh. Now, he required a steady source of blood, and death. Hours were spent driving to and fro, spinning out his needs, to make them invisible. Days had been lost, in travel and preparation. He had begun to consider that he might need to travel to Paris, and buy his kill there. The cost of dealing with Violette had stayed that hand, for the moment, but unless he began to feed from her…

And there it was: the source of the pain.
The thorn in his pad.
The catch in his throat.
The poison painted upon one half of his apple.

Unless he began to feed from her…he put it to one side, and thought of more ways she brought him pain.

Sex. There was sex. All the feeding, all the death, all the beatings… his groin was stirring. When her blood blossomed up through his senses, fresh and enticing, more things awoke than delicious blood lust… the dead rose. He hated this need arising, and preferred it sealed off in decades of isolation. His instincts changed when his sexual power asserted itself. He had begun to concentrate on females in his hunts. This brought danger; encountered far more risk. Males were easier to kill. Easier to hide. Easier to have forgotten. Less fuss was made of males. Especially the dispossessed, the very young, or the very old. Not that old ones were good for hunting. But for the occasional needed death, the occasional quick dispatch... the old did well. But to sustain this kill score, he would need to leave the country, sooner rather than later. The desire for female blood, death, just made it all more complicated. Female kills were for palate change, not a staple in an increasing feed pattern. If he kept needing to kill females, he would have to travel to where their lives were much cheaper.

He could not do this, with her stored away. Things happen. Landmass can always be travelled. Sea, ocean... could not always be mastered in time. He was stuck with a problem.

...unless he fed from her...

Instinct was what drove him, made him safe. Keeping her like this, defied instinct: it was always impossible. Reason had to be brought to the table when he let himself slip like this. Plans made, kept. Timings were important. Teachings had to be kept in rhythm. Reason and rationalising over training could let mistakes into the rest of his life. Mistakes could threaten his peace.

...unless he fed from her...

Sleep brought fire and sword. Sweat and blood. Yearning, longing and contempt. *She* was back in his mind, and eating his soul once more, as *she* feasted upon his body.

...unless he fed from her...

He sighed. It was rare for him to speak his thoughts to the air, but he sighed, a sharp exhale of breath.

He would have to feed. Feeding from her, it was no big thing. It didn't mean anything. He could still kill her in a moment, a thought, a careless happening.

She was not meaningful to him...

However... she was innocent of what he was. He enjoyed that. It was part of his control of her. Part of the anonymity that he had locked them into. Sitting there, on the other side of the door, she was clueless. Utterly innocent. Completely naïve.

No matter how well trained... no matter how well schooled... if... when... he told her, revealed himself... there would be change. There was always change: it was not usually for the better. Why was he hesitating?

It was not as if this was not a known, worn, path. It was not as if this comfort, this contentment, could last for ever. Not telling her... that brought its own change. Nothing could stay as it was now. She would crumble into madness soon enough. And once that happened, he would kill her, and be left... be left... *alone*? No, left empty. Having lost his rhythm to her captivity he would need to find it again.

It was very annoying. Always.

He wanted a bit more time. A bit more of the path, before he ended up having to reinvent things all over again. He would have to start feeding from her, and use her blood, and body, to control the lusts. It was either that, or kill her now.

Which was tempting... but no, not yet. There was more to be had here, she had a lot more to give.

So few had ever found the silence...

By the time he had finished the last of the calls, and tidied his records, she had drifted off to the kitchen. He followed, in order to start dinner, and to see how he could test out the conversation he wanted to have with her. How to make the most impact, get the most fear for his revelation. He was tingling with anticipation, now his choice was made.

He was preparing Oriental, so there was lots of chopping to be done. It was 'Oriental' as there were far more dishes she didn't know about than did, and he didn't like her commenting on how good the Chinese was, for it to turn out to be Thai, or Vietnamese. So she thought of it as 'Oriental' and let him tell her, if he felt like it. He put the wok on a high gas jet, so she moved it up to 'Stir Fry' of some sort.

It was one of her favourite types of dish to watch being prepared. So much done in advance, and then out into the wok in very quick order. The colours and smells, the different vegetables. It was a real feast for her starved senses, even if it didn't always taste as palatable as she would have liked. Watching it made was enough satisfaction for any day.

She was sitting in her accustomed perch for the kitchen, on the passageway side of the little breakfast bar. He was standing on the other side, his chopping implements and the vegetables between them. He was razoring through some crunchy green vegetable, somewhat like a long thin cabbage, but thicker, at mesmerising speed. He chopped like a TV chef, his blade never faltering.

It faltered. A nick of blood appeared on his index finger. The chopping stopped, the knife laid down. Tension shot through her, everything suddenly much more dangerous. She schooled herself not to react in any way, and stay coolly attentive of him.

He very slowly lifted his finger, with its beal of welling blood. He studied it, dispassionately, moving it slowly to his mouth. Before it reached his lips, he stopped and made direct eye contact with her. She dropped her gaze quickly, ducking her head down.

'Look up.'

She moved her head up, her gaze finding his finger, concentrating on it, and not his eyes. He moved the bloodied finger to her lips.

'Suck.'

Everything fell apart in her head. This was completely new. He never addressed her like this. Her mouth opened as she drew in a startled breath. He placed the finger on her lower lip, slowly smearing the blood across it, like lipstick. He then pushed the tip into her mouth, wiggling between her teeth.

The feeling of invasion was absolute. Every fear she'd had of sexual assault, that had been slowly lulled over the months, sprang into life and slammed through her. Her head moved back slightly, and she caught the movement, forcing herself to stay still. Her gaze locked into his, and there was nothing she could do to stop the panic she was feeling from showing.

His eyes were also showing his emotions: pleasure, triumph, arrogance.

She blinked, as he pushed his finger through, onto her tongue, caressing it in small circles.

'Suck.'

He whispered it, in a soft caress that lifted the hairs all over her body, as if ants were tramping over her in their thousands. Tears pooled in her eyes. His blood tasted brackish, bitter. She closed her mouth down on him and swallowed. With his finger deep in her mouth, she felt the ululation of her tongue and muscles as it clamped on him, pushing him up to her palate as her tongue convulsed. His face transformed, as if in orgasm. She closed her eyes.

'Harder.'

She swallowed again, pushing back the instinct to gag. Her mouth was bone dry, his finger also, there can't have been much blood at all. She fought the panic, and the muscles of her mouth. She'd never realised swallowing was such a complicated, or painful, set of actions. She felt her tongue curl up around his hard finger.

Please God, please don't let me be sick... throwing up on him just wasn't going to happen.

One more swallow made it down, but nothing more was going to happen, not in her mouth, at least. He pulled himself out, abruptly, smiled, then placed the finger in his own mouth, and sucked down on it. The smile on his face, the knowingness in his eyes, was obscene.

She dropped her gaze down to the work surface, desperately trying to find something innocent to focus upon. The staccato of his chopping resumed and he carried on preparing the meal as if nothing unusual had occurred.

CHAPTER TWELVE

As he carried on preparing the meal, moving to the very quick cooking stage, she tried to get her head around her fears. The issue was not about *if* she was going to get a belting that evening, it was when. That was inevitable. Anytime the pathways changed like this, she'd get a beating. At some point this evening she'd be slammed onto the floor, and he'd cut into her with one of the belts. Nothing was going to stop that, given the state she was in, and the air of self importance he was now giving off, the air shimmering with his build to explosion.

All she had left to her, was to delay it somehow, try and minimise the events. Keep her own control, and carry on with the evening's normal pattern as much as possible. Allow time to carry them further into the evening, where he may just lose a little of his fervour.

A girl could only hope, after all.

Unfortunately, this required she eat the meal now sitting in front of her. She'd sat at the table perfectly, attending to his prompts as he placed the plate in front of her. Perversely, however, he'd given her a huge portion compared to normal. Normally, she'd have been cheered with the pile of food, as he kept her always slightly hungry. However, with the feel and taste of his finger still in her mouth, she didn't want to eat one morsel, never mind the massive pile of vegetables and sauce now mocking her. Lifting up the chopsticks, a skill she had learned quickly under his tutelage, she set herself the task of getting half way through the plate and seeing if he'd let it go at that. The meal tasted of slime, which didn't help in the slightest. One mouthful at a time... She schooled her face to remain politely interested in both the food, and his presence, as she attempted to chew and swallow as she thought through the pattern of the evening to come.

The issue wasn't the belting. The issue was what might also happen out of the ordinary. She felt chilled, physically chilled, by the turn of events. Her bones ached with it. Whilst she'd normally be trying to work herself into an acceptance of what was about to happen, and hope this time, tonight, she'd manage to fly away from it, or that he didn't kill her... all that space in her head was filled with something else. A fear so large she didn't feel her body could contain it all. It was trickling out of her pores, and down her back, even as she tried to push it away from herself. She could even smell it, rancid, upon her body. Her eyes stung with it, her ears were blocked by it, her breath robbed by it. As her muscles and bones remained schooled and calm, her pores oozed out the sweat and fear. She'd noticed the smell before and had supposed in some way there was a chemical smell to fear. Hormones, adrenaline, what was the other one..? Cortisol? Cortisone? They'd had a talk about work stresses, under health and safety info, her own boss being a great believer in the ticking off of boxes to prove no fault in her management. There had been a chemical in the blood that signalled very intense stress, she was sure it was cortisone … she felt sure she knew how it smelled... as she did now, in fact.

One morsel at a time, and the dinner was going down, but the fear levels, were rising up, up, up. Her body was rushing her head long into catastrophe: she must keep it under control a little longer.

'Is it flavoursome enough?'

Her head jerked up, a bad thing for it to do. Showed she wasn't paying him attention.

She recovered: 'It's fine, thank you.'

'Good. I did not use any oyster sauce, and wondered if it was a bit... bland.' He left it open, inviting response.

'Not at all.' *Think! Think! Think!* What would he like to hear? 'It's a very good balance of flavours, actually. Oyster sauce may have overwhelmed it.'

He considered.

'Which part?' His voice was a cat, and she was the mouse. *Shit!*

PanicPanicPanic No opportunity here for prevarication for asking questions back to spin out, find out, what he was after. 'The lettucey vegetable, I'm sorry, I don't know what it's called. But it's very... fragrant. Very… fresh.' Her voice tapered out... she was doomed. In an odd way, she was relieved: at least the wait was over.

'Pak choi. It is called pak choi.' There was a long, considered pause, as he ate another mouthful himself. 'Yes, you may be right, it would have been drowned.'

The silence between then stretched out once more. It was a sound, or an absence of sound she hated. The very air carried the weight of the silence, and there was just so much of her lifespan in that vacuum of fear. Literally. Totally trapped, she sat, chewing but no longer swallowing. She concentrated on just getting rid of the one tiny mouthful... *just get rid of it!*

'And yet... it still tastes a little flat. Something is missing.' He put down his utensils, placed his napkin on the table, and rose to his feet. 'I will just fetch some more sauce, excuse me.'

This was also totally new, and completely unexpected. She'd half risen from her seat when he did, and then had to sit down again quickly. What was the protocol, for the host leaving a guest at the table? Where was *Miss Manners* when she was really needed? So much of her *education* at his hands had been about the social niceties of... what, living? As if this was living? But she now knew how to set an elaborate table perfectly, and how to drape a napkin according to the meal. But did she rise when he came back to the table? She could hear him moving about in the kitchen, but kept her gaze firmly locked on the plate in front of her when he returned.

Stay seated and swallow this mouthful, swallow this mouthful...

He moved back over to the dining room, and entered on her side, passing behind her to reach his place, set at the head of the table, backed onto the window. She shuddered as he passed behind her, and she was aware her top was now sticking to her lower back, so much sweat was pooling there. He stood at his plate as she managed to finally clear her mouth. She reached for a sip of water as he spoke to her.

'Give me your hand, please.'

Her left hand reached over to him, automatically, as the right one froze on the way to the glass. She tried to look away, as he grabbed it in a firm hold but the flash of searing pain in the palm, brought her to her feet, gasping for breath. She fought down cries and tried to get hold of her fear, as he held her hand over his plate. Blood was gushing from her palm, onto his food. Aghast, she pulled away instinctively, and fell sideways a step as he released her. The table was all that kept her upright. Her left hand curled into her chest, and when she pulled it back to see, her top was stained with blood. Blood was pulsing out of a deep cut, in the fleshy heel of her palm. She grabbed her napkin, and pressed down, looking up for him at the same time. He was standing at his chair, his face giving clear signal that he was awaiting her reseating. She sat, quickly, continuing to press down hard on her hand. The now cold sweat bathing her body, made her shiver.

He seated himself with a flourish, and placed his napkin across his knees. Picking up his chopsticks, he expertly used the tips to mix through the ingredients on the plate. Her blood mixed into the vegetables. He picked up a large mouthful of food, sniffed appreciatively, and stuffed it into his mouth. A smile lit his face as he chewed thoughtfully, giving a good performance of a gourmet at a banquet, or a wine taster at a demonstration.

'Ah yes, I was right, it was not quite salty enough.' He lifted his wine glass of water and tilted it to her, saluting his thanks.

She threw up. It wasn't possible for anything else to happen, there was no other pathway. Her eyes blurred with stinging sweat, her body convulsed, her throat retched and gagged... and she spewed onto the table... the delicate porcelain plates, the fine crystal glasses, the silver cutlery and the damask linen. A torrent of bile let forth. Somewhat like a cat ejecting a fur ball, she jumped up and back, knocking her chair over, as she vomited.

There was a moment when they just looked at each other, with the horror of the vomit lying between them. She turned ghostly white, then turned... and ran.

It was a totally futile thing to do, she knew that. But she had to escape what was going to happen. She just had too. She reached the bottom door, the one she was not allowed to go near, and tried desperately to open it. Nothing. She could hear him calmly walking down the corridor. He was opening the cupboard door, fetching a belt... in her desperation she tried to make it through the living room, back up and round, heading for her cell. He never used the belt in there, ever, if she could just reach... the door was locked down shut. She screamed as he came back round the corner, a thick heavy belt snaking between his hands. The hand was slippery with blood, on the handle of the door, as she backed away. What to do, what to do?

She turned back into the wide open space of the living room, her feet slipping on the smooth wood, blood drops splattering on the floor from her cut hand. She was almost half way across, when something inside her changed, flowed up to the surface. Rage flashed through her: the feel of him pushing his finger into her mouth, his cutting into her hand. Rage at the awfulness of the change, the tearing away of another layer of safety. Rage at everything he was doing to her. Without thought, she turned, so quickly she almost slipped, and as he walked slowly to meet her, her right hand flew out and she punched him hard, on the chin. He took a step back, startled.

Her hand hurt from the impact, as it was like slapping stone. Another moment of complete suspension between them, and then she was turning to run again...

...what on earth had she been think...

The thought was obliterated by the savagery that slammed into her back. She was felled, instantly, and lay on the smooth flooring, the back of her mind analysing the detail of the wood grain as she tried to breathe, but couldn't. This had happened to her many years ago, when she was a young child. She'd fallen off a donkey, on Blackpool beach, and had lain in the sand, face down, unable to breathe. Her father had come and picked her up, whole, and the action had started her lungs again, as she'd been lifted up into the air to start wailing in panic. The action was repeated, now, as he picked her up as if she was a tiny child, and gave her a gentle shake. Her lungs burst into life, but the scream was short lived as the pain that tore through her back was too much for her system to cope with and she blacked out.

He laid her back down on the floor, careful to avoid bleeding on the couch, but placing her firmly on a rug, to contain the blood. What had he been thinking of? He really had lost his temper. He cursed himself for his own stupidity, on several levels... what on earth had possessed him? It had gone so well, and he had thought his introduction to his nature was quite inventive. He had never done that before, and had been pleased with himself when it occurred to him to try it. It would have been far preferable to get her to clean up the mess herself, with his leather on her back to aid her concentration. But no, his reaction had been as spontaneous as hers had been, and he had hit into her with the buckle end of the belt, in temper. His hand had held the leather end of the belt, and had just swung; putting everything into it.

Her shoulder was a ruin of torn flesh. He fetched supplies and cut off what was left of the fabric. The buckle end had dug into the soft flesh on her left shoulder blade, just to the left of her spine. It had literally dug out a lump of flesh as it scored down, on a diagonal. She had a crater, a deep hole, in the flesh, and on the very edge, bone from her spine glistened through. A huge blister of straw coloured fluid was collecting on the impact edge. This was what he meant by problems being brought to the table. The humour in that, given the ruin of the table, roused him a little. Oh well, it was begun, may as well just follow the dance where it led, for a while. He soaked up her blood with towels, and used a scalpel to dig in around the wound, slicing open the blister, then slit his own wrist over the mess. She started to rouse, so he shot her through with sedative and painkillers, then carried on dripping his blood over everything. The blister reformed, but he cut it back once more. When the raw flesh was closed in, and beginning to heal over, he placed a dressing of his own blood over it. The skin was healing puckered and torn: he really was an idiot, and he was annoyed with himself.

Such critical thoughts did not survive long, however, and by the time she was stripped and clean, and was back in her bed, he'd returned to silently berating her weakness.

Whilst he cleared the table cloth and its contents into the rubbish, scrubbed and cleaned the rooms, and parcelled the dining room rug off to a specialist cleaners, he plotted and planned. He fetched identicals of everything, from the loft storage and redressed both rooms. He did not actually possess an exact match for the Persian rug, but a good enough copy would do until he knew more of the original's fate. The living room one was consigned to the furnace and simply replaced with its twin.

Retiring to his own suite for a long soak, he determined that the issue was her mind. She was physically trained, now he had to tame her inside her head. Why had he never seen that before, at least, not this clearly? He must break her to his truths, in her mind and soul, not just her body.

It took a week of care and recovery, before she could be up and dressed as normal. No amount of his blood on the wound would create new flesh where there was an absence of it. It was a mess, but he did his best to keep it pain free whilst the skin and muscles underneath mended as well as they could. She could not see the wound, of course, and reacted stiffly and with resistance to his changing the dressings with his blood on them as he applied them. Again, he recognised the battle over his true nature was about her mind, not her body... he thought long and hard on how to move forward on the matter.

When the shoulder wound had recovered enough, and she was up and dressed as normal, he bade her join him in the dining room for breakfast. She had dressed in her more formal clothes, and her hair was meticulously restrained. Her face was composed in an excellent marble slab of complete attention to him. Her right hand was occasionally rubbing the healed wound on the left palm: he was pretty sure she was unaware of the action.

They very rarely ate breakfast in the dining room. Either they did not share the meal, or they ate on the breakfast bar in the kitchen. He had laid out the breakfast ware formally, and placed bacon and eggs on her plate. She was moving them around her plate, with just enough being consumed to avert comment. Not that anything was going to avert comment today.

'I am pleased that you are feeling better this morning.

'Yes, thank you. I'm much better.'

'Good, it was unfortunate, that you became so... indisposed.'

She managed to get another scrap of bacon in her mouth, taking a drink of water to try and drown it down.

'Joanne, I have been meaning to have a talk with you. Perhaps now would be a good time?' He sat back, settling into the chair, the meal dismissed.

She adjusted her own pose exactly, sitting in quiet attention, moving her body slightly to angle more to him.

'First of all, let me say that I do understand your... reticence... in the matter of your time here with me...'

She tuned out everything, but listening. If he was pontificating, best not to let something important go unheard. She found if she focussed tightly on his lips, and how they formed his words, the rest of the room would fade from her view. Slowly blink out to nothingness, and dim in colour and detail. Something she often worked on when left on her own for any length of time: how long to stare at a fixed point long enough, and watch the room fade from her peripheral vision.

'...do you agree?'

'Yes Jonathan, I do agree.'

Best just to repeat his phrase. If she embellished, or reduced, he could get testy. *Testy?*

'Good, then I am happy for this to be out of our way. You really do have to accept this.'

She was nonplussed. He'd not mentioned whatever it was she'd have to accept. *Had he...?* He was looking at her for a response. She felt her way along the words, slowly.

'I will, of course, accept anything you say, Jonathan.'

'Excellent! I should never have doubted you.'

He really was acting totally out of sorts. She clamped down on following that thought, using her energy to keep focussed on his lips.

'It is important you accept my true nature utterly. You should, after all, feel privileged. It is a rare, and exceptional honour, to know a vampire.'

The room exploded back into colour and detail. So sharp, and so fast was the change, she felt she'd heard a shock wave. Her breathing was faster, her palms sweating up. She ordered her body to remain still, whilst she sought to bring her focus back purely to him.

Her eyes had flared so wonderfully... the pupils expanding so quickly, it was if they were devouring the light. This was much more like it...

He leaned forward towards her.

'I am content that you understand so well.' He timed the pause to her heartbeat, moving into the silence as her body tipped into panic. She would taste wonderful! He reached out his hand. 'Give me your hand.'

She instinctively raised her left hand and offered it to him. She didn't like that this is how her body had reacted, but equally, she didn't want to argue with it. She was still trying to work out some way to hear, and process, his madness. She had worked very hard, at refusing him the label of mad. It wasn't a label she could cope with. Faced with such evidence of his own delusion, there was little escape: he was mad and she, in turn was utterly doomed.

He grasped her hand firmly, pulling her into his space more completely. His left hand holding it from underneath, the fingers of his right hand trailing over her opened palm, in that obscenely suggestive manner he'd first displayed last week in the kitchen. She felt her mouth flood with saliva, as the bile rose. She swallowed hard, again aware of how complex and difficult it was, to swallow down fear.

'I had wondered, if you had not wondered before now? About how special my gifts were?' His index finger was tracing a tiny circle over the mark on her palm. 'About how well you heal?'

Everything dissolved. Her blood; her bones; her brain. She felt the slump as her body began to list. His hand kept her trapped to him, even as the rest of her sought to slide sideways onto the floor. She had fought thinking about this so hard, so completely. Her memories of how much damage he'd inflicted, had never been matched by her awakenings in a body different from the one her mind had fled. Bruises would look days old, and cuts and welts old and half healed. She'd known he was playing with her mind somehow, and had guessed that more than once, she'd been 'asleep' longer than she thought. But the inconsistencies had grown, especially since her release into the flat. Day and night had a meaning once more, and the rhythm of 'outside' could be glimpsed. Many times she was very sure of falling asleep in an agony of fire, and wakening with the duller pains of healing, when only one night's sleep had gone by. Just as she'd been equally sure that sometimes many many nights had gone by, and he was giving play that only one had passed.

She had chosen to ignore it utterly, lest she go mad herself. This had been a conscious decision, made when she began to wonder if he'd actually really hit her that hard, after all. Had she really bled? Had it happened? Was this life real? Was she in a mental ward somewhere? She'd locked it all out of her mind: to hold it in even the slightest measure, would be to drive herself insane. To question how much pain she'd endured, was to question everything: she did not question on this.

Ever.

It had been exceptionally hard to keep to this, during the past few days, whilst her shoulder had burned and ached so. The memory of lying on the floor, not breathing, the fire that had laced across her back. Yes, it had hurt, but nothing matched the memory of the hit...

'Do you not wonder about all the little injuries, all healed up? Your shoulder?' He raised her hand up, and licked his tongue over her wrist, the tip of his tongue playing over the veins.

She looked away, had no choice. All was needed to deal with the scream, to stop the scream: the scream could not be released. She must swallow the scream.

The movement on her hand became more playful, more... sensual. He was licking and tonguing and teasing her skin. The licks became slow, playful bites. His teeth pressed down on her here, there. His mouth took control of one of her fingers, and he sucked down then moved on. She kept her face turned away, still working on the absence of scream.

When he finally cut down, into her left wrist, she hardly felt it. She was so far into adrenaline overload, he could have done much worse, and she'd still not have felt much. The rush of her fear-soaked blood into his mouth was ecstatic. He drank down eagerly, licking and pulling the wound open bit by bit. Sucking out every drop he could without actually opening a vein. He deliberately smeared his game out, along her hands and fingers, and his mouth. He felt the tingle as her blood settled onto his lips. He finally drew back, dropping her hand, and twisting back in his seat to sit more normally at the table. He dabbed his lips with the napkin, making slow and deliberate show of her blood staining up the cloth.

Her hand stayed where it fell, on the table between them. Her head was bent away from him, her body slack against the chair. She could have been mistaken for a corpse. The fire her blood had poured into his stomach was utterly, utterly divine. She tasted wonderful.

'Pass the water jug please.'

Once more, her body instinctively did as he bid, with no reference to her mind for consent, or refusal. She was so terribly glad of this, so happy for the instant obedience, she forgave the betrayal. How could she have fought this so? Obedience to him was such a wonderful relief... the burden of choice was removed from her. She took the prompt and poured water into the tumbler at his setting. Some for herself. He was using his napkin to dab the blood, her blood, from the corners of his mouth and lips. Then, he tucked it back onto his lap, and began to butter a soft morning roll.

She re-seated, also fixing her own napkin in place. The cold and congealed remnants on the plate defeated her, and she pushed it away, reaching instead for a pastry. That could be moved about and pretended at with ease.

She could not help drying her hand and wrist upon the napkin, removing the last of her blood, and his saliva. There was a small cut on her wrist: it was not bleeding. There was no need to wrap it, to compress it. She pushed her hand onto her lap, under the table, and drank from her water glass with the other. She could be fine, could obey, as long as she did not think. She would not think about what he said, and how there could have been pain, and blood, but no injury there now. She would not think on it. It was a trick.

'Do not worry. There will be no infection, or bleeding. Vampire blood protects against all that. It will heal very quickly.'

As she slowly forced the pastry into her mouth, and down into her guts, tears welled up into her eyes, and spilled soundlessly down her face, dampening her blouse and the napkin.

CHAPTER THIRTEEN

The next few days passed in torpor, her actions supported by her routine. Her mind appeared frozen. Her body moved through the different phases of the day, the meals counter pointing the emptiness. When he spoke, she obeyed. When he moved, she followed. He spoke to her incessantly about his being a vampire, and what that meant for her. She took everything silently, passively. Three times he took blood from her left wrist. Three times she didn't react. He beat her twice, both times savagely, as her heat in his veins was causing him immense problems with his temper. He managed to not feed from her, after the beatings, which could have killed her. She took the beatings silently, and for once, he cursed that. That had not been what he was looking for: he required reaction from her, some sense of independence. He was not going to allow her such a total retreat: he knew this was as much game plan as anything else. Her heartbeat, breathing and scent betrayed her: she was aware. She was just choosing not to show it.

After a week, when her appetite was failing badly, and she began to show signs of serious dehydration, he acted. He was not happy with how fast he was having to act, he felt his hand was being forced, which did not sit comfortably with him. However, he would not be deceived in this fashion; the word 'fool' was not one to be applied to him, under any circumstance. Besides, she would sink into real atrophy if this kept on: that he had seen before, many times. Sitting her at the breakfast bar, he poured a large glass of raw goat's milk in front of her. Her hand reached forward automatically, to do his bidding. He staved her off, and she sank back in the chair. Lifting his wrist over the glass, he slashed it open, and his blood spilled in. Nothing came from her, not even a flare of her pupils. He stirred the glass until it became an even pink colour. Then he pushed it towards her.

'I am both vampire, and your master. Drink of me. Take of my body, my blood.'

She stood up, turned her back, and walked to her room.

Well satisfied with his judgement, that he had called her out, he placed the glass into the fridge. There was to be no hiding from this. She would accept his authority. She would bend her will to his, even as she sought refuge in closing down her mind. If she wanted to dabble with melancholia and depression, he would supply it for her in abundance.

The fridge and cupboards took a little while to empty, but he wanted that done first. Second was closing down the steel shutters on all the windows, locking out the light, hence the need to empty the fridge first. He took the light bulb out of the fridge, and from most of the sockets, leaving just enough light that she could not fall over her own feet every two seconds. The heating and hot water went next. Finally, he dimmed the lights in her room and bathroom, and spent a few fiddly moments getting the cameras to switch to infra-red, just in case. There would be no wrist slashing or rope swinging when he was not present.

His plans set, he moved through the days with exactly the same rhythm as before. Three meals were laid out, all of them in the dining room, and she had to sit through them. Not that it took long to eat a slice of bread or a small bowl of boiled rice, or a cup of gruel. Her forcing herself to eat had been cured by a few days of actual hunger. Hunger will not be denied, and she had never really understood, or experienced that. She now ate everything in front of her, and scraped the bowl clean. When he had not objected, she licked the bowl out. She drank copious amounts of water, to try and stave off the hunger, but soon found this made her ill and did not fill her as she had presumed. Water was not food.

She tried not washing, or dressing to his standard. He laid raw her lower back, without the subsequent benediction of his blood, and left her to heal as best she could on the calories allotted her. She had resumed grooming.

He made a point of telling her he had not used his blood to heal her quickly, and that he would continue to leave her to heal without him. She had been soaking the blouse off her back in a cold water shower for a week, before it healed enough not to leak and stick to her.

Every day he filled a glass with the milk and his blood, and left it in the fridge. At every meal, it sat by her plate.

The long hours she had spent sitting in the living room, watching the sunlight, had become long cold cramped hours in the hall, looking at the faint line of daylight that he allowed to spill under the closed study door. He kept the shutter up in there, and left the electric lights to blaze, so that when he opened the door, light spilled everywhere into the darkness that enclosed her. Which was then firmly closed off from her when he closed the door behind him.

By the end of the second week, she was talking and crying out in what little sleep she could manage. She often burst into crying as he left a room. Silent sobs and a flood of empty tears, spilling down her cheeks, unchecked.

He took blood from her every two to three days. He would flick open her wrist with a scalpel, and drink a toke: a token. Again, he would comment that he would not be gifting his own blood to heal her, and left each little cut to heal on its own. He explained that he could take blood without pain, but since he was rejecting his truth, he chose to do it this way. When infection took hold, he administered antibiotics. Each time she had to swallow a capsule, he reminded her that if she accepted his blood, his nature, she would be healed by now, and out of pain. She never commented, but the hand was always raised to him on request: he had her body completely. Her mind, her spirit, was almost his.

Almost...

Three weeks in, his sleep was disturbed by a slight ping, and he quickly took the back route into the study and the screens. She was in the kitchen, standing in front of the fridge. She opened and shut it several times. Her hand reached in once, but withdrew. She closed the door and returned to her bed, curling up in a ball under the sheets, crying and rocking.

Almost there.

She lasted another two days, which somewhat impressed him. It was at lunch, a bowl of plain rice, when she broke into wracking sobs. He remained calm, letting her take the lead. Her hand reached for the glass. She was shaking so much she spilled some as she tried to lift it. She needed to use her left hand, to steady her right one, as the tumbler was lifted, and brought to her lips. Again, some slopped out the sides, staining her top. It took a few moments before she could stop crying well enough to let the glass touch her lips. She drank, and swallowed. He let her have two mouthfuls, before taking the glass from her.

'Not too much. You will not cope with the richness, right now.'

She nodded to him, tears continuing to spill down her face, her chest rising with the effort of trying to calm.

'Go through to your room, and lie down. I shall bring you something else in a few moments.'

She retreated, still holding onto her sobs. He basked in the glory as he set the flat back to rights. Shutters up, heating and hot water on. Light bulbs replaced, although he switched them all off. Her eyes might take several hours to re-adjust. The restocking of the fridge and cupboards took a little time, and he heated through some clear broth for her and put it in a flask as he went. Finally, he moved the light levels up in her room, before going in with a tray containing the flask, a yoghurt and a banana.

She was under the sheet, silently rocking to and fro. He placed the tray down, and lay down beside her, gathering her in his arms, she turned to him, and cried some more. He stroked her hair, and sang lullabies to her as she shook.

As she fell out of the defeat, into exhaustion, he rose and went through to the bathroom, running a flannel under the now hot tap. Taking it back through, he washed her face and neck, drying her tears. He pulled his fingers through the tangles of her sodden hair, and pushed it back off her face. He gave her the yoghurt, and a spoon, and sat silently whilst she ate it. When she was finished, he reached down to her left wrist, and raised it to his lips, kissing it gently. He caught her in his gaze, as his tongue began to lick slowly over the scabs and half healed cuts. She was easy to catch, in her state, and she began to moan softly as he carried on caressing her. At the moment of penetration, when he tore open her wrist, and let the vein flood him, she moaned and convulsed in orgasm. He drank swiftly, the drop in blood pressure causing her to faint into her tiredness. He withdrew, and cut into his own wrist, smearing his blood liberally over the torn flesh. He held her until the faint transitioned into a more natural sleep, soothing her distress by stroking her hair, her face, her arms.

He stayed by her side, and watched her sleep for longer than was logical.

In the morning, she found her bathroom filled with wonderful smelling baths salts, in large spheres called 'bombs' and an enticing array of fruit and spice derived shower gels. Exotic face creams and cleansers filled the shelves. After her pee, she returned to the room to eat the banana and investigate the flask. The warm clear liquid tasted wonderful. She sipped it slowly, in between mouthfuls of the banana, and marvelled that anything could taste so wonderful. She tried to ignore that she rocked as she ate.

After running a hot bath, she exploded several of the 'bombs' into it, and found it would have been better if she'd been in the bath at the time. She got in quickly, before all the fizz ran out. It tickled, as the jasmine, rose and lavender bloomed around her. The water turned a deep purple, as all the dyes mixed. She luxuriated in the feel of the hot water, the scents, and the freedom. She dipped a flannel into the water, squeezed it out and placed it over her face, as she floated back, feeling her hair move around her. An image came to her, of Anne, pretending to be Elaine, laying herself out on a dory on the Lake of Shining Waters. She smiled, shying away from the Elaine part of the image.

As she cleaned herself off, she refused to look at her body, and how thin it was. How hard the bath had felt on her bones.

She peed again, and took a hot shower, to wash her hair through and apply some deep conditioner. The lights had gone up enough for her to clearly see her wrist. She could not help but run her hand over it, and feel both the ridges and bumps of the scars, and the soft feel of the new skin. It no longer hurt: the ache which it had carried for weeks, gone. A memory whispered of something that had happened there, on her wrist, last night. She pushed the memory away ruthlessly. She was crying as she towel dried her hair.

Attending to dressing herself and her hair, calmed her. In the light, she was back with her own routine. When she was sure she was presentable, she peeked out the door. Daylight! She almost danced out into the hall. She went straight through to the dining room, to see if she was required for breakfast. He was sitting eating warm croissants and butter. Her plate held sliced fruits and a bread roll. Both water and apple juice were laid out. She said good morning as she sat, drinking in the light. As she took breath, the light flooded her, it sat on her skin, and oozed down into her pores. He said good morning back, and moved on to talk of fripperies.

It took her a couple of weeks to recover. She found she was very weak, and subject to dizzy spells. He was careful to build her eating back up slowly and surely, and her weight slowly moved back to slender. Several small snacks were added into the meals routine, and she was given permission to eat from a range of foods he stored on 'her' shelf in the fridge. When he truly began to feed from her, she would be required to eat a great deal of food, to sustain her: it was best she had some control over calories now, when she was so pliable, and eager to maintain the companionship between them. This would not last, but access to extra calories would be established by the time the honeymoon was over.

She spent hours sitting on the couch in the living room, resting and rebuilding herself. She loathed leaving the light, and often slipped out of bed and pulled on a dressing gown, to come and greet the dawn. He would come across her, asleep and would place a blanket over her. She would wake, snuggle under it for a moment, and then return to her room to dress.

He relaxed clothing and hair rules. She had a wider range of colours and styles, and was allowed to wear her hair loose: she could never use it as a curtain between them now. There was no curtain possible between them now he was in her mind. Almost literally, in fact, as she succumbed to thrall so easily when he fed, that he began to fancy he had finally developed the ability see thoughts. It had long been a bane that the dark gift had not brought that talent to him. Night bastards had it, but not he. It was both outrageous in the general, and very annoying in the personal.

He was not feeding often, or deeply. She needed building up a little more, and he was wary of letting her become too aware of what was going on, quite yet. The befuddlement was useful, as was her unease about exactly how pleasurable the process was. Every cut, he cut her cleanly with a scalpel, every time, he gave his own blood to the wound. He was not sure she truly understood his nature...

How could she?

...or that her acceptance had gone beyond complete capitulation in principle: what he said was true, no matter what he said. There was no real difference between the two, in terms of his control of her... but there was in terms of what her survival might be.

Survival?

Now there was a curious thought.

Her survival?

CHAPTER FOURTEEN

Curiously, she felt as if she was emerging from a nightmare. It was curious, as the opposite had occurred. She had fallen into his nightmare. She had given up and accepted his madness.

At times she even believed it.

At times, it was such a *seductive* thought, that it could not be denied. It certainly made no more, or less, sense, than the rest of it. That a *vampire* had stolen her, was certainly more comforting, in many ways, than a simply deranged human. However the thought that a murderous human who *believed he was a vampire* had taken her... that was not to be contemplated. But... well, that didn't make sense either. How could being in the hands of a human, no matter how mad, be worse than... *slipping through the worlds into a parallel universe?* A rupture in the space time continuum? Hello Scotty, all is forgiven, full warp drive home please. Or perhaps The Doctor, who could reveal that *he* was an alien creature, who did, after all, drink human blood. And take her out of here in the Tardis. She'd become a new companion, and travel the Universe!

Well, it was just as feasible, wasn't it?

Well, not really. That was the problem. That was the nightmare she was falling into, not emerging from. There was the pain, the healing. No matter how confused she was, no matter how disoriented... she couldn't deny that, not in her guts. Yes, there could be other explanations, far more plausible, far more believable. Yet none so practical. She could see the healing happen. She could certainly feel it, especially when it was not there. She had puzzled endlessly about the problems of how she was taking so many beatings, and still walking, talking; was whole. She had fancied far worse scenarios than this, including her own insanity and incarceration in her own deranged mind. She had posited that she'd died, and this was actually hell. A real devil and endless torture for not going to some Church once a week, or for not actually being baptised in the first place. She'd gone into the bathroom one night, quite early on in those thoughts, and made a sign of the cross over some water in the bowl, and blessed herself. It had seemed logical at the time, especially given how much of her time she'd suddenly started to fill with prayer... which had been quite a challenge, as she barely knew how to stammer out *Our Father*. She had only done it, as at that moment, she believed there would be a loud crack, a bolt of lightning, and *shazam*... she'd be in heaven. She could dismiss the thought as ridiculous now... but at the moment she'd done it, back then, she had believed in it.

Utterly.

Just as when, she'd lifted that glass to her lips, she believed he was what he said he was.

Utterly.

No other explanation would have gotten her to swallow that blood, his blood. Blood was not good stuff. It was dirty, it *carried things*. Infection, it carried *infection*. Swallowing his human blood, it wasn't an option. Rotting her insides with his disease... it wasn't going to be. What if he had AIDS? Okay, that might not be a good thought to be having, giving how much of her blood she'd shed... but she still wasn't willingly drinking it. She really would rather die.

But it was curious, she knew, that he didn't beat her over it? If he'd belted her, repeatedly, she'd have drunk acid if he wanted her too. She knew that. She'd thought about it quite often...

Why don't you just belt me you moron, then I'll drink the stuff? She'd sat in the gloom, glowering the thought at him... *belt me and this will be over.*

That's why she'd deliberately provoked him by refusing to wash in his stinking cold water, and leaving her hair uncombed. But he'd not done as she thought... he'd belted her all right, raw and bleeding and broken... but it had not gone anywhere near the glass, the drinking. It had stayed where it was, and he'd left her on the hall floor, crawling slowly back to her cell, on her hands and knees, barely able to move. Nowhere, had it come anywhere near... *drink or I'll hit you again...* that, she would have done.

But he hadn't done that.

She'd believed it was vampire blood she was swallowing. Utterly believed in it. Had actually wanted it to be true, for maybe it would take away her pain. Maybe it would... make her strong. Maybe it would let her find a way to fight back.

...if it was vampire blood...she had a chance...

This was the nightmare. As she sat in the living room, basking in the air and light, wasn't it interesting that daylight changed the quality of the air you breathed? This was the nightmare she was emerging from. Right here, right now, she knew it was perfectly ridiculous of her to have thought like that, back then, in the darkness. Now, with the warm light and food and some comfort... it was madness to have thought him speaking the truth. Madness to drink the blood. Madness to consider it as a sign of hope, not humiliation. Humiliation was what she felt now, as she remembered believing him. Humiliation and worry, fear. Fear of what infections could have been in that glass. What was he giving her, when he smeared his blood on her wounds?

...how it hurt less when he did that... how it soothed and healed...

She rubbed her left wrist, oblivious to the action, as she concentrated on thinking *less*... thinking wasn't good. Just being, in the moment, that was good. Warm baths and a full tummy, that was good. Being able to help herself to cheese, or a fruit juice, that was good. A pair of trousers to wear, and a red top, that was good. Her hair flowing round her shoulders, and not needing to make sure it was perfect before emerging from her cell... that was good.

...as was how she felt when he picked up her hand and looked into her eyes and...

She broke the thought by rising up and fetching a glass of that smoothie stuff she was now allowed, which she really liked.

She took the glass through to the dining room, and sat at the foot of the table, so she was staring over the length of it oval, out to the huge netted window behind. The window with the most light, and the most car noise, and the green and blue smudges. Or brown and blue smudges – she was sure they were trees, the smudges under the blue sky. She had poured it into a knickerbocker glass, for all things for him to have in the crystal cabinet, and was spooning it up with the requisite long handled spoon, although never had she seen one in wrought silver. Spooning it made the pleasure last longer.

He came out of the study, and went to the kitchen. She heard the tap run, and a glass filled. It would be a glass, as he only drank water and only from crystal. This made her think of how she longed for tea, or coffee, or a vodka and coke. Or a coke! She'd forgotten coke existed.

...how was that possible? ...how could you forget coke, or chocolate or...

She carried on spooning the banana mixture into her mouth as he took a chair beside here. The other 'empty' chair, the one that sat opposite from her chair, for meals.

They sat in silence, as she studied the light at the window. It was late afternoon, and the shadows were growing as they moved to evening. There was a lot of rain, and each day was slightly longer than the last. It had been chilly when the heating was off. Chilly, but not cold. The light was mostly grey and blue, with some days heavy cloudy and some days bright and sunny, but not hot.

She was pretty sure it was spring.

'It's been a year.'

The words popped out of her thoughts, into the air. He appeared to consider them. Everything felt raw, unknown. Certainly she'd not intended to speak first, or in such an odd way, but the room didn't feel heavy and dangerous... it felt open, *hesitant*. He looked to the window, his sight settling past the thick netting.

He knows what's on the other side...

'Yes, almost. Almost a year.'

His voice was normal, low key, quiet. Almost introspective. It invited response. Her own voice was just as calm, just as low key. Ghosts were dancing in the room with them, brought to life by their voices.

'It was so warm, I remember. Far too warm for April, for London.'

'Yes, it was. I remember that too.'

He glanced back at her, smiling, before returning to gaze through the window.

'Global warming?' Her smile was genuine, just as she had not been fishing, merely musing.

'Perhaps, although it is not that hot now, or predicted to be anywhere close to it.' There was a warmth in his voice now. He sipped his water as he chatted. 'I am not convinced on that theory, but the weather in London changes consistently. That is all that can be said of London – it always changes.'

The limitations of her situation closed her down. There was nothing she was allowed to ask, and nothing she knew to give any context to his answers. She began to flounder on uncertainty, fear pricking into the air between them. He rescued her, a most gallant, and unpredicted, act.

'How long have you lived here?' His voice was even, not distant, not particularly interested: social chit chat at a party. Just the right soothing tone to build her a platform, something she could use to climb out of the panic.

Again, her thoughts were in the air, spoken, before she had thought out a reply. Social chit chat, after all. She was actually quite good at that, or had been.

'Here? London?'

He nodded.

... London...

'Nearly two years. The lease on my flat was due, and I wasn't sure about staying.' She concentrated hard on the conversation. Silly to feel elated... but...

'In London, or the flat?' He genuinely seemed interested. How strange that he too could do chit chat...

'The flat. It was noisy and dirty and cramped. But I was lucky to get it at all, and without a pay rise...' her voice trailed off.

The pay rise had been out of reach and she'd known she'd re-sign the lease, even 'tho the rent was going up, and her pay staying the same. The memory took her off in thought.

'And London..?' He prompted her back to the conversation.

…in London…

She paused… was it such a surprise to learn she was indeed, still in London? Not really, not with the grandeur of the flat here. But that was silly in its own way. It's not like outside of London was all council houses and country cottages. She could have been anywhere.

But it always *felt* like London. Even sillier, given how long she'd been in her cell.

'I liked London, a lot. It was so much better than before, at home. But it was lonely, and I wasn't sure if I should try for another city. Move around.

He drained his glass, prompting her to finish hers. As they moved to the kitchen, to clear away, he carried on.

'I have always loved London, since the first time I set foot here. There was something... exciting about it. I have moved around, of course, but I always come back here.'

The crystal was always hand washed and dried with a special cloth, and returned to the cabinet. It only took him a few moments and they moved to the living room. She settled in the corner, under the window, and he sat just across from her, facing into the room. Physically close, in the same conversation, but not too intense. She watched his profile, with the darkening shadows chasing across it, as he spoke.

'I have lived all over the city, including areas that were not part of the city, but which the city grew into. I have observed the city grow and made much money on buying land cheaply, and waiting a few years, sometimes decades, before selling in profit.' There was a little pause before he carried on, somewhat ruefully. 'I have lost huge fortunes, equally.' He smiled. 'The city is capricious. Once she has wooed you, she will not let you go, but she is not always easy with her favours. Every time you think you have her measure, she takes you by the throat.' He turned and smiled to her.

Once more, there was nothing she could offer, but silence. She was used to listening, and schooled in it, but the subject had never been so personal. She pondered on 'decades', as she had always considered him to be young. Late 30s, perhaps early 40s – no older than that. How many decades would his delusion allow him to mention?

...still in London...

'This apartment...' he paused to sweep his arm to the splendour of the living space around him,'...was deemed folly at the time of the build, so much so, that it was almost never begun, never mind completed.' Energised, he stood up, and began to move around the room as he spoke, his face alive with memory. 'It was, I have to say, one of the biggest gambles I have ever undertaken with London. It was an unholy amount of money, and no one felt it would ever be repaid, least of all the banks.'

'My boss said that banks only lend you money when you don't need it.'

He stared at her with that searching look, the one where she always felt her mind was being tested. No, not her mind... her intellect. Her brains. He continued, turning to walk the room again.

'That is often true. However, I have witnessed banks go under, from lending too much. Sometimes they need your money so much, they will lend what they do not have, to keep you in their pocket. Conversely, no matter how much capital you have with them, if they sense war in the air, they will lend nothing, unless you manufacture weapons. They are extremely fallible and unpredictable institutions. Never the less, I am more than happy that they exist. Life was much harder to juggle without them.'

...am still in London...

He was enjoying the freedom of discussing his life openly. No need to censor or avoid... no need to pretend that he was something else. This was liberating, and so rare in his life... this made it worthwhile, did it not?

'They are like any business – you can never trust in their permanence, but can always take advantage of human greed. Banks are greedier than most, so they are more... more malleable than one might think.'

'I couldn't even get an overdraft!' The words were out before she'd thought; genuine, actual conversation.

He smiled at her. 'Of course not, they do not need you. You have nothing for them at all. Banks need money. If you have none, or no promise of any, you may as well be a beggar in the street for them.'

He smiled again, a genuine smile. One of those moments, where her world, met his. She had been a good worker, and had a sound mind. He understood the need for work in the mind of those with nothing; drifting in the winds of change with little to bolster them. Utterly penniless if the week's wages failed to materialise. Whilst this generation seemed to exist in unbelievable wealth – she lived on her own, after all, in a two roomed apartment – they were just as likely to fall to the gutter with no notice, as any other. It was a more comfortable gutter here and now, than it had ever been, of that he was sure. But when in the gutter in her world, they did not seem to notice the soup kitchens were also there. In fact, he had observed the truly destitute becoming angrier, and more belligerent about their status, the better their welfare support had become. It was a puzzle he had not managed to cut through, as of yet. But then, it was not one he spent much time upon.

She reached for a cushion, and cuddled into it, folding her feet up under her. It gave him pause to think, and he sat down beside her again, dampened down his reaction a little, making connection again, individual to individual.

'Before the banks... before the banks, it was incredibly hard. Even for me. Even although I stayed here, in London, for so long. Storing money, riches... spreading it about and hoping... it could go horribly wrong. You never knew what might happen. Even fields in the middle of nowhere, would be dug up. People you had lodged fortunes with, would die, or be killed in raids. Nothing was secure... before the banks.'

... I am still in London...

'But surely…?' She hesitated. He was so animated, and she did not want to unsettle the moment, change the tone.

He nodded her on, eager.

'Surely banks fail too? Surely they crash and you lose everything?'

He did not smile: he grinned. It was actually a pleasant sight. How could she have forgotten he was so handsome? Those liquid brown eyes, the faint curve of warm brown hair, the fine features and pale skin: he was such a good looking monster. How did he manage to change himself so? Sometimes he was so beautiful, you could barely breathe in his presence, other times just the pretty side of ordinary. Now, right now, he was enchanting. So different from the one that filled with rage, and pain and terror. Yet he was always compelling, even at his most ugly.

'Yes! Of course they do!' He exploded into emotion and energy. 'Some do... but there are so many different types of banks! Some will never fail. My bank will never fail, not now.' He was back up on his feet, his enthusiasm for the subject sweeping them both along.

She felt as if she was on a merry-go-round, being spun round by his passion.

'The trick is the right type of bank! It took me many years to sort it out. I did invest a little here, a little there, when they first developed. Abroad mainly, sometimes here for business advantage. But it wasn't until Nathan came along... oh Nathan, how I miss Nathan!'

A shadow briefly passed through his eyes and his voice dropped. His thoughts were so clearly turning inwards, searching his memories. 'Nathan taught me how to make a bank work for you. To truly make a bank work for you.'

He searched her face, for understanding, for acceptance of what he was saying, then continued, much quieter, more contained, but still very involved in the moment of what he was experiencing.

'To take risks when it was safe, and to dive under the floorboards when it was risky. That is what he would say you know...

'Time for the floorboards Marcus... time for the floorboards!' Time to take it all out of the bank and put it under the floorboards. Turn paper to gold and land, and dig the gold under the land, and put some floorboards on top, and sit and wait. Hide the gold. He was a genius.'

... Marcus...

His flourished his arms again, indicating the room around them, the apartment.

'I owe all this to Nathan. He was long gone, of course, dead many years, before this building was begun. But Nathan taught me how to take a risk, and how to make it safer. How to keep a bank afloat. I often think this building is a testament to Nathan... and no one knows.' His voice dropped down, both volume and tone.

The memories were no longer so much fun, there was hesitance, and bitterness... and loss?

'When we were trying to get the backing for here, I knew. I knew that Nathan's advice would see me through, and this place would be a triumph. I knew it worked in Paris, apartments like this. I knew it would work here... but if it had failed, like they all predicted...' He looked back at her, her gaze meeting his. 'I would have lost everything. Everything. I put everything I had into making sure the bank had enough to cover the entire build. Every brick, every shovel of earth moved... I put the funding in place, personally, through the bank and some other companies. But it all came from me, from everything I had.'

As he stared, she saw the pain, the sudden flash of pain.

'When it all came through, all those years later, when the investment turned to solid gold, as if the bricks had been gold themselves... no one knew. So much time had passed... no one was there to recognise I had been right. No one.' He slumped down on the couch facing her again, his head in his hands, as if he'd lost the gamble, not won it. 'No one knows. No one was ever there to share the triumph, for me to tell of Nathan, and how much I owed him. Except you my little one, except you.'

The softness in his tone, the longing, the grief, it was all bare in his voice, his face, his features. He was a man, hurt and alone, lonely. It hit her like a blow, and she felt her skin drain of blood, her breathing quicken, her skin crawl.

... lonely and afraid...

'I...' He stopped, his voice clogged with emotion. He stood and turned to walk away, speaking was easier when he was no longer looking at her. 'I have never... never told anyone of all this. Never had someone here, like you little one, to explain the truth of it all too.'

... lonely...

Damn him, how did he keep shifting her world like this? She could barely keep hold of her thoughts, as her mind tumbled in free fall once more. *Lonely and afraid?* He's lonely and afraid...?

...or very good at making show of it...

There was nowhere for her to go with this, nowhere at all. She nodded, keeping her face composed, but not too distant. He turned away from her, his hands going to his face, pushing up through his hair. Dropping his hands back to his sides, he turned suddenly, swiftly, and she jumped a little in fear.

'Would you like to see?'

Confusion naturally clouded her face.

'Would you like to see my building?'

She nodded automatically. His manner had changed utterly... he was still not presenting her with direct threat, but she trusted nothing from him. Her heart skipped a beat as her pulse began to race.

'Excellent, come with me.'

CHAPTER FIFTEEN

He signalled her up and out of the opening on the left hand of the room, by the seating. Into the oddly shaped hall and The Door. Which is how she thought of the door she was not allowed near, and which she'd never seen him use. With barely a thought to slowing himself down for her, he opened it and was through. She followed swiftly in case he closed it on her. She emerged into a perfectly even and balanced hallway, large and shaped like a t-junction. Directly in front of her, on the other side of the large hallway space, was a double set of outside doors. Light flooded in from both left and right. She glanced back, the partition that she had walked through, looked like a wall on this side, the proportions and décor not revealing its true nature; it was balanced on this side, and did not look odd at all. She was in the narrower confines of the bottom space, and he had moved forward over to the far wall, with the doors. He opened cupboards to one side, and rummaged. She kept moving for fear of being caught out in doing something wrong. Emerging into the central space, she saw the large outside facing windows on her right, and the inner facing windows on her left. There were clearly two rooms on either side, she'd walked up their length. She daren't stop to look. The far wall, apart from the doors, contained built in wardrobes and cupboards, ceiling to skirting board. The outside doors flush with the panelling. In front of her, centred exactly, was a small rectangular dining table with six chairs. Three aside apiece, and none on the ends. It was narrow, but fitted perfectly into the space. Above it was a chandelier, and on the shining mirror like table top of dark wood was a display of carnations and tea roses: pinks and white and baby's breath. The scent from the flowers was gentle and delicate and in perfect balance with the space. Her heart was hammering as she stepped around the table, to where he still rummaged in the deep-set closet.

'Here we go,' he turned round back to her, his hands holding forth a winter coat in bottle green. 'This should fit you perfectly.'

He flourished it open at the shoulders, and she automatically put her arms in, and twisted round to the other arm. Three large buttons fastened easily, and a tie belt. She was shaking, but controlling it. He shrugged the coat up onto her back, and patted her forward. She could see two doors on the now right sided, inner sided, room. They were open, and she could see into a large formal drawing room. Like this hallway with its dining table, it was furnished in period style, suiting the sweeping style of the architecture. She thought it might be Georgian, but didn't know enough to know. There were two doors on the room on the other side, the street facing side. Both were closed. One must be the elusive missing bedroom.

She took it all in, in the moment she had to flick her hair over the back of the coat, and turn back to him. He had put on his own winter coat, dark grey wool. He was pulling gloves out of the pockets as he addressed her.

'Put your hands in the pockets.'

She did so and found soft leather gloves, one in each. She pulled them out and stuck her hands in them, glad of something to do to try and hide how much they were trembling. Forcing sweaty hands into the soft lining was tricky and took longer than she wanted to. As if oblivious to her struggle, her turned his back and opened a drawer in the wardrobe space, which was at least two feet deep. He pulled out a red cashmere scarf for himself. Another drawer opened and a muted green scarf, which matched the gloves perfectly, was handed to her. She placed it over her shoulders, leaving it loose.

'Are we ready?'

There was nothing she could say, as he turned and closed the door. He walked forward and pushed a button on the side of the main doors. There was a 'click' and when he heard it, he pushed the left handed door open, and signalled her through. Her breath caught in her throat her heart hammered in her chest. Her legs felt weak and shaky, but she did not hesitate; she walked through.

She emerged onto a communal hallway. Quite narrow and tiled on both walls and floor. On her right, was a massive outside window, with no coverings. But the bottom half contained frosted glass. Street noises came through clearly. She could see sky, real sky, through the top half. In front and to the left, was a stairwell. Ornate and in keeping with the grandeur of the place. Everything felt Victorian. Black and white tiles, black ironwork and dark wood. They were on the top floor, the stairs only led down. Across from them, was the identical doorway to the one they had just exited, with a letter 'H' in brass plaque on the wall. She glanced back, and they had emerged from 'G'. On the left, further back than she expected, was an old fashioned lift, with sliding metal gated doors set into a mesh cage. He directed her to the lift and pressed the button. Ancient machinery whirred and whined.

'It is a long way down, best to give your legs some leeway.' He spoke totally matter of fact way. Nothing unusual about this, not at all.

Her mouth was so dry she wasn't sure she could keep swallowing, yet her back was plastered in sweat. She could feel her blouse sticking to her and pulling as she moved. She resisted fidgeting. The lift rumbled into view. It was quite large and plush, much more posh than she had expected from the age and Victorian feel. It would easily have taken a grand piano and a few people to carry it. He slid back the outer gating, then the inner, and indicated she should go in. She did so, and he closed both gates behind them. He pressed 'G' on the enamel buttons, blue on white, with faints line of age across them, on the side panel. The top one was '3'.

The descent was slow and steady, and they passed down floors 2 and 1 with enough time for her to see the same layout and design and flash of window as the top floor, but the stairwell in the centre obscured the view. The ground floor arrived too suddenly, adding to her disorientation.

Such was the tension in her body, the slow slide to stop was physically painful. The massive windows at the far end of the lift were windows no more. An outside door beckoned beneath small stained glass panels of solid colour. The light coloured the hallway, reds and ambers. It felt dark and crowded. The lift was in shade here, some of the light obscured by the stair well that began a few feet from the doorway. The hallway, as they emerged from the lift, was actually wider than those above, to accommodate the pathway to the lift from the doors. The doors to flat 'A' further back, and delineated with red floor tiling, to give it some privacy from the troop to and fro to the lift. As they walked past she wondered... had she always seen the world in such detail, or was it only now, after being locked away for so long?

The thought was broken by the tremendous noise that threatened from the outside doorway. She hesitated, as bus and car and lorry noises attacked her in waves, as if she could see the shape of the sound as well as hear the roaring shrill screeching and rumbling. Like giants fighting in an alley. He ushered her forward gently, linking his right arm through her left one, as he flicked another button on the wall, and on hearing the 'click', pushed opened the heavy swing door. Traffic, thick London traffic was in front of her, and for a moment, they waited on the top of some shallow stone steps. She felt so tense, she was beginning to worry she might vomit, or stumble and fall. His arm was a reassuring presence and pressure. The noise felt deafening... how could she have thought fondly of this racket?

Across the busy road, trees burst into her view. Trees in late evening shade. They were that fresh brilliant green of early bud, the brown starting to be obscured by new growth. She was too scared to feel elated, too intimidated by the noise to speak. He led her gently down the couple of steps, whilst she stared across the traffic to the trees. As she stood transfixed, he unlaced his arm from hers, and slipped it around her waist. He gathered up her left hand, in his, and slowly directed her body to the right, as they moved down the pavement. The shock of what she saw buckled her knees, and she did stumble badly. His arms held her upright, allowing her a few moments' grace until she got her legs to work properly again.

People rushed past on both sides and she shrank from their bodies as the noise continued to bore into her. She'd closed her eyes as she faltered, and she kept them closed as she moved forward, feeling the motion and power of his body as it kept her upright, and moving. She leaned into him, grateful for his strength: it was so impossible. Her eyelids flickered back up and she confirmed what she had thought she had seen. There, on the left as they walked down, across the road, and in the park, was the Albert Memorial. In front of her, as they emerged from the shadow of the building they had exited, was the Royal Albert Hall.

There was nothing she could say, nothing she could think.

His muscles and bone and flesh kept her muscles and bone and flesh, moving. They proceeded down the pavement, out from the shadows into evening sunshine in the spaces around the Hall. Then he turned her again, this time left, and guided her across the busy pedestrian crossing, in front of the exasperated traffic. The keening whine of the signal to walk cut through her, and she tensed against him. He lulled her across the road with gentle sighs and promises it would all be fine. In front of her, the Memorial loomed. They entered the park and she found there was another tarmac road, with traffic, between them and the Memorial. They crossed it carefully, and he led her to the base, stopping on the pavement. Looking up briefly, she did almost fall to her knees, and he gently turned her round to look at the road they had crossed. She was grateful to no longer be engulfed by the Memorial, but could not come to terms with the views directly to the Hall either. He guided her down to the right, past the Memorial, and they crossed from pavement to grass. The uneven surface felt alien beneath her feet, her soft pumps feeling every leaf and branch and root they stood on as they passed. He led her to the trees, and allowed her to lean back upon one. She was facing out to the street, and the building they had left, but he obscured that view with his body. Looking into his eyes, trying to find some truth in them, she was startled to realise that he was smaller than her. Even slumped against the tree, her knees shaking, she was looking down slightly to his eyes.

...we must look like lovers, embracing in the park...

He leaned closer into her, his left hand brushing her hair back off her forehead. She felt the strength of the tree behind her, the rough feel of bark through her gloved hands. His body's weight in front of her. The noise and panic diminished slightly.

'It is all right little one, you are safe.'

...he was such a good liar...but...

The 'but' was too uncomfortable, so she pushed it away and concentrated on breathing slowly and evenly.

'Is this...' She had to stop, breathe deeper, restart. 'Is this Hyde Park?'

He smiled, and his eyes darkened and enlarged. Normally, she'd look away, but those eyes were all she could afford to focus on. The world was too frightening for her too look away from the strength in those eyes.

'No.' His tone was gentle and loving and slightly pleased by her naivety. 'Well yes, but no.'

She tensed, expecting some sort of anger to come with the conflicting answer. His right hand caught hers, reassuring, as his left hand once more cupped the side of her face.

'Hyde Park is the north end of where we are. This part is called Kensington Gardens.'

'Oh.' It made it worse. She tried to formulate the thought, her memory said this... was it true? 'Isn't that where Princess Di lives?'

'Yes. He indicated over her right shoulder. 'Over there, further back, in their own grounds. Kensington Palace.'

She knew she was ashen pale, from the feel of her skin. She knew she was panicking from the heartbeat and her breath. She knew she was going to faint, and the thought filled her with dread.

He stood back, a grand flourish, a statement of showmanship. He finished the flourish with a bow.

'You, my lady, are far more beautiful than she.'

The slight mocking tone gave her something to hang on to. She swallowed down her panic as best she could. His face was her only anchor, and she thought she'd make it, as long as she didn't look around too much.

He stepped back into her space, this time playing with her hair, as if pulling leaves from its grasp. The sky was so heavy, so huge, it was bearing down on her. Thank goodness she was under the tree. She felt the sky would crush her if she stood under it alone. A tear formed in the corner of her right eye, and began to trickle down her cheek. He brushed it away gently, and leaned forward and kissed her cheek. Without thought, she folded herself into his chest, and buried her face in his coat.

His arms embraced her, and held her tight. 'It is perfectly fine, everything is perfectly all right.'

He carried on soothing her, as she tried to get hold of herself. The traffic noises were just so loud, she couldn't think.

'It is a lovely little park. We will come over again in the summer, and walk around all the statues. We can look at the pond, and I shall tell you stories of how it all came to be here.'

As he spoke little things of nothingness to her, and stroked his arm down her back: she concentrated on the softness of his voice, the scent of his cologne, on the pattern on his coat. Anything, anything to keep her in place.

'But first...' His enthusiasm had erupted again, he grasped her upper arms, and gently pulled her back up, to look into his face. He looked so... happy? 'First, I shall show you my building!'

His grin was infectious, and she smiled automatically. He took this as his cue, and flourished his left arm up and around, and stood back. Across the road, Joanne could see the building they had left. It was a huge Victorian mansion of some sort. Dozens of grand flats and apartments. The Royal Albert Hall was to its left, centred in the middle of the taller housing that surrounded it. The building they had left, matched the one on the other side of the hall, similar size and design, obviously built together to set off the Hall. A matching set, not quite the same; siblings not twins. She'd seen them before, these buildings, from the bus, and had marvelled at the apartments in those two facing the park, and the other triangular shaped ones curving round the Hall. Red bricked and high, very high. Looking now, she thought they must be several stories, and she was suddenly aware that she was looking into the huge glass windows she was used to seeing from the other side. She took a step back and met the tree again, sinking down slowly on the grass. She dipped her head down low, to prevent a faint, she was sure she was going to black out. He sank down beside her, his arm snaking over her back, and he held her close until her head came up again. It was as if he was pouring his strength into her, and she responded. The black dots receded, and she could focus again. She settled her back onto the tree, and drew up her knees and grasped them. That way she was small, not so exposed. He matched her movements, and they sat under the tree, looking at the buildings across the roads.

…lovers sitting in the park, talking small talk…

It took further moments of silence, of feeling the bark behind her, his body warmth on her left side, the feel of the hard cold ground beneath her, before she could find her voice.

'Do you own all of this?' The words were so small, she wasn't sure she hadn't just thought them.

'All of it?'

She nodded.

'No. Just the one building. Just that one.'

The silence drew out, as did the shadows. It was quite cold, the traffic noisy, people and dogs hurrying past.

'Shall we go get some tea?

It was the mundaneness of it that allowed her to nod, to be helped to her feet, to walk back up past the Memorial, across the road, and back into the building. As she walked up the steps, she read the sign she hadn't noticed as she left.

2 Albert Hall Mansions West

'The one on the other side, is Albert Hall Mansions East.'

'But you don't own that one?'

'No, just this one. Just this final slice of Kensington Gore.'

'Gore?' She was shocked.

…how fitting was that…

'Yes, Kensington Gore. It's the name of this strip of land, the one we built the development on. Kensington Gore.'

'Oh.'

The lift was waiting on the ground floor, and they entered silently. As they emerged onto his floor, and he was inputting a code into a door lock, she asked another question.

'Jonathan?'

'Yes.'

'Jonathan, when you said your bank would never fail.'

'Yes?'

'You meant… you… I mean… Jonathan, you meant the bank you own, didn't you?'

His delight was once more plain across his features, his eyes alight with pleasure. He opened the door for her.

'Yes. My bank. The bank I own.'

She walked back into her prison, the door closing silently behind her apart from the faint 'click' of the automatic lock.

After they'd eaten, and he'd made it clear she was still never to approach the conjoining door without him, or go nearer the windows than she was normally allowed, she asked for permission to retire to her room. He gave it, and retired to his own rooms.

For once, he was not disturbed to awaken with an erection in the middle of the night. He stole back to the study, and watched her sleep on the infrared cameras, and masturbated over the image.

Life was good. Life was very good, indeed.

CHAPTER SIXTEEN

Doubts and regrets, rage at her own stupidity, crashed in almost immediately. How could she be so dumb? Why hadn't she screamed her head off as soon as they'd gotten outside the damn door?

She stripped off and turned the shower jets up as high as she could bear, and scrubbed herself ferociously. How could she do that? How could she finally get out of this stinking hell hole...

...worth what, a million pounds...

...and not *do* anything to get away? It didn't matter how damn rich he was... she was out in the open for god's sake! What was she thinking?

...fear terror panic fear terror panic fear terror panic...

And as for falling for his stinking lies... what was she, a moron?

...lies...lies...lies...lies...lies...lies...lies?...

Of course they were lies. A vampire... *a vampire...* building a mansion on Kensington Gore? Was there even a street *named* Kensington Gore? Huh? What was this, Hammer Horror Week? Well yes, it had been Hammer Horror Year, hadn't it?

She couldn't get any peace. If she calmed down on why she hadn't just started screaming and run off... she started up on who he was. If she throttled down on his lies...

...he still owns this apartment... that's at least a million, maybe more...

...then she kept coming back to her own stupidity. Her complete inability to *do* anything once he'd walked her out that door.

There were moments, terrible moments of clarity, where she started to see the shape of what had happened, what had been done to her... but she snapped off all thought in that direction the second she found herself looking at it. As if there was another Door, another locked door she could not approach. And this one was about her, and fear and…. well, he didn't have to own this apartment, did he? He could be renting it…?

…and… that makes a difference… because…?

He could be squatting in it and be on the run, and any second now, now they'd been out, the police would…. the police would what? She got out of bed and went back into the bathroom, ran a hot bath and threw in loads of smellies.

After all, he could afford it.

Did it really matter? Did it really matter how much more rich he was, more than she could have possibly suspected? It had been a year… *a year…* and he had to be wealthy. Had To Be. Did it make any difference? Knowing she was in London… knowing she was in Kensington? Kensington for gawd's sake.

Kensington.

Did it really matter?

Yes, it mattered. Rich people… rich people… *got away with things…* She moved back to his delusions. Safer for the moment. No, he didn't own the entire building for goodness sake, or a bloody bank. All she knew was that he had possession of this place.

…possession… good word… that's not all he possesses, is it…

She punched the side of the bath, hurting her hand. She would not go there, the pain helped her focus. He did not own this entire building; he did not own a bank. For one thing, this apartment was nowhere near that level of wealth.

…what… he should have a house maid running around clearing up the blood after him… perhaps have the butler give the odd beating for him, to save his hands…?

For another thing, as far as she knew, most of the posh bits of London were leased or something. She'd see the adverts 'with 80 years to run' sort of thing.

…so he owned the lease… or the bank owned the lease… does it matter…?

It did matter, it mattered a lot. But she couldn't work out why. But she knew she had to reject everything he said. This brought her back, again, to how she'd felt when she'd stumbled, and he'd help her upright, kept her walking. She'd been grateful, comforted... her fist hit the side of the bath again.

It was useless, nothing would get her anywhere. Thinking about it all was totally not worth doing. She had to shut down her mind, had to walk away from all this. Had to Get A Grip.

Get a grip of what? She was lost, utterly lost, and it hurt and she... cried herself to sleep.

In her dreams, warm arms held her as she cried.

Morning was very strange. Nothing had changed, the world could no longer ever be the same shape again. Their routine continued... but... there was a pressure in the air between them. There was a ghost in the flat with them, the ghost of the outside, the ghost that had been kept out, on the other side of the door. As she moved through the day, her gaze kept returning to the conjoining door. He finally lost patience with it all, and locked himself in the study to do some work: selling a modern business took forever, it seemed. She sat in the living room... and looked at the door. He half hoped she would rise and try to walk through it, but she stayed seated. Looking. Over dinner that evening, he found himself once more engaging her in conversation, real conversation, and she responded well.

So they moved into a quiet courtship that thrilled him, and horrified her.

First of all he dealt with her fascination for the outside, and how that door had been opened up to her mind, by giving her new possibilities within the apartment. He opened up the concealed storage on the end living room wall, revealing the viewing screen, videos and CDs. She devoured anything he allowed her, and he rewarded her with new videos, new music, as and when she pleased him most. They would lie together, on the couches, and watch films of an evening, in comfortable companionship. Slowly, with extreme delicacy and grace, he evolved a situation whereby his arm would naturally fall around her shoulders, and she would lean into him and they would converse as they watched movies. She had clung to him for strength in the park, and he used the body memory of that reassurance to build more of it. He also allowed her mind to become more stimulated, encouraging more independent responses. She liked old Hollywood movies, just as he did, and they spent many hours talking through ridiculous plots with bold and brave men and hysterical woman who screamed incessantly. During these discussions he slowly broke down her resistance to being touched, and she opened up to him.

She was the desert, he the oasis. She was hunger, he was bread. The terror of his touch was soon dissipated by the desperate need within her for human contact. For skin contact, for gentle caress and comfort, for conversation and inter-change.

When she was utterly calm about the casual contact of their bodies, he slowly extended his control to not so casual touching, and he began to take blood from her, openly, and with no pain. He would play with her hand, as they watched the film, and raise it up to his mouth, and suckle upon her veins. He used thrall to begin the process, bedazzling her into acceptance, but the need to do so quickly diminished. His footing on the path of her seduction was swift and sure. When she recoiled, he left her. Would just calmly stand up and leave to his study, and hence to his own rooms. The next day would move through its own rhythms normally. It was a relief that he could get on with a great deal more work whilst she watched movies all afternoon on her own, he even managed out to meetings and signings at lawyers. The camera record proving what he had known: she carried on as normal, oblivious that he had gone out.

In the evening, after dinner, he would go to his spot on the couch, and discuss what movie to watch that night. She had complete freedom to leave him, to sit where she wanted, to retire to her room. From the initial refusal, she began to comply voluntarily. Anything was worth the contact, it seemed and she would settle down with him, and keep herself under control as he slowly feasted on her blood. It was tiny sips, to be sure, and he was very careful to make them as pleasant, but not overwhelming, as he could. This was actually a very refined skill, and few could have taken from her so regularly without losing themselves in the blood thrall. He thrived on her blood which was remarkably refreshing and invigorating: had that happened before?

Within two months of her visit outside, she was donating blood to him every evening.

This required a huge amount of tinkering in her diet, and she had been allowed to cook and prepare elements of their meals. He began to encourage her in making a series of more substantial snacks during the day. She was still very weak from the starvation during the dark punishment, and he was taking calories out of her that she could ill afford. Her muscle tone was wasted from the lack of exercise and the trauma of her confinement. Her skin tone worried him, especially on her back and the left wrist where he had taken such pleasure in slicing open the flesh routinely. She was not healing well, and even with his blood having been applied – mostly – on injuries, scar tissue had formed in several places. He needed to have her begin to exercise, and he brought a running machine through into the laundry room, and gave her the task of first walking, then slowing starting to run, on a strict schedule.

This precipitated the first major blow to their new found relationship, moving her swiftly back down the ladder several notches The room, that they both referred to as the laundry room, was the 'empty' bedroom that was opposite the main bathroom, by the conjoining door. It was mostly a bare space, with nothing going for it at all bar a washing machine, a dryer, and packed cupboards of supplies and materials. Essentially, the running machine just sat in the middle of an empty space. However, she took to being allowed into that room on a regular basis, with some rebellion. It was as if adding a room to the territory allowed her, somehow emboldened her mind, empowered her in some way. She began to resist his companionship. Whilst she did fulfil his exercise targets, she also began to explore the cupboards and cabinets in there. Thus, she found the secret doorway into the other side of the apartment, and its stairs upward.

He came to regret not having installed a camera in that room, when he realised she had discovered his deceits. She could never escape that way – doors that opened out for exit, also opened in for trespass, and both the connecting door with the drawing room on the other side, and the trap door through the ceiling at the top of the narrow stairs were sealed shut. However, her finding her way through the fake cupboard into that in-between space, gave her new strength. She began to walk away from any opportunity for him to feed. She grew distant. At first he was mystified as to what had derailed his carefully crafted plans: why was she changing? After analysing how often she went to the treadmill, and how much activity was being done on it versus how much time she was spending in the room... it was obvious. He should have been paying more attention to the noises as she moved around in there. He let her have her way for a couple of days whilst he placed wiring and cameras in both the in-between space, and the laundry room. Sure enough, there she was, opening and closing the cupboards, sitting in the stair well, sometimes trying to run her hands over the door and trapdoor lines, seeking how to open them. Sticking her fingers in the keyholes, trying to see through them. But mostly, curiously, just sitting in there, calmly. Then leaving and pounding on the treadmill to make up the 'lost' time.

He mused upon it. He came to the conclusion that she was 'escaping' him when she sat in there. It was a tightly confined space. No natural light, very stuffy when the doors were closed. It had never even been painted, it was bare plasterboard walls. It was a 'passing through' space. There was nothing in there to attract her. She could not go further. She was just as imprisoned as she was anywhere else in the flat.

Except. Except that he was not in there. She was free of him, when she was in that space. She was stealing the space from him. She was taking control, when she sat in there. Hence her retreat from him.

He planned it out meticulously. He made show of going into his study, and telling her he'd be there all afternoon, something that was his habit to do, so meal times could be arranged between them. Should she cook then? Yes, that would be lovely, could she cook and set the table, and he'd appear when dinner was ready? Wonderful.

He locked the study door behind him, and swiftly made his way through to his bedroom, out into the far vestibule, in through the drawing room and was in the passageway, from the other direction, before she'd even done the pretence of her running. When she opened the doorway a few minutes later, she walked straight into his embrace.

During the struggle, he lost his temper. He was acutely aware of that afterwards. He'd been furious with her, for tricking him. Although part of him admired the ingenuity, the dominant emotion was rage. When she struggled, when she screamed, that rage surfaced. There was no room for more than fists and feet, but she was a bloodied mess in moments. He should have stopped. He knew he should have stopped sooner, but had found it so satisfying, letting go. He had planned to just leave her there, in her own blood, and let her wake up in the tiny suffocating space, and leave her there for a couple of days. Let her hunger and thirst in there, foul her clothes and the air. Experience the space with him in it.

When he did pull back from her, he did, in fact, leave her, and barred the door firmly from the cupboard side. He went to shower, and change his clothing, and stopped to check on her on the monitors on his way through the study to the kitchen. She had not moved. He flicked the lights off in there, and switched to infra red. He could hardly see her image, so hot was the air in that tiny, sealed space.

Panic touched his senses. His own heart began to beat a little faster, just a tiny fraction. He took a sharp intake of breath, and tried to make sense of his reaction.

...what if she died...

With the air so hot and still, her body barely registered, the temperature of her body and the air, matching. Beneath her however, was a pool of different colour. Slowly spreading, slowly cooling.

...she could be bleeding to death...

He switched the cameras back, and the lights on. Yes, there was a dark stain of blood all around her, soaking into the chipboard floor.

Sweat was beading on his brow by the time he opened the doorway. The stench hit him, she'd voided her bowels. Was that before, or after, he left?

When he turned her over and picked her up, she was limp, pale. Lifeless. Thick drops of blood oozed out of her left wrist. She was in danger of bleeding out. He had no recollection of feeding from her, but the wrist was torn open. Her heart was faltering, her breathing laboured through obstruction. He placed her down on the floor, by the treadmill. This was the right room for this emergency, and he took a line and saline drip out of the cupboard they were stored in: he had full stocks. He had difficulty getting the line in, as her veins had begun to sink, and he only just managed to get one into her leg. He hung the bag from the treadmill, and adjusted the flow. Her wrist still oozed, so he slashed his own forearm with a scalpel, and his blood sealed that wound shut. Just as it had on the shoulder, the ruined flesh would heal over...but would never be anything other than a scar. A scar on a scar.

Damn.

Her face was a mess. He palpated under the swelling, and found her jaw broken. Her nose had seemingly escaped his rage, but she had petechiae flowering across her lower jaw and neck. Had he strangled her? He intubated her as a precaution. There was no reaction as the tube went down into her throat but it seemed to go in easily enough. The saline was doing its job... but not enough. Her heart was still hesitating. Not really a surprise, given the damage that the year had inflicted and she had just been starved most severely.

Looking down on her, her swollen face utterly unrecognisable, covered in blood and stinking of her own shit... his own heart faltered.

He could not lose her. He could not. Later, he would tell himself that it was because he did not wish to lose his investment. All that time and effort, all that expense. But it was a lie. As he knelt by her, feeling her battle for life slipping away, he knew he could not bear to lose her. Could not bear to left alone once more.

He stripped open a 250 ml syringe and slipped it into his own veins. Pulling back, he filled it completely, then drew it out and injected his own blood into the saline drip. He repeated this three times, as the bag slowly drained down into her. He felt along the jaw, located the break, which felt clean to his probing fingers, and he reshaped the jawline, supporting the break. Within about 20 minutes of his blood going into her, the swelling on her face began to subside. Her features took on their normal shape and the skin slowly cleared of hematoma. He continued the support, and only let go of the jaw when he was sure the break had healed, probably only a fracture. He'd get her x-rayed at some point, and any misalignment could be dealt with then. He removed the breathing tube.

Fixing another saline bag to the same line, he once more emptied his own blood directly into the bag as it drained. Her heart was no longer suffering, its beat more powerful than it had ever been. She had emerged from oblivion, into sleep. Her breathing was even and regular.

He left her to fill the main bath tub with luke warm water. When the second saline bag had finished its work he removed the drip and carried her into the bathroom. He stripped her, cleaned up what he could, and then bathed her. The water turned pink from the dried blood upon her, and her hair stained the water dark red. He drained the tub and refilled it, with her still oblivious, and searched through her scalp. Whatever injury had been there, was gone, but it had been severe, as her hair was totally caked in blood. He did the best he could with the showerhead without drowning her. Then he lifted her up, and into the bedroom. He had hesitated, thought to take her to his own bedroom, but pushed the thought aside. She would be disoriented enough, when she woke this time, when she woke... *changed*.

He left her on the bed, on a pile of towels, whilst he cleared up the various messes. The flooring in the passageway would need replaced.

There was no need of drugs or pain killers, with so much of his own blood in her. He contemplated a sedative, but was not optimistic it would work under the circumstances. He would have to be very careful about her getting any more blood from him.

Which meant he had to control his temper.

At a loss with what to do now she was settled, and safe... he lay in bed with her, and cradled her in his arms. She slept for the best part of a day, with him holding her in his arms.

Whenever she began to stir, to moan, and to struggle, he stroked her head, her hair, the line of her shoulder. She unconsciously moved into him for comfort and he responded by cuddling into her. The word felt alien in his brain. Spooned into each other, as any normal couple, he slept also.

The feeling of his body, behind her, enclosing her in warmth and comfort, came through in a dream. She was a child, feeling poorly in bed. She'd crawled into her parents' bed in the morning light, and snuggled up to him. He cuddled her close, and stroked her hair and sang lullabies to her. The memory was so strong, so vivid. She knew she would open her eyes and be at home, in their little flat, and her Mum would be in the kitchen making breakfast, and her Dad would be giving her one more cuddle before he got up to go to work, telling her to stay in bed and do as her Mum said.

The weight and length, the scent... it was all wrong, and the terror crashed in with wakefulness. She extricated herself out from under his arm, and fled to her bathroom, retching. Tears flooded down her cheeks unbidden, and she stood at the sink shaking. Her memories were confused, and confusing, and she knew bad things had once more happened.

...what had happened... what had happened... what had happened...

There were memories of pain and blood, and death and fear. Memories of agonising smashings and the sounds of bone crunching and grating... her hands flew to her face, and felt her nose and cheeks... what had happened...? Something had happened. She couldn't explain then, how her body seemed fine... shaky, weak, but not broken. She felt her throat, where she remembered great pain and terrible pressure, the sense of falling unconscious, of being strangled unconscious. There was nothing there to feel, nothing to see in the muted reflection from the marble tiles. She was naked, and pulled on a towelling robe, as she went through to the kitchen, to examine herself in the kitchen cabinets. The crystal cabinet gave a good reflection if the lights were positioned properly. He was still asleep, and she moved past him quickly, quietly.

If anything, she looked well. She couldn't fathom it. The only thing wrong with her – different – was that her hair was utterly matted. Bird's nest, as her mother would have called it. She stood frozen between intangible memory, and the image of her wholeness. Surely…?

…what had happened… what had happened…what had happened…

Something had happened. Something bad.

…no…no…no…no…no…no…no…no…no…no…no…no…no …no…no…

Something bad, something terrible… and here she was, looking fine. All that showed something had happened was her matted hair. That can't be, because if she was fine, and something bad had happened….

…no…no…no…no…no…no…no…no…no…no…no…no…no …no…NO!

She took a sharp knife out of the drawer, and began hacking at the matted locks that straggled about her face.

He came to her there, where she stood, slashing at her hair, and he gently took the knife from her, and held her in his arms. She sank slowly to the floor, sobbing into his chest, and curled down into the foetal position upon the hard tiles. He held and rocked and shooshed, his hand stroking down the length on her back. She gave into it utterly, accepting what comfort she could from him. He was all she had, and she was grateful for the feel of his skin against hers, for the sense of being cared for. He moved to pull away, and she responded with a frightened yelp, and pulled him back down to her, closer. She wanted that moment again, when he had held her straight and strong in the street, and his arms had carried all her fears. She was drowning in pain, and memories of pain, and his arm was all that held her from the abyss: from dropping into blood and pain and emptiness. He was all she had, and she reached for him, and folded herself into his arms and cried in despair of her acceptance. There was no escape, none. He was inside her, completely, and there was no way out, no way past him. She needed him.

Would accepting that make it easier?

CHAPTER SEVENTEEN

That day was spent in resting, and eating, and crying. He held her whilst she cried and she couldn't bear to be alone for a second. Panic engulfed her when he left the room, to make drinks or food. He slept the night in her bed, holding her tightly. She gave into this gladly, more terrified of being left alone. Something had shattered and only his presence kept her together.

He smiled as he stroked her to sleep.

The next morning, when she had recovered herself a little, and they had dressed and eaten, she was taken back outside the apartment, her massacred hair tucked up into a loose ponytail and a scarf over her head. Her left wrist was bandaged lightly, and the white peeped through her sleeve edge. She pulled at it frequently, pulling the dark fabric of her blouse over the white.

She was weak, and shaky, but they did not go far, just off Kensington High Street. He took her to a salon, a very expensive salon, where each customer, each *client*, was dealt with one to one, in small and impeccably fitted out rooms. She couldn't imagine how he'd got such a long appointment so quickly, and a very quiet and utterly dedicated man she did not recognise at all (she kind of thought she should have known who he was) cut her ravaged hair perfectly. The snipping took forever, as they teased out all her knots, treated her hair, coloured it, super treated it, and then snipped up and along very very slowly, working around the problems until her new 'style' was revealed.

All the old perm came out, and a sleek and chic shoulder length masterpiece of waves and shimmering chocolate colours emerged from the ruin. Jonathan had surveyed the entire transformation, and been consulted several times on treatments and styles, on conditioning colours and on the nature of the food and drink brought into them at regular intervals. She herself had been invisible, to both the stylist and the younger male assistant who had washed her hair, rinsed out the colour and swept up the cuttings as they fell.

She was grateful for this, as it was so overwhelming to be in the presence of others, and to see herself clearly in the wall of mirror in front of her. To be touched by alien hands. She spent much of the time, and it was long hours they were in there, devouring her image. Who was she, that splendid woman who looked back at her? The perfect features, the pale and slightly glowing skin. The piercing brown eyes and the high swept cheekbones. She was beautiful, that became clear as her hair was cut to complement her face. A beauty she had always sought, but which had previously evaded her. It wasn't just the lost weight, it wasn't just the suffering. She could see her suffering had made her more attractive...how her skin lay stretched upon her bones like a model on the catwalk... but there was something else? Something else she could not quite fathom. She turned away from it.

Twice, the speed of the changes, the complete shock of being out of the apartment, of sitting having her hair cut, overwhelmed her. Twice tears rose up from her eyes, unbidden, unstoppable, and flowed down her face. Both times the hairdresser left the room, without a word, followed by his apprentice. Both times tea and coffee appeared, and tiny pastries. Both times Jonathan had poured her a drink, and they'd sat until her tears dried. Both times he'd held her close until she'd stopped shaking, whispering courage in her ears. Then he would return to his seat, call the staff back in, and they would pick up where they left off as if nothing had happened.

He'd escorted her to the toilet, he'd held her coat for her, he'd paid the bill without a word. He'd made every decision that kept her safe, and smiled when she needed reassurance. Later, much later, she was to recognise that the staff had thought her in recovery from drugs, or anorexia, or some other ailment of the rich. That their deference to her complete isolation from them was, in some way, utterly normal. That she was not the first high class, high priced, docile but fragile package to be groomed in their little booths, never out of sight of a minder. That her presentation to them as a silent doll to be dressed up, was quite normal for some of their clientele.

The walk back to the apartment exhausted her, and she remembered little of it. Everything in her itched to be back, safe, secure. She slumped into his body and allowed him to half carry her back into their side of the apartment. He settled her on the couch, a rug over her legs, and brought her soup and snacks. They watched a movie, *Stella Dallas*, and she sobbed into his warmth at the end, her throat tight with longing and pain. He lifted her up and took her through to the bedroom, and once more slept by her side.

The level of her shock was quite delicious. She was utterly malleable and completely controllable. It was delightful to have such complete and utter dominance. He used his advantage ruthlessly, the rhythms of the days picked back up, but with more and more frequent trips out. He carefully expanded her world to accept and absorb every element he'd want in place, when her Turning was complete. Clothes were bought, lunches taken, shoes made for her feet, her hair kept in perfect order. He ordered body sleeves to be made, in fine flesh coloured cloth. They were originally for healing in burns victims. He had them moulded to her back, and one as a short sleeve for the left wrist and forearm. The one for her back was off set over her left shoulder, then swept in under her breast, like a halter fitted back to front. It was far more expensive that way, but he wasn't having her breasts covered and hidden. When wearing the sleeves, the scars were safe from irritation, and she could safely change and be pinned for fittings with no one to see what was under them. No shop assistant would be gauche enough to mention them, and would automatically work around their presence in selecting items for perusal.

He ordered a new identity for her and when it had finally arrived, filled a purse with credit cards and a provisional driving license. It hung in the coat closet next to an ever expanding collection of matched shoes and handbags. He would not give it to her yet, but soon, she would be ready. He installed a beauty mirror in her bedroom, and filled the shelves with grooming and make up supplies. He booked two sessions with a professional makeup artist, who taught her how to spend hours constructing a natural yet polished look. He began to pick out jewellery. By the time she'd started to recover from what had happened in the crawl space, she was perfectly groomed to his tastes. He sent a message to Paris.

She grew accustomed to taxi trips to and fro, for shopping and meals. She rarely spoke when they were outside and she was always grateful for their return to safety. There was no joy in buying things, or eating food in public places, but there was comfort in returning indoors. He saw to it that her strength was rebuilt slowly, and she returned to the exercise machine in the laundry room, with him always beside her. She was utterly lost to explain how good she felt, no matter the exhaustion which dogged her. Just as lost was an explanation of what had happened to her when she had blacked out in that tiny crawl space... waking up in bed with him, whole. She refused to look at the memory, or to think on anything other than how good it felt not to be covered in bruises, or blood. He'd not touched her since, in anger or in any other way.

By the time the summer's heat was starting to let loose its grip on the city, he began to feed of her again. She had made the offer first, one evening, lifting her wrist to his mouth. The tension over when he was going to start again was getting to her, and she preferred to have it over. That was what she told herself, as he drew her blood into his mouth.

She had never tasted so good.

He rewarded her surrender by allowing her access to the rest of the floor. They explored his own bedroom, and the other sitting room. She picked it up quite quickly.

'So you can have visitors here, and they think this half is your entire flat?'

'Yes, exactly.'

'So no one that visits here, knows just how rich you are?'

'Exactly.'

'But rich enough, successful enough, to have this couple of rooms in such a grand building.' They were standing in the hall, by the dining table, which was adorned with red and white roses.

'What do you say about the door?' She pointed to the conjoining door that accessed the real apartment.

'That it is a fire escape, and it is electronically monitored, so they may not have a quick peek out to the emergency stairwell.'

She nodded. His bedroom was the far left doorway, and the near left one was a tiny bathroom, that was en suite from his end, but also could be used by visitors from the hallway.

'But where is the kitchen? You can't have guests without food?'

He was immensely pleased by the gasp as he opened the cupboards to the left hand side of the main door, and swept out the extending cupboards and revealed a perfect, tiny, built in kitchen.

'My goodness.' She had never seen such a thing, and her surprise delighted him. He pushed everything back to seamless perfection.

'In truth, I never cook in this little area. If I am feeding guests, I get in a caterer.'

'But it's enough to show anyone that you actually live here?'

'Yes, exactly.'

She turned back to his bedroom again, and explored it all.

'Where is the door?'

He did not hesitate, and carefully pulled the switch inside the bureau drawer, so she could track his movement. The bookcase that had defined the end of the wall, as it met the outside window wall, swung open into the corridor. He invited her onwards with a nod.

This in-between space was very different from the one on the other side. To begin with, it was fully decorated in the style of the apartment, and was very long, if not that deep. It too held a spiral staircase up, but it also held one of the massive outside windows. She observed the electronics on the small work area, and the injutting boxed in room shape. She looked up to the air conditioning ducts, and the various wires trailing on top of the lowered inner ceiling.
She touched the inset cuboid.

'This is my cell, isn't it?'

'Yes, it is.'

'Which means…' She walked on past the window, into the narrow corridor leading on, and came to the seeming stop of a wall. She turned to him. 'Which means through here, is your study?'

He nodded. 'Just push.'

She leaned into the wall, and pushed. The wall moved forward and swept to the right, opening in front of the window in the study. Thus, she entered it for the first time, from the secret door.
He joined her, and pushed the door back into place.

'It's incredible.'

'Why?'

'It's silent.'

His pleasure was great. 'Yes, it is silent. That is the bit that costs a great deal of money.'

'But all the books, they must weigh a lot?'

She was so wonderful, sometimes, in her intellect. He really did admire her, in fleeting moments such as these. He pulled the bookcase back from the fake book spines, and shut it again, soundlessly.
She turned to view the room, from the vantage point of his desk. She was looking up at the long shelf of monitors that sat above the real door. They were all switched off, as he had no reason to track her through them, now.

'You can come in and read the books, if you wish to.'

She spun round to him.

'Really?'

'Yes, really. We should go book shopping, and get some more videos too.'

She sat down at the desk, looking at him with tears in her eyes. 'I'd love to be able to read some books.'

He sat on the desk's edge, and trailed his finger along her cheek. She flinched slightly, which he accepted. She was emerging back into herself, and there would be more troubles on the path. Looking at her now, however, he was absolutely certain that everything would work out perfectly this time.

'Then we shall go shopping tomorrow, and get some books for you. I doubt anything in here will be very interesting.' He indicated the wall of reference books.

'I'm sure there are some nice things in there.'

'Yes, there are, but later, not now.'

He stood and indicated he wanted her hand, then led her out of the study, through the normal door. Over dinner, she grew more distant, and she did not offer her blood to him that night. She did not object to him taking it, but she did not offer.

It was time.

The first part of the plan was to introduce her to the real residence. He had hoped to move in there with her when they were in London anyway. She needed to be unsettled before he left for Paris, and opening up the space would do that. He had considered moving her directly into the small cell in the other side, as she knew her own so well, and how it was utterly false. In the four days he planned to be away, she may have broken out somehow, although it was unlikely.

So he considered the other cell, which was larger and encased in brick. He dismissed this, however, as wanting to leave the memories of her confinement, to the inner apartment. So he decided to maintain the real residence as a cell free zone.

The next morning they went out book shopping, and between them they picked up a good 400 books. She actually got a flush of pleasure from just picking up book after book after book, and adding them to the growing pile. Foyles had seen it all before, of course. That was one reason they had gone there. He made sure that there was plenty of children's classic in the piles. She did not appear to notice this, or at least did not comment on it, which was fine by him.

They returned to the flat by taxi, with just two large carriers. The rest were being sent on the next day, by courier. She was quite chatty in the cab, which was not like her when outside, and this was more evidence that she was approaching an equilibrium.

Which shattered when he stood her in front of the seemingly benign and utterly innocuous picture, hanging on the wall between the kitchen and dining room. She had gone to put the books into her own room, and he had stayed her hand, instead bringing her to the end point of the corridor. He stood for a moment, allowing her confusion to build, then leaned his hand under the tiny shelf that seemed to provide an end point for the décor, on that brick wall. The door swung forward, soundlessly. He had made sure the lights were on, and the glare made them both blink. Then he stepped through. She did not follow, which pleased him immensely, and he had to step back, grab her arm, and pull her forward.

The walk through was always awkward, and for this reason he almost never used this entrance. Up either of the spiral staircases, into the attic storage rooms, and across and down, was far easier. The entire point of this entrance, after all, was that it was completely hidden: there was no hint it existed in the architecture. So it was awkward, pulling her round the tight bend, along the narrow corridor, and pushing out the sealed door on the other side, to emerge into the very real and dedicated laundry room. When she was clear, he sealed the door shut behind them, and it disappeared into the tiled 'wall' that was utterly seamless on this side too. Without giving her pause for breath, he carried on out into the main kitchen, through the formal dining area and out into the vestibule.

He did allow her a moment to gawp, speechless, at the sheer size and scale of the atrium. The sun shone in through the glass roofing, and the central chandelier glimmered and glistened in the most beguiling fashion. It was quite warm, the air conditioners struggling, as they always did in this central space. The ceiling window blinds had been left open deliberately. He started off again, and pulled her up the main staircase, moving down the mezzanine landing swiftly. He opened the door to their bedroom, her new bedroom, and took her in.

'The book cases on the left hand side of the bed are yours.'

He indicated the empty shelves, positioned perfectly for reaching from the comfort of the huge, custom made bed, and then moved himself to his side of the room. He busied himself with the business of walking into his dressing area, and made great show of taking off his shirt, and changing into a casual sweater. She was rooted to the spot, where he had left her, tears cascading silently down her face.

He very kindly, and gently, relieved her hand of the burdens of the bag of books and emptied them into the shelves. Then he guided her to sit on the edge of the bed, and he opened up the dressing area on her side of the room, and allowed her to see the treasures within. Every morsel of space was already stuffed with clothing, shoes and accessories. He rambled on about how much of it had been made for her, to his design, and finally bade her to enter the room, when he reached the jewellery carousel. She came, and he seated her on the chair, and flipped up the lid. It became a perfectly lit mirror, and he gently slid to one side the seemingly plain white counter underneath. The first tray of impeccably laid out jewels was revealed. He let her take in the sapphires, before sliding them out of sight to reveal the ruby tray, then the emerald one. The final layer was plain metals – gold various, platinum, some antique silver. She was shaking by the time he finished and replaced all the layers, and the lid.

'Of course, you are not quite ready to wear any of this yet. It takes a particular skill to wear real jewels out and about in London, and one you will have to have some advice on it. The insurance agents insist.' He prattled on as he again pulled her behind him into the main sleeping area. 'As it happens, I dislike diamonds, so that makes street insurance a lot easier.'

He crossed over to his side of the bed, and opened a small drawer. From it, he took a ring box, and took out the hematite ring that had been so missing from his left hand since the night she had been stolen. He slipped it on the middle finger, and flexed his fingers. That was so much better. So ingrained in him, in them all, was a ring upon that finger, he actually itched when it was absent. It was exhilarating to reach this point with her, to begin to dress himself in his own identity.

'When you are fully Turned, you will need to wear a ring on the middle finger of your left hand, always. It is one of the few laws of the Kin.'

He showed her through to the en suite behind the curved wall that partially encircled the bed. The 'his and hers' Jacuzzi was perfectly centred under a circular ceiling window, which was domed and lined with soft spotlights. Behind again, was the showering area, all laid out as a wet room, and then the personalised toileting stalls.

It was clear when she stopped taking things in, so he led her out of the master bedroom suite, and down the corridor, to the small breakfast bar come kitchenette that was sandwiched between the master and the other bedroom suites. He poured her a drink of water and handed her a banana. She ate in silence as he watched. His left thumb slowly spun his ring around.

Her blood sugar somewhat restored, and her composure brought back under control, he continued the tour. They went downstairs again, and he pulled her by the hand once more, through the various great rooms, the library, the gym and the private cinema.

'It is only 15 seats, but they are very comfortable.'

They glanced in the projection room with its stacks of reels, and moved on. The entrance to the other cell was in there, and he did not wish to draw attention to it. She would spot the slight dissonance in the wall structure, he was sure, if she spent more than a few minutes in there. She worked a lot out from where windows were, and the lack of them in the cinema and booth would not fool her for long.

They returned to the atrium. He was wondering if she recognised it.

She was wondering the same thing. Incredibly, it was the plants that were claiming most of her attention. Starved of anything living at all, on the other side of the wall, this place was filled with plants. Bright green splashes everywhere. Every room had fresh flowers and perfectly cultivated plants. That meant care. Lots of care. Tending. This reception area, what had he called it, the atrium? It was part rain forest. Huge green plants, feet high, flourished in the sunlight bathing down on them.

Plants meant staff.

The size of the dwelling meant staff. Everything glowed impeccably.

Money wasn't even a consideration. This made her think of the trays of jewels and she slammed the thought down.

...the lift... the lift... the lift... the lift...

She allowed this thought in. Survival meant she had to understand the lift, and the rest of the ...*mansion*? Only word that fitted.

The atrium was semi circular, facing out to the flat edge of the far outside wall. It contained the central reception area, and the balcony off the main stairwells, above them. That level was recessed back, to allow this main area double, triple height, all the way to the roof. It was a bit like being in a glasshouse at Kew, although the roof was part brick as well, with the glass in sections. The stair way up to the bedroom areas was grand and sweeping and curled down to one side. The lower rooms began only after the balcony, and so were somewhat recessed. But downstairs was a much higher room height, which matched the other apartment. Upstairs was lower, a more normal room height. She wondered if there were smaller attic rooms somewhere. In this central well of space, the roof was 30, 40 feet above them.

Central to the entire design, on the outside wall which did not have any windows, was the lift. There was a glass wall and heavy doors between the atrium and the lift area. Stairs clearly curved around and down the lift shaft. The atrium doors were thick and ornate, wood and metal. They were offset, and sat to the side that the internal stairwell met. The glass walls allowed perfect vision of the lift area, and it was curious how heavy and solid the door was, settled within glass walls. The individual glass panels were huge and set into thick shining metal sills. The doors were set in what looked like wood, and the sill and above was solid wood. In a small semi-circle, the glass wall curved around, away from them, to create the quite small entrance and exit area for the lift. When you left the lift, you were contained in a small curving space, with the doors to the left of you. Except the glass walls meant you also saw the huge expanse of the atrium. It was odd that the doors were so heavy and out of place.

'I don't remember glass walls.'

He moved to the side wall, and flipped up a panel of switches. From each of the thin metal sills supporting the glass panels on the lower levels by the lift, bronze/brown fabric flowed under the glass. It took a few minutes, and then the area of glass that actually met with the lift vestibule, was closed off from view. The doors now looked in keeping with the fake 'walls' that held it.

'Voila.'

Another switch flicked again and lighting hit the fabric and turned it into a shimmering, opalescent wall of light. It was quite beautiful.

'But you do remember?' His question was gentle.

She nodded.

'The lift. That was how we came in here, the lift.'

'Yes, it was.'

He touched the now familiar numbers pads, set on the edge of the door frame. The huge door, she'd thought them doors, but it was only one, swung inwards. He stepped through to the vestibule. She followed. Another touch of the pad on the outside, and the door swung shut behind them. On this side, there was no hint the wall was glass, unless you touched it. The fabric on this side, was textured and gave the impression of a non-descript plaster wall. Only on touch, did you feel the glass and notice the smear left by human hand. She looked up. A fake ceiling had also been put in place, that gave out concealed lighting. You'd never guess it was fabric.

'Is it like one way mirrors, that sort of stuff?

'Almost, although more sophisticated. It is a fibre optics design, in bullet proof glass. There is a coating on both sides, inside. The fabric is protected by the sealed atmosphere, and the lighting manipulates the look of it. It is very technical, very new. We sell it all over the world, where people wish to protect themselves, and their art, whilst also allowing both to be viewed at times. The really tricky thing is keeping the fabric moving smoothly.' He sounded both annoyed, and proud.

It really did feel like a small and enclosed space, totally normal and solid. She remembered how the door had looked, from this side. He pressed the button for the lift, the door slid open.

'The lift is always where I last exited it.'

He entered, but she hesitated. He looked back sharply at her, and she followed. Rather than just pressing a button, he used a code pad, just like the doors. The lift had two sets of doors, the one they entered by, and one opposite. He'd walked in and stayed faced to the closed doors. She took this as her cue and did the same.
Being inside the lift was torture.

...keep it together... keep it together... keep it together...

Why? What difference would it make?

...a beating always hurts, that's what difference it makes...do you really think the beatings were over...fool...

The silent glide to a stop was only just noticeable. The opposing door slid open, and they were once more in a glass panelled reception area.   Sunshine streamed into the dark shadow carved by the overhanging building. People were moving to and fro outside on the pavement. The building's exit was a very tall, open brick archway. Inside was a glass vestibule, cutting off the noise. Normal glass, it looked, although thick. They stepped outside the lift. On the left and right, was a small hallway, with a desk with a phone on the left. A small bank of monitors were in a line above the desk, about six feet up. They were switched off. He walked to the front door, which was a very clean and clear single glass door, set in the large glass wall. The huge open archway was the exit point to the building, the glassed in area they were stood in, separate and contained. Outside, she could see the people hurrying up and down and the main entrance to the Royal Albert Hall, to the right.

'Did we come in here?'

'Yes.'

'Oh.'

She didn't say another word, as they turned, went back into the lift and ascended to the private entrance of 1 Albert Hall Mansions West.

CHAPTER EIGHTEEN

The move into No 1 threw her terribly. She was completely bewildered and confused by it all. He stood back, adding to the space around her, and let her flounder. He moved them into the main bedroom that day, and took her through the housekeeping routines. Everything was attended to by a team of cleaners from an agency, under the stern direction of a German housekeeper, also employed by the same agency. He spoke fluent German when he spoke to the housekeeper on the phone. She never came into contact with them herself, always being somewhere else when they were working on sections of No 1 in rota.

Meal times became more formal, as he would never eat in the commercially equipped kitchen. Movie watching was less intimate, less cosy, in the cinema, and working out in the gym, as opposed to the tiny space of the spare bedroom in the apartment, was a daunting and unnerving experience. Not least because of the huge mirrors, in which she'd see herself, and wonder who she was? For she was not of her own image; she did not recognise herself. She was too thin, too pale, too subdued. Not to mention the scars on her wrist and back. She'd look down on the treadmill, and did anything to avoid seeing herself. She often wore the body sleeves to work out, but found just looking at them made her look away, too.

He carried on with the trips out and the grooming, moving up her clothing and style to that of the uber rich. Private fittings were held in the most exclusive salons, with much of the clothing from the wardrobes in the master bedroom being altered to fit exactly. There was no relief from the tension of such outings, as coming back to No 1 was not the reassurance of safety she needed. She began to unravel. She started to have nightmares, and he would hold her in her sleep, soothing. The only time they had, which was as it had been, was when they lay in bed in the evening, and watched videos on the huge screen that rose up out of a recess in the bed end. They would lie together, and he would wait, and wait, and her wrist would raise up and be offered to his mouth. He would reward her with pleasure, muted and distant, through his bite. Not too much, but enough to keep her addicted to the closeness between them.

He began to talk to her in terms of her transformation, the Turning, and she was left with nowhere to go, and nothing to say, upon the matter. Survival skills were foremost, and he taught her all the various exits and entrances for hidden escape from No 1 and the apartment. He schooled her in only ever entering No 1 from the apartment via the roof spaces: the fake wall door was never to be used and he did not teach her how to use the catch. He gave her private access codes for the main doors and lift, and took her through the basement exit, for unseen admission to No 1 via a dedicated fire escape.

In addition to safety, she had to sit through lectures on hunting, and nutrition. Long, detailed explanations about what blood she could take, once she was fully changed, and what she could not touch. He referred to her as 'his Changeling' often, but equally talked about how she would be *Turned* to 'a Changeling', and be New Blood. She never asked, just absorbed, and tried to avoid missing anything.

During one rather boring lecture on how important multiple identities were, he had handed her a small, soft black leather purse and a small rectangular gift box. She had grown used to gifts, if not in the middle of lectures, and accepted them quietly, examining the purse first. She felt the fine grained leather and hand stitching, turning it over in her hands to examine the detail. He approved of her noticing and commenting on quality, so she began to discuss that it was obviously Italian, designer, and not a fake as she opened the purse to examine the lining... and her breath was stolen by the contents. Neatly slotted in rows, were several plastic cards. Credit and debit cards, in golds, silvers and black. Very black, with gold imprinting. She took them out, one by one. The name on them all was the same: Helene Blanchard.

'Turn them over.'

She did so automatically, although she had just been about to do so anyway. Each strip was blank.

'Now open the box.'

This time she had to think about what she was doing, as she was still stunned by the cards. Inside the box were two items. A long thin tube of black velvet with a cord tie, revealed an elegant pen in gold. The other item was a small A5 sized notebook. It was expensive paper, but plain and unadorned: a notebook.

'I want you to practice signing your name, as often as possible, before you sign the cards. Once signed, they are yours.'

'Thank you, they are lovely.'

She knew better than to mention anything other than her gratitude, and obediently opened the book and started to write 'Helene' several times. Her skin was crawling, sweat was beading along her spine, but she patiently sat and wrote Helene... Helene... Helene...

'Take your time. Best not sign the cards until it is second nature to write your signature. A few weeks at least, until you sign that automatically.'

She had taken the purse and put it in her dressing area, in the jewellery carousel, and she used the pad to sign her name in sporadic bursts, as any reluctant child will do their homework: just enough times and in just enough time, to escape punishment. She was sure the pen was actually made of gold, and was very sure of where she kept it, returning it to the black velvet sleeve after every use. That too, she kept with the jewellery. The thought of signing the cards made her ill, and she concentrated only on her signature, and not what it might mean for her, to own those cards. What had happened to Helene Blanchard...? Would her own name be on the back of a set of blank cards for another.... she firmly closed the door on such thoughts, and carried on writing out the name.

His delusions, however, were terribly compelling, if also gross and obscene. When he'd calmly explained that the blood of a very young child would make her ill, and the blood of a baby could kill her, and to also be wary of those very old... the skin on the back of her neck made as to crawl off under its own steam. She'd actually felt a physical shock, as her system reacted to his monstrosity, in even a fantasy of such things. It made it hard for her to ignore her own fears about the depths of his madness, and depravity, and throttling such under was becoming more difficult with each 'blood' lesson.

Blood was life and also death and...

She continued to push it all away, as fast and as hard as she could... but it was getting harder. She was more needy, and shaken, and more clingy. She recognised this, and that it was dangerous... but there was nothing to be done. She learned his lore as well as she could, which for her, in her position, was completely. There was to be no danger of him getting angry that she could not remember any pertinent point of information. Particularly when he would begin 'Your life may depend on learning this...'

Conversely, whilst she recoiled from him during his *teachings*, as she came to think of it... she missed him greatly at other times. Her panic at not being by his side had not decreased, if anything, it had increased. Lost in the huge spaces and many rooms of No 1, she was spending a great deal of time on her own. Just as she had in the apartment, she was often to be found hanging around outside his study, waiting him to finish work. Whilst she had books to read, and films to watch, she was intimidated by the size and scale of No 1. She found herself yearning for the smaller spaces of the apartment, and was then horrified by herself for thinking such thoughts. He took great delight in forcing her apart from him and watching her struggle on the monitors, whilst also noting her return to physical strength. She continued to give blood in exchange for contact. Continued to need his physical presence, at all costs, even that of casual physical touching and blood letting.

He booked passage to Paris.

When change did come to the routine, it came swiftly, and sharply, and she didn't see it coming at all. She'd been in the upper attics, going through boxes of old books and files and papers. He let her do that, and she'd found them to be fascinating.

And very scary.

There were fire safe drawers, and fire safe boxes, and fire safe chests. She'd wondered why they were stored here, and not in professional premises, but like everything about his operation it made sense. Why have them in storage out of his control, when they were safe here, as anywhere, and he could control the fire risks? The building was practically fire proof, and the proof of that was in the massive archives he kept. She'd found the architect's original plans, buried deep. She'd found the plans, the alterations... everything. Well, not everything, there was not enough time to look at everything. There was too much of everything, but she'd found enough. Enough to know he had the paperwork that showed complete control of the building, since before it was built, from the very foundations.

It was quite ingenious, actually. The building was owned by a company, that was owned by another company, a property company, that was owned by a bank that was registered in Switzerland. She presumed it was his bank. Every property in the building, and there was a lot of them, was hired out or long term leased. Most of it, by the property company that owned the company that owned the building. Other small companies sub-let from others, and she had no doubt it would all trail back to the Swiss bank, eventually. She'd also found a few things he'd not mentioned. Escape traps were not only to be found in No 1 and the apartment...they were everywhere. Built into the fabric of the building. Some had been used up over the years, for laying air conditioning, cabling, more water pipes etc. But others were still clearly spider webbed all over the place, particularly from No 1. You could crawl into the rest of the building a dozen ways, from No 1.

She did wonder why he'd allowed her access to all this.

Well, she didn't, really. She knew... *it proved he was speaking the truth...* He'd let her have access to it all, to boast, and to prove his claims. He was incredibly proud of this building, and all the subterfuge. He adored that he'd designed such a masterpiece. He loved boasting about it. He loved showing her the detail, the painstaking detail. He had practically wet himself when he'd walked her up the stairwell that snaked around the lift. Every aspect of The Atrium, was revealed slowly as you emerged from the top of the stairs. The entire atrium, was built around that view, that was why the doors and the staircase, were off set to the opposite side of 'the reveal'. That's why the walls were glass, to preserve the view from the top of the stairs. And he claimed its splendour for himself because, of course, he designed it. The apartment on the opposing end of the building, was no where near as grand and did not boast the Atrium. He'd designed this place, and he kept it entirely the way he wanted: updating never got in the way of the original grand layout.

The plans proved the continuity so he was happy to let her rummage.

She was happy to rummage, as it made the time go faster. She could spend hours in here, doing nothing.

...being alone... being alone... being alone... being alone... being lonely...

It made things easier. It filled time. Time dragged greatly. There was so much more things in her life, and time was so much more oppressive than it had been. It didn't make sense, but she couldn't look at trying to make sense of it. She could just look at... *old books and paperwork, and deeds.*

And try and keep his voice out of her head, whilst she did so.

'Of course we can go out in daylight, have you not noticed I do not disappear, poof. If the sun is strong, keep out of its rays, or use sunblock. Otherwise it will hurt, and do not let your skin burn from sun – it takes weeks to heal.

'We can survive perfectly well on raw animal blood, remember that. It tastes vile, especially rats, but they are very useful, rats. Especially if you are caught short *in extremis*. No matter how bad it is, there are usually rats.

'We do need to feed off human blood several times a year, or we fade. Look older. This is very useful. Some of us go through entire decades, slowly aging ourselves, to fit in with a life span. Then they 'die' and suddenly a new young relative arrives, to inherit, who has the look of the old man.

'There are not many of us. There are few true hunters at the top of any food chain. Not many lions to deer. You will be an empress amongst us.

'You must kill a human at least once a year. Drink them dry as their heart fails. Without it, you will fade for real. Hunt and kill, it brings you life.

'We shall start you on my blood soon...make you my Changeling complete.'

On and on and on. She was expected to remember the answers, and to ask questions. She found the latter difficult. It implied she believed him. Being bored and unoccupied allowed her to obsess about such things. So she retreated to the attics, and sorted through boxes, whenever she could, ever mindful that she was sometimes trying to search for evidence of other girls, evidence of Helene.

At first, she had only gone to the attics when the staff came in, three times a week, to clean and attend the plants. The housekeeper supervised everything, and the dry cleaning, laundry and food deliveries came whilst she was here. It was obviously how he'd kept the apartment well stocked, just carrying things through from No 1. The property company also owned the cleaning agency, so it was a very elegant use of resources. She would have liked to retreat to the apartment at cleaning times, but that was forbidden her. So she'd gradually drifted into the attics as they were absolutely safe from the staff. Her visits had become more frequent over time, until they were also her refuge when he was working in his office. She had tried to while away her time by sitting in the atrium, on the balcony, and looking up at the sky. She thought she had missed it so much, she could watch the clouds go by and dream, as she had as a child. But it had panicked her, and made her heart hammer against her throat, just as it did when he took her outside. The sky was so heavy. So she came to the attics, and played with the boxes, when he worked. Acutely aware that the boxes provided distraction, but little comfort.

Acutely aware that every room had a camera somewhere.

Madness did run in families. His *family* could have owned all this, for this amount of time... but why did it feel so good, when he took blood?

...how could she heal with his blood... there was simply no denying that...

She went back to ignoring her thoughts, by moving out of the records, to the rooms further back, with the 'stuff'. He has such an amazing amount of stuff. It was like a museum's attic, some of this stuff up here, and she liked... the end door opened and he walked in.

'Would you join me downstairs in the apartment, please?'

She nodded, and followed as he turned and retraced his steps. She'd left him in No 1, where he was working in his office, and now he'd approached from the apartment. They were on the south facing side of the building, which meant they went down the spiral stairs into the formal drawing room, and through the conjoined doorway. She hated those stairs, and never used them. The blood stain was still on the floor, and she swore she could smell...

...la la la la... fingers in my ears... la la la la...

But he zigged, rather than zagged, and they descended the spiral stair case down the north side, the Park side, and into his study. He motioned her to sit in the spare office chair, whilst he seated himself behind his desk.

'I need to go away for a few days.'

Her heart slammed into her throat and she found it difficult to breathe.

He flipped open one of the desk's panels, and started to flip switches. Behind her, the monitors flickered to life.

'It will only be for a few days, three at the most. There are things I need to arrange for your Turning.'

He switched his office lamp on, and continued to flick switches. The electronic shutter in the window behind him, began to descend.

'I did think about what to do with you. I have decided, the best thing, the safest thing, is for you to stay here.'

She couldn't trust herself to speak. There were no words anyway. He pointed to the monitors. They were on around the apartment, and in her cell.

'I shall be recording everything.'

She could hear the shutters going down in the dining room next door. Panic seized her. He couldn't, he couldn't leave her in here, like that? She stood up.

'I am sealing the apartment down and I have rescinded your security access. None of the doors will open for you, anywhere.'

She felt the wet on her blouse, and realised her face was streaming with tears. Her blouse was also sticking to her back, with sweat.

'Do not worry. You will be quite safe. I have taken care of everything. Of provisions, and your safety. However, nothing...' he looked at her, like death, that evil mask of complete coldness that she'd not seen for months.

...not since the...

'...nothing out of the ordinary is to occur.'

He finished with the desk switches and closed the flap. He stood up, and moved to the study door, indicating she should go through first. She did what she was told, instantly.

The apartment was completely closed down. All the shutters were in place. The electric lights fought the gloom.

He pushed open the cell door.

'I shall see you in a few days.'

She hesitated. He looked at her, straight through her, straight into her soul.

'Now.' His voice was neutral and calm.

She went into the room automatically. Her body did as it was bid. She'd forgotten that happened: that her body responded no matter what her mind was doing, or saying to herself.
She went into the room, but he did not follow her. She turned, and he was still in the hallway.

'There is to be nothing out of the ordinary. If you try and escape this room, I will make you regret it. Even if you do get out, you cannot leave the apartment. Attend me Joanne, I will make you suffer if you try anything.'

Hearing him speak her name was terrifying. He never ever called her by her name. She took a step back as the taste of bile rose up.

'Be good.'

He closed the door.

She threw up.

Which was, as she reflected over cleaning it up, totally dumb. The stench hung in the room for hours and hours. She'd crawled on the bed, and cried and moaned a lot, initially, leaving the mess on the floor. But the smell had just got worse, and mingled with the stench of her fear, and the sweat. A very familiar set of smells that did nothing to calm her down. Just as lying crying and rocking on the bed, was very familiar, and no comfort what so ever.

Eventually, she'd had no choice but to get up and clean the mess up, scraping it into a hand towel, flushing it away, and washing the floor with the towel.

She'd discovered a few very unwelcome facts. The water was cold. The bathroom had been more or less stripped. There was a very basic shampoo, some conditioner and some solid bar soap. A travel toothbrush, tiny and pathetic and a travel tube of toothpaste. Some toilet rolls and some sanitary tampons. She was due on. She hated that he not only knew that, but supplied her with what she needed and removed the surplus afterwards. It was completely humiliating and she tried very hard never to think about it.

The towel cupboard was empty. Only the set of one hand, one medium and one large bath towel that had been hanging out. She hand washed the clean up towel in cold water and bar soap, and rinsed it and left it to drip in the shower cubicle. It was unlikely to dry.

The bedroom has also been stripped. The wardrobe contained a dozen boxes of various breakfast cereals, several cartons of UHT milk, and three cartons of UHT apple juice. A plastic bowl, spoon and a cup. There was fruit on the table.

Her dresser top clutter was gone apart from a wide toothed comb. The mirror had been removed. The top drawer contained a pack of 6 black knickers and 6 pairs of thin, black cotton pyjamas. The next two were crammed with books; children's books. She was grateful to find the books but was totally bemused by the type.

She was already very stressed, sweaty, stinky and mussed. So she stripped, folded her soiled clothes and put them in an empty drawer and took a hideous cold shower. With her hair towel dried and combed through, and in fresh pyjamas, she felt better.

How to survive without going mad?

He left as soon as he had bolted the cell door down on her and checked through that all the shutters were fully down and sealed. He pulled down the apartment's exit door shutter, which she had never seen of course, and strolled over to the opposite apartment. He called for the previously booked taxi and checked that 'H' was set up for his return. He was hoping to bring back two couples, and had made sure everything was well stocked for immediate occupancy. The taxi company called up and he picked up his case and took the lift down.

The journey to Paris involved him in trying to put his worries to the back of his mind.

What if...

There were no 'what if's. She was as safe as she could be, short of the building burning down. Even if she did try and break out, it would take her a week to get out of her cell and then the apartment. Everything that could cause a problem, such as heating and hot water were switched off. Even if the air fans failed, there was now enough air access for the room to support life... that lesson had been learned well. If she went mad, she went mad: better now than later.

She would not, he was utterly confident, attempt suicide. If that had been a pathway open to her, it would have been used already.

He used the flight to De Gaulle, to compose his features and body signals. That Parisienne bitch could read a stone, and she would not get a shred of emotion from him.

She had agreed to him staying at one of her town houses, and it was costing him a fortune. But they needed time and space to select a team. One of the coven met him at the airport as twilight descended, and escorted him through to the house. As agreed, Violette was there in person. It grated that he had been forced to agree to that, but she was not going to give up the opportunity to make his presence in Paris a huge event for her own people.

He put up with the social introductions, the formal acceptance into her home, his formally making clear he would not kill, maim or feed from any of her people without permission. She, in return, had arranged a snacking boy for him, and he took the barest lick, before passing him to the others. The youth was clean, presentable and biddable. He added him to the bill. He would nicely do for his *little one's* charade.

Once the pretence was over, they went straight to business. Violette had brought him four couples, and, interestingly, a triad. Two tall and muscular men with an extremely assertive and equally physically adept female. She controlled the men, and they all appeared to copulate with each other with no rancour: a real working partnership of three. They appealed immensely from the very beginning, and after barely a day of watching them respond to his routines and working on a hunt with them, he settled for their suite and the others were sent away. They were excellent trackers in the city streets: silent, unseen and dedicated. They worked exceptionally well as a team and were practically invisible when tagging.

The bargaining began.

Violette knew that they would never return to her from the mission, so the bargaining was high. They, in turn did not know this, nor that he was of a completely different nature to the rest of the night turned filth that Paris contained. They had real respect and some element of glamour for working for him, and they had been seeking employment with one of the wealthier Kin for some time. Violette has inducted them individually in Paris, through her covens, and then they had hired themselves out as a group. They had been in South America on a more or less feudal estate but travelled back to Paris when Violette had advertised the position with her contacts. They were seeking employment in more sophisticated climes. She was English, which was exceptionally useful and all three spoke it very well. They would not look out of place anywhere in London, or in Wiltshire. They did not flinch when put through their paces on a couple of sewer rats Violette's people had gathered for the task. Most importantly, neither did they seem to enjoy it. It was a job, nothing more, nothing less They showed absolute disciplined restraint all the way through, only doing exactly what was ordered in both the beatings and rapes, and then the deaths and dismemberment. Both men had been mercenaries in Africa, one was South African. The other was Swiss. She had been a business consultant and had drifted to the darker side of life in Amsterdam and had sought out the Paris covens via the S&M clubs. This had worried him, but she was as impeccably responsive to his commands as the males, and showed as little interest when told to leave off, as they did. They liked fulfilling orders and she controlled the men well. Between them, they spoke eleven languages fluently and enjoyed keeping themselves fit enough to run a marathon every week, if that had been a requirement.

This was an exceptional skill base, for most Kin who would have employed them as hunters, but that was not the task he had in mind. They were nonplussed when asked to cook, clean and keep the town house in orderly fashion, but did all well. They were not personally sexually active outside the trio and accepted that once employed, Dreyfuss owned them until the contract expired.

Terms were agreed and a year's payment made up front. Technically, they would all return to Paris in a year and a day, and Violette would witness the dissolution and arrange terms for a new contract if required. In reality, Dreyfuss had already paid Violette the forfeit for their accidental death, which would be given over to whoever they had nominated to receive it, minus Violette's handling fee. Doing it this way also gave her a year's interest on the capital. Her lilac eyes sparkled at the amount of bearer bonds he handed over to her, and he could smell her musk in the air between them. Common whore, was

Violette, who fantasised that money gave her class. Just that she fancied her occult talents gave her powers beyond the merely undead. Dreyfuss has fantasised about ripping her limb from limb for centuries. But she always remained too useful. Besides, her very presence in Paris was a thorn in the Lord of the River's side, and that was worth keeping.

The four of them, Dreyfuss and his new slaves, travelled back to London together, with the snacking boy in tow. They told him he was being brought back as a gift for a new vampire, which was very nearly true. He was delighted at the thought of having a master of his very own.

Violette did such good work.

CHAPTER NINETEEN

They settled into the 'H' well, and Dreyfuss spent several hours with them going through his plans and orienting them into the design of the building. He showed them their own access point to the attics above the apartment, and on into No1, just in case they were needed more quickly than anticipated. He took them through the release point they would be using, and they undertook to do a full evaluation of proposed routes and likely refuges. Snacking boy, whom he never named as one did not name food, he gave to the trio, whom he named Mary, Mungo and Midge. Mungo was the South African and Midge, slightly smaller than Mungo, the Swiss mercenary. Mary understood the references, and smiled. This annoyed Dreyfuss and he had slapped her down so hard she fell. Mungo and Midge stood impassive and Mary righted herself, and apologised.

This was going to be fun. He'd never bought willing slaves before.

He made it clear that snacking boy was to be kept alive and still useful whilst they made themselves familiar with London and the plan, and returned to the apartment, retracing the steps that had been made in shutting everything down. He checked on her, and she was asleep.

Excellent.

He showered and changed into a robe, before resetting everything to rights. The housekeeper had filled the main fridges as requested, and he took through to the apartment what they would need for the next few days, as she would fare better being allowed the safety she felt there.

He slipped into her cell, and her bed, without her waking. As soon as he leaned into her, however, touching her skin, she was awake and sobbing in his arms. She smelled clean, and the room was stale but not obnoxious. He soothed her and stroked her, and as she dissolved into absolute hysterics, he opened her veins and drank deeply. He had deliberately not fed in Paris and was truly hungry. He brought her to orgasm in thrall as she fainted from blood loss, then settled down with her for a nice long nap. Here, he could sleep deeply.

He woke first, as he sensed her stirring. He had taken a lot of blood, and whilst he was sated, she would be weak. He fetched hot soup and spooned it into her grateful mouth whilst she was propped up on pillows. She sobbed continually. He let that be and continued to give her what material comfort he could. When she finished crying herself out, he took her to the bathroom, and showered with her, helping her stand under the hot water. Wrapping her in her towelling robe, he took her through to the living room, and settled her on the couch in front of a movie. Then he prepared scrambled eggs and hot toast, and brought her tea. She wept and wept, and he once more just let it be.

It took two days before she stopped crying, and moved into withdrawn. This was useful, as he got a lot of very good nutrition into her, to counter the four days of crap, and gave the team enough time to orientate in London. They agreed with his assessment of where she was to be let go, and they brought both cars up to London. As a tag team, they made their way around the zone several times. He kept her in the apartment whilst she recovered, although they slept in his bedroom. He doubted she would ever walk willingly into the cell ever again.

Which was fine. There were always more cells.

As she emerged from her withdrawal, he was careful to be kind, very very careful. A couple of times her unbidden tears and sobs, and her clinging to him as he sipped from her veins as they watched a movie, annoyed him. But he schooled himself ruthlessly: she must have comfort. He had bought several new films whilst whiling away time at airports, and he allowed her to sit on the couch and watch them endlessly, as he brought hot food and restorative drinks, and spooned them into her. He stroked her hair and petted her shoulder, and encouraged her to weep on his shoulder when she began to shake. She began to talk to him of how lonely she had been, and how scared he was never coming back, and how she thought she would starve to death in there... and he continued to soothe her. She babbled a few times, and where he would normally close her down, he allowed her freedom. He said little, but made the right sort of noises that encouraged her to continue.

On the evening of the fifth day of his return, he fed without any thrall at all, and she moaned in his arms, and snaked her leg up around his waist. Such was her need for comfort, and to know that he would not leave her, she offered herself to him utterly. He was not fool enough to think she was genuinely aroused by him, but her desperation to make connection with him, to prove to herself that he would not leave her again, was marked and apparent. He thought through taking her there and then, and dismissed it. However, he gave her full attention from his hands, mouth and tongue, and by the time the movie finished, she was in a torment of longing and loathing in equal measure.

He knew that nothing would have made her reach for him, for her to take action on his body, but he delighted in plunging his fingers into her, and hearing her moan. Feeling the wetness and how she opened herself wider and wider to him, desperate for her emptiness to be filled by something, anything, even him. When he withdrew, part of her objected, and she tried to grasp his hands, his shoulder, anything to feel the connection with him, as living flesh to hold her. She wanted him fully, to confirm the pact she had created in her mind, that he was never going to leave her locked up and alone, again. Her need for safety drove her to offer all she could, in keeping him. He resisted. It would do her good to remember this moment later, this moment when she had fallen to him physically and actually taking her would ruin that. If he did actually take her, she could not be so harsh on herself afterwards. He did not leave her, however, just refused to go further and he took time and effort, and brought her to a tremendous orgasm with his fingers digging deep inside her, and his thumb upon her clitoris. She shrieked and flailed as her spine buckled and her head thrashed upon the cushions. For a second, she was only pleasure and release, and then all of her fear and pain and longing swept back through her. There was a faint heart's beat in the Universe, a pause, a moment of silence, and she crashed into tears and despair and howling. It was very sweet and he fed upon her despair like a cat lapping cream from a plate.

Sleep was not possible for her that night, and he lay awake, feigning sleep, listening to her trying to cope with what had occurred, knowing how much she must hate herself right now, and sensing the pain she was in from her heart beat and respiration. She spent the entire night almost having a genuine panic attack, and pushing it under, no doubt from fear of what he would do if she woke him up.

It was time.

In the morning, he announced it would be good to go and exercise before they ate, in order to build up her body. She automatically said *'Yes, of course.'* and dressed in the clothes he was pulling out of drawers for her. *'We can shower after we return, after all.'* He smiled as he said it, and handed her the clothes. There was a plain designer tracksuit in standard grey. Three pieces, with bottoms, vest and hooded outer top. For underneath a form fitting half vest as sports bra. Black running shoes and grey socks. He was wearing similar. She almost queried, but he quelled her with a look. There was even a plain black band to tie her hair up into a pony tail. When she had finished dressing, he took them out of the apartment door and down the stairs which completely disoriented her. They always used the lift.

She knew that each stop on the lift was actual double storeys on stairs until they reached the first floor as she had seen the plans. That everything above the first floor was double layered apartments was not new to her. But walking down the empty spaces of the stairwell was eerie. It felt like moving through layers of ghosts, with the echoing and the complete absence of any evidence that anyone lived there.

Outside, plunged into the noise of the traffic, they crossed the busy road and entered the park, exactly as many others were doing, and began to run in the frosty air. She was terrified of the outside all over again, with the huge open sky above her, and the cold air pressing into her. As she tried to still her breathing, she realised it was late autumn…where had the summer gone? He swept her up in his arms, and began to run. She leaned into him, once more taking strength to cope with the outside from his body. She was soon tired, and aching, and sweaty, but he harried her on and kept her moving, stretching and jogging, for what seemed like hours. Every part of her began to tremble and ache, but she daren't complain. He let her slide to the cold ground, with its thick carpet of leaves, every now and then, and rest. But always, always, back up and keep moving. Eventually, as the morning moved into noon, he walked them back to the No 1, but he insisted they walk up the stairs. She was almost glad to be in the Atrium, when she finally staggered in. He directed her to the main kitchen, which was odd, and then placed a glass of hot water with lemon in it in front of her.

'Time for a detox, I think. It is important you know how it feels to be hungry, and to know how to feed after you have Hungered.'

She said nothing, but sipped the glass to quench her thirst. When she'd finished it, he took her to the gym room, and set her up on the treadmill.

'Walking I think, in order to build those leg muscles.'

Her leg muscles were trembling and her head faint and her heart pounding, but she walked on and on, with him doing the same at her side. When she'd walked four miles, he let her rest, and gave her more water.

'Fluids are the key little one. If you have not eaten, drink. If you are running from an enemy, drink. If you are in fear of your life, and cannot stop to feed or sleep, drink. Water will give you strength once you have Turned.'

Of course, she had not yet turned, and there was to be no strength for her from water, not just yet. She began to pale, significantly, and he allowed her to rest for an hour, still in her wet, sweat stained clothing. He carried on his monologue about hunger, and thirst, and the need for an iron will to overcome.

'Hunger is your friend and your enemy. It is always about food, and the need to feed. You must learn to discipline yourself, in times of starvation. When you are at your most hungry, your most vulnerable, you must find the strength not to eat. Falling into a feed when you are in danger… is the worst thing you can do. Control, it is all about control.'

He started the treadmill again.

By about 4pm, with the day's light dying on the windows, she reached her limit. She had begun to sob openly, and was very near to fainting. He stopped the treadmill and she fell to her knees, panting. He helped her to her feet.

'I know it is hard, but it is necessary, to keep you safe. Turning is hard work.' He kissed her cheek, and smoothed back her hair. 'True hunger is a test, one which you will have to pass.' Then he smiled, and pulled her to her feet. 'But do not worry, today is not the day for that test. That is far in the future. Today, we eat!'

He pulled her into his arms and walked her back down to the Atrium, helping her shaky legs cope with the stairs. They did not, however, go near the bedroom, and he pulled her into the lift with him. In the tight space of the lift, she was aware of how smelly she was, and glimpses of herself in the glass vestibule showed what a physical wreck she looked. What on earth was he doing, where on earth could they go eat, looking like this?

It threw her even more when they turned right outside the main door, into the back streets, and he got into a black cab with darkened windows that was parked there. He hadn't phoned for a cab, something she was used to. The driver was hidden by black glass, both in the outside windows and the large inner one that separated the passengers from the front of the cab. She'd never been in a black cab where she couldn't see the driver before. It was extremely luxurious inside, with what looked like a private bar. There were no registration documents or meter. She sat down on the back seat with him, but slid over as far as she could. She looked out as London passed. She felt completely swamped, entombed in the darkness.

...just another cell... everything was just another cell, different shape, different size... who was driving...?

He stopped his monologue as she huddled in the corner of the single long couch that was the back seat. He was composing himself for the performance, and he wanted her to be as disoriented and insecure as possible. Mary was driving as she was the most competent in London traffic, so he had no concerns about their journey. Mungo and Midge were already in place with snacking boy, who had a slightly different version of the script than the rest of them. Mary timed it well, and even as they crawled through the traffic to reach their destination, they were settled in the side street by the peak of rush hour.

'One of the things you will have to learn to do, little one, is to hunt well. Hunger and hunting go together. Hunting works best, when you are riding an edge of hunger. Hunger can give you life.'

She automatically turned her attention to him, and gave good show of being happy to concentrate on the lesson. At least she was sitting down. Every muscle in her legs throbbed.

'Hunting is not what you might think. Hunting is often best done in a crowd.'

He indicated the streams of people and traffic flowing in and out of the streets around them. She thought they were parked quite near an underground station, but the area was generally very run down and the place looked squalid, even as busy well dressed commuters hurried past.

'To begin with, there are many eager to be hunted.'

He pointed to the youths loitering at the edge of the street where they were parked, by a broken fence on waste land. Mostly young boys, with a few aggressive looking girls. They were hanging around, yet being isolated from each other, moving slowly into the stream of people, and back out again a few feet later. Some peeled off with those they approached: rent boys. Working the evening commute. She'd read an article about it in Cosmopolitan.

The evening's shadows were lengthening, and a lot of the street was in deep shade. It was cold out there, from the look of the people as they passed by. Some of the boys were shaking their hands, moving about to keep warm.

The click of the door opening terrified her, and she shrunk back. Was he making her go outside here, what was he going to do? The doors locked down as he closed it, from the outside, and he walked off, leaving her in the car.

...just another cell...

The thought of being locked in a cab with a strange person driving it, distracted her. What if she knocked on the window, and...

...and what? Did she think this was just a normal cab?... idiot...

What if she knocked on the window, and demanded he let her out?

...what if she ended back in the cell on her own for a week, in punishment?

Tears started to stream. She simply wasn't up for this... she knew she was going to crack wide open any second.

The door locks clicking back up, and the door opening made her jump. She didn't scream; was too well trained.

A young man got in the back of the car, and she practically levitated. Jonathan followed in behind the newcomer, and the cab doors locked and they began to move off. Both of them sat down on the back seat, the young male in the middle, beside her. The contact freaked her enough for her to shoot over to the flip down seat, so she was now facing them both, her back to the driver. Jonathan said something in French, and the young boy laughed.

...control it control it control it control it control it...

There wasn't much left to control of anything. They chatted away in French, laughing and smiling, and the completely surreal nature of what was happening started to eat into her. Jonathan was talking about how pretty the boy's eyes were, the boy was totally star struck by him, and just kept giggling. She was sure she was going to start screaming and never stop. Where was she really and was this actually happening? She had a totally physical flashback, and part of her, just for a second, knew she was back in her cell, asleep. She could feel the sheets on her skin. She closed her eyes, and began to lift her knees up to her chin, and to tuck her head down.

'Little one?'

...there was no voice... there was no voice... there was no...

'Open your eyes.'

Her body did as she was told, even as her mind sought refuge in pretend distance.

He was sitting directly in front of her and his left hand was stroking the back of the rent boy's neck. The boy was smiling dreamily.

'Thrall can make them enjoy it.'

Jonathan looked straight into her eyes, and without blinking, pulled the boy down onto his lap.

'Which makes it easy, and therefore much safer. For you.'

He lay there, with that dream look on his face, the back of his head on Jonathan's lap, his legs awkwardly sprawled along the seat and trailing on the floor. She could see that under his thin trousers, the boy had an erection.

'They can have a happy death.'

Jonathan leaned down and licked the length of the boy's Adam's apple. It was awkward in the space, and their eye contact was broken, briefly. She couldn't look away.

'It is such a beautiful thing they do, give life...'

Pulling back slightly and smiling back up at her, Jonathan raised his hand over the throat. She saw the gleam of metal, and he pulled back sharply. Blood welled up. The hand moved again, and the blood gushed over his hand. The boy had not moved, did not protest. Jonathan leaned down, and thrust his face into the gaping wound... and tore the throat out.

She was screaming, she was screaming, she knew she was screaming. She was also punching and kicking the glass, and then there was a tide of blood flowing down Jonathan's legs, and onto the floor, and coming towards her. She moved back up the wall, climbing on to the seat. Still, she could not look away.

He was ripping the boy's neck to shreds, and his hands were covered in thick red blood. The boy was not moving, he hadn't really moved at all, and still Dreyfuss worried at the torn flesh. There was an appalling silence as she stopped screaming, her voice gone in the terror of the image. He looked up, and met her gaze once more, the lower half of his face was covered in blood; thick red clots drooled down and dripped back onto the ruin.

'Would you like to taste, feed your hunger?'

She was screaming again and punching the doors and the glass, and trying to get out. The cab screeched to a halt, and Dreyfuss tipped over the boy's body and fell clumsily to the floor, into the blood pool there.

'Fucking hell!'

He was not happy, as he tried to pull himself up and untangle himself from the boy's body and his hand slipped on the blood and he went down again, his hand hitting the door. As he went down, Joanne heard a 'click; as the driver's door opened behind her. She glanced at the door opposite... it was unlocked. She leapt off the seat, hitting her head badly on the roof, but her hands reached the door handle as she fell down. The door pushed open and she fell out onto hard stone ground. Behind her was a shout of rage.

'*Noooooooo!*'

She scrambled to her feet, and ran.

Her panic took her for several minutes. She was aware that she'd banged her knee and shoulder and hand, falling out the cab, but it didn't matter to her. All that mattered was running. She was on waste ground somewhere and she just kept going, pitching over a couple of times but getting straight back up, awaiting the feel of his hand on her shoulder.

She didn't look back, she didn't think: she just ran. Her lungs gave up first, and a slashing pain in her side buckled her over. She tipped forward and went ass over tip painfully. She sprawled on the cold hard ground and tried to breathe.

Dreyfuss watched her disappear over the waste ground, as he wiped himself down. Mungo and Midge were positioned perfectly, and were tracking her without effort. Mary was swiftly double bagging snacking boy waste. She laid thick towels on the floor: too risky to have fluids drip from the cab as they drove. When the flood was contained, they drove off. The garage was only three streets away. He showered quickly, and changed into street clothes. Mary put the meat into a freezer for later disposal, and hosed out the cab. She would then swap the number plates with its twin prior to returning to the streets in case they needed to pick her up. Not a drop of blood had ever been spilled in the twin. When the chase was over, one of the trio would take the original cab back to Arden Coombe for more sustained cleaning.

Invigorated, Dreyfuss struck out to join the other two. The game was afoot.

Whilst trying to bring her breathing under control, she'd started to cough, and then to vomit pure bile. It burned the back of her throat savagely, testament to her screams. She thought she was going to choke to death before she managed to both stop retching, and breathe properly. Tears coursed down her cheeks. Her hands were caked in dirt and saliva and vomit. The need to get up, and keep running, over-rode everything, and she staggered to her feet, standing in the vomit pool, and set off again. She rubbed her face down with her sleeve, and rubbed her hands down her legs. Ahead of her, the waste ground ended in a chain link fence. On the other side were lights, street lights, and a pretty deserted road. She reached the fence, and realised it was really high, about 8 feet tall. For a second, panic stopped her moving, then she thought she heard something behind her, and took off to the right. There had to be a gate somewhere. A broken section of fencing emerged, and she made it to the pavement. She carried on running, oblivious to the stares and hasty road crossing of any who spotted her. Sweat was dripping of her again and she felt her skin burn with heat.

She would not be caught.

Turning a corner, she ran into a main street, full of commuters walking towards her. She tried to keep running, but only managed to barrel into a couple who hadn't noticed her, and the woman fell to the ground.

'Oi, you stupid bitch, what do you think you're doing?'

But she was off before the man's shout had finished. She dived off to the right again, into a smaller side road. Too many people, too much lighting. The run slowed to a jog, and she carried on pushing. Up ahead, she saw what she needed, what she'd been looking for without really knowing it: a phone box.

It was empty, and she opened the door and buckled over from the waist, her lungs exploding. She tried to slow the rate of her breathing, increase the depth, pull herself under control. Fainting was a real possibility. It took a few moments, moments where she kept expecting the door to open, but she could finally breathe properly, and speak. She looked around to check if he was there, but there were only the swiftly moving walkers, heading home.

She picked the receiver up and dialled 100, then asked the operator to make a reverse charge phone call. She gave the number, and then the operator said

'Who shall I say is calling?'

'Say it's...' she hesitated. 'Say it's...say that J...'

What could she say? How could she phone her mother after all this time, and just say it was her?

'I'm sorry caller, I need a name. Who shall I say is calling?'

She slammed the phone down.

Who shall she say is calling? Who? Tears overwhelmed her. She started to sob. She couldn't she just couldn't. She picked the phone back up. She dialled 999.

'Emergency services, which service do you need?'

'I... I ...'

'Emergency services. Please answer, which service do you require?' Her mouth moved, nothing came out.

'This is the operator. You're calling from call box ...'

She slammed the receiver down, turned and ran.

The running was less frantic. Confusion had her, confusion and turmoil and fear. Tears. Wracking, sobbing, tears. Everyone who came near her, turned and walked to one side. Her crying, the clothes, the dirt, the blotched face and the smell of vomit. She was a junkie, a runaway, a trouble maker looking for trouble. A wide berth was given as she wandered on. She turned again, into a wide street, and found herself once more in the middle of a huge walk of commuters, hurrying out of an underground station. It was Whitechapel. She couldn't make sense of it, couldn't make sense of anything. There was the Tube station, and people hurrying to and fro, and there was here, where she was stood in the street, somehow not quite in the same place as everyone else. She turned back down to the Whitechapel Road, and headed back down into town, wary of getting deeper into the East End.

Whitechapel. After what she had just witnessed... Whitechapel. He did have a sense of humour...

As she slowed, she cooled. The sweat which had drenched her, cooled. The air was cold, the night underway. She started to shiver. Her feet hurt, her back ached, her shins had sharp stabbing pains. Her left knee ached and her left hand burned. She looked, and she had dirt and stones driven deep into the heel of the hand, the blood from the scrape had dried. She needed to pee. Once the thought was in her head, she badly needed to pee. She found a small children's playground, abandoned in the cold evening, and climbed into a hut that formed a platform above a slide. She huddled for comfort, and cried, howling inside but only sobbing gently outside. She didn't want to draw attention to herself.

Eventually, as she began to shiver badly, she had to make her way back down the steps, and find a bush. Pulling her pants down to reveal her naked backside to the world, was so terrifying, she fumbled and much of her pee soaked her right trouser leg. The warmth turned cold, and dribbled into her shoe. She pushed off again, trying to warm herself by walking, ignoring the growing pain in her legs.

There were crowds in the streets as she made her way down Aldwych, unsure of how she'd gotten there. The pubs and clubs were starting to fill and people were in their evening finery. Queues were starting to form outside the theatres. She knew people were looking at her, staring. Everyone moved out of her way as she walked towards them. Two policemen were walking down The Strand towards her, as she crossed the road. She ducked down Savoy St and headed for the Embankment, she'd always loved the Embankment.

Dreyfuss took the lead as she entered the Embankment, sending the others North. She'd hit out North at some point, he was sure.

She staggered around, trying to settle on a bench and catch her breath, but moving off as soon as anyone noticed her. It was still too early to be out in such a state, and the revellers recoiled from her quite openly. He could smell the vomit, urine and fear clearly. Even if he had lost sight of her, she could have been tracked her by scent. She lingered for a long time by the river, crossing over to the Southbank when it started to rain, haunting the various nooks and crannies. A couple of the youths skateboarding, made to make friends with her, but he appeared in the edges of their vision at the right moments, and they backed off. She crossed back over Hungerford Bridge and was heading North by about midnight. She was limping.

She headed straight for Leicester Square, and stood in the square staring into the windows of the steak house he had stolen her away from. It was perfectly delicious, and he was pretty sure where she would go next, so sent Mungo and Mary on to spot out the route. Midge took the other side of the Square.

The Square was home turf to many of the younger drifters and lost children of London, and there were a few anxious moments. Several spotted her distress, and her shock, and began to initiate moves to see if she needed aid or information. She was oblivious to their streetwise overtures however and when one young lad set himself the task of approaching her directly, she bolted into the back alleys of Chinatown. A couple of hustlers, looking for types such as her to befriend and aid into prostitution spotted her and moved in. Midge moved in faster, and they backed off with such speed one of them tripped in the gutter. She left the Square just before the troops arrived with soup, bread and bibles.

The long walk up to Archway took her almost 5 hours. There was the cold, her distress, her getting lost a few times, and frequent stops to rest. Two other stops to urinate, and one to defecate. That had been an almighty drama, and there had been moments where they had all thought she was going to have to be picked up, between the desperate actions on trying to find somewhere safe (impossible) and clean (more impossible) and her general humiliation, which was radiating off her in waves. She had finally given in to nature, in the doorway of an abandoned shop which had a broken hardwood panel flapping off to the side. She had hurried away from her spoor.

At first, she entered every empty phone box she could find, and stood in tears looking at the receiver. Once she had picked it up and replaced it without dialling anything. Another time she placed her hand on the receiver and stood for over half an hour, before leaving the box. As the night went on, she stopped going in to them, or even seeming to notice them.

Dawn was the only time London ever felt less than busy. It was never empty, but at dawn, it always stilled, as if there had to be a moment of indrawn breath before the burst of the day. It was at dawn that she stood in the street and looked up to where she used to live. There was no evidence that whoever lived there now, was resident. No lights were on, although the curtains were closed. She stood for a very long time, and then moved off as the street around her was becoming daytime busy. He was surprised, and somewhat pleased by her next move. She shuffled off around the hospital grounds, and slowly made her way down to Highgate Cemetery, just a few minutes away. It took her a good hour to find her way into the cemetery and settle down for some sleep in the bushes around a very old and deserted area of the necropolis. They discussed it and were confident she would rest there for some hours. Midge elected to stay this round, and the rest returned to Kensington for food and sleep.

Refreshed, he rejoined Midge in late afternoon with Mary, who came out to replace Midge. Mungo would follow later. She had been busy, waking from her sleep at Highgate and making her way over to Hampstead Heath, where there was, it transpired, an old drinking fountain. There were several actually, that he recalled but had been surprised any still worked. Midge reported she had drunk so much so quickly she had thrown up. Hardly surprising given the water was hardly of drinking quality. However, there were also public toilets free of charge. and she soon moved to them. She emerged cleaner, but wetter, and shivering. No hot water, of course.

Water found, food became her focus. Rather intelligently, she had taken empty bottles from the bins, and filled them with water from the toilet taps, so she kept slowly sipping as she limped on. She had also attempted to scrub up but would pay for it as her clothing would still be pretty damp come dark. She garnered a few calories from the park bins, but nothing major. Her hunger was still too tame to overcome her revolt enough to really raid the litter bins dotted around.

Keeping track of her was both easy, and a little tricky, in the parkland. Easy to keep a spot on her, much more difficult to protect her from approach. Dreyfuss brought Mungo in a little early and the three of them triangulated around her immediate vicinity.

It was Mary who alerted him, that as dusk fell, she was in real danger. She had drifted over to the West Heath, some remnant of common sense telling her she was going to be safer in the gay quarter. What she had not considered, was that the West Heath attracted those who would delight in attacking any lone male they found, intent on a good kicking, in modern parlance. They found her instead. Four stalwart skinheads were drinking and 'patrolling', looking for someone to teach a lesson to. They had beer cans in hand, and came across her huddled on a bench. She was too defeated to run, and they were quite openly supportive of her. They offered her a drink from one of the cans, and she accepted. They offered a cigarette, she declined. One offered her a bar of chocolate, which she devoured.

It was terribly predictable. They were a pack and she prey. As darkness fell, the two lieutenants fielded out, and took point on the pathway that passed them. When they were safely in place, the lead skinhead dragged her into the bushes, followed by the young apprentice.

Dreyfuss had made sure he was in place, and had a good vantage point, with Mary just a few feet away. It was a good stroke of luck, so to speak, as it meant he did not have the bother of setting it up, or dealing with her reaction if she subsequently recognised either Mungo or Midge. But it would be crucial to make sure she was not actually harmed and as no knife had made an appearance so far, the odds were good.

The leader took her first, of course, with his hand over her mouth. Then he sent the apprentice off to get his first mate, and he came and took her next. Well trained, she had stopped struggling after a few heavy slaps, and just lay there. This was to the good. When all three of the main players had had their turn, they offered space to the kid. He did not have it in him then, having ejaculated whilst watching the others, but urinated on her instead, making sure he got a stream into her mouth. They laughed as he buttoned up, and they all moved off, the final insult being a beer can emptied over her and dropped on her. He sent his two in pursuit, with orders to maim but not kill. They went off with good humour, Dreyfuss having been sure he had detected the scent of Mary's musk as she watched the sport.

CHAPTER TWENTY

He watched as she lay on the ground, and shuddered into herself. It was cold, bitingly cold, and she was soaked in more ways than one. She was half naked, her jogging pants around her knees, her knickers torn off. They had just pulled up her top and the sports vest over her breasts had survived, but she had both claw marks and bites on her breasts and stomach. She had the two water bottles in the jacket, and she searched around in the pitch dark for them. Then she washed herself out, as best she could, rinsing out her mouth and in between her legs. Then she dressed herself in the sodden garments and limped off. The toilets were shut and locked, but the fountain was running, although in a wide open and exposed area. It was quite dark however, with only a little moonlight through the cloud cover, and she slowly and methodically soaked and rinsed every scrap of clothing, the socks and even her shoes.

She was silent, at all points.

It took a couple of hours, by which time Mungo and Midge had returned; their knuckles in a satisfying state of bruising despite their leather gloves. Mary confided that the young buck leader may never father children and they had left two of them out by the bathing pond. With luck, others would exact more justice: they were too confident of their territory for this to have been their first successful attack.

Joanne was blue with cold by the time she and her clothing were as clean as could be but she did have his blood inside her, and she was nowhere near the hypothermia a normal human would have been in. Vampire blood was in her veins, and it was so clear when you saw her like this. Although it would not help her on feeling cold, yet, and she must be so exhausted that the cold would be like knives in her flesh. Her shoulder injury must be agony. When she was redressed, but totally sodden, with both water bottles refilled, she headed back down to the lights and Hampstead Heath underground.

It began to pour with rain before she reached the streets, and this worked well for her. Wet was wet, and she looked drenched and sodden, but without undue alarm in the casual observer. She pulled up the hood of the jacket and trudged on. He peeled off the chase and went to eat when Mungo arrived to take his point.

They swapped around, fed and rested over the next few hours, as she once more trudged through the streets. Her speed slowed right down, her limping grew worse; there was something wrong with her right foot. Blisters, no doubt. The heavy rain served to keep her both isolated from the few fellow travellers braving the torrent, and to keep her moving. It was impossible to settle, even when she found steam giving evidence of warmth, and she kept to the shadows as much as possible.

She arrived back into the centre in the dead quiet hours. The homeless were battened down in their cardboard boxes and plastic sheeting, the soup vans gone and police and street cleaners in abundance. She ducked and dived as she stripped the bins behind bars and restaurants, working ahead of the cleaning lorries, always evading being noticed at all costs. That pleased him. She had thrown herself into finding food properly, and was devouring any scrap she could find. Inevitably, she threw up. Before dawn began to break she climbed over the fencing at Soho Square, and climbed into a tree: she was learning.

Dreyfuss once more returned to Kensington, accompanied by Midge and Mary. Mungo stayed at the Square, parked up in the cab, where he would escape notice. They discussed her progress and the other two were of the opinion that she would crack that day. Dreyfuss was less sure, and they laid out several possible rotas. It was Friday, and so she was walking into the weekend, which changed the dynamic.

The day dawned clear and unseasonably warm, with quite strong sunshine. Dreyfuss rested until after noon, when Mungo returned for his rest, and then struck out. She spent the entire morning and early afternoon in and around the square, moving only to avoid approach by gardens people or officials. She had successfully managed to somewhat dry out her clothing and to eat, and was toileting and refilling her water bottles at the nearby Tube station.

She spent most of the afternoon dozing upon a park bench in Soho square, soaking up the warmth in classic hobo fashion. Her crumpled and stained clothing carried the look of desperation. The bruising on her cheek and jaw, the still strong smell of vomit and urine and beer that no amount of water would shift without soap, kept all away. Oblivious to the implications, one of her recycled water bottles was a black plastic one that would have held orange squash. It was battered and the label ripped off. She was completely unaware that it made it look as if she was swigging booze like all the other alkies. In the late afternoon, as the sun and warmth again began to fade, she began to stir. A young man entered the gardens from the opposite end to her: a priest. Dreyfuss eyed him warily, he had the energetic feel of one still young enough to believe in the ultimate power of redemption and his own role in that process. He spotted Joanne's distress within seconds, and moved slowly forward, preparing for a full assault of holiness and understanding aid. Dreyfuss tensed, action may just be required. The priest's shadow reached her first, the failing sun lengthening his physical reach. She was still sleepy, and not sure of what was going on, when his shadow blocked the sun from her eyes. He slowed, and sent on a reassuring smile, but before he was within a dozen paces of her, she had startled from the bench and was in the streets like a rabbit escaping a trap. The priest had experienced enough of a cynical world, to know to leave well alone, and he contented himself with a small prayer before passing on to his original task.

Dreyfuss was indeed happy with the day's sport.

She had fled, instinctively, to the tunnel around Centrepoint, where her appearance would not be noticed or commented upon. Huddled by the south stairs, she shook and cried as quietly as she could Commuters passed on quickly, immured to the sight of another pathetic homeless bum cowed down in the tunnels: she did not even have her own sleeping bag. She was too old for any of the tunnel's permanent residents to approach her. She was more likely to be kicked off a prize spot, than accepted. Presently, the sense of danger she had begun to develop, fear of being picked up by the police, moved on, discovered, prompted her to rise and resume her walking. She passed quite close by him as she stumbled up the stairs, and he noticed the cracked lips and clammy skin. He added antibiotics to his list as a precaution. With his blood beating in her veins, it should not be needed, but best to be sure.

She headed down back to the Embankment, a place of infinite possibilities and dangers. Regular patrols were made by the Godly in those areas, handing out cards to present to overnight hostels with dry, warm beds and a team of counsellors. Homeless support workers converged there, eager to get everyone still somewhat salvageable inside, at least for the night. The truly feral were left alone, always. She did queue for hot soup and bread, and gladly took a blanket, but refused to speak or to respond to any other request. Used to this, they just gave her what they had, and left her to her lonely path. *She knew where they were if she wanted them,* and he had observed this mantle of lies as a protector of the charitable, for centuries. It had always made his life much easier, as it did now.

As darkness fell, she was once more on the South Bank, sitting on a bench, looking at the river. She was wrapped in the Salvation Army blanket and had taken her shoes off to rub her feet. There was pain and evident stickiness as she slowly pulled off her socks. She placed her naked feet on the cold paving, perhaps to salve blisters, but replaced the socks gingerly on feeling the cold concrete. She tucked her feet up under her and carried on staring at the lights across the river. The middle of night came and stole her strength, and she lay down on the bench to sleep.

Whilst she slept, another bum crept forward, and slowly, with infinite patience, stole her shoes. It was an impressive performance, taking many measured minutes, and the most delicate and gentle movements, to free them from her hands without waking her. The sleep of the dead, indeed.

The pre-dawn cold roused her, and after a few attempts to wrap her feet into the blanket, she woke to discover her misfortune. Her sobs were audible. She tried to start walking on her socks, but October was turning to November, and the paving was icy cold in the morning air. She sobbed into the blanket wrapped around her, taking comfort in its warmth. Then did the only thing she could do: ripped it into long strips and wound them around her feet. He checked the sky; no sign of rain, she may survive long enough to get back to him. She headed off.

He stayed with her throughout the long, rambling morning. The limping and lurching along was becoming a problem. The loss of her expensive trainers, replaced by rags, changed her status. As she staggered along, he worried someone was going to offer to help, regardless, and he did not want a medic or ambulance being called. Grass was easier to walk on, however, and she meandered through the parks where she was more easily ignored. It was easier to strip bins as well, and the central parks had left over fast food in abundance.

She staggered from St James's Park, to Green Park and crossed Mayfair as the morning was slipping into afternoon. She became completely disoriented in Hyde Park and wandered up from Belgravia, into the north of the park and Speaker's Corner and then had to wander back down again. She was keeping going for longer than even he had thought, and he thought the trio had some grudging respect for her.

As she sighted the Albert Memorial, and used that to navigate, he slipped ahead to prepare.

She kept him waiting. It was hours before she shuffled into the stoop, moving down to the basement entrance. She had shuffled around the Gore endlessly, limping on and hiding in doorways when she could. Evening had started to fall and there had been serious worries that the police would be called to deal with her vagrancy, given the wealth of the housing. The overt CCTV cameras dotted on his building was probably what saved her from being reported. He had noted in the past, the more cameras he put up, the more he could do anything he pleased as it was assumed that someone was watching, and dealing with anything. The entrance to No 1 was already pretty suspicion free, as it was not directly overlooked by any residence, the Hall itself more or less ruining the views from anywhere else in the Gore. Crowds and staff milling in and out of the Hall were not in a position to notice traffic to and from the housing. The shared No 2 stairwell was much less secure, hence why he kept such iron control on the tenants, most were company lets with ever changing executives. The basement level at the base of the stoop that was under the stair way arch to the front entrance, did attract derelicts. But the fire exit doors and the cameras moving to track them as they settled, moved everyone quickly. There had never been any trouble. She had slipped down into the well area with no problem, London crowds, even to the Hall, never took one jot's notice. She stayed there for a long time, however, about two hours, huddled in the corner, before using the keypad to enter what looked like another shared fire escape door, but was one dedicated to No 1. Again, she stayed on the inside for a long time, before key padding into the stairwell. She could have accessed the lift then, but chose not to, and she began the laborious climb up the eight flights of stairs.

He instructed the trio to cease duty and to retire to 'H'. They would overnight there before decamping to Wiltshire. He expected to join them with her, in about a week, but it may take longer.

It was very late in the evening, by the time she dragged herself up the stairs. He had closed the curtaining, and she was enclosed in the vestibule area, the way it had been when he brought her home the first time. She sat, her back on the wall containing the lift, and stared at the front door for another hour or so. Finally, and his impatience had been starting to grow, she let herself in.

He was on the balcony, looking down on her, and she looked up at him in complete silence. She sank to her knees, sobbing. He came down and gently picked her up, and took her up through to the bedroom, carrying her into the wet room shower area. She wept into his shoulder as he carried her, like a heroine being rescued in a fairy tale. He had prepared a chair under the showerhead and some essential supplies. She moaned as he gently unwrapped the rags on her feet. He left the socks on, and placed her feet to soak in warm water and antiseptic, and carried on cutting the rest of the clothing off her, bagging it as he went. She flinched when the warm water hit her, but did not object in any way whilst he washed her down. The lice shampoo would sting eyes badly, so he had to talk her through what he was doing to get her to tip her head back and help. She said nothing when he bade her stand up, take her feet out of the soaking tub, and wash her pubic area with the lice shampoo. She complied as she would normally do and within half an hour she was clean and in a towelling robe. He settled her in front of a sink, again on a chair, her feet immersed, and attacked the mess of her hair, checking thoroughly for infestation. He had been giving her sips of watered down juice as they went and then as he let conditioner soak into her hair, he spooned some warm broth into her. She accepted everything silently, this being an old routine between them. He also allowed her some banana, a yoghurt and a pain killer, after which she brushed her own teeth, violently, and used an entire bottle of mouthwash. Finally, he carefully cut off the socks, and she cried pityingly as he peeled fabric off her abraded skin. Blood blossomed in the bowl when he returned her feet to it and when he wrapped both her feet into a towel, red spotted through. He picked her up and took her to the bedroom, deliberately laying her down on his side of the bed.

Neither of them had spoken a word, apart from the odd command for help from him, given in soft but non-committal terms.

He dressed her feet first having prepared some vials of his blood earlier. He was prepared to take the conventional route with everything else, but he wanted her walking quickly. He pierced the several very ugly blisters and dribbled blood over them before dressing. There was an infected tear of skin around the little toes on the right foot, from repeat blisters being torn open and a weeping sore on the heel. She lay on the bed, staring at the ceiling, not looking as he again treated and dressed. He finished both feet with light bandaging for support. Then he asked her to open her legs, which she refused to do, pulling her knees up, despite how much pain this caused her feet.

'Now.'

He had meant to be kinder to her, he really had. He was exceptionally happy with her few days on the hoof and was proud of her. He knew care and gentleness was worth a lot now, but... he was irritated by the silence. She responded to his tone and instantly opened her legs, but turned her head away from him. He was not rough, but neither was he gentle, as he examined her for damage. Bruising to the thighs, to be expected, no sign of a tear. He lubricated the speculum and as he inserted it, she moaned in fear and her hips rose off the bed in the need to escape. He pressed her down on the stomach and told her to relax her muscles, which was a pretty futile request. She returned to staring at the ceiling, and tears streamed out of her eyes. There was some swelling, some grazing, no tears, nothing to be worried about. He inserted a swab to be sent to the lab, just in case. He withdrew the speculum and moved on up. He soaked her pubic hair in what he knew was a freezing wash, and then dried it off. Then he moved up over her stomach and to her breasts. There was a small line of infection on a deep scrape on her right breast, which he cleaned and covered with a dressing. He cleaned and swabbed the various cuts and bite marks, but there was already some sustained healing. There were no flea bites on her, which was excellent: both in terms of the bedding, and in the signs of how her blood was responding to his. There was a slight infection in her throat, but hydrating and eating well would likely deal with that. He told her to sit up, slowly, and pull down the top of her robe, which she did. He backfilled the syringes in front of her.

'This one is an antibiotic, just in case.' He injected her in the upper arm. 'You shall require three more, but this will be enough for 48 hours.'

He swabbed down the other arm, as the next one would probably leave a bruise.

'This is to prevent conception, just in case.'

He knew from her cycle, there was little chance of anything like that, but she probably did not know this, as she seemed as woefully ignorant of her body as all modern women appeared to be. She tensed as the needle went in, and he had to grab her upper arm to stop her flinching back.

He disposed of the needles on the bedside cabinet, where the supplies were laid out, and turned back to face her. She was flushed an angry red, her fury flaring out at him. My my, temper temper. She knew that he knew, and she was rage, and poison, and aggression. It was delectable.

He should have resisted, he knew that, but it was so tasty, what she was offering him. He responded with light mocking tones and a wry smile.

'I was not aware that you liked skinheads, if you had simply asked...' his voice trailed off in mock invitation.

She flew at him. He was completely unprepared for it, and her body slammed into him and pushed him backwards, he fell, with her shrieking fury driving down into him. She punched and hit and screamed and used her knees to drive into his lower body when the pain in her feet prevented kicking. It was utterly divine and completely refreshing and sheer exhilaration. His laughter rose up, which drove her even more.

'You bastard, you complete bastard, I hate you!'

The words were fired like bullets, and he responded with more laughter. This was so much fun he was actually getting an erection, with her writhing on top of him like that. Oblivious to everything in her rage, she drew herself up and straddled him, her robe completely open. He found himself appreciating the view just as she drew her right hand back and punched him hard on the face.

Ouch!

He had felt it, so it was quite a strong blow. It hurt her hand badly, and she folded down to cradle it. He took advantage and grabbed her shoulders and pushed her over onto her back, flipping himself up and over, his body completely covering hers. Trapped under him, she reacted simultaneously defensively, and aggressively. Her eyes flashed rage and poison and she screamed in denial of him. Her body tried to curl under and turn away. Her hands started to flail out, and he trapped them both on either side of her head. Their faces were only a few inches apart. He was still greatly amused and totally enjoying her tantrum. She spat in his face, which thrilled him less. He let it drip back onto her, which sent her into spasms of rage once more. Her breathing was ragged, her pulse and blood pressure going through the roof and her strength waning. Adrenaline would only take you so far and she was starting to physically suffer for her anger.

'I would calm down if I were you.'

She tried to swallow her anger and failed. She spat the words out without thought, seeking only to wound him in any way.

'At least they were men and not a fucking eunuch!'

His amusement carried on. 'Oh, is that correct?'

She was aware she'd done something incredibly stupid, dimly, at the back of her brain where the fire alarms were ringing, but her anger was still too strong too clear, too direct.

'Fuck you!' Everything in her that rejected him, spewed out in the words.

His face calmed and stilled, and the mocking stopped. He gazed down at her anger for a heartbeat, then acted. Springing up from her body, he picked her up from the floor, and tossed her like a rag doll onto the bed, she landed face down, and began to scramble away. Her ankle was caught by him, and she was pulled back down the length of the bed and flipped over. He was taking off his belt and she screamed and tried to crawl away, but his knee came down on her thigh and trapped her. He finished unfastening his trousers and leaned over her so she could see the size and strength of his erection. As her head twisted away, he pushed down into her open legs and was fully in her in one long stroke. She was caught awkwardly on the edge of the bed, splayed out in a diagonal, and he was able to make good use of his position to ram into her to absolute depth.

'Always. A. Pleasure. To. Oblige. A. Lady.' Each word was given at the end of a ram.

Her mind folded up and tried to fly away, her body tried everything to escape… to no avail.

… stupid bitch… stupid bitch… stupid bitch… look what you've done now, you stupid bitch…

The worst of it was that it was completely dispassionate. He carried on, relentlessly, with no anger or turmoil, no seeming involvement in the occasion. It was what he was doing, and that was that. He was unstoppable, and whenever he came, or flagged, he simply leant down and plunged his teeth into her, drinking her life back up into himself, and carried on. It just did not stop. When she was raw and bleeding at the front, he picked her up, turned her over and entered at the rear, using her own blood and his semen as lubricant. On and on and on, until she felt herself tear and she spasmed in agony. She couldn't scream much, as her face was buried deep in the bed and breathing was the trouble. When his rhythm faltered, his mouth found the back of her neck and he took more blood. Each blood taking had been hurt and sharpness and pain, and then the return to the pounding, pounding, pounding. She could feel his engorgement rise within her again, as he drank. He withdrew when he was hard as stone and simply turned her over and slid her onto the floor, so she was sitting upright against the bed. He pushed himself into her mouth as she gasped for air, so she was tasting her own shit mixed with blood and his sperm. He deep throated her so swiftly, she didn't have time to gag and her head was pushed straight back onto the bed edge as he carried on pummelling into her, his feet on the floor by her own hands, his hands on the bed either side of her head. She thought she was going to suffocate but he knew what he was doing and although her neck and throat were in agony, she could breathe through the awfulness of it, although the smell in her nostrils was unbearable. There was no question of trying to fight when he was lodged in her like this and she went completely limp.

He appeared to come again, and withdrew, and then, as his penis moved back up and out of her throat, the explosion of vomit came and she sprayed the floor and him with everything in her.

He waited until she was empty and dry retching, picked her up and walked her back to the showers. He pushed her back onto the chair and hosed himself, and her, clean, hosing out her mouth and between her legs. Then he pulled her to her feet, pushed her over the sink, and entered her vaginally from behind, and pounded away. Her head came up as he grabbed her hair and she was faced with the image of him raping her with a calm and contented smile on his face. She tensed, and anger started up again, and her reward was for him to withdraw and plunge into her raw and bleeding anus on one savage stroke. She writhed and screamed and he let go her head to fasten her hips to the sink with his hands, whilst he carried on and on and on. She'd started to beat the sink and mirror with her fists, and to bash her own head down on the porcelain, such was the awful tearing pain. He grabbed her hands and fastened them behind her with one of his, and then he grabbed her hair again to bring her head back up to the mirror. She was completely trapped; powerless: possessed.

She closed her eyes and crawled into a hole inside herself and simply left the scene.

It was blood loss that determined he stopped. By that time, she was pretty near unconscious anyway, and he let her fall to the floor from where he'd had her pinned up against one of the wardrobe doors. Her body was a welter of bites and bruises under a shining red sheen of sweat, blood and darker streaks of excrement. Blood flowed from between her legs, clinging thickly to everything it touched. He left her there, breathing laboriously, whilst he stripped the bed off and threw everything into another room. Then he showered himself clean and sluiced her down for the what... fourth... fifth time?

That would teach her.

CHAPTER TWENTY-ONE

Her draped her out on the bed on a thick layer of towels and slipped a line into her am. He shot morphine into her buttock, sending her to oblivion. Then he put the needle in his own veins and pulled back. He filled the saline bag with three shots of his blood, checked her breathing and went to get himself some food. He was ravenous.

She was torn up pretty bad, but the blood worked its magic, and by the time she showed signs of rousing about 30 hours later, she was bruised and tender and sore, but more or less physically healed. He kept the line in for a long time, and had made sure she was fully hydrated, having donated a bit more blood to the cause along the way, before he took it out. Worried by the lack of calories, he put a feeding tube in briefly and made sure she had plenty of nutrition and fibre. He had shot her through with a great deal of morphine, as his blood would fight against its effects.

He then set about cleaning up the mess: a laborious and boring and annoying task, as the master bedroom in No 1 was not designed for this service. This should not really have happened in here, and it was not what he had planned. Not at all. He had planned gentleness and compassion and seduction. He had planned reward. When she finally staggered into the Atrium, he should have been an old friend, quietly anxious for her, and pleased she was safe. Comfort and healing, as she came to terms with her lot in his life.

The anger though... her anger had been deeply satisfying and very welcome. Her strength was quite surprising, considering her ordeal on the streets. She impressed him, and excited him, and pleased him. Now to bring her to her own true strength, even more. They would recover from what had been done, what he had done. After all it was only out of sequence, that was all. The lessons would have to have been learned, regardless, if she was to survive her Turning.

The thought that it had not been about *her* anger, he pushed to one side. The thought that it had been his need to possess her, to take her in all ways after the skinheads... to mark her in every way as his... to prove she was of his blood and therefore take anything he decided she could take, in any way he wanted... that, he also pushed to one side. That he had wished to own her, completely, to satisfy his own needs... that he refused to see. Thus, he committed the final obscenity, unawares.

As she began to rouse, he had slipped into bed with her, so she did not wake alone. His intent had been to console and comfort her, and to be what she needed: a gentle human touch. That she had no need of

214   *Morgan Gallagher*

such, of anything to do with him at all, had not occurred to him. He had done worse physically and still she had woken gratefully to his arms. That she had begun to fight with him, before fully awake, did not unduly disturb him. It had happened before, and he had taken her rightful return to him under her own direction as the sign that she was won. She was broken to his hand.

So the strength of panic and avoidance and fear she displayed as she came up through the layers of healing sleep, caught him unawares. He found himself struggling with her, physically having to hold her from harm, before she shed the last of her sleep. After the responses he had driven from his own body, in order to break hers, the struggle aroused him. For every measure of her panic, he matched her in need, and by the time she was fully awake, he was locked in a tussle for her body, as much as her obedience. As she struggled, he used thrall upon her, to calm her to his touch. She softened under him, and moved from fear and panic, to pleasure and longing. This pleased him, soothed him, and, once more denying it had anything to do with his own needs, he raped her again, this time filling her with all his sweet and subtle powers, to bring her to maximum enjoyment: he took her mind as well as her body.

Thus, they were locked in a complete eye line embrace, their minds matched, when he came and brought her to simultaneous orgasm. Deep in thrall, with him using far more of himself than he suspected to control his own feelings and thoughts, he revealed his true state to her, when she was as deeply in his mind as she had ever been, or was ever likely to be.

In the most primitive parts of her own mind, under his hypnosis, Joanne had been fighting every move and every advance. Her rage could only take her so far, however, as the shock and trauma of the previous few days were locked into her bones. Shock written so large upon her, that it caged much of her sense of survival. With the traces of morphine in her system, she had sat back, powerless, and watched her body react with pleasure to his call, and had sat in the ashes and dust of her psyche. When she awoke, she would not remember the strength of her resistance. Like all abused, she would concentrate on her weakness, and torment herself with how her body had yearned for his touch. How it had responded to his embraces, even as he opened freshly healed wounds within her, and blood flowed out of her once more. She would flit back between this rape, and his fingers bringing her to orgasm just a few days earlier. How she had need of him inside her, and how she had gotten what she deserved. She would dwell on how complete and overwhelming, and welcome, her physical orgasm had been, not how much her mind had desperately fought to prevent it. He was the stronger. Her will, like her body, fell to his control, and she would blame herself first and foremost for the rest of her life.

With his gaze locked so deeply with her own and her so ravaged by violence and fear and hunger, his preternatural will conquered all her conscious mind, tearing into her thoughts and feelings. He deliberately connected with her longing and hurts, promising sanctuary in his own touch: *come with me and I will make you safe.* Her body responded to his call and her mind blossomed as she came, reaching out to him for communion and absolution. They connected, wholly, honestly, and without barrier, in the endless timeless moment of shared orgasm.

She slipped into his mind more thoroughly than he had ever managed in hers. Whereas she had always blocked him from her true thoughts, she was suddenly privy to his.

In his eyes, she saw all he was: his pain, the devastation, the loneliness and the hurt. The betrayal that drove him and the terror that blighted every part of him. She rose above her own body and mind and fear, and looked deep into his. Her heart, which was warm and human and exceptional, responded to the bitterness and loneliness it witnessed. She connected completely with his devastation and loss.

For his part, she became someone else, in the fleeting moment of transfer, in the moment of infinite dance, he saw only whom he wished to see. She was what she had always been, a simple cipher, a vessel for his image of someone else. In the immediate aftermath of the pleasure, she was overwhelmed by sorrow, pity and compassion, her own situation swept away for the moment, as she had seen the hollow in his soul. She reacted to another human being also in endless, awful, pain… with compassion and tears. She showed him sorrow for his loss, sorry so strong and so complete, that for that one long second, he could see her clearly.

The expression in her eyes was too much for him. No heart beat could contain that look within his soul, and no breath speak of it. He rejected her eyes, and her compassion, and the warmth faded until all he could see was fire, and death. Her features melted into another face entirely. Eléan lay under him, laughing and mocking as she demanded he service her again and again and again… or suffer the consequences. The physical memory, as he felt her hands, her knives, upon his body, and smelt her harsh breath upon his face, was so complete, so absolute, he threw himself off her, tears streaming from his eyes, his erection withered by terror. The memory of what once had been was locked in his body, and rode him as hard as she ever had: he ran.

The leaving of her, at that moment in her journey, wrought the worst damage of all. She had come to an ending within her own mind, where she felt she could sink no further, and then had been betrayed again by her own body. She had come back to this place of her own accord, and he had given her what she deserved. In her desolation, she had seen through into his humanity, and responded as one human being to another, in the most desperate of circumstances. She had felt real concern for him, for one moment, one heartbeat. She had somehow reached past what he'd done to her to see him as something other than a monster. He had left her, abruptly, and left a body that sang with the imprint of him and had cherished his touch... empty. That thought, the thinking of that as something to be sorrowful over, something that was lost and empty, crashed through the endorphins, shattered the remnants of the thrall and the morphine. The despair and her own pain came crashing down and engulfed her.

Self disgust and loathing lit through her. How could she... how could she have come back... how could her body have...? She turned away from it, from herself, but the pain could not be denied, could not be swallowed. Unable to deal with the now, her body moved her back to similar moments, and the memories this sort of pain wakened within her. The brief moment of connection with him had only brought her back to her own primal pain and longing; her own loss. She turned into the pillows and sobbed, the heart-broken sobs of a child who has just been told her father was dead and there would never be another moment of happiness in her life. A child who would have given anything for someone, anyone, to hold her, and rock her gently as they sang lullabies into her ear, softly stroking her hair. A child who had smelt her father's aftershave in her dreams, and had cried afresh every morning, when she'd woken and found he was no longer there.

In the dark hole of the cell, he cowered, sweating and rank and naked.

...I will get hold of this... I will get hold of this... I will get hold of this...

His hands gripped and twisted incessantly. He would get hold of this, and he would tear her out of him again. She was dead, and he had killed her, and he had won. HE HAD WON.

...I will get hold of this... I will get hold of this... I will get hold of this...

His voice echoed against the cell walls.

Her sobs died, as they always did, and her broken heart kept beating, as it always did. Her body was in pain, and the pain awakened her to herself, as it always did. The pain was mostly a sharp stabbing between her legs, and finally, resignedly, she had to attend to it. Every time, when she was driven to this level of despair and bleakness, wrapped in pain and shame and misery and all hope had died... she wondered the same thing: why not just kill herself? Why not end it here, and now, and simply kill herself, and let it be over?

Every time previously, the thought had been alien, and dead, and somehow redundant. What would that mean, really? That he had won, and she would never allow that. That she would have escaped? Hardly, she'd be dead, not free. Lying there, this morning, this pain, this overwhelming damage... she knew parts of her were broken, she could feel their loss... she knew he'd broken her, and killed bits of her, and she was lost... she knew she still couldn't do it. It sounded sensible, and safe, and *desired*, for the first time. She could see the sense in it, this day, when she'd not ever seen that before. It was *sensible...rational...her only escape...* but it was stupid. It was empty and hollow and useless.

A bit like her.

Death was not an answer. He'd won, and taken her, and broken her, and it still wasn't an answer. She'd accepted what he was, and that she was his, for him to toy and play with, but that wasn't the same thing as taking her own life. Not at all. She had nowhere to go: that was true. And that nowhere, included death. Death was nowhere for her to go. Death was what had happened to that young boy... and that was not part of her, and she would have no part of that. So death was out. Utterly.

And therefore getting out of bed, and attending to the pain in her body, was in. There was blood everywhere in the bed, and between her legs, but it appeared to have stopped. The pain increased as she stood, but steadied a little as she waddled to the toilet. Her feet were sore and tender, but in between her legs hurt more. Peeing was agony, and stang viciously. She ran a shower, and forced herself to stay under it, before forcing herself to get dressed. Naked was not an option.

As she bent over to pull up her knickers, fresh blood spotted them. All the bathroom contained were tampons, and that was so not happening. She stuffed two face cloths into her pants, and then put on a pair of trousers. She was shaky and scared and in pain and... she needed food. She needed food, and she would have some. The little kitchenette was always well stocked with fruit and pastries, and she sat and pushed them into her mouth and swallowed them down with juice. She barely tasted anything, but her body was so hungry and she needed food. She would have food.

She was tired of being hungry.

The terrible call for sustenance that had completely overwhelmed her, abated somewhat. How bad she felt was allowed in, and it was not a blessing. Her body was wasted and ravaged, in all sense, and tears sprang into her eyes as she contemplated the bleakness of her life, and the pains in her body. Her life was his and a pitiful life it was. It was, however, the only life she had. She made her way downstairs, to see if there was meat in the kitchen.

He was gone for three days. Two nights. She spent the time eating and staying warm. Huddled up on a couch, watching movies, a warm blanket around her. She sat in the flickering dark, drinking hot chocolate and ignoring the tears that slid down her face. She washed her body a great deal, but resisted it becoming a compulsion. She moisturised with every expensive potion and lotion she was supplied with. The bleeding and the pain between her legs, stopped. Her feet still felt tender, but were otherwise perfectly healed. Every time she dressed, she contemplated moving her belongings into one of the other bedrooms, but decided it would be a futile move. She slept only when she passed out with tiredness, and slept where she fell. She'd waken, wash, change clothes and carry on reading, eating, sipping soup and watching movies. She spent an entire afternoon gazing down at the traffic flowing past in clogged streams of impatience.

He appeared late on the afternoon of the third day. He was just there, as if he'd never been gone. She had been in the main kitchen, eating a plate of cold roast chicken, when he sat across from her at the work unit. She said nothing, and he said nothing, and they both said nothing together as they ate.

Later on, when she was changing into night attire, she took the black purse out of the jewellery carousel, and slowly and carefully signed every credit card.

She was no longer Joanne.

They slept without touching, or speaking, at separate ends of the wide bed. If he noticed that she did not creep towards him in the night, needing the comfort of human touch as she slept, he did not mention it.

The next morning, after breakfast, he asked her to pack an overnight bag, and bring what things she'd need for a weekend. She was so far in shock, it never occurred to her to be scared, or fearful, or even amazed at the instruction. It was just what he said and therefore just what she did. Whilst she packed into the matching luggage that he'd brought from the wardrobes in the spare rooms, he settled some final business in his office.

She showered and dried her hair, the cut ensuring it would look good, although the roots needed done, and then dressed and packed. Filling a case was easy, choosing what to take, more difficult. She took more toiletries than clothing, making sure the best of the creams and lotions went with her.

She genuinely did not wonder where she might going. For all she knew, it was back to the apartment, and this was just another cruel test.

She was at a loss on what to do with all the jewellery. Trays of it, and surely he'd intended her to pack or wear some of it? She'd dressed in simple black linen trousers, with a black knit ribbed cashmere sweater, and an oatmeal jacket in raw silk. Understatement coupled with impeccable style and tailoring. Without jewellery, she was unfinished, and that would be noticed if they were going out.

Why was she thinking of such things...? How were these thoughts in her head? She put it aside to think on later, and returned her attention back to the trays. Her experience on the streets was something that would be obliterated by luxury and comfort: she was determined about that. He had money; she would take advantage of it.

Finally, she put on simple gold earrings that were just a bar with a Celtic knot design, a gold chain, a very slender gold bangle around her wrist. The earrings took a fiddle to get in, and she realised her ears had almost healed, so long had it been since she'd worn anything in them. The array of rings was so overwhelming, she just couldn't think what to do. She fetched gloves, scarf, and shoes in a complementing coffee and cream colour, and sorted through the handbags for something that matched the outfit. As she knew it would be, a small clutch purse that was the exact colour of the gloves and shoes, emerged from the shelves. She switched the scarf to a cream that matched the jacket. It occurred to her she had only packed indoor things, but really, was that going to be a problem?

She placed the black purse with her cards and the pen, in her clutch bag. The pad would not fit. As an afterthought, she returned to the toiletries and packed make up, which she had missed, and selected a lipstick to match the outfit. She smeared her lips and then dropped the stick into the clutch bag.

He entered the bedroom as she finished, and he stopped and looked her up and down. It was the appreciative glance of a man to a woman. She did nothing, but waited silently for her instructions. He studied her for a moment, then moved to the jewellery drawers. He flipped a couple of trays, before selecting. In the silence that was to be a feature of the next few days, he lifted her left hand, and slipped a gold ring with single sapphire onto her ring finger. As she looked at it, she realised her hands and nails were a mess. No one with any sense at all, would be fooled by her clothes, when they were worn by someone with those hands.

'I need a manicure.' He examined her hand, and then bent down to kiss it.

'That can be arranged.'

He then picked up her case, and walked out the bedroom; she followed three steps behind.

She was a little surprised when they turned right as they left No 1, and turned into the back street again. Her heart lurched at the thought the black cab would be there. It wasn't, and he beeped his key ring at a smart silver sports coupe, Mercedes Benz, parked right by the corner. He placed her case in the boot and opened the passenger door for her. As she seated and clicked the seat belt, she had fancied they were going to drive to a railway station, and board a steam train. It was a moment of fancy in a long drive.

When he started the car, music started up: something soft, soothing and classical. Then he drove out from the shadow of the Albert Hall Mansions, turned into the traffic, and headed West.

CHAPTER TWENTY-TWO

The drive was quite uncomfortable. It wasn't the silence, which was fine, and it wasn't the seating, which was plush. It was being outside, and seeing so many people, and travelling past so much life. The car also appeared to be moving extremely fast, even in built up areas: when was the last time she'd travelled in an actual car? She genuinely could not remember. It was also unsettling as she had no clue where they were heading. All she knew of London was going North and exiting from either train or bus station. The bus she'd taken 'up' to the Big City, had driven in via the M1. She'd never travelled outside London, in any other direction than back up North.

She studied the sign posts as they made their way out, and finally they hit a flyover and climbed onto the M4. She'd heard of the M4, dimly, and had known from the signs that it was 'The West' they'd been heading for.

It gave way to green and countryside very quickly, and they zoomed along. Traffic wasn't heavy, and it thinned as they passed, and he cruised at roughly 80 miles an hour, only slowing slightly at junctions. The trees were in the last fall of autumn, and the countryside looked empty and worn around its damp and muddy edges. She thought she should be enjoying the sight of open land, but she wasn't, and once more the sky was too big and threatened to crush her. Everything started to blur in green and grey snatches, as they sped on.

Afterwards, when she'd learned this route so well, she wondered about how she'd not noted the names of the town as they passed, that first trip. But she'd been oblivious until he'd indicated they were turning off, and they dived down left towards Hungerford. It was a name she had never heard before, and that it was written on the road signs, as they passed, shocked her. All she could see was 'Hunger', and she wondered again that he owned part of Kensington Gore. Did he was also own part of a place that started with the name 'Hunger'?

They turned right and drove through a series of buildings and some such, that suggested a village, or a series of villages, and then were back through once more to open countryside. The road was wide, and winding, and dotted with pubs and hamlets and strange and curious sights. It was all very Enid Blyton and Agatha Christie, and there were lots of thatched cottages. They entered a long stretch of road, bordered by dense tree cover on either side. The sign said 'Savernake Forest'. She almost spoke, such was her fascination, but he slowed and indicated left, and then turned into the forest itself. Signs on the roadway warned this was private property, and others that the Forestry Commission took a dim view of damage to their trees. They finally turned into a long and narrow driveway, that didn't seem to lead anywhere. The reveal was after a few moments drive, up and round to the left, and suddenly, there it was: a country mansion fit for any murder mystery one could envisage in the depths of gentrified England.

'Welcome to Arden Coombe.'

Exactly as the stereotype demanded, he drove his sports car to the front of the drive by the steps, and got out. He then went round to open the passenger door for her. She was stiff, and bursting for the loo, and it was awkward to get out. He did not hold out his hand, and she did not look for such. The smells that flowed over her were utterly alien. The air was raw with cold that was never really felt in London, and it was clean with green undertones, like moss. She was never aware of smelling trees and bushes in London, no matter how big the park. The silence was startlingly loud. Their footsteps on the gravel were amazingly sharp and distinct. When she was on her feet, he led her to the front door. The building was very large, and square, with two floors and small dormer windows on the roof. Above the small portico of the doorway was a large triangular section of wall extended from the roof, containing a circular window. It was the window of all childhoods, a window to look out onto gardens and see the world and read books beside. An attic window of mystery and adventure. She'd read many murder mystery books as a young adult, and the window she was now looking at had always been part of her dreams. One story, she couldn't remember which one now, had a house like this with a large wall around it, and all you could see from the bus that passed by... was the circular window set in a triangular arch. Over the years, when she'd caught sight of such a window... she'd sighed with longing and desire for money and wealth, and an attic with a circular window that looked out over the drive.

He touched her elbow, a gentle reminder to move on, and she shook herself out of the reverie. The house was still waiting for her, and she stepped forward. There were about five steps up into the main doorway, and green something or other plants had grown thickly around the wall on the ground floor. Shaped green bushes, round as balls, were in pots along the front line of the building. They went inside, to a glorious and quite breathtaking cream and gold hallway with marble flooring and ornate plasterwork on the walls. Centre to the square, and going up to the first floor, was a huge wooden staircase. Her eye-line naturally followed its lines as it ascended, and so moved to view the ornate plaster ceiling, with its rich load of leaves, vines and grapes, all painted in cream. A massive central rose held a crystal chandelier. He moved up the stairs, and she followed, her feet sinking into the thick mustard coloured carpet that ran up the centre of the treads. At the top, he took the right fork as the stairs split into two sides. On the balcony he entered the single set of elegant double doors that were centred exactly in the wall. She entered the main bedroom, which had a double aspect… and it was simply beautiful.

Despite the formal features and the ornate plasterwork, the whole room was elegant and simple and utterly charming. A very modern look and feel that echoed the comfort of the living room at the apartment – low modern furniture and simple lines in lemon, cream and white. Thick cream curtains framed the windows, and she realised what was attracting her so much to this room: there were no nets obscuring the view. The windows were tall and wide, and split into layers of squares. She knew it had to be a period style, but hadn't a clue what it was. It was not the Georgian of Albert Hall Mansions. The room contained four massive windows, two over the front of the drive, and two at right angles, the outside wall, facing out over gardens and woodland. The large bed was centred between the windows facing the front of the house. Elegant furniture also made the room a sitting area, with two armchairs and an occasional table in the space made by the other windows. The bottom left wall was a line of fitted wardrobes, floor to ceiling, with simple panelling that echoed the room's lines. Two doors were on either side, matching perfectly the symmetry of the room and the windows. She knew one would be an en suite.

'May I go to the bathroom?' She indicated the doors.

'Right door.'

It led into a small rectangular bathroom with more windows, but smaller and higher up and facing out to the back gardens, which were more domestic than the formal gardens at the front and to the side. Once a walled kitchen garden, if she knew her television gardening knowledge well. She tipped toed up to peek out. The forest was very close at the back of the property. No doubt how she had not spotted the house as they curved around up the slope into the dip this house was nestled in. The bathroom itself was a perfect study in making a small size function elegantly. It had double sinks and mirror splash back, toilet and a triangular bath with jets in the sides, tucked in the corner underneath the back window. White had taken precedence in the smaller space, with touches of lemon. His usual taste in marble had been abandoned in favour of immaculate white tiling. Everything was very modern, and very perfect.

When she returned to the bedroom, he helped her off with her jacket, and opened the right hand side wardrobes. They contained a scattering of random outfits, which she knew would fit her perfectly.

She left her bag, gloves and scarf in the closet, and also slipped off her shoes. He had done the same, and was actually padding on the thick cream carpet on bare feet. She had hose on under her trousers, so that wasn't an option for her. He opened a drawer to reveal a line of house slippers, all in her size, obviously. She slipped on a plain black pair that reminded her of her gym shoes at school, had gym shoes been made of silk and bottomed in soft leather.

He casually opened the other door in the wall of wardrobes to reveal the wet room that contained the double shower, with a glass panel that slid over a towelling area. She just peeked in. In was an entirely dark cream coloured marble with white veins running through it, apart from the brown flooring which was some sort of in-dented rubber. It was very masculine, in contrast to the bathroom, which had been light and delicate. He closed the door and moved them out of the bedroom, across the balcony the long way (to avoid having to go down some stairs and back up). The mirror image of the double doors that had entered the main bedroom opened into an interior hallway. He took her into the first room on the right, which faced the back of the building. This was the real dressing room and was very similar in design to the units at No 1. Centre to the room as you walked in, tucked under the windows, was a double vanity unit. The right side of the room was for the male, the left, the female. This was a house for whom the word 'symmetry' had been invented. The doorway they'd entered was recessed, to accommodate the storage on either side, and when she walked in, she found that storage doors were mirrors, to add to the light and to aid dressing. The room was utterly neutral in colour – it matched the oatmeal of the jacket she'd just taken off. She supposed that was a blank canvas, for the clothing.

He looked at her with that look that said 'Be smart. Say something smart.' She didn't need to think of what to say as she'd been working it through in her head any way.

She walked to the bottom right hand corner of the room and examined the wardrobes. Yes, there it was. Inside the bottom corner unit, was a small spiral staircase, leading up.

'Very good. You may go up.'

She didn't actually want to go first, but now had no choice. It was a very tight squeeze. So small and tightly wound was the stairwell, obviously bespoke and in white wrought iron, that you had to keep going up after you went up through the ceiling level, and move out of it sideways, into a doorway opening. She entered into the back corner of the attic space that held the circular window.

It was also his office. A single large space, that ran from the three dormer windows of the back wall, all the way up to the circular window.

…that was the word, lattice, all the windows were latticed... was that right...?...

The space was immense, but didn't feel threatening as the roof was much lower, and filled with his usual office equipment. It was also in clean white lines, and... the circular window actually had a boxed window seat built around it. She had to move into the room to allow him to enter behind him.

'The other staircase is slightly off set, to avoid the shower room.' He pointed to another panel on the opposite wall. The concealed storage he favoured lined the back half of the room. The other hidden stairwell would be in there, somewhere. He flipped overhead lights on, and the brightness and simplicity of the lines became apparent.

'It's very beautiful.'

'Yes, it is.'

She was drawn to the upper half of the wall at the circular window end, which was covered in a series of prints and paintings. They were all of houses or forest. Two oil paintings were side by side, one of an Elizabethan type mansion, and the other, the house they stood in. The older one had 'Arden Coombe' written under it, and the modern one 'Arden House'.

'That was the original house I had built here.' He pointed to a smaller ink drawing to the far left. 'I had the land for a long time, and finally built a house on it. That was the first...' It was a small single storey house, perhaps a large cottage really, with a thatched roof. 'Then came the Elizabethan Mansion, and then... the house as it is.'

'Arden Coombe... Arden House?' She looked quizzically at him.

'Coombe means a little piece of land that has a hollow in it. Or rather, Coombe is the hollow. This land in the forest, had this coombe. When I built a house, I named the house 'Arden', after the Forest of Arden, Arden Coombe.'

He enjoyed explaining it all out, and also referred to a smaller charcoal and ink line drawing on the opposite wall. 'When this present house was built, 'coombe' was old fashioned and not of the times, so it was referred to as Arden House. There is also the farm estates, all named Arden Coombe. There is Arden Coombe Lodge too. The estate remained Arden Coombe, really, when the main residence changed to Arden House. I never think of it as Arden House. It is either Arden Coombe, or Arden.'

She examined illustrations of farms and farm houses and workers clearing forest by hand.

'The de-parking drawings are probably the most valuable, actually. No one recorded real work, in those days.'

His every action and word was about reinforcing his age, and power. If anything, he had more of both, here, than at Albert Hall Mansions. He was letting her know that from the outset. That was why they'd come more or less straight up here, and why the lecture.

...everything is just a bigger cell...

She returned to the framed oil of Arden House. Nothing seemed to have changed since this painting, well, from her brief glimpse of the front anyway. From drawings that were framed and displayed lower down, she could see there had been an extension added to the back of the house. She went back to the dormer windows and peeked down. There, on the left, the Victorian extension from the plans made the back of the house into an L shape. She returned to the painting. It was signed, and dated, in the mid 1700s. She played to his ego.

'What style is it?'

'English Baroque is the more correct term, but some refer to it as 'Queen Anne', as she was on the throne when it was built.'

She nodded, but did not have a clue about anything he'd said. She'd have to work on this slowly. Was there going to be help in the attics?

'Of course, at the time, it was just 'in the new style'. All the houses I have built have been in 'the new style'. This one was new style classical, really. Anne was not on the throne when I began the commission, but she was when it was finished, just.'

'Oh.'

'I did not commission the oils until the house had settled, and I was sure I was going to keep it like this.'

She said nothing... what was there to say?

'We should go down and eat, the staff are waiting.'

His words fell through her world like a stone plunged into deep water: swiftly, silently, and with maximum impact beneath the surface.

There was, from that point on, a surreal quality that made thinking, moving, breathing... very hard. He took her down the 'real' stairwell, which was at the end of a corridor which mirrored the one below, splitting the attic office in two. Smaller rooms led off from them, just as they had downstairs. She almost stumbled twice, as she descended, the dreamy sense of not being there fudging out the detail of the world she moved in.

As ever, she was delectable. And delicious. And very very smart. He had made a small bet with himself that she would sniff out the staircase in minutes, and had been right. She was thoroughly and completely inducted into basic survival habits in terms of accommodation. All those lessons in the attic had been fruitful. She naturally thought 'Where is the escape?' at every juncture. She knew he would put them in, that was one level of good... but she was also seeing where and why they would be in that place. That was very satisfying.

All she could see in the kitchen was the three people standing there. A man and two women. No, that was wrong, it was a woman and two men. She closed her eyes for a moment, and took a deep breath. Yes, two men and a woman. They were standing, somewhat stiffly, on the other side of a large workspace in the middle of the kitchen. Faced with other people, real people, in front of her, in a domestic space... with him...

...what nice flowers on the table...

He signalled to the three to come forward. They did so as servants, keeping their hands to their sides and not offering a hand shake. His little one was clearly unable to respond anyway, but it did please him that they were so impeccably presented.

'This is my lady, Helene. However, I do not think that she will require that you call her Madame?' He raised an eye to them all, and referred back to Helene for guidance. She didn't react.

'Perhaps Miss Blanchard...?' Mary spoken in quiet and reassuring tones, and gave a show of a quiet and unassuming smile.

'I think Helene would be best. Helene, this is Mary...' Mary made a slight head bow and smiled, then stepped back.

'Then Mungo,' Mungo, who was the more taciturn, remained quite motionless, 'and Midge. Midge is slightly shorter than Mungo, if that helps you.' Midge smiled the same innocuous smile that Mary had. The moment stretched, and she had not moved, so Dreyfuss took the lead again.

'Mary, you have prepared us luncheon?'

The three split into a working team. 'Certainly Master, this way...'

...MasterMasterMasterMasterMasterMasterMasterMasterMaste rMaster...

One of the men led them back out of the kitchen, past the backstairs they had entered by, and through to a large formal dining room. He carried on into the next room, which was a formal drawing room sort of thing, and then they were back in the main hallway. Back into the main living room she'd first seen, and then at the bottom of that, by the back of the house, doors opened into a conservatory she'd not noticed. It held a circular table with two place settings. The glass doors of the conservatory led, in turn, to a wooden platform thing... what was that called...? Decking..?

She sat down, and was very wrong footed by the man then pulling *his* chair out for *him*. *He* sat there, whilst the man... what was his silly name...? Lifted the napkin and placed it on *his* lap for *him*. Anxious that he did not do the same to her, she lifted hers off the plate and settled it for herself.

Being in the company of others was making her think of holding a name in her head for him. That wasn't good. He didn't have a name in her head.

...as good as you being called Helene...?

No, that wasn't good either. She no longer felt like herself, but she certainly wasn't this Helene creature...

'Helene?' He was calling to her.

'Yes?' She automatically replied.

'Would you prefer the salmon to the soup?' His tone relayed the info that he had asked this at least once prior.

...ohmygoodness... ohmygoodness... was that the alarm bell ringing?

She better get back on track, or this could be painful.

...what could be more painful than this...?

Plenty.

'Soup, please.'

The meal lasted forever. She tried to force her attention to everything, but failed. She had required several prompts to stay in rhythm with the meal, and to answer his conversation. So distant was his voice, she had stopped worrying about not paying attention. The damn bell rang all the time anyway, may as well ignore it.

He allowed her to excuse herself afterwards, to freshen up and change. When she went to the main bedroom, she found her suitcase had been taken up and unpacked for her. She ran a bath for herself, and got in. Three hours later, he came in and lifted her out. The water was stone cold, and she'd noticed it, but ignored it. He lifted her through to the bedroom, and lay her down on the towels he'd laid on the bed. She just lay there, as he dried her off. Then he slipped her under the sheets. She lay there motionless too.

It was still light, so he pulled fast the curtains and the room became dark. He put on a lamp, and sat in one of the armchairs, and read a book. After another few hours, she fell asleep.

The rhythm of life at Arden Coombe evolved around her. She was lost in cobwebs and nightmares, and he was perfectly happy to let this run its course. Melancholia was something he knew well, and he was not in the slightest nonplussed. The trio, had they felt it was strange what was occurring, were wise enough not to comment or react. It suited him very well that a routine of normal going about business was conducted, with the trio moving invisibly around them as very good servants. Every morning she was woken, she got showered and dressed, and meals punctuated the day. She stayed close to him at all times, as without him, she was at the mercy of encountering the others. He did not feed. On the contrary, he fed her, a constant stream of light meals and titbits and warming drinks. The hollows filled. He fed off the trio who gave without reaction, but found each bitter to his taste.

She took to sitting in the window seat by the attic window, gazing out at the drive and forest beyond, whilst he worked. He was not engaged in much work, having unloaded most of it before they moved down, but she was not to know that.

November slipped into a wild December. The lashing rain at the window finally drummed into her enough for reaction.

'It's raining again.'

'Yes.' He'd raised his head from his desk, where he was actually reading a book, and answered normally. 'It is a heavy winter.'

'I used to like walking in the rain.'

'Do you want to go for a walk?'

She didn't reply. But it was sign enough.

He left it another day or so, and when he was sure there was a chance she might emerge, he booked some beauty treatments in Marlborough. A very discreet private parlour operated out of one of the High Street's hotels. Whilst her hair was being re-cut and highlighted, her hands were manicured and her nails shaped and painted. He purchased a set of manicure materials and several nails colours. Three days later, when one of her nails chipped, she took off the colour and repainted.

He sent Mary out to find mail order catalogues for nail care, beauty products and clothing. These were left in the main bedroom and by the window seat.

After about a week, she picked one of them up, and glanced through it. A day or so later, she fetched a pen, and circled a couple if items. A pack of nail colours and a lipstick to match. When they arrived he had them unwrapped and simply placed in her dressing table. She used them.

She slowly ticked or ringed more article and items, which were automatically obtained. He matched this with small outings to the shops in Marlborough, moving her gradually to meal dates in small and intimate restaurants. He raised the level of the catalogues, by adding in Harper's Bazaar, Vogue and Cosmopolitan. This was the first time she'd had access to the outside world, in real terms. All the magazines also carried gossip and news of a kind. It didn't appear to have much impact upon her and she appeared to only study the fashion.

One afternoon, she ringed an article on Hermes and their Birkin bag. He put two agents on it, and had arranged an assorted delivery of 6, in different colours and sizes, 3 plain and 3 crocodile, arranged within a week. The agents flew between three continents, to find them in that time, and it had helped that she had not specified a colour. He made this knowledge available to her, as she helped him unpack. It was important she knew none had actually been stolen, which would have been the quickest way to obtain them, and about the only option for someone less wealthy than he, in that time scale. Her now impeccably manicured and flawless hands, unwrapped the bags within bags, to reveal the scents and colours of such a unique king's ransom, even his breath was momentarily stolen away. It filled him with a quiet satisfaction to see her cherish the treasures he had brought her. He could not recall a similar moment.

'Thank you.'

It was her first spontaneous words in weeks.

'You are most welcome. In a moment, we shall detail the key and lock numbers, if you are content, for insurance? You can check them against the receipts if you like.'

She nodded; he was making it clear again, that they were not stolen: that he'd moved heaven and earth to give her what she'd wanted. That he'd had the power to do this. That he knew that she knew what it had cost, and how effortlessly it had been achieved.

'Can I ask a question?'

'Certainly.' He moved back from the unpacking at the bed, and seated himself on the furthest arm chair, giving her space.

'Why do you never have anything engraved, or inscribed, with 'Helene'?'

He considered a moment before answering.

'I think that is probably the most intelligent question you have ever asked of me. Could you explain why you ask it?'

She wasn't afraid of him asking her to explain, he sounded genuinely piqued. The silence between them, these last few weeks as she'd ghosted through Arden, had given her a stillness inside. She was aware the stillness wasn't natural, but it was comforting, like a warm shawl around her shoulders on a cool night. Something to keep away the chill. How to answer? She sat down on the bed, her hands still holding one of the bags, a white crocodile.

'The gold pen you gave me, when you bade me start to sign 'Helene'. It had an engraving section, to hold a name. It was blank. It made sense to me that if you were requiring me to change my name... you would make sure that name was on everything. Likewise, the purse it came in. It was very expensive, like these... and yet, there are no initials anywhere, even on the inside.'

He smiled his pleasure.

'Very good thinking, I applaud you. However, I was not giving you a new name.'

She looked a little puzzled, he drew the moment out.

'I was giving you a new identity.'

She continued in her stillness, listening.

'Identities can be, and must be, swapped around all the time. To move swiftly from one, to another, is often a price of our living, here, amongst humans.' He pointed to the bag she was holding. 'If I had that bag stamped with your initials, or have them engraved on the locking plate... you would have to leave it behind, in a hurry, if you ever had to go on the run.'

She looked thoughtful.

'If you ever mark anything you value, as truly yours – be prepared to lose it.'

'I see. That's very clever, I hadn't thought of it.'

'You would have, the first time you had something precious that you treasured, and had to leave behind. To take it, is to risk being identified as the old identity. Also... and this is sometimes a serious consideration, marking objects of great value, diminishes their resale value. Investment in things such as First Edition books, Portfolios, that sort of thing... you must always keep them mint. Assets must always remain assets, and not personal possessions. It is not really a consideration for you, but it is a lesson that is part of our lore.'

She thought hard for a moment.

'Jonathan?'

Oh how wonderful, his name!!! Moving to Arden and bringing in staff had been a fertile exercise. He pushed down his smile.

'Yes, little one?'

'Why is keeping assets intact not a consideration for me?'

'Well, that is simple, you will never need to worry about maintaining your wealth. When you are Turned, my Changeling, you will receive half my fortune, in your own name. It is my obligation to split everything I have – money, property, business... and give you exactly half. Something we need to start setting up quite soon.' There was a long pause. 'Would you prefer to have Arden Coombe or No 1?'

She didn't speak, merely rose after a few moments, and carefully took all her new bags through to the dressing area. She returned to perfect silence and stillness within, although she continued to behave impeccably. He carried on with no regard to it.

Theatres and art gallery trips were re-introduced. They ranged about the local art centres, the M4 corridor becoming familiar to her. He liked having the trio as drivers and escort, so he could sit and point out interesting facts and information along the way, building up a picture of the sort of world she could inhabit as his Changeling. He used the word a lot, and explained out the different uses of the words. When she started to drink from him, to set in motion her Turning, she became his ward within the Vampire world. Once Turned fully, once she was drinking human blood and the change had occurred, she would be his Vampire recognised possession for one hundred years. He would be total Guardian to her Changeling status, and everything he did now was about preparing her for survival come her change. Changelings rarely made it to independence, for they were rarely trained in how to survive. Changelings were weak, immature, and it took time to mature from a Turning. She was his responsibility for that Century. After that, she could choose her own path. Very few Changelings made it to maturity. That was not an issue for her, who had the best master there was. He would ensure she survived.

He was so expansive as the trio were always listening, and absorbing information. Sometimes he and they chatted around her, in French, German, Spanish... he was enjoying keeping his languages up in modern registers. When they were talking in another language, he would often respond in it without realising. She would withdraw further at these times, but, again, he took no notice of it.

He had also been keeping her to a timetable of real lessons. Actual slots of work dedicated to teaching her essential survival skills. Driving lessons had come first, and he gave her the provisional driving license that had been prepared. He also let her see her birth certificate and passport, in case she ever needed to answer any questions if she was stopped by the police whilst driving. She examined them carefully. Helene Blanchard had been born two years prior to herself, in the same region she came from. Same month, different year. It prompted genuine curiosity, the first for some weeks.

'They are all quite fake, aren't they?'

'Yes and no. Yes, the identity has been created for you. But all the documents are quite genuine. You do exist as she. It can take a good year to get genuine documents processed. It can take just as long for actual fakes that look that good. Work within the systems of law and record that exist, if you can.... but I fear for how long that will be possible. Computers and electronic storage are soon to take over. I am unsure how often in the future it will be possible to do this. Mostly, it is easiest to find the name of a child that died young, in the year you want to be born, and then apply for their birth certificate, and from there, a passport. However, that is all going to get much more difficult in the next few years.'

He stopped for a few moments, to gather his thoughts.

'When you are up and running, you will get the hang of starting a couple of new identities from scratch, twenty or thirty years before you plan to transfer. It is very hard to keep track of your assets otherwise. Having your new identity born abroad, with British citizenship, has been useful. Again, I am not sure how long that will continue. It is always a challenge, in an ever moving world. And, lately, change has been so rapid... I think there is soon going to be a time when only those born in the United Kingdom have citizenship. That is why I went to the extra expense of giving you a real identity, from here. Also, it is easier to keep some details from your original persona open, until you are used to moving your sense of who you are, to the new identity. Hence the birth place and month being roughly approximate. Your voice should not betray you whilst you gain your confidence. That all said, Helene is as real as you are, now.'

The words chilled her, but she was relieved that 'Helene' had never been a real person, or, more importantly, wasn't dead at his hands. He said 'Helene' with a slightly more pronounced accent than was usual in Britain, but then spoke the 'Blanchard' as it would be in England, and not in France. It puzzled her. It also puzzled her that 'Savernake' was pronounced more like 'Savernak'. You say tomato...

The driving lessons were very hard work. A thin faced and slightly built man named Mr Postlethwaite, came out from Marlborough and picked her up in his driving lessons car. One of the Three Stooges sat in the back of the car. Mr Postlethwaite did not seem fazed by this in the slightest, and never spoke or referred to them. After a few trial runs, lessons were booked for two hour slots, four times a week. She wondered why he had not just ordered her a driving licence too, but supposed it was that it was quite important, somehow, that she actually learn to drive. Lessons were nerve wracking, and difficult to survive without speaking. Mr Postlethwaite was, for all his quiet and unassuming manner, a hard task master, and he would not stand for her not answering questions or relaying observations. If she should show fear, or nervousness, and once she dissolved into tears at a roundabout when she'd stalled the car, Mr Postlethwaite just rode by her emotional reaction, and carried on as if it had never happened. He would remind her that a lot of money was being paid to fast track her through the test, and pushed her to succeed. His quiet but clipped Northern tones were deadly in her ears, and she knew his type as honest but hard and brooking no resistance. She passed first time. Afterwards, in the guise of a vampire lesson – how to control and manipulate people, she'd asked Dreyfuss how he'd managed to buy Mr Postlethwaite's obedience, especially when it came to a 'minder'. Dreyfuss had explained that he'd confided in Mr Postlethwaite, that Helene's prior heroin addiction had meant she required both a minder, and for those who dealt with her to ignore any emotional disturbance. It was then that Joanne had rerun her early visits to the hairdressing salon in Kensington, and subsequent shopping trips and theatre and restaurant dates. Dreyfuss held all the cards.

After she passed the test, she was directed to take longer and more complex drives in the wide range of vehicles in the garages so she could cope with all sizes of vehicle and all driving conditions. Often, she was woken in the middle of the night, in pouring rain, and made to drive a car, or land rover, for hours, before being ordered to drive back and not exceed the speed limit once.

She was also learning to ride a horse, and master computer accounts at the same time. The horse riding was a genius stroke, and Dreyfuss observed her thaw a little when sitting on warm flesh that obeyed her commands. He had brought three animals to Arden, for her instruction, and Mary and Midge taught her basic competency so she was capable of their care and riding safely. By the time summer took hold, she could control a gallop, rise to the trot well, and cope comfortably with a jump of a five barred gate. She was never going to be dressage material but if push came to shove she could survive a fox hunt. He himself rode out through the forest with her regularly. Horse riding was unlikely to be the survival skill for her, that it had been for him over the centuries, but it was a traditional skill to be passed on. He was careful to keep her from making too emotional a connection with any of the horses. That would not do. He wondered about teaching her to fence and shoot, but decided she could always decide those skills for herself after she Turned.

Accounts, business matters and computing, she excelled at. She had, of course, arrived with a good basis in that, and he built on her skills with ease. It was during the early sessions in the office, that he had begun physical overtures again, sitting closer and closer, touching her casually as he leaned over to open a book, or pass her a pen. She accepted everything with no reaction, and shortly thereafter, he resumed his blood taking. She was utterly passive, and offered him no emotional neediness and appeared to have dispensed with her need of physical affection or touch, even when he used thrall. He found her passivity delicious and new, as this had never happened before. After a few weeks, he began to have sex with her on a regular basis. She continued to be passive but obedient. This disturbed him a little... in a way he would not look at... but pleased his ego greatly. He told himself that that had been the entire point, that she needed to learn to override her own instincts and fears of rape or sexual congress. A functioning vampire with modern day hang ups about sexual autonomy and body control, holding fast to the concept that she, and only she, controlled access to her body... that was simply absurd. She was female, and that was something that could neither be denied, nor resisted. Her status was determined by her body, for all the shallow pretending of the world that had raised her. She had to come to the reality that her body could be either barter or possession, depending on circumstance. Both, often, if the times were difficult enough. He could not have her ending up like Violette, could he? He enjoyed the sheer wickedness of that thought.

That he was genuinely enjoying the sexual congress, and beginning to talk gently to her, and whisper sweet nothings, and bring her lover's gifts... he did not see. That he had always sought reaction, and proof of dominance from all he had ever bedded... and this was not happening now... he did not see. He was aware it was ... different... but he did not dwell upon it. The difference was in his mastery, and how completely he had conquered her. All had finally come to be his, as it should always have been.

CHAPTER TWENTY-THREE

Her physical training also progressed. The trio, who lived in the staff cottages at the back of the stable block, took turns in first walking, then jogging, then running her around the estate. They also oversaw her use on the fitness machines in the gym room at the back of the extension. She hated these times, it was clear, for all her passive outlook. The work outs were slow and methodical. She would need a great deal of muscle tissue for the next phase.

Tissue was a bit of a problem, actually. Her scar tissue, to be precise. He had been a little shocked when he had actually noted her body, and the passage of her journey that had been written upon it. Her left wrist was a crumbled mound of scar tissue on scar tissue on scar. The crater in her back, where he had torn open her flesh with the belt was still there, and was likely never to fade. Numerous scars and welts littered her back, buttock, thighs and arms. Some of her skin was puckered and tight, and it interfered with her fitness regime. She was in pain when asked to do certain things, both in the bedroom and the gymnasium. He had always resisted putting a swimming pool into the Arden Coombe estate somewhere, never thinking he would need it enough to make the problems with planning it out with the other wardens of the ancient forest, worth it. He regretted it then, and knew he should have done it in the 30s, when everyone else was jumping on the bandwagon. Short of burning down one of the barns overnight, he could not manage to slip one in now. He had planned that the next accidental fire would be Arden House itself, as he was somewhat tired of working through the restrictions from it now being listed. It had taken a lot of work to keep re-inheriting this area of land in the forest over the past 800 years, and he was somewhat taken aback when the little one had elected to keep it as part of her portfolio. But it was wrong to get too attached, especially to a place that had, unexpectedly, stayed locked in a time bubble. So he had begun the hand over process, and had moved her into the position of controlling the fake family inheritance that had been in place for generations. He would miss owning this pile: it was so secluded, and so peaceful, and just so damn convenient for London. He set in motion some renovations of a manor house he owned in Suffolk, which had been leased for the past 200 years.

In terms of her back, and the issues of the scarring, they had begun a regime of massage to complement the physical training. He used his blood where and when he could, but also relied on cortisone creams to reduce the swelling and pain when exercising her out. All three of the trio undertook the massage regime with her regularly, and once or twice he had to cut tight skin open with a scalpel, and then pour his own blood directly onto the wound and hope. They held her down whilst he did it. It helped... but that back, and the wrist... he had broken a rule there, and did not like the taste of it. He toyed with considering plastic surgery, but doubted it would work. It was also too risky; he could easily lose his total control of her in a clinic.

Her confidence grew, well contained within their collective shadow, but it grew nonetheless. She began to engage again. Her first request had been to go and buy scent for herself. He knew it was her time on the streets that drove her to new clothing, fashion, looking good... and smelling good. So he was happy to oblige. Shopping for scent was something he detested, and he sent Mary with her. She spent a few hours in Marlborough, and used her shiny new credit cards for the first time. She ventured out more and more, doing her own shopping and sometimes bringing him back gifts. They extended their joint excursions, and soon they were dining at the best restaurants the region could offer, and occasionally staying over in London for shows.

Handing over a share of the businesses was increasingly taking up more of his time, and as the summer turned, they were spending a lot of it in London, with both of them working with lawyers and accountants. Everything took a great deal of time, and a lot of signatures. Endless signatures. He never mentioned who she was, and everyone assumed she was his fiancée, as he always ensured that finger had an appropriate ring. When she was not shopping, having an endless stream of clothes refitted and made perfect for her, she was helping him in the office, gradually taking on more and more demanding tasks. Much of her encouragement out of the silence was the need to communicate officially with more and more business operations and executives.

It was, although he never realised it, one of the happiest and most settled times in his life. There had never been a single beating since they had taken up residence in Wiltshire. He relished in the thought that this was because she had never provoked his anger: she was fully broken to his will. The actuality, that since the night he had mind raped her and fled to hide in one of his own cells... he had never felt the *need* to hit... he could not see. He was content with where he was, for the first time in a very long life, and he went with that, utterly. He was lulled into a routine of training and preparation that made him feel satisfied, settled. He knew that it would, must, change. What they were heading for would break it all down again, and she would fight and rebel and they would be back to hate and anger in short order... and that this must occur. Turning was impossible in this contentment... he would have to break it and move on. But it was so... relaxing, this unexpected bounty. He knew he was indulging her, and this phase, and they had already stretched past his original plans for transformation. He considered that he should forgive himself the over long stay in safety and security. He had worked hard, for centuries, to refine his skills to this point in the journey. He should be rewarded. Therefore, he indulged both himself, and her, endlessly.

Part of the indulgence was supporting her in some quite incredible spending, in a wide selection of stores. Mungo turned out to be her favourite shopping companion, and she dragged him around the most exclusive of department stores incessantly. He suspected she chose Mungo, as he hated it, and would sit in stone silence in the outer dressing area whilst she had personal shoppers run in with this, run in with that. Given her scars, he quite understood that shopping for, and refitting, clothing, was a demanding task. There were no low cut evening gowns in her future, and the art of concealment was crucial to her now impeccable styling. He genuinely appreciated the effort. When an antique clothing store opened in Marlborough, she then developed a passion for vintage fashion and accessories, and began to fill the spare bedrooms at Arden with her finds. He indulged it all, especially her penchant for vintage Chanel: it could only appreciate in value.

Her shopping outings became part of the routine of all her other training, with trips for beauty treatments and salon visits. Men of his class and distinction required a woman who was impeccably polished and well behaved in all aspects, all the time. Therefore he ensured that she was groomed from tip to toe, to reflect his status in her every hair, every line and every thread. He was pleased with how finally honed she was, and impeccably presented on any occasion he chose to set up. The sex was wonderful and he grew somewhat addicted to her blood. He had never looked younger or fitter, reflecting the age he had been at his own Turning, and had never felt so completely victorious in everything he touched. As autumn approached, he drew wistful over what was about to occur, but drew his resolve around him. He settled with the trio that their contract would be extended by another six months; he had not prepared for such long months of gathering resources before moving on, and reconciled himself to just another couple of weeks of play before the real work began.

It was therefore, a complete shock, when the phone rang one September afternoon, and for him to be delivered of the news that she was gone.

It was Midge that brought the news to him. Mungo had phoned from Marlborough, she was gone, nowhere to be found, and the others needed to get there fast. Had it not been so urgent to act, Dreyfuss would have killed him on the spot. As it was, he punched the man so hard, he fell down and stayed there for several minutes.

Mary came up to the office, to say three cars were now in the drive, and to hand them all wireless radios. She explained what Mungo had told them. Mungo and Helene had been shopping, in their usual routine: Helene had shopped for handmade toiletries she could only get in Marlborough, then spent an hour combing through the vintage clothing shop. They had left there and crossed the main road to the Hotel, where it was her habit to take tea and scones before returning to Arden. As they passed through the parked cars that lined the centre of the High Steet, she had stumbled and her shopping had spilled everywhere, with bottles and bombs and bars of soap falling in the path of the cars cruising through the street. Mungo had retrieved some items, and stood up to hand them to her... and she was gone. The shopping lay where it had fallen, and she was vanished. The High Street was busy, very busy, with a lot of cars passing fore and aft, and he'd scanned for her, but there was no sign. He'd collected the bags in order not to arouse suspicion, and returned to their car, which was parked just a few feet away. As usual, he'd held the keys, so the car was still there, and she was not. He'd dumped the bags and phoned on the car phone. She'd been gone no more than three minutes when he phoned. He told Mary he would go directly to the train station, but the others would need to cover the bus routes. He'd take the wireless radio kept in the car. Mary had sent Midge up to tell Dreyfuss, and gone to bring round three cars and collect more radios and set them to the frequency they'd agreed on.

Dreyfuss took a radio and told Mary and Mungo to cover the bus routes. Buses into and out of Marlborough were long and slow and lumbering. A quick look at the timetables, kept for emergency, showed that only two buses could be possible for this time of day – both moving along the A4, one East, one West. Mary and Mungo were to drive out to find the ones that had just passed, driving back down the A4 to the High Street, checking any that lumbered into view as they did so. When they reached the High Street, he would have new instructions for him. If she was on a bus, they were to leave her on it, and call him, following behind in the car.

It was of eternal regret to him that he had not just sent them straight to the airports. But who would have thought...?

He drove straight to Marlborough himself, and checked at the station with Mungo. The big man paled when he saw him approach, as he knew that Dreyfuss was not going to let this go. He assured Dreyfuss she had not left by train, and would not. Dreyfuss left him there and went to the High Street, and tried to think. Where could she have gone in such a short time?

He knew the crossing they used and he went and stood on it and surveyed the long thin High Street with its parking on both sides, and straight up the middle. He realised quickly that she had been, as usual, extremely clever. The High Street was packed, far more than usual. The traffic so thick it ground to a halt a couple of times in front of him. Not only was it high tourist season... Marlborough School was returning from the Summer Holidays. The roads to the West end of High Street, where he stood, were clogged with limousines, Range Rovers, Rolls Royces, Mercedes Benzes and Bentleys. Large cars parked in every possible space and vehicles clogging traffic as they moved into and out of the school courtyards at the West end of town. The streets were thronged with boys of various ages and their various Guardians. The tourists were in a frenzy. Where could she have gone? How had she disappeared?

The question was not fully answered for several days, by which time he'd beaten Mungo half to death and nearly killed Mary for interfering. After two futile hours in Marlborough, he'd sent them to the airports, whilst he drove first to Arden to check the safe. As far as he knew she had never seen the safe, never mind knew the combination, but her passport, and a couple of thousand pounds cash, was gone. She always kept her own driving licence, as it was required by law when driving. Where could she have gone? How had she disappeared so swiftly?

The answer started to become clearer when he phoned the banks and frozen the credit on her cards. An impressive amount of money had been spent on them in the previous two weeks, starting from the day after the last statement had been sent. Most of the money was to airlines, for tickets. It took him a couple of hours to break down an airline employee, but then determined that the tickets had been ordered electronically and were for pick up from the check-in desk. It was impossible to get flight information: had she picked up the ordered ticket and boarded? Nothing would furnish this information from any of them. He then launched into the computers in the office, which were private line networked both to London, his bank's London office, and Switzerland. By the time he located the back door she had created, it was going on 7 or 8 hours, and he knew she had flown by then, literally.

She had only been granted user password privileges into the accounts packages he was teaching her, so he went into the administrative level and searched deeper. His little one, his little well trained pet, had worked herself into the administrative passwords and had been through the systems like the proverbial thief in the night. She had used his networked connections to set up a pay account that did not show up on his normal systems, and had purchased about a dozen airline tickets out of the country, charged to her legitimate credit cards. Most for them for that day, all in the name Helene Blanchard. A couple were later flights from other airports, such as Luton. There was one for two days hence, from Glasgow. Insurance in case she had not reached Heathrow in time. Insurance in case she had had to race across the length of the country, to get to an airport. All the booked flights were short haul to Europe, various destinations: Paris, Milan, Rome, Amsterdam, Brussels, Munich. Working out which one she had taken was going to take time.

Credit, as it turned out, was easy to steal from him, using the damned systems he had both set up, and had partially taught her to use. He had no inkling on just how good her computer skills had been. But she would be lost without a lot of cash, and what was missing from the safe was nowhere near enough... how the hell had she gotten into the safe? She had to have more cash... how?

He checked through the wardrobes, and found that a lot of the higher end items that had been purchased were not there. After a discussion with the others, he realised she had been buying stuff on the credit cards, and returning it, for cash. Her minders had been oblivious, trained as they were for force and terror. They thought she was returning clothes for alteration, or on whim, and had, obviously, never seen cash being given to her. She had spent months going to the same stores, doing the same things. That was always a problem with bodyguards, routine. He realised that as the trio knew they were protecting her from escaping, they had not bothered as much as they might about routines than if they had been genuinely worried about her being attacked. Routine had been the perfect companion to them all these past few months.

There was also the issue of her going to the same personal shoppers again and again. Meaning she had spent a great deal of time with staff, behind closed curtain, the trio sitting outside, oblivious. She had used his own designs of her total control of her, to defeat him. The realisation stabbed him with a thunderbolt of fury.

...the little BITCH!...

She had outwitted him. The more he looked into the accounts, the less confidence he had that she could be found quickly.

He had been forced to leave the house, saddling up one of the horses and riding out in temper, before he maimed or killed one, or all, of the trio. It was too dangerous to hunt in this mood, and he resorted to galloping through the woods for hours, smashing himself, and the animal, into trees, bushes and walls as he passed. When the animal finally fell beneath him, pitching him into the soil, he snapped its neck and walked back, the hours and hours of tracking to work out where he was, and how to get back unseen, finally banking down the anger.

He was exhausted when he returned, but calmer. He dispatched the Stooges to reclaim the body of the horse before the alarm was raised, and lay in a steaming tub of water, washing off the dirt and fury, and plotting revenge.

The bitch was going to pay.

He lay, calm and still, in the cooling water, and thought it all through. How had she gotten cash? She must have had cash, a great deal of it. The cards were useless to her once she'd left Marlborough. A thought trickled into his mind... an ugly thought.

He went to the wardrobes again, and pulled out the Birkin bags. As he suspected – they were all fake! She'd done what many a mistress and wife had done over the centuries: taken expensive gifts, commissioned a sales assistant in a store that sold similar to find fakes to replace them, and then handed over the originals for cash for a fraction of what had been paid for them. In fact, the only thing she'd taken with her, he'd already worked out, was the most expensive Birkin he'd bought: the white crocodile. That had been her handbag that day, and she'd left with only that and the clothes she stood in. She'd taken it out with her as part of an investment, that and a lot of gold jewellery.

He'd taught her well. That bag had obviously been the only one left that was the genuine article.

Even if she had only gotten ten percent of the true value of the bags, and only a share in the returned clothing... he reckoned she had at least fifty thousand pounds in cash on her when she left. That was impossible for her to have gotten out of the house with, without notice, and too much for one handbag, even a fucking Birkin.

And how had she got out of Marlborough?

The answer was in the final set of bills on the credit cards, although it took combing through the paper copies to spot it. There was a payment to a limousine company in London. He'd contacted the firm by phone and had a chat. Paying upfront, she'd booked them to drive from London to Marlborough, and pick her up on the afternoon of the escape. They confirmed that she'd been picked up from the front courtyard of one of the dorms at Marlborough School, which was drowning in a sea of such cars moving in and out of the gates all day long, and then she had been driven to Heathrow.

He spoke to the driver, and after discussing with him how his sister had stolen some family heirlooms in order to run off with a lover they suspected of being after her money... he was more than happy to offer the information that she'd had a couple of bags with her. She'd paid him a cash tip from her handbag, and had also had a small suitcase of the type that had wheels and an extending handle. Small enough for hand luggage. The man believed utterly the story about the runaway sister and her lover, as when she'd booked the limo, she'd given instructions it was to park in a very certain spot, and to arrive early to ensure it could do so. He'd been there two hours before she turned up, and she'd then slumped down in the back seat, looking harassed, and not really sitting up and not paying attention to anything until they'd driven onto the M4. She'd told him to drive West, meaning they didn't pass through Marlborough High Street itself at all, and they had then driven up to the M4 via Avebury and then had cut back across at Wroughton rather than go on at Swindon. Used to rich people doing weird things, the driver had not commented, and the High Street itself had been very congested. Driving out the wrong way had probably saved them time to the airport, in the end, he'd reckoned. Besides, he'd not known the area at all, and the lady had: so he'd done as instructed. Dreyfuss left him with a large tip to pay for his discretion in the matter.

The carry-on luggage took him to one place, and one place only: the vintage clothing shop. When he'd entered, with Mungo at his side, the owner, a middle aged woman had blanched, and stood back behind the till area. Her hand had reached for the phone on the wall behind her. He smiled, and moved to look through some men's clothing that was on a small stand to one side of the window. He'd made small show of selecting something, and brought it forth to pay for it. He paid cash. She rang through the jumper in quick time, and would not make eye contact with him. They left.

He had the trio pick her up when she closed the shop for the day. She broke, in all sense of the words, very easily. Unable to trust himself, he'd let Mary do the work. Deirdre told them everything. Yes, Helene had made contact with her, and asked for help. She'd slipped letters into items she returned, and begun a correspondence with Deirdre, through the items she then purchased, and the swapping of notes in the fitting room. Helene had explained that her very rich boyfriend was abusing her, and she was trying to escape, but could not. Deirdre had offered to inform the police, but Helene had refused: she'd been to the police and they had not acted, since her very rich boyfriend was also a local magistrate. Deirdre was appalled, and promised to help. The ever looming presence of Mungo had helped persuade her that Helene was in need of an escape route. Helene had been siphoning money to Deirdre for months, and Deirdre had been collecting it in a small suitcase. She'd also been helping herself to a little extra along the way. Something she kept apologising for.

On the day of the escape, Deirdre had been in the back alley behind the shop, holding the case waiting for Helene. She'd taken it off her, given her a kiss, and disappeared.

Had she told anyone else about all this? Yes, she had her husband Brian, who would be at home waiting for her, and who would call the police if she didn't come home. Mungo and Midge went to fetch Brian.

Brian was broken even quicker, as he had Deirdre to look at. No, Brian had told no one. They had no children and had moved to Marlborough to open the shop, for their retirement. It had been a bit of excitement for them, really. And apart from the money collecting in the case, he suspected they'd never actually considered the situation as 'real' in any sense. Deirdre had certainly been shocked to find a note saying 'meet me in the back in 5 minutes with my case' that day, and had been looking in the local newspapers for news. She sobbed endlessly about how she should have gone to the police.

Deirdre and Brian were bundled away by Mary and Mungo, Midge following in their car. They were put back in their car, slightly dead, and the car was spun off the road into a brick wall, and then it caught fire.

It was such a tragic accident.

What was not a tragic accident was that Dreyfuss branded Mungo with a red hot blade. A slice of punishment.

As such had been written into their contract, for negligence, no one complained. Had he not needed them all well enough to carry on the search, he would have done far worse. As it was, he took out some of his spleen on Mary, who had to lap that up as well, as that too had been written into the contract. She was slightly mollified when he'd told her that she could take it out of Helene, when they found her.

That it had felt good to beat a woman again was a thought that was ruthlessly pushed away. He just needed to keep them mindful of their contract, and take the edge off his temper.

Finding her was proving to be difficult. At first, he was sure that she'd have gone straight to France. But after three weeks, he managed to satisfy himself that the ticket that had been used had been to Madrid. He sent his agents to see if they could track down a white crocodile Hermes Birkin bag for sale in the hands of a private trader in Spain. Yes, one had exchanged hands recently, and was sold on in Italy. The lock numbers matched.

He had no way of knowing where she'd gone on to. But what was clear from his investigations, was her computer skills had been much better than he'd known. When he got a security expert from the bank down to take his system apart, he was shown the hidden programme that had logged his keystrokes as he'd given his passwords to the main admin areas. He'd never heard of such a thing, obviously, and determined his own computing knowledge must now increase dramatically. It was a matter of rage that he'd used his computer password for the safe combination. It had been convenient at the time.

Such skills were not the only ones she had kept hidden. An investigation into her background, rather deeper than the one he'd commissioned at the time of her kidnapping, gave a much fuller report. The bitch could speak French fluently, and get by in Spanish. Had he known that... had he even suspected it! He wasted no more time on regrets, or recriminations.

He phoned Violette.

CHAPTER TWENTY-FOUR

The landing into Bogotá was bumpy to say the least. As she'd learned over the past couple of months, aircraft standards were extremely variable, as were runways. She'd flown out of a bumpy crater strewn stretch of concrete in Costa Rica, and landed on a larger but no less damaged piece of concrete here.

Her spine ached from the cramped seats and she felt she would never be clean again. It had been three weeks since she'd showered in hot water: she needed a modern hotel. She booked into one at the airport, washed thoroughly, slept, and then ate as much as she could hold. Her cheap and local clothing, well, local for Costa Rica, she dumped as soon as she'd outfitted herself in cheap Bogotá clothing. Then she found the bus depot and headed out on the next bus. Anywhere the next bus was going. She ended up in a town in the mountains called Muzo, where she spent five nights resting up in a pension. Resting up was very important, for she found her body was in a perilous state sometimes. Cold, and cramped quarters badly affected her scars, especially her back and wrist. Used to a great deal of exercise, her body rebelled if she did nothing but sit on seats, or hide in rooms. Stretching every day, and finding some way to exercise every other day, had become vital. She'd not had the money to waste on gyms, and some of the places she'd been were dangerous for running in the open. When she was exhausted and tired, she needed sleep and somewhere safe to exercise. She tried to walk in the hills around the town, and very quickly came to appreciate, that this country was far too dangerous for her, with the constant tales of gun battles and drug lords she picked up from local newspapers and from the talk of people as they moved about. She only needed to keep her head down for a few days, then head back to the airport. She did a lot of sleeping and eating.

The eating had shocked her. Away from his grasp, she'd learned to read her body better, and had found it was undeniable that his blood ran through her veins. Vampire blood was part of her, and she endured overwhelming hunger if she did not keep her body fed regularly. A Changeling she was, undeniable. Feeding herself was one way to keep that knowledge at bay, but it was hard work. Exercising also burned up calories, as did tiredness and fear. So stopping to eat a lot was also part of the pattern of escape she'd honed down to a fine, if uncomfortable, art. Escape was hard work. As was ignoring the poverty and terror she'd found on every street corner now her eyes were open to it. She'd found escaping from her time on the streets was just as hard as escaping from him. Everywhere she went, pale frightened hungry faces haunted waste lands and fed from bins.

The pattern of flight was almost ingrained in her now. Fly in, preferably on the smallest airline that serviced that airport. Get out of town, wait a few days, come back, get on another plane. Or cross country by bus and then get another plane. Whatever worked for the least way of being recorded. Each time she'd done this, as she hopped across the world, from Madrid to Quebec, Quebec to Ontario, Ontario to Vancouver, Vancouver to Belize City, via Mexico City Airport, Belize City to Panama, Panama to Bogotá... she'd ground down her presence smaller and smaller. It would have been so much easier if she could have gone anywhere in the USA, in any of its States. But a visa was required, or a holiday tour package, and then she'd found both Mexico and Puerto Rico required paperwork too. So she'd concentrated on losing the chances of her journey being logged by paperwork and computer, by skipping endlessly down countries and facilities. She was finally in South America, which had taken weeks, and, where she was sure she could find some place to hide for a long time, simply given the sheer size and the lack of electronic infrastructure.

Time to set up a new identity properly, and leave Helene Blanchard, and *him*, behind.

Money was becoming problematic: it had all cost so much more than she'd thought possible. She knew where she was heading, she'd done a lot of reading and research as she'd moved on. From her initial panic to just get out of Europe, she'd whittled down her options as she'd slogged slowly through Canada. She'd decided Argentina was probably her best bet, despite the small matter of the Falklands. Of indeed, because of it. It had taken her weeks to get to this point, as she'd zigged and zagged, hoping to leave no paper trail, now was the time for a large jump. She was so tired of running, and not sleeping.

She boarded another bus and headed back over the bone breaking mountain passes to Bogotá. There she had to decide how to make her way down what was proving to be a vast country. Yes, she'd known the world was big... she'd no idea how big until she'd been forced to move through it like a mouse chased by a panther. No, she wasn't going there, she put that to one side.

It would have been sensible to continue the hopping a little, but faced with a lack of flights, and a lot of military with very large guns at the airport, she booked a connection through to Montevideo. She'd give Brazil a miss, as she didn't speak one word of Portuguese. Literally give it a miss, as the flight took her to Lima, and then Santiago, and then across to Montevideo. 32 hours and several of those in cold dark airport waiting rooms, sleeping on her single rucksack with a poncho to keep her warm. She was grey and shaking by the time she landed and managed to make it out through customs, which was rudimentary to say the least. Coming in from Santiago on a pit stop flight had helped there.

Montevideo was huge, and modern, and assaulted her thoroughly. As did the heat, which was more than she was expecting and it was that wet heat that makes you sweat. It wasn't until she arrived that she realised that it was so close to Buenos Aires by boat. Faced with either going back on a mountain bus, or staying in Montevideo itself, she elected to go down to the ports, sleep for a night in a cheap hotel, and board the ferry to the Argentinean capital. A long bus journey in this heat was not happening. She was driven by the need to feel a little safer. Her rudimentary Spanish was not servicing her as well as she'd hoped, amongst the various accents, dialects and linguistic developments she'd encountered since landing in Mexico. She had to find somewhere to rest, and recover, and learn to speak the language properly. Escape had been pointless, if life was going to be as futile as this. She found even the later afternoon sunshine painful on her skin, something he'd warned her about in his lessons. Yes, he could go out in the sunshine, but only with sun block on if the sun was strong. As she'd moved through the city sorting it all out, she'd found a chemist and bought both sun block, and some more hydro-cortisone cream.

She got the early morning peasant ferry out, and spent 5 hours with chickens and goats and fat babies. She was getting used to every form of transport having chickens, goats and fat babies. And some very badly smelling men. She'd also learned, very fast, to always cover her hair, and as much of her face as she could, both by woolly hats, shawls and keeping her head down. In many areas, a single female traveller making eye contact with men meant she was fair game. It had been a hard lesson. Twice she'd had to get off buses or trains in the middle of nowhere, to avoid rape or murder by a bunch of men who'd seen their wives and daughters off at the station, and then promptly sat down to work out if she had any protection, and could they have her? Then she'd had to survive in the middle of nowhere, a single female traveller, until she got on another bus or train. There had been some close calls, and so, there were always fat babies in her life now, as she'd learned never to board a rural bus or train, unless there were women with smiling fat babies in their arms. She'd sit close to them, and end up making eye contact, and occasionally hold the baby whilst the mother dealt with older children, or settled an aged relative. Or a chicken. She'd also grown to be wary of the baby handed over quickly, as it invariably peed on her. Nappies were not a feature of rural peasant life, and the mothers developed a sixth sense in dealing with waste on long buses. Goats and chickens were not so well trained.

On the ferry, the babies were held over the railings, so she was still clean and dry when she landed in Buenos Aires... and promptly found it more unbearable than Montevideo. Hotter, wetter and more congested. It took her the best part of the day to sort out the bus station, and a sense of where she was going, and she hesitated to travel in the dark. That was bad for a whole slew of reasons. So she found a hostel and did manage some sleep, even with one eye open and her bag wound tightly round her hand. Her money and travellers cheques were wrapped tightly around her body, but losing your bag could lead to more trouble: it made you look weak. Hostels were not good fun, but even pensions in the big cities often kept registers, and took your name and passport number from you, so she'd learned cheap hostel survival skills.

She got to the bus station early, and bought a ticket to Mar Del Plata along with a cheap straw sun hat. However, as the bus was filling up with a lot of men and few women, a local bus parked next to it was filling up with fat babies. As it was revving up to drive on, she jumped on, and thrust notes at the driver, who looked around, and stuffed them in his pockets. The bus moved off and she settled down between the fat babies and their Mamas. The bus stopped every few kilometres, as local buses do, and much time was spent with loading and unloading. The heat built until she was in an oven. Her clothes were still Bogotá clothes, and far too warm for the sub-tropical air. She dare not take layers off. It could invite unwanted attention, for a woman to strip layers. Even if each under layer was still covering everything. Three hours after they'd left the City, in the middle of the morning climb to noon day heat, they arrived in a place named Magdalena. The name appealed to her, as did the beauty that unfolded as they drove along. It was small and perfect and clean looking, and the sun shone and the blue waters of the coast could be glimpsed... the streets were wide, like boulevards, the houses were white and grand and pretty and sweet at the same time. Massive trees lined every street. The bus stopped at a market square and the fat babies and their Mamas got off. So did she.

It took a week or so, but she settled in Magdalena, over on the port side, at Atalya, where there were enough tourists and travellers that her presence as both a single woman, and a foreigner, was not of note. She found a little tiny hotel that struggled to compete with the larger tourist places, and haggled for three months food and board. The haggling was important, if she was to have local respect. Her room was modest but clean, and tucked back out of the way, with a window that looked out to a small courtyard. She'd already bought local clothing, and moved as seamlessly as she could amongst the local people, never venturing far into the areas where the rich foreigners drank too much and wore too little. She never met the gaze of any male who addressed her, and she played with the children who pestered her for sweets. Babies were given to her to cuddle and kiss, often, and she watched all the women work very hard, all day long. She had bought some cheap reams of paper and a box of pens, and gave show of being a writer, settling away to work on some great novel. She sat in the cool shade of trees and looked out at the glistening waters and drank fresh fruit juice and spoke respectfully and quietly to everyone. Truthfully, she had planned to hide out somewhere far more remote, and less desirable. But the reality that she had to be somewhere where tourists were, in order to be unnoticeable, had hit home very early in her travels. She attended the local Catholic Churches to further cement her neighbours' good views of her, and observed with wonder and awe, the amazing rituals that swelled the town over the Christmas period. She kept an eye out for an appropriate job, as she slowly soaked in the language. She'd have to start to earn money soon.

Night-times were the worst. She wondered if the others ever heard her scream, as in her dreams, she never stopped.

In early January, she went to the local market, as was her fashion, to buy fresh fruit and bread. On her return... she smelled vampire in the room. He'd been here, he had. The room was untouched, and for a moment, she doubted herself; it was panic, that's all, the stench in her nostrils, the trilling across her nerves; it was sheer panic. There was no way he could have found her, no way at all. He wasn't going to find her either. It'd take two minutes to pack, and she'd be gone. She almost didn't notice it, such was her hurry, but when she reached for her alarm clock, on the rickety bedside table, there it was, neatly centred upon her bed: a newspaper. She stared at it for a moment, confused. Maybe that's what was wrong with the room, the cleaner had been in, despite her instructions, and left a paper for her. But this wasn't the sort of place that gave complimentary newspapers. It took a moment for her to recognise what was wrong with the paper: it was in English. It was, in fact, a British newspaper. She picked it up. There! There was his smell, he had been here, or, at least, he had touched this rag. And it was a rag, a scandal sheet at its worst. She stared at it, unknowing, uncomprehending. What on earth was this about?

There was a full page headline, under the title BUTCHERED! was a grainy picture of a woman, a small photo blown up way too big. Joanne looked at it, and puzzled at what this meant. The woman was old, drawn, grey, she looked as if she was terminally ill. The monochrome eyes stared up at her... and then the vampire blood drained from her face. She frantically scanned the text, her panic blurring the words, making them jump and jumble in front of her. She read the name, and suddenly everything was calm, controlled. She could hear her own breathing in the silence of the room. Hear her own heart beat, hear the blood pulse round her body. Hear her life's pulse continue, as she read of what he had done, how his vengeance had reached her.

'Police were baffled today over the horrific murder of a Leeds widow who lost her daughter in mysterious circumstances nearly three years ago. Mrs Margaret Maitland (45) was found in her home last night when neighbours became worried after milk had not been taken in off the doorstep for three days. Those who witnessed the carnage inside 26 Colchester Road described how it appeared to them that Mrs Maitland had been 'hacked to death by a madman'. The police described the attack on Mrs Maitland as 'savage and uncontrolled' and refused to comment further on exactly how she had died. The results of a full post mortem are expected within the next few days. Mrs Maitland, who was widowed nearly twenty years ago when her husband was killed in a drunk driving accident, came to public attention in April 1987, after her only daughter, Joanne, (then 23) disappeared from her London flat. Despite extensive police inquiries at the time, no trace was ever found of Joanne, and the worst was feared. Close friends of Mrs Maitland's described how she had come to terms with the loss. 'After a while, when it was obvious that Jo wasn't coming back, Margaret became convinced she was dead. She did her grieving, and got on with her life. That this should happen to her, it's just horrible, horrible.'
Detective Inspector Harold Patterson, said last night that police were not investigating the daughter's disappearance in light of Mrs Maitland's death. 'It is a tragic coincidence that one family should be wiped out in this way, but we are reasonably sure there are no connections between the two. We are anxious to speak to anyone who had spoken to Mrs Maitland in the last week. It goes without saying that we consider the person who attacked Mrs Maitland as extremely dangerous, and should not be approached by members of the general public.'

The story continued on a double page spread, and she read in fascinated horror a reprise of her own disappearance. It had never occurred to her that there had been so much fuss about her, never thought that she would have been newsworthy for any time. There were two pictures of her, and three of her mother spread over the pages: one of her at school, one of her eighteenth birthday party. She stared at those pictures, and wondered who they were of, for they bore no relation to her. It was as if she was reading about someone else's life, someone else's disappearance.

Could she even remember that far back, to that warm April evening? It had to have been warm, for she was wearing a white dress, with no jacket: it said so in front of her. Had she? Had it? What had that evening been like? She couldn't remember, couldn't remember one single damned thing about it, other than Dreyfuss, and the wine she had sipped when she first saw him. Couldn't remember what she'd being doing that day, what she did the day before. Nothing of that life was open to her, accessible. All there was, of that girl in the school uniform in the photo, was a few scattered memories of childhood. Sitting there, in the quiet dusty room of a foreign land, in a place that she had thought she felt safe in, but that was now utterly alien to her... she read about her own life story. She found it had less to do with her than the faded cotton bed cover she was sitting on. The hotel was more real to her than the people in the paper.

When she did think of her family, her home, it was always her father she thought of, not this woman who stared up at her from the page: not this woman whose death she had caused. The thought closed her heart down for a few moments. Had she suffered? Had he drawn it out? Of course he had, he'd taken his rage out on her mother, made her pay for the defiance that had brought her to this hotel. The real horror broke through to her there, splitting her head with panic, sending sweat cascading out of her body: what if he'd told her? What if he'd told her mother who he was? What if he'd said he was the man who had taken her, that she was alive, and had never contacted her, never told her where she was? She closed her eyes, and tried to close her mind to such thoughts. She couldn't afford it, couldn't afford to lose herself into that fear. She must get out of here, must *go* before he came back for her.

On the bus back into Buenos Aires, with her bag hastily packed and her mind desperately trying to work out where to go next... she realised she had nowhere to go. He knew where she was, had found her with ease, and had been in her room. She looked around the bus: for all she knew he was here, with her at that moment. He was right: there was no running, no hiding from him. She wasn't free of him, wasn't safe from him, wasn't in charge. If he hadn't spoken to her, approached her, taken her, killed her, it was because he didn't want to, not because he couldn't.

She was as captive to him now, as she had ever been

She made the decision there and then, that she'd prefer to be toyed with at home, in her own world, than lost out here. There wasn't enough money to go far more than once: she may as well go back to the UK.

It took her two days to get a flight back to Europe, this time, making no pretence at covering her tracks. By the time she touched down in Brussels, she had lost all sense of time, of urgency. She connected for Heathrow with little thought for where she was going, and arrived in a snow covered land, to discover it was Sunday, and Britain was to all intents and purposes, closed. Reluctant to go into London, she took the Rail/Air link to Reading, and checked into the Ramada, to sleep off her jet lag, which was far worse than it had been in the opposite direction Sleeping through most of Monday, she emerged just in time to do some shopping for clothes.

The noise and confusion was welcome for a change, for everyone pushing for a bargain, and talking loudly in her ear spoke English, and she felt less alienated than she had since her escape. She was nearly freezing to death in the only clothes she had. Standing outside Debenhams, she looked at the prices and shuddered. The room at the Ramada had cost a lot, but she'd wanted some luxury around her before... before he found her. She went in and found a thick warm coat in wool. As she took it to the till, she had a thought, and instead of handing over cash, dug around in her bag for her useless credit cards... for his credit cards. She handed one over, scared it would be removed and the police called. But she had to try.

The card was accepted and the machine spat out a counterfoil.

She signed, wiping tears of relief away discretely, and headed back out the door. With the tags off and the coat on, she determined to make as much of the cards as she could, for as long as she could.

As long as she kept moving...

She moved through some other stores, and bought warm, practical, comfortable clothing: jeans, sweaters, padded jackets and gloves, boots and thick socks, a couple of warm, stylish hats. When she returned to her room, she ordered dinner in her room, and settled down for another night's sleep. In the morning she inquired about hiring a car, then realised the impracticality of that as a long term plan, and went off to buy one. That proved more difficult than she had thought, and she ended up paying a lot of her dwindling cash for a second hand estate car with 80 000 miles on the clock, and the promise that it was mechanically sound, if a little battered looking. She found a Youth Hostel shop in the town, and loaded up with all manner of strange items intended for world travel: a tent that unfolded from a circle of wire flicked in the air, towels that fitted in a match box, lethal looking torches in various sizes, and a sleeping bag that you could sleep on water with, if you were so inclined. It was more expensive than the car, in the end, but as it was his credit, she couldn't have cared less. Finding an AA shop right next to the hotel, she registered for car insurance and recovery services from the Wiltshire address, and left Reading with less idea of where she was going than when she'd landed at Heathrow. Caught between the twin devils of Savernake to the West, and London to the East, she drove north, picking up the M40 as she went. Finding herself heading into Coventry and Birmingham, she turned across country and headed onto the M1. Sheffield was upon her before she really took stock of her position, and stopping at services for tea, she realised it was inevitable that she was going home.

Not that she'd ever considered Rothwell home, they'd only been there a few weeks when Dad had been killed, and she'd never settled there, always wanting in her heart to return to Chorley and her old school and her friends. But her mother had hated Chorley, and had taken comfort in the fact that her husband had managed to get them away, to their own little detached home, before his accident.

Jo had been too young to appreciate it, but his death within months of the taking out of a mortgage, had left them in comfortable straits compared to most. Her mother had adored the bungalow. After the cramped quarters of a one bed roomed council flat above a grocers, she'd considered it a comfortable retreat from the world at large. It was a house that Jo had rarely been allowed to bring friends to, and in which few visitors had ever been entertained. That eighteenth birthday party photo in the newspaper had been one of the few occasions. Her mother's unerring instinct for social mores had told her that you didn't ignore an '18th' and not be talked about. Mum had had the front room, which she called 'the parlour' redecorated. Everyone else referred to it as 'the living room', which it most definitely wasn't. All the living in Jo's childhood had been done in the kitchen, where a large table and some battered armchairs chairs provided what comfort they could. A portable black and white TV had been added at some point, which helped. The grander and larger TV in 'the parlour' was never switched on except on Xmas day, when they both occupied the room as ghosts at their own feast. When the opportunity had arisen, Jo had been more than happy to escape to London, returning infrequently at best, unwillingly in truth.

It was late before she got into Rothwell proper, having lost her way a little as she'd transferred off the motorway. She kept away from her old streets, there being the very real danger that someone might recognise her. Besides, she had no wish to see that house, and stand in the road, imagining what had taken place behind that door. What she did want was the cemetery, a place forbidden to her as a child. She'd been caught there twice: an exhausted little girl who'd walked her little legs off in the long trek from her own house. Dragged back by a truly irate and harried mother, who'd desperately explained, again, that not only was her father not really in the cemetery, but that little girls could not go walking alone in the night, no matter how much they had wanted their favourite fairy story read to them. The cemetery had become a battle ground between them, and was territory that she'd had to concede to the contrary adult in charge of her life. She found it with little difficulty, although she hadn't been there in years. The cold and the dark served her well, as had her meticulous physical training, for she was over the high fence and disappeared into the depths in seconds. This graveyard had been far easier to break into than the last one.

Finding her father's resting place was less easy, graveyards she realised, constantly grew, changed shape, particularly when an adult sought to recognise a child's pathway through the headstones. It emerged eventually, and she found it little changed. The stone was granite, and therefore prone to less weathering than soft marble.

HERE LIES
JAMES WILLIAM MAITLAND
BORN
12/01/41
DIED
12/01/73

BELOVED HUSBAND AND FATHER

It had been his birthday, and he had gone out during his lunch hour to collect cream buns for tea. In a twist of fate that you couldn't make up; the man who killed him had also been enjoying his birthday. A shift worker, who had been working all night, and then gone to the pub with his mates for a celebration. As her father had been crossing the road back to his office, the man had gone through a red light, and hit her father, and a woman who was walking next to him. The woman had been newly pregnant, and she lost the baby, and her leg. Her father had died in the ambulance, whilst the woman had miscarried, and the ambulance men had been dealing with her. She'd read all the clippings as she'd gotten older, and knew them by heart. The driver had gone to prison, where he had hung himself in his cell one Christmas Eve. She hadn't found that out till she was twenty, when her mother let it slip, probably too worn with the memory to carry it on alone any longer.

It had never escaped her since becoming privy to that final secret, that in all likelihood the man had killed himself over regret for the scrap of unborn flesh that was mashed by his car, not the man whose head had been broken open on the kerbside. The unborn do not have friends and lovers to grieve for them, they don't have responsibilities and children of their own. They don't tuck scrubbed clean children into warm sheets at night, telling them of princesses and dragons, enchanted castles and magical talking dogs. The unborn, however, appear to carry more sorrow, more significance, than the born and truly adored. She swallowed the familiar bitterness hastily, unnerved at its continued strength.

She knelt on the grave, and traced her bare hands along the stone. It was freezing cold in the January wind, and even with Dreyfuss's blood in her, she found it difficult to feel where the chiselled edges began and ended: her fingers were numb. She leaned down and kissed her father's name, before standing up to shake the ghosts from her mind. The stone held room for another inscription, as the grave held room for one more. It would be filled soon enough, and she wondered who would attend to her mother's inscription. Who would bury her? It was that thought, more than any other, that drove into her as she stood there. Who would bury her own mother? Chant the prayers, cry the tears, leave the flowers upon the opened earth? Shaking, she headed back for the car, the cold cutting into her bones and ravaging the scars upon her back. Rejoining the motorway, she traced her steps back to the last service station, checking into a Travelodge for a fitful night's sleep.

CHAPTER TWENTY-FIVE

It was still dark as she set off the next morning, taking the straggly line of the M62 as it skirted the southern edge of the Pennines. She was tempted to skip across through Rochdale and Bolton, but there was still snow being blown in drifts across the motorway, and side roads might not be safe. She peeled off the M61 into Chorley about 10 in the morning, just as the grey sun was becoming visible through the heavy cloud cover. She found little she recognised. Her old school was gone, as was her original home. The street itself had disappeared, making way for a dual carriageway. One thing was still there, and that was her grandmother's grave. The irony was not lost on her, as she searched for it in the frigid daylight.

MARY JEAN MAITLAND
2/08/1919 - 14/08/1961
HE WILL SWALLOW UP DEATH IN VICTORY

Her headstone had not fared as well as her father's. One corner was split, and the mildew and moss made it hard to read. It was tucked into a neglected corner of the municipal cemetery, few of the graves around her giving evidence of living relatives to care and tend.

Jo had never known her: she'd died before her father had stumbled on the dance floor at the Locarno and tripped over her mother, tearing her best and only dress and breaking the heel of her best and only pair of stilettos. She died before she saw what her son had made of himself, and before her only grandchild had made her entry into the world. It was strange, that she lay here, so far from her home, with no one beside her that she knew, her son so far away over the snowy hills. Jo had never thought of that before, at least her mother would lie with her father. Was that his wish, for it had been her mother who bought the plot that held him, ordered the stone for two? She'd been brought here every year as a child, to put flowers on this grave when he was alive. Why had she not been allowed to do the same with her father's grave?

She shed Chorley, finding little to hold her, and found Blackpool so quickly she was completely disoriented. She'd remembered an endless bumpy ride on old buses, that seemed to twist and twine forever, before that first magical glimpse of glistening sea. The town came upon her before she was ready for it, and driving up the long front shore, she felt no connection with it at all. She didn't stop the car, driving straight back to the motorway, turning north once more. She knew roughly where she was heading for, but had no idea why.

The M6 just kept on unfolding before her, and she found herself driving through the snow as she drove over the border at Gretna Green. She discovered that drivers travelled in packs. Slow down on the motorway, and a pack would zoom up and overtaken you in sequence. Speed up, you'd overtake the pack and then find the next one ahead. It was a curiosity to her. When she was tired, she'd tuck into the middle of a pack, and drift along.

Perversely, the temperature rose over the afternoon, and by the time she reached Glasgow, the rain was drumming on the roof of the car. Sick of driving, she spent a few days exploring the city, and found it far prettier than she had expected. He didn't turn up, and the credit cards still worked, so she carried on. She wondered if she really thought she could take to the car, and the tent, when the cards stopped working? How much of her world was real now, and how much imaginary? She wasn't sure. Driving around Britain felt far less real than escaping across three continents. Not that that had felt real.

Monday was clear, bright with winter sunshine and brilliant blue skies as she turned to the M8 and drove across to Edinburgh. The drive over the Forth Road Bridge was simply stunning, and she felt she was so close to the age old sight of the Rail Bridge, that she could have leaned over and touched it as she drove over the Road Bridge. Romantic memories of steam trains and dramatic chases across Scotland played out in her head, as old black and white movie memories were triggered by the flattened diamond shaped bridge. The journey around the coast road to her grandmother's home town took much longer than it had looked on the map, and it was late afternoon when she turned into the tiny winding streets of Pittenweem. There was a bed & breakfast house with stunning views right on the harbourside, and she booked into it. It was named 'Gyles House' and it boasted that it had once been the home of Captain Cook. It was set slightly apart from the other buildings in 'The Gyles' row, and faced onto a side way slip that was, essentially, its own harbour. There was also a tiny slip way on the other side, so the house was truly 'stand alone'. It appealed to her immensely, and she looked no further after spotting the B&B sign in the tiny catchment window as she'd parked the car. She entered through a huge oak door, and straight into a spiral staircase, and then up, to the main floors. Her room was the long run from the front eaves, to the back, in the attic spaces. She was lucky they were open in January, it transpired, for most of the tourist houses were closed against the winter gales.

She had an en-suite bathroom and a log fire in the slanted roofed bedroom. The lady who ran it promised she had a sea view of the Isle of the May, but nothing could be seen through the rain. She also informed her that the 'g' is Gyles was a hard 'g', not a 'jee'. Everywhere she went, people spoke things funny. After unpacking, the landlady recommended a restaurant higher up in the village, and Jo slogged up to it: the streets were so steep the main road had to wind back on itself for vehicles to make it.

The seafood turned out to be spectacular, and she enjoyed her meal for the first time in many days. The evening was blustery and rain sodden, the wind driving the rain in off the shore. She returned to her room and hid from the wind, wrapped up warmly against the draughts, listening to the dark sea roar directly onto the house walls and watching the flames dance in the fire.

The reason for the quality of the meal became clear as the noise from the boats unloading their catch in the dark of the morning woke her. It had never occurred to her that such a small community would still boast a working harbour and fish market. The tiny winding alleys, called 'wynds' – she didn't ask if that was blowing air or winding bobbins – led her to believe she would find what she was looking for quickly, and she left the guest house in little more than jeans, sweater and a sturdy jacket. The rain began with a steady grey drizzle, and she found that whilst it was light and pretty looking, it penetrated her clothing very quickly. This meant she was soaked through and shivering by the time she was half way up Cove Wynd, just a few yards from the harbour. So steep was the Wynd, there were handrails attached to the walls, and it only emerged at the top, by the library, by the addition of steep stairs. There was also some kind of cave grotto of some sort that she passed by on her way up but ignored. Past the library, after the Church, was the graveyard. It was very odd, as one graveyard was serviced by two Churches. Or was that two Churches, serviced by one graveyard? She supposed it depended on how one viewed God, whom she was personally sure did not exist; therefore it was not an issue to her.

The Church of Scotland building, at the Cove Wynd end, was much larger and grander than the Scottish Episcopal at the other. She had no idea what either denomination signalled, in the grand scheme of things. The graveyard was caught in the middle, and also wound back around the larger Church, to meet the library. Some of the wall plates were on the library wall.

She pondered on this as sudden squall blew in from the sea and nearly tipped her over a headstone, cutting into her bones till her marrow ached. She could barely see through the rain as it slammed into her horizontally, driving into her eyes like flecks of ice. When the squall blew out, a mere five minutes later, she felt more drowned than dead from the cold. Her hair was plastered against her head, the ends whipped around in the wind, smarting as they lashed her face. Not surprisingly, there wasn't a soul to be seen. She staggered back to her room, peeling off sodden layers with difficulty, her body wracked and blue. He had warned that whilst she was changing, cold would be her enemy. Not that he'd admitted she'd started turning yet. All those lectures about 'When you start to feed...' and she'd had his blood first, what, two years ago? Not only was there the whole 'Drink this glass of vampire milkshake now' mess, there was the blood that had poured over her wounds. Also, she suspected, but would not look at too closely, the whole 'miraculous healing whilst you had a good night's sleep' thing. But she 'hadn't started on his blood yet', had she?

He was quite mad.

It occurred to her, then, in that warm room with the wind and rain driving on to the roof, pummelling the tiny windows and the sea pounding against its walls... that maybe he was just a vampire... that happened to be insane? That he'd been an insane human too? Not that all vampires were insane... just him? Were all the others like him? Could it be that he was mad... but there were actually other, sane, vampires? The thought was incredibly new and rich and fertile. She never ever thought about the other vampires. He never talked of them. She only knew of this Violette, in Paris, and that there were others. But no names or details.

Nothing useful, of course.

Her back was demanding attention, so she put the thoughts aside to concentrate on forcing herself into a hot bath. The very cold bits of her, especially her legs, did not want this, but her back and wrist screamed for heat. She forced herself down into the water, trying to stop the warring parts of her tearing her in two. It was of no consolation to her that pain killers no longer worked so well, as they would have if she'd been wholly human. Just as it had been little consolation to her, that, as she'd removed herself from his influence and had time and space to look upon herself... she'd realized she did have a body that was substantially different from the one she used to have. A somewhat super-human body, in her eyes, at least. She was stronger, she was faster, she felt less pain. She could sleep on concrete and continue to walk for 10 hours solid with no food. She could stay awake for 72 hours, and not lose her thoughts or concentration. She could carry a heavy back pack, and not tire from the weight.

It was only that The Hunger, the ever present hunger, made all of this a torment. The savage desire to devour all, if she allowed her calorie intake to drop. She might feel less pain, but when she did hurt, like this pain in her back now, it was overwhelming, all encompassing. For everything that had been given her, in this changed body, more had been taken. She allowed herself some weakness, and cried silent tears until the worst of the pain eased and she could crawl out of the bath and dress for lunch. She found a roaring fire in the pub down the harbourside and sat so closely to it she thought she smelt smoke from her Aaron sweater. There she returned to the startling thought... that he was actually a vampire who was insane, and sanity may actually reside in others of the Kin.

Forced to look at it for the first time, she realized that his information on vampires, as opposed to being vampire, was very sketchy. A lot was being left unsaid, about actual Kin, as opposed to The Kin, capital letters, exclamation mark. Thinking back to that day she never thought back to, she played through the memories of what she'd seen in his eyes. What she'd then often glimpsed later on, at Arden, when he was playing lover and she fool. Those moments of honesty that she'd catch, when his guard was down. If it was simply that he was insane... he'd been that way when he was Turned. Of that, she was sure. Which begged the question... who would Turn a madman?

Again, a whole new way of looking at things suddenly opened to her. It had never occurred to her that Dreyfuss had been *Turned* by someone else. She'd never looked past *him*, past his madness and his violence... she'd seen what he was as... what it was to be Dreyfuss. Now, she realised she'd seen that as being *vampire*. But what if it wasn't? What if that was *him*, not the... *condition*? Yeah, sure. You have the drink the blood of other humans to live, and you had to kill them at least once a year doing it. Or yes, you could be sane doing that.

...loads of humans kill...

She turned her attention to the fish and chips on her plate, which was something more knowable: hunger, and then feeling full. Concentrate on the little things, like how nice it tasted and how wonderful it as to get the needy feelings out of the way. Little things that will get you past the bigger things in your way. Sated and warm, she returned to the car and searched through the purchases from the Youth Hostel shop. The North Sea, indeed. She had never met it before and was suitably chastened by the experience. Her second visit to the grave yard was more successful, as with the aid of heavy gloves, felted hat, padded water proof jacket and thick boots, she retained enough of her body heat to search systematically. Her legs were less well covered – she hadn't bought weather proof trousers, but she managed to hold her own against the wind that threatened to knock her for six. Many of the headstones had been similarly battered by the elements and the whole grave yard looked somewhat drunk and disorderly.

She searched diligently and found two stones dedicated to Maitland families. All the headstones told their own stories. The most common one was that until very recently, there were few adults buried there compared to the number of children. Many of the older stones were over six feet tall, and detailed the passing of entire families. One Maitland family, on a single large rectangular stone, about five foot high, had many names. Two parents, both dead by 45 years of age, with six children dying before them: the youngest one day old, the oldest six years and four months. Agnes Elizabeth Maitland, nee Boyd and James William Maitland. The stone itself had been raised on the death of the mother, in 1933, and after her name, had been roll called all her dead children. Many of the stones around had taken similar advantage: named predeceased children when the mother had died. It was very sad. What was different from the majority of stones, was that the children had been named fully and their ages added: most headstones just said *died in infancy*. It was a lot of carving and called for a large stone.

Had it been a promise? Had Agnes made James promise to name their children properly, give them full honours? Or had James determined they were to be remembered with their mother, no matter the cost? James himself was the next name, following Agnes in 1936. Another two children followed in 1937 and 1939. There was no sign of the surviving child, Jms Byd, who had inscribed his name as the loving brother of the last child, and son of his parents. James Boyd Maitland could have been her grandfather. Her father's father.

In her head, she rechecked the dates. Agnes Elizabeth Boyd, wife of James William Maitland, had died in 1933, aged 38, and had been buried with her son, John Malcolm, aged one day. The five previous deaths then recalled. Then their father had died. Then came Anna May, daughter of Agnes and James, buried in 1937, aged fifteen years and three months. *Buried by her loving brothers.* Thomas Andrew, followed in 1939, aged nineteen years and nine months, *lost at sea.* She thought of the fish being unloaded at the harbour every day and the strength of the wind battering in on the village, the thickness of the harbour walls and how the moored boats still bobbed violently. Thomas, unlike the other seven, wasn't in this grave: the memory of him was. Thomas had been commemorated by his loving brother, Jms Byd. There was space for his name after this, but it did not appear. With Thomas Andrew, it appeared that the Maitlands ceased to be buried in this graveyard. All the women buried had their maiden names on their stones as well as their married. She couldn't find a female *nee* Maitland that matched the timescale. Nor James Boyd. She thought this through over another excellent dinner, and combed her memory for clues. Her father had been born in this village during World War II, and been taken away to England by his widowed mother when he was five years old. She was sure her grandfather had died before his son was born, but could remember no more about him. She wasn't even sure of his name, other than it was Maitland, but she was pretty sure it had to be Jmes Byd. Her own father carried that Jmes Byd's father's name – James William Maitland. She found James Boyd the next day, on the War Memorial that stood in the churchyard by the main gate: she'd had to walk past it to get in and out.

Sgt James B. Maitland, died between 1939-1945. No other dates, of course, no sense of how old he might have been. He was Army; most of the dead of the village were in the Merchant Navy. She thought of Thomas and the sea. Was that why he'd chosen land forces? She mused on this as she entered the library, which was only open part time. It was one large cramped room, with some local records kept safely aside. The roll of honour was easily found. James Boyd Maitland had died in Libya on 30th March, 1941. He was 24 years old. He had been born third, when she checked the microfiches, born only a month after the first son named James had died. His mother's pride and joy? The longest living of all her children: the survivor. How must James have felt, going off, leaving his pregnant wife? He'd only just buried his last sibling, his brother Thomas, and then there was war. How did James Boyd, her own maybe grandfather, view the world as he'd set off? What had he hoped for in the chaos? Had he suspected, feared, he'd never see his child, never to know if he had a son or daughter? He'd never held the baby, never carried it in his arms. Had he even known that there was a baby on the way, before he died? It seemed unlikely to her.

She drove over to St Andrews the next day, and the main library, and spent the day pouring through the parish records, knitting together the births, the deaths and the marriages. Proof of her lineage was there in the marriage certificate of Mary Jean Ross to James Boyd Maitland. They'd married in August 1939, on the eve of war. Thomas had been lost in the June. Her grandfather's marriage appeared to be the only one that existed for his own generation: all his siblings had died before they could marry. Or so it appeared; the librarian had pointed out she could have missed a birth, and a marriage could have taken place elsewhere, although that would have been unlikely for the times. But that James Boyd was her grandfather... of that there was no doubt.

Exhausted and drained... she still had no idea why she was doing this... she returned to Pittenweem, and walked back up to the War memorial in the slating rain. Looking at all the death it contained, so many names for such a small village, it was no wonder to Jo that his widow had left to become housekeeper to a doctor in England, taking her son to a different future. There was nothing to hold her here after all: not even a grave to tend, just his name, carved with all the others in the Memorial Cross. He had gone across the sea to a far land, and never returned. She ran her fingers over his name, in the same way she had done with her father's and her grandmother's. He was her grandfather, and she was nothing and no one. As the rain froze to sleet, she walked back to the other end of the cemetery, to the headstone tucked behind the far wall, with a view over the sea. By the grave of her great grandmother, Agnes Elizabeth, Jo found her tears for her mother, although they fell reluctantly. It was a strange feeling, to know herself kin to all those silent names, and that as far as she knew, she was the only living Maitland from this place. There must be many cousins, great uncles and aunts spread throughout this area, Boyd and Ross, but the line that James William had gifted Agnes appeared to lead only to her. She ached with the pain of it; the waste. So many births, so much joy, promise; and it had all been worn down to her: a Changeling. The line ended here.

Agnes Elizabeth had mixed her genes with James William's and birthed that mix nine times. All but one mix had failed, and she was the result of that effort. Both James and Agnes lived on only in her. The stone was worn with the wind, and the rain and the snow had pelted it for decades. Agnes Elizabeth had lost Elizabeth May first, then James William, her firstborn. She must have wanted her husband's name continued badly, to then gift it to another son, the next born. Hoping that child, and the name, would survive. She thought of her father, named she now realised, for his own grandfather, although he had never known it. Or at least, *she* had not known this, for how much of her father was really left to her? Her mother had hated to talk of such things, and Jo was lucky to have remembered what she had of her grandmother, lucky to have made it to this remote fishing village. Family and blood had not ever been part of her mother's life.

Jo's mother, Margaret Smith, had been born, like her husband, during the war, but she was not the child of a soldier died valiantly on the front. Not that she knew of, anyhow. Born, and then abandoned in a home for unmarried mothers, Margaret had been named for the midwife who had delivered her, and grown up in a Barnardo's home. Rescued by a man who had married her despite her illegitimacy, and who had no living relatives to cast pity on her indignant head, Margaret had relished the isolation that her tiny family shared. Jo had never understood her mother's shame over her past, her silence on such matters when she had tried to raise the issue. Now, shivering in the bitter wind that whipped off the sea, she understood a little of her mother's wounded pride: her silence and independence from others. She wondered what Agnes Elizabeth would have thought of Margaret; the wife of her grandson, the mother of her great granddaughter. Wondered what she would think of her great granddaughter, and how she had brought about her mother's death. She broke open completely at that thought and sank to the ground sobbing, huddled against the granite that had written upon it her family's doom. The wind took her hat as she slid back on her knees. She tore off the other glove and ran both hands endlessly over the names before her. The soaked grass stole all the heat from her legs. A squall came and went, then another. Still she cried, cried for her butchered mother and a bitter world of regret for what might have been.

Eventually, her body's desperate signals overcame her grief: her teeth began to chatter so loudly she could no longer hear her own sobs. Her back spasmed. She fell silent and used the family stone to drag herself back to her feet. She was tired of crying. She left what she hoped was her last tears behind her as she shivered her way back to the guest house. Left her tears for Agnes Elizabeth, for her father, and, finally, for her mother.

Another hot bath seemed the fastest way to bring her body temperature up, but after three abortive attempts to force her body into one, she settled for soaking in luke warm water instead. The chill didn't leave her for a couple of days, and worse, it set off her wrist and shoulder scars. As ever, the left wrist was the worse, a maddening itch in the reddened tissue, but she could salve there, whilst her broken shoulder was out of her reach. She locked herself up in her room till the worst of it was over. She slept badly, the lack of physical activity affecting both mind and body. All she could think of was Agnes Elizabeth, and the death that had come to her family. The death that was now carried, physically, in her. Dead blood, vampire blood: death and pain.

On the Saturday, she checked out early, ignoring the pouring rain, and headed back over the bridge, across the M8 and down to the M74 once again. She cleared Scotland before stopping for the night, and was in Leeds by the following morning, dizzy and sick with the driving. She checked into a first class hotel in the city centre, and paid extravagantly for the services of a sports physio and masseur, who worked the knots out of her body in stunned silence. She paid the man well to work massive amounts of hydro-cortisone cream into her back, and her skin felt much better by the morning, which she spent in the gym. By evening, she was feeling less battered and she repeated the routine of exercise, massage and rest for another two days. On Wednesday, the local newspaper carried a full feature on her mother's death, and the police investigation. Once more, her own disappearance was gone through. She gleaned from the article three interesting facts.

Her mother had been involved in running a missing persons emergency phone line since her own disappearance, helping out at fund-raising events and speaking in local schools. That she had met a local man, Mark Wilson, whose son has also vanished ten years earlier, and they had established some sort of relationship. The paper described him as a 'close friend' and Jo wondered how he was faring. Finally, the police were close to releasing her body for burial, and a collection was being made for flowers. That made sense to her; she knew her mother had paid for her own funeral, at the Co-op, many years earlier. But with no relative to bury poor Mrs Maitland, flowers would have to be furnished from the community. This filled her with morbid doubts. If she came forward now, declared herself to all and sundry, she could bury her mother. But there would be all those questions, all that fuss. Where had she been, what had she done? She knew that people sometimes did disappear for years, and suddenly turn up, but doubted if she could do so. All the fears she had ever had about her sanity returned, and in this, her scars were her only solace.

She *could* have imagined Dreyfuss, been in some mental breakdown all these years. Could even, conceivably, inflicted the damage on her arms and wrists herself, but she could never have done to her back what Dreyfuss had done. She could just imagine explaining herself to the police, the authorities, explaining her disappearance, her life on the streets as a tramp, and her decision to return on hearing of her mother's death. But she couldn't imagine how she could carry it off, how she could even be in the same room with people who knew who she was, who she had been, without wanting to rip the clothing off her back and graphically reveal the changes in her. She couldn't imagine her *not* telling them who had killed her mother. A *vampire*. A vampire had killed her mother. A man who had been alive for centuries, killing for centuries. It was obscene. It was insane.

It was impossible.

The thoughts tore through her mind trying to find some escape, some way of being heard. All the moments of isolation she had felt since returning to Britain, moments that had been totally different when abroad. Moments of being amongst living people, real people, but being set apart from them. The casual interactions with cashiers and waitresses check in clerks and maids. The moments of standing at her car, filling up with petrol, watching other people in their cars, in their own world. Of being of these people... home... but totally separate from them. The desire to talk to them, to reach and touch them, the sadness at the distance, thousands of light years, which separated her from them. The silence within as she had returned to the car. The blood and pain that divorced her from all of them.

On her flight across the world, she had been isolated from others as she was foreign and strange: alien. In Britain she was foreign and strange and alien... as she was no longer quite human. It had taken escape from him, and then return... for her to see she was no longer part of this world.

She was having increasing difficulty in keeping apart her two lives, the two versions of herself: Jo and Helene. Jo's world, the normal one, where people went to work, came home on the bus, lived and laughed together. Helene's world: the world of Dreyfuss, and blood, death and immortality. They just didn't meet, could make no sense to her. The sense of schism she had felt on that night when he had fed from the boy in front of her, returned. What she was living through *could not exist*. It defied all sense, all logic, all she had ever known about her world. It was possible as she fled him abroad... in the strange new worlds that were out there... it was *possible* that he could exist and track her. Here... here it was *impossible* that the great granddaughter of Agnes Elizabeth Maitland had been kidnapped by a man who was alive on the day that Agnes herself had been born. Had been alive when Agnes's mother and grandmothers and great grandmothers had been born. It was impossible that she was being Turned to his blood, becoming one with him. Such things did not exist in this world. Could not exist. They did not, could not, meet.

Faced with the possibility to standing up and claiming her mother's body... she could not face the shame. The shame of who she was and what she'd done. Of how she was responsible for finding solace in a maniac's arms, of how she'd been weak and needed him, no matter what he'd done. Of how she'd offered herself to him, and been grateful for any gentle touch. Of how she'd not been strong enough, when she'd picked up that phone on the first night after the death, and screamed '*Tell my Mum I'm here!*' Nothing about explaining what had happened could be done without admitting her culpability: her weakness. She wouldn't shame Agnes Elizabeth by speaking a truth that connected Dreyfuss to her. The world that contained Agnes did not contain him. It was inhumane, to bring what she now was, to her own blood. Her own blood no more. She could never tell anyone else what had happened to her. Not humans, at least.

She wasn't going to be sectioned either. No psych was going to try and persuade her out of her delusions. Dreyfuss was no delusion: he was nightmare, and not one she could share with others. No matter how she'd intend not to mention him, she would be driven too. Pretence was not an option. The pain too real, the scars too fresh, literally.

She had nothing to do with this living world, and she would be best to leave it behind utterly.

Nevertheless, she found herself, in the dark of that moonless night, standing in the street outside her mother's house, that which had been her home. Inside that house were all manners of things that proved who she was, marked the passing of her feet in this world. There was her birth certificate, her baby clothes, school photos. Her school uniform probably still hung in her closet, wrapped carefully in the dry cleaning bags that her mother managed to keep for years without tearing. Her school books were in the loft, her toys in the cupboard under the stairs. In her mother's jewellery box lay the coal black curls from her first hair cut, along with her first tooth, dipped in silver. Her parent's marriage certificate was somewhere in that house, with their birth certificates, and her father's driving license. Her own birth certificate and school records, her exam certificates. In some senses, she existed in that house more than she did outside it.

The woman standing in the street called herself Helene, and signed that name on every card receipt, every hotel register. She presented to the living world as such. *That* was what was in that house, in those records and photos and memories: the living world, Joanne's world. She moved through this world like a ghost, a spectre forever haunting the feast. The hundreds of miles she had driven, surrounded by people, sleeping in rooms next to them, eating at tables across from them, watching their children smile and chatter: they were as dead to her as her mother had been all these years.

She could break into that house now, find all those memories, those traces of her presence, wrench her life back: but it would never be a living one. For along with her toys and games, her father's braces and her mother's handbags, there was something else in that house now:

Dreyfuss. He had taken her mother's life in that house, in the kitchen. In the place where she had eaten fish fingers and frozen chips, sneaked biscuits out of tins, and moaned about doing the washing up. He'd split her mother wide open. He'd used the knife she'd used to peel potatoes, chop carrots for stew. She'd died alone, not knowing whether her only child was alive. She'd died in agony and terror.

In that kitchen, where she'd done her homework, and sat on her father's knee as he'd given her pocket money, Dreyfuss had split her mother's body open and spread her wide. In that single, violent act, Jo's life path had been changed, just as it had been on the afternoon her father's head had struck the stone kerb. A catastrophe even greater than the one that had occurred on the night she'd missed a train on the way to a party. Imprisoned in his world, she could block this reality from her mind. She could distance herself from what was outside of his walls, never dwell on such thoughts as what her Mum was doing, or what had happened to her cat. There was no room for such domestic niceties while she was watching him feed, her blood filling up his veins. She could take the changes, the punishments, the rewards, and accept what he was, and not let it touch this other place. Now, they existed together, and all she had ever been was eaten by his savagery. There was only one world now, one existence, one dimension to her life. He had pulled her completely through to his side. The question was what she did about it. The part of her mind that always whispered survival was silent. Other areas of thought must be engaged.

She stared once more at the house seeking some sort of answer. What would her father have said? How could she possibly know? She closed her eyes, blocking the house and its ghosts out. This place was only giving her more pain, eating her up from the inside out. As ever, there was only her, she must make the answers for herself. Lives torn asunder cannot be repaired, restored; they can only be made over into something new.

Before leaving the next morning, she almost left a cash donation for the flower fund, but a sense of outrage prevented her. An awareness that she'd be trying to buy off her mother's memory. Besides, it was his money. Sickened by the car, and driving, she parked at the railway station and left it unlocked, keys in the ignition. She abandoned everything, taking only her hand bag. She was thoughtful enough to leave the registration documents in the glove compartment. Someone was going to enjoy the unexpected bounty of a tent that could withstand 20 degrees of wind chill. Leaving on the next London train, she was long gone out of the station before Mungo and Midge arrived.

Dreyfuss's instructions had been clear, take a train to Leeds, locate the cars parked side by side in the station car park, her keys locked in his. Take both cars straight back to Wiltshire. He'd barely had the time to lock both cars before boarding her train.

She put all thoughts of Joanne's mother's funeral to one side. Joanne wasn't here, and had been gone a long time. Helene didn't have a mother, and therefore would never need to attend a burial nor order a headstone carved. Helene could never escape Dreyfuss, just as Joanne had not been able to. Now that Joanne was gone, Helene was determined to make living possible amongst the dead.

The train hurtled on to London.

CHAPTER TWENTY-SIX

King's Cross assaulted her with noise and chaos. After the privacy and freedom of the car, it was a tremendous shock. People rushed her from all sides, swooping past, banging into her, battering her with their presence. She queued for a taxi, longing for the isolation of the cab whilst people pushed and shoved around her. When she finally gained the space of the cab, she found it little comfort, locked in endless queues of traffic, and made the driver pull over and release her. Whilst the night air was cold and sharp it was substantially warmer than the north had been. The city air smelled of fumes and oil, and the light splattering of rain felt abrasive, stinging her face. She walked for a little while, then braved the tube, which immediately encased her in anonymity. She emerged at Bond Street, with a fair idea of her destination, although she ended up walking the wrong way, and it took her a while to find it.

The staff at Claridge's were too well trained to raise an eyebrow at a young woman arriving rain soaked, pale and luggage-less in jeans and hiking boots, but with funds to order and pay for a suite for a month. They certainly made no connection between her, and the rather more elegant gentleman who arrived less than half an hour later.

He'd been immensely relieved when she abandoned the car and bought a rail ticket. All that driving had been tedious and it made feeding difficult. He'd almost starved in that rain soaked rat hole they'd called a village, and his temper had been wearing thin. He had always detested Pittenweem and his shock that she'd ended up there was considerable. Spending days hiding from her in the rain had not helped, as there had been too much time doing nothing not to end up thinking about all the other times he'd spent there, and how he hated the entire East Neuk. He was furious with her for dragging him up there and had regretted his trick in her hotel room with the newspaper once or twice. Who knew startling her in a bolt hole in South America would have driven her to the shores of Fife of all the god forsaken areas of the world? God forsaken, that was right, on so many counts.

It had been fascinating though, he had to admit that. He'd had no idea how she'd react to the newspaper he'd had sent through, and it had been all been so much more interesting when she'd touched back down in the UK, to track her himself. Violette always charged more than she quoted and the bill for finding her in Argentina was immense. He owed her more than money, and she would not let that pass. So the return to London had pleased him immensely: home turf was easier to play in. Here, he was in charge. That was why he'd rewarded her by opening the cards back up. That, and made it clear she was being followed. She'd coped with it all rather well, he'd thought, just as how he'd grown proud of her afresh, the harder she'd been to track. Rage and fury at her leaving, had been replaced by admiration over what he'd created. She'd done exceptionally well, but had been starting to slip up badly though, by the time she boarded the train. The police would have been called in over the car within hours, and leaving her registration documents and her keys would have made a murder scare by morning. He wasn't terribly convinced about Claridge's either, although so far, her instincts had been good on such things. Well, we'd see what the morrow brought, but he didn't think it was going to last much longer.

She started off early enough, proving his misgivings by appearing that morning in the creased clothing from the night before. Not that she'd had much choice, he supposed, since everything had been left in that awful claptrap car. She remedied that immediately. He quite liked the smart suit she bought in Selfridges, consigning the jeans to the bins in Oxford Street. Her next stop surprised him, and it was hours before she emerged, almost giving him the slip as she did. He hadn't been expecting the cool blond that emerged with a shining cap of hair: collar length, and cut asymmetrically to one side. She looked stunning. Harvey Nichols was next, which was much more like it, although the hours she was in with the personal consultant dragged. He filled the time usefully enough, choosing quite a few items himself. The woman who was paid extremely well to fetch and carry whilst her clients reclined in the splendid isolation of a dressing suite was having a hard time. Being a class act, she'd started from the bottom up, so to speak, and the lingerie department alone took an hour of flitting in and out, here and there. The woman had started off with that blasé composure of the professional at work, but after a few rejected lace bras and knickers, she'd emerged pale and trembling, her scent signalling her discomfort. He wondered how little Joanne was coping with the woman's attempts to mask her reaction to seeing that body uncovered. There had been no sheer body sleeves in her world for quite a while. How had she coped? The assistant disappeared back into the dressing areas with an armful of silken teddies and body stockings. There were ways around everything.

By the time they had gotten to the shoes, he was itching to see what she'd bought. The procession of clothes in and out had seemed never ending, and he'd not been able to track everything as it had come and gone, needing to be seen to be served himself. As the store was beginning to close down for the day, she emerged, and he realised he'd missed a beautician going in. He couldn't quite believe it was her, this tall cool blonde with impeccable grooming and a sheen of personal style that was both younger, and more daring that he'd witnessed before. The not quite recognising her was mirrored at the hotel when she asked for her key and she had to give the number before the startled clerk realised which guest she was. Very bad form for Claridge's. He at least, had seen the transformation in stages, whilst the hotel clerk was seeing it in one go. She ate in her rooms again, and he went out to feed himself, his exhilaration making a pleasure out of necessity.

The next morning saw a stream of boxes and designer bags delivered to her room. He listened at her door to the ripping and shredding noises before returning to his own suite to call the bank. It wouldn't do to stop her in mid-stride at this stage and he was smirking as he cleared through a massive amount of credit for her.

She was his again.

The extra credit was a precaution he was thankful for as he followed her into Mappin & Webb. She was wearing a Chanel suit in green linen, which settled upon her trim body like a glove. Her hair had kept its shape, a testament to perfect cutting, and she'd done an excellent job with the new makeup. Even in this store, well used to money and power, she shone out like a beacon, sending them here, sending them there. They whisked around her eagerly, sensing the size of the sale. She didn't disappoint them. The emerald ear studs had caught her eyes first, and she'd had to try them on. This was followed by the matching necklace, then the bracelet, which licked green fire around the curve of her wrist. She then chose an impeccably matched pair of diamond studs, which no necklace in the store could compliment, a fact she recognised quite quickly. A series of simple, elegant gold necklaces followed, from which she chose three: pale, rose and white gold. A platinum art deco brooch. An exquisite ring of woven gold bands. The significant factor about that ring, he'd missed, and would not discover for a few days. He'd had to leave then, afraid of making himself obvious, but the receipts informed him later of her other purchases. Another four brooches; amber, coral, gold and silver. Three more rings, a solitaire, a sapphire ringed by diamond chips, and a gold thumb ring. Two anklets, one gold, one platinum. Three silver and crystal perfume bottles. Two lipstick holders, gold. One powder compact, gold with jade inlay. A wrought silver purse mirror.

Whilst they were ringing the purchases through, he'd stood in the street and switched on his mobile phone. Just as the bank called, once again, to check it was all acceptable. He barked at them that he did not want another call, no matter what occurred on any of the cards.

She lunched briefly, grabbing a sandwich and a tea, then spent some time in a theatre ticket booth. At this, he phoned Arden, ordering Mungo and Midge into London. She spent the afternoon in Liberty's, although she bought little more than a handful of extravagant scarves. This amused him immensely: she was toying with him. Whilst she was changing for the evening, he went through the credit card faxes, and sifted out the ticket purchases. She was spending that evening at St Martin's in the Field for a candlelight concert, tomorrow evening at the Haymarket for Arcadia, and Monday evening at the National for a Pinter retrospective. The trolls, as he had come to think of the two men, could follow her to all those, although he had intended to pick up Arcadia at one point. He was bored with standing in rainy streets. It was also becoming increasingly difficult to control his libido when seeing her, and erections were not useful in undercover work.

Leaving them both to keep her in their tracks, he took the car back to Savernake. He found Mary in the living room, acting like she owned the house. She returned to the staff cottages with a timely reminder of her boundaries in his employ. They'd been stuck without tasks for too long, and were forgetting their places. Once more, it annoyed him he needed help with her Turning. He enjoyed a trip into Marlborough for both food, and feed, then unpacked his own selection of boxes from Harvey Nichols, relishing the synchronicity. After a good night's sleep, he drove to a local spa and spent the morning working out in the gym, and the entire afternoon swimming. He'd done this frequently over the three long months she was gone. He was missing her blood badly, and exercise took his mind off that. He'd grown used to her taste, her scent. Everything tasted a little flat without her. That had been a serious revelation to him, in the ashen weeks after she'd disappeared. At first his rage had taken him through it, fury at her defiance propelling him along in her wake. He'd not been at all happy that he'd been forced to ask for help in tracking her down. He'd had to sit back, and wait, dependent on others; that had been the most humiliating part. But that had been worked through, and in the absence of her, he'd discovered how much comfort he'd gained from the presence of her.

When reports had started trickling through of her move down through the Americas, relief had been the dominant emotion. So he'd worked on finding all the reasons why he was pleased – in the name of her Turning – that she'd escaped. It had taken iron self control on his part, to allow her to continue her flight, and not intervene until she'd settled, and was feeling secure. Although it was useful, to display his superior understanding to Violette and her trash. Ordering them to stand down *and do nothing*... had been satisfying.

It now didn't concern him so much that she'd gone, that she'd fooled him, which was good in its own way. Neither did he really worry that she would not be found, that was never at issue. What galled him, what really drove spikes into his eyes, was that he'd had to sit and wait for others to find her first. That she'd managed *such* a clean escape... his ego still required retribution for that.

But it had been useful in some ways, for it had focused him, given him time to plan things out meticulously, even if it had also embarrassed him initially. His Turning her had provided the Kin with enough gossip, enough opportunities to discuss his life between them. Some of them would have laughed at him losing her, the stupid ones that is. The rest would have understood that her actions had only proven him right in his decision: that she was equal to the challenge. Equal to Dreyfuss. That made him smile.

Yet he had been forced to ask filth like Violette for help, and that was never part of his plan. Paying for her services was one thing, but owing her favours quite another. That would have smug bastards like Jordan chortling over their feed. He didn't wonder if even Agrippa had heard about his little faux pas, and that *incensed* him. It wasn't the debut amongst the Kin he had planned for her, and it sure as hell wasn't how things were going to be left. But it did mean he'd have to deal with that Parisienne witch at some point, and that was going to be difficult; now he owed her.

He'd owed her for finding him the trio, of course, but that was business. Needing her network to find his *little one*... that was galling. It never bothered him that he had nothing to do with any of the rest of them. He was their superior, as they were all night turned and inconsequential. He was one of only five left Turned the old way, the correct way, and none of the others had been seen for centuries. The known Kin were peasants one and all, even the old man. They were nothing to him... and that he'd had to use Violette of all people, to send out her brats and orphans... it galled. A powerful amount of frustration had built these past three months, and now she was back, he felt it just might find release. Not on her, of course, that was futile, but it would be nice to get back on track. Afterwards. After it was over.

Now he must concentrate on bringing her home, so he could finish. She had to walk through the door of her own accord. At least, that's what she had to think.

That he needed her, that he wanted her...for herself, and not what she represented... that was pushed under. In the months of her absence, he had found himself waking in the night, the scent of her in his nostrils, the sound of her in his mind. Waking to physical desire, wanting to feel her softness under him as he penetrated her, not for the fear of it, for the control of it... but something akin to pleasure, comfort. He was so used to her, so completely at ease with her. She'd been with him now for such a long time, enough time for him to notice, his body adjusting to her rhythms. None had ever survived this long, and she had done more than survive: she had thrived.

He thought of that long cool blond, impeccably dressed, totally in charge, who had sent them running in London. Who had nodded this way, then that, and everything had been brought to her. He thought of how she looked in those clothes, how she had moved through the streets. How her eyes had scanned the cases, her mind weighing the options, looking for quality. It was refreshing to see her act like that, to watch her in charge. It was exciting. He concentrated on his stroke, another ten lengths, then he'd feed. Mary was in need of some more humility and he had a suspicion that she'd struggle rather well.

The enjoyment she'd been taking in being free of the worry of who she was, and free of the need for flight, and free of the need to worry about money, took her a week to work through. She may be free of what had been crushing burdens of worry... but she was still lonely and trapped in the overall nightmare. She stopped enjoying the time out, and turned to much more time in. After so long in flight, rest and comfort were a salve to her. He could walk in at any time, but that had, essentially, always been true. On registering, she had not required the in-house butler service, but had needed help in unpacking and caring for all her shopping as she'd progressed, and so she'd had a maid service assigned to her. It was not the full service of the butler, but it was a half-way house of seeing the same person, semi-regularly, who attended to making sure her clothes were dry cleaned and returned to their hangers and drawers, and that her suite was kept impeccable. The identity of the maid changed with shifts, but consistency was kept to, where possible. As she spent more time in, reading, and curled up on the chairs and ordering snacks and drinks throughout the day, she would sit and read whilst the primary maid worked in the other room. She was a young Canadian woman, Minette, who was impeccably trained in the non-committal standards of care that servants charged well for. Whilst working within her professional boundaries, this young woman was capable of letting Helene know that she could see her distress.

Connection had been almost inevitable, given that with the names they carried, the maid had assumed Helene was French, and she had assumed the same of the maid. In clearing up that neither were actually French, although both, clearly, with French origins, they started with a slightly less formal tone. A series of smiles, and passing references to the clothing and the jewels, which Minette helped unpack and put away, then opened a slight passageway of communication between them. They would speak French to each other at times.

Minette was discreet and exceptionally well founded in not offending her employer by being too familiar, but by the end of the second week, it was clear to Helene that the maid thought that she, Helene, was on a respite break from love. That in first of all spending an obscene amount of money to fill empty wardrobes as she'd arrived with only the clothes she wore, and then spending time going out alone to shows and concerts, and then locking herself in her room to read books and watch a lot of television... that she was pining for a lover. Or dealing with a lover's transgression, and was awaiting rescue. This was all conveyed in the gentlest of touches, and very little was actually said between them, but the young woman... why did she think of her that way, the maid was probably her age, if not older?... was clearly sensitive to her need for solitude, whilst over reading the part of *l'amour* in the situation.

So when the gifts began to arrive, Minette was quite excited, in an understated and unobtrusive manner. The first bouquet, of exquisite white lilies with jasmine and tight white rosebuds, was breathtaking. There was a slight flush to the maid's face when she appeared with the display, and said merely, 'A delivery for you Mam'selle.'

Helene's own reaction, which was to wave her away with a dismissive hand and return to her book, only reinforced the idea that this was a lover's tiff. So whilst Minette was not the only one to bring the gifts to her suite, she was the only one whom Helene knew was reacting. It was actually slightly amusing.

Dreyfuss had been careful with the gifts, and she did both note and appreciate it. When once it would have been ostentatious displays of wealth and status, it was now delicate and discreet personal tokens. A bouquet of flowers, a box of favoured chocolates. A book she'd liked. A gift of a box set of DVDs of her favourite melodramas. Her preferred handmade toiletries from Marlborough. A gift box of the handmade body sleeves that truly, she had missed. That one, mistakenly opened in front of Minette, had brought tears to her eyes, and she'd had to turn away to hide her face. Minette had been too well trained to say anything, and had withdrawn, but it reinforced the narrative the maid had running in her mind, about the lover in the wings, awaiting to be allowed back in. Ironic, given the tears were over the grief for the need for the body sleeves to be worn. And that he who had given her the scars, seemed to be the only one who knew where the sleeves had been made, and therefore was the only one who could furnish the means to disguise them adequately.

It was about two weeks into the gifts, a good three weeks after she'd arrived, that the invitation came one morning. It was a card, wound into another white bouquet of jasmine and lilies. The card was as simple as it was elegant:

L'ortolan, Tomorrow Evening, 8pm.

It was an impeccable choice. Just outside Reading, therefore between the frying pan and fire of London and Arden Coombe. Public space, yet discreet. Somewhere both of them would have to travel to, and from. Double security. And on departure, a choice to be made, which direction to travel back; London or Savernake, alone, or in company?

Was it possible she could not attend? Was it possible she could say 'yes' but change the date or the hour? Minette tweaked the bouquet and settled the display as she sat and thought. The excitement and tension the aide was displaying was palpable. Perhaps best to let her go after all, and request a service change? That would be a black mark on her record, Helene was sure, and so she resigned herself to a little more interaction with Minette than she would have liked.

'You may go, Minette, but please come back tomorrow afternoon and help me prepare. Please inform the concierge team I would like a limousine for tomorrow evening, let them know the destination.'

'Oui, Mam'selle.' She was almost glowing with anticipation.

Helene returned her attention to the card. It was inconceivable that she not attend. A choice offered more or less freely, once spurned, would not be a choice. Yet was that a choice at all? She considered the options, few that they were. She could refuse him, make him come to her, as no doubt Minette thought she was doing by staying here in the first place. How many of the other staff believed this of her? Probably a few, those who could be bothered to fathom the actions of the pampered rich.

She smiled at the irony of Minette's fantasy on her behalf, the love-lorn lover waiting... waiting... waiting. He'd hardly be a lover if she failed to attend. He'd come to her all right, but not in a form she'd appreciate. Did she appreciate this, the invitation? Sorting through her wardrobe, deciding nothing would do and that, bothersome as it might be, she'd have to shop, she decided she did. It was nice of him to ask her, like a normal woman, rather than turn up... turn up and what? Throw her over his shoulder, drag her out of the hotel by her hair? It was a series of such ludicrous thoughts that kept her entertained throughout the afternoon's search. The reality was she could be whisked into a car by the Three Stooges at any time. Swallowed up once more in the city's bustle, an anonymous snatching, undertaken in seconds.

She had no illusions.

She headed up to Bond Street. Searching out the right outfit was not easy. It wasn't the first time, when shopping, she bemoaned that her left shoulder blade had been destroyed. She'd never found a one sleeved gown that would cover both shoulder and wrist, and wasn't looking forward to finding anything suitable. Fashions had changed in her absence, however, and she was happier with some of the new sleeker dress shapes with less tailoring and no shoulder pads. She had good legs, so went for a short glimmery silver-blue mini dress with matching jacket. She'd just have to keep the jacket on. The same dress, with long sleeves as opposed to spaghetti straps, would have been ideal, but that wasn't on offer. It came with matching clutch and shoes, so all she needed was the right tights, with no top edges.

She returned to the suite and brooded.

Minette turned up at 3pm as requested, and helped her prepare. Helene had no idea why she'd requested such help, but it was somehow comforting. She'd just showered, and put on her knickers and body sleeves, and she was wearing her dressing gown. Minette helped her choose the jewellery for the dress, agreed that the diamond studs were the best earrings, and that nothing was required round the neck at all. Then she'd busied herself with tidying up as Helene blow dried her hair, the bob falling back into line perfectly. They exchanged pleasantries, as girls do, when one is dressing for an event. Even service could not remove the basic connection of preparing to greet a male. Her eye make-up was slightly heavier than normal, to cope with the sheen on the dress, and she'd genuinely required feedback and aid from Minette. Was this the correct shade, should there be more blusher? It was bittersweet to

Helene, who had so missed normal human companionship. To Minette, usually behind the reserve of staff... what was it, Helene wondered? An afternoon distraction whilst she got to see Helene prepare for her romantic renewal? Staff at establishments such as Claridge's were there to mimic that their suites were the home of the client, and the staff their own personal staff. Was she over reading Minette's manner? Was Minette a successful mimic, to all her client's needs? She pushed away the over thinking... that was Dreyfuss, in her mind, and she wouldn't play the game. She chose to believe Minette was genuinely concerned that she, her client, was well turned out and happy. After all, you didn't aim to be a servant at this level, unless you enjoyed service.

She had bought tights that had a seamed back strip, as if they were stockings, but with no top leg line at the thigh, and was actually grateful for Minette's hands on attitude, as, never having worn them before, she had had little idea of how hard it was to get them straight. The sectioned heels alone took 10 minutes fiddling with to get perfectly centred. With the tights on, and her makeup done, and her hair perfect, and with not that long to go, Helene took off her dressing gown as Minette held up the sheer dress.

Helene heard the unconscious catch of breath as the other woman spotted the body sleeves. Of course, she did not react in the slightest and simply carried on slipping the dress down. Its informal lines needed no zip. Helene looked in the mirror, and liked what she saw. In the reflection, Minette's eyes betrayed that all she was looking at was the curve of the body sleeve on the left shoulder, and the one that covered her left arm, from wrist to elbow. The silver-blue spaghetti strap sat in the middle of the beige sleeve fabric. Looking at it now, as she moved slightly to see how the dress flowed, Helene realized there was no reason why that part, the part that showed on her neckline and shoulder... could not be transparent. The arm sleeve needed to cover the scars. The same with the panel on her back. But the shoulder line could be much more sheer.

Helene looked at... Helene. Minette slipped the jacket over her shoulders. Yes, at the meal, she could have the jacket loose like that, rather than wearing it, if she wanted, without exposing too much. They were sure to be in a private room.

'You look amazing.'

'Thank you.'

'Do you mind if I make an observation, Madame?'

Helene was taken aback for a moment... then answered that no, she did not mind. But she noted she'd moved from 'Mam'selle to 'Madame'.

'It is only that I thought I should mention... full length gloves never go out of fashion.'

Minette turned and busied herself with tidying up as Helene stared at her reflection. Why had she never thought of that?

The answer came to her as she was sitting in the limousine for the ride out. With rush hour traffic to contend with, they'd left at 4pm, so she had plenty of time to stew.

She'd never thought of it, as Dreyfuss had never bought her long length gloves. He'd brought her a body sleeve: she wore that. It had never occurred to her to respond outside his direction. With the exception of the things she'd bought since moving into Claridge's, everything she'd ever bought had followed the lines of fashion he had set up for her. She'd never noted it. Well, really, how could she have? It's not like she'd had much bother, or fascination, or budget, for clothes before he took her. And everything had been so set in advance, his favoured style, his sense of taste. Why was it so surprising?

She determined it wasn't... but it was interesting. Especially when she emerged from the limousine at the restaurant, and saw the look on his face.

Saw how he'd stared at her legs, and how he'd reacted to the swish as her very short dress moved along her thighs.

He had been a perfect gentleman, and booked them into the main dining room, if in a discreet location. So they were still in public, but could speak privately.

'Thank you for coming.'

She was, she had to admit, simply terrified. But oh, that was getting so old.

'Thank you for inviting me.'

She looked over to him, taking note of him properly for the first time, as she made pretence of looking at the menu. He looked well, but slightly older. There were a couple of lines around his eyes, and his hair had a suggestion of grey.

'You've not been feeding well.'

'You have not been here.'

It was, simply, the most bizarre thing she had ever done. Sit and chat with him, as if they truly were lovers, and they were truly setting out a path to see if they could be reconciled. The room saw that was who they were, and gave them privacy. The table was set in a slight alcove of sheer drapes, and the other tables far distant. Discretion was a by word here, for all clients.

They chatted over the starters, over the main course, over the dessert. They discussed all sorts of things, things of no note or meaning, but interesting in their own way. The old groove of social chit chat between needed little help in being established. It was, after all, a primary method of remaining safe from him. As coffee arrived, she did something so unexpected, that even she had not seen it coming.
She slipped off her jacket.

He was totally nonplussed. The body sleeves were there for all to see, should anyone glance in their direction. She looked up at him, and carried on as if nothing had happened. He hesitated, and froze. She had the advantage. He simply hadn't expected her to have taken hold of something, something he thought should be hidden, and present it. In that moment she realised something important. Dreyfuss was all about illusion. Everything about him, the wealth, the status, the power... it was illusion. He cared greatly for how things looked. Not just from a perspective of power... but from one of conformity. She'd never seen it before. How could she have, never having truly stepped out from his gaze? He had captured her whole, and she'd only seen herself through his eyes. Only seen him as he presented himself to her. She put down her coffee cup.

'To business, then.'

He raised a quizzical eyebrow, and signalled her to proceed.

'Much as I appreciate the invitation, we both know there is no invite here. We both know I have no choice with you.'

He nodded.

'Likewise, we both know… I hate you.'

He nodded again.

'And it is of no importance to you, at all, really.'

There was a hesitation. He chose his words with considerable care.

'I do not quite agree, little one. I do…' the pause was long, as he searched for an alien word '…care… for you.'

How to answer that? She felt along the words, trying to fit an impossible reality into normal, everyday words that would make sense.

'When you care for people, you want them to be happy, to be safe. You don't care about my feelings. You don't care for my suffering. You don't care for my pain. I am a dog to you, obedient and loyal, and to be chastised when appropriate.'

He put down his own coffee cup, and sat back, thinking long and hard.

'Your verdict is somewhat accurate. However, you are not a person: you are a pet. You are a possession. Something I own. One can care greatly for a pet. I never have, but I know others do. You mourn when they die. You miss them when they are gone.'

Genuine emotion again. Her own emotions were more genuine, and of rather more weight.

'You beat them when they misbehave?'

'Yes, you do.'

She felt stalled. Where to go with this?

He took the lead.

'Dogs stay with bad masters, as well as good ones.'

Okay, she'd started in the wrong place.

'You are not my Master.' It was a little too defiant.

'Yes, I am. Otherwise you would not be here.'

Touché.

That was the actuality. The part she could not escape from. The pain was immense, but held distant. Perhaps it is true – carry a pain long enough, it gets lighter. Or maybe you become less... these were not good thoughts to be having. She concentrated on him again.

He took the lead when her attention was back on him.

'Joanne...' She flinched, broke eye contact and looked away. He smiled, and sat back. Oh this was sweet. He looked to her, and made an assessment. He began again... '...Helene...?'

She looked up. Such was the sweet contentment, he felt an erection stir.

Oh this was divine. *Divine.*

It was not just the surge of power that came from knowing he had broken her with her past... it was that in doing this, he had brought her a significant step closer to him. He relished that taste whilst still continuing to ignore why it was important to him that she return.
Loneliness was not a state of being he recognised for himself.

'Helene... I respect that you escaped. I respect that you are more than I thought. That does not mean I do not own you. It does not mean I will not mete out pain and suffering when I will it. It does not mean I will not punish you for transgressions. You know I will punish you. You know that not to punish you is not an option. I am your Master. That I care about you is part of being your Master. Punishing you is part of that care.'

She held her poise, her skin blanched, her pulse sped... but she kept her composure.

'It is also my pleasure. I like what I do to you. Sometimes, it is true, you drive me to distraction, and I have, I will admit...' Helene felt the nature of the air in the room change. Time was holding its breath. '...that I have sometimes damaged you further than I should have. I know that I have a temper, and not everything I have done has been honest.'

Every hair on her body was standing straight up to attention. All the quiet background sounds in the room fell into silence. The waiters around had disappeared. She expected the air to crackle with static. Did he have any idea he was leeching power out into the air? Physical, tangible... she could taste it on her tongue, breathe it in. His eyes had become dark pools of liquid... she glanced around and saw that the other diners had unconsciously stopped noting their presence. They had disappeared from everyone's view...

...that's how he can follow without being seen...

Oblivious to what he was doing, he carried on with his speech.

'But honest or not, it is mine to act that way. My will *is*. You are subject to that will, and you will not escape, on any level. Nothing but death will change our relationship. You know that.'

It was her turn to nod. Yes, she knew that. The power she'd just seen manifest in front of her, power she'd felt and understood from the first... but never actually witnessed in this form... that power was her doom. There was nothing she, or anyone, could do, to stand against that. Would it have been easier, if she'd accepted that earlier?

Had she accepted it?

She turned her head from him, pretending to look down to her cup. The tension had to break, and she broke it by clattering the cup onto the saucer, his attention was drawn to it. His gaze broke from hers, and the gentle murmurs in the dining room returned. A sharp uncomfortable laugh from a table signalled that someone had understood there had been a problem, somewhere, but it was gone. That night, the restaurant had many who said they had felt uneasy, and not enjoyed their meal, but no one could quite put their finger on why.

In the corner, the loving couple on a date continued to discuss life and death.

'If I could kill myself to escape you, I would do so.'

'That, I know. It is not an option for you.'

'And you have already punished me.'

He let his silence answer.

'You killed my mother.'

'No, I did not. Mungo killed your mother.'

Her head jerked up and she stared straight into him again. He was not mocking her, simply utterly quiet and unassuming.

So this had been his punishment to her, for tricking Mungo... getting Mungo to kill her mother? He read her look clearly.

'Yes, that was my punishment for how you managed to fool him. Although he did enjoy it, so that part was not punishment for him. But he did not enjoy what I did to him. Get him to show you the scar one day.' He raised his hands and signalled the waiters back into the fray.

'More coffee please, and cognac, for us both.'

She liked to think that she could be outraged, to get angry and aggressive, argue with him and flounce out. It was an appealing, if hopeless, thought. She swallowed her anger down, with the last of the coffee. Somehow, she would begin again. They both waited whilst the waiter refilled their cups, and placed cognac glasses in front of them. Dreyfuss signalled again, and the bottle was left on the table. He left a decent silence for her. She took it, and worked with what she had.

'Fine, let us have honesty between us.' She took a deep breath. 'I have no choice, and therefore, therefore... you are my Master.'

He acknowledged her bravery with a tip of his glass... saluté.

'But I am not happy with that, and I do not like it.'

Again, he nodded his acknowledgment, and made as if to speak. She gave way to him.

'Your happiness is not required, and I do not care if you like it or not. It is. It simply is.'

It was her turn to nod assent.

'However...' She hesitated, to allow him the choice to let her speak... he nodded her on. '...however, I do wish to understand something from you, prior to my return, if I may?'

'Certainly, I have no problem with discussion with you. In fact...' he paused to ensure she was looking straight at him, 'I have missed discussions with you. I have missed you.'

Oh, how to deal with that? How to look at him and see genuine emotion on his face, as if he was a puppy dog? How could he have changed so much since she had gone?

...who has changed... is it him, or is it you... she'd never spoken to him like this... if she had, would he always have answered...? But he did change, didn't he, that night, that night she'd seen inside him... he'd run off... he'd not beaten her since... but how much of that was part of the move to Wiltshire...part of the plan...?

She could not see how him not beating her, for that length of time, was normal to him. Something had occurred, but she did not ever look at the events of that time, she closed them down and sealed them off. Something she tried to do again, now they were in her mind. She failed and the words tumbled out.

'I cannot say I have missed you, I cannot say I have missed the man who is my rapist, my abuser.'

He displayed no anger at her words. He was calm and softly spoken.

'Everything you have is mine to take: one cannot rape what one owns. One cannot abuse that which is only an extension of your property. You are only what I decide you are. For as long as I decide it.'

She swallowed hard. She needed to have the strength to take the opening he'd just given her.

'That is the crux of the matter I wish to discuss.'

It had been refreshing for him to discuss all this so openly. He was intrigued by her manner, and her questions. It was liberating to be so free about his identity, and hers, in open communication.

'Carry on. I am enjoying listening, and find the conversation stimulating.'

She put the compliment to one side, and carried on carefully, building up to her point.

'You own me now, as I am Changeling? No one can come between us, amongst the Kin?'

He considered for a moment... he had not foreseen this turn of events.

'Yes, by right of law, that is correct. You have not begun to feed really, but I have you in my ownership... you do hold my blood within you. So yes, you are *Changeling*. You are mine, utterly, and no Kin can interfere in anyway.'

She took another sip of cognac, aware she was starting to sweat and this needed finished.

'Would that be true if I was still human, still simply human?'

There, there was her mind at work again. What an amazingly intelligent question.

'Actually, no. If you were not of my blood, by now I would have broken a rule. I'm impressed that you have spotted this.'

'Thank you. What rule would you have broken?'

'That to torture humans for the sake of torture, is forbidden. It must be feed, or Turning. You can capture and keep feed for a time, or make humans work for you, as slaves. But to take one aside, and do what I have done to you, for simple pleasure, that is forbidden. It would be deemed to be madness.'

There was a rueful tone to his voice. She did not pursue it, could not reveal what it was she suspected. She moved along in the direction she needed to know about more.

'You have said to me, that I get one hundred years to mature, from when the Turning occurs?'

Once more, an unexpected question. How entrancing.

'Yes, that is correct. You are mine utterly for those hundred years. You are still Changeling.'

'No one else can interfere? None of the Kin?'

'No, none.' His irritation at the thought that anyone of the night turned filth could stand against him, filtered through a little. The waiters once more disappeared from casual view.

'You can kill me in that time, keep me to you, I am your possession utterly?'

'Yes, I have explained that. What is your point?'

'What happens when the century is up?'

He smiled, and sat back on the chair, laughter on his lips, and in his eyes. He raised the glass to her again.

'I salute you. That is a fine question and a fine bit of thinking.' He drained the glass, before pouring himself another one.

'What happens, my little one, is that after one hundred years, if you are still alive… you are free. Utterly free.'

It was her turn to swallow the glass in one. Then she too leaned over and refilled it.

'In fact, not only will you be free… it would be my death if I tried to keep you. The Kin will not stand for enslavement of their own. You are Changeling for your own protection. As a Newborn, you will be immature, and what you do in those first few decades… is my responsibility. As my ward, it is my duty to keep you safe, alive and well. If you go mad upon your Turning, it is my duty to kill you. Vampires are not allowed to fight and kill other vampires, not without excessive cause, and that cause must be proven. But I am allowed to kill you, in that century.'

That he relished that power, that it meant something to him, something personal, was obvious to her. She filed the information away.

'If I deem that you are not safe, that you might endanger our kind, I can end you. Just as I could kill you now. Once you have proven you have the maturity to survive on your own, I must stand back and let you go. If that is what you desire.' His voice intimated she would not go.

She looked at him fully on, square and unflinching. 'I will leave the first second I am able to go.' The challenge was clear.

'Do not be so sure. A hundred years is a long time. By then, you will never want to leave my side. Ever. We will spend our immortality together.'

He snapped his fingers, and the waiter appeared by magic.

'Tell my staff to bring the car around please, and inform the lady's limousine driver to do the same.' Dreyfuss was never gauche enough to pay a bill in front of her, it was always arranged in advance.

'Very good, sir.'

They were done. He had had enough, and they were leaving. Her pretence that she had freedom, disappeared in the click of his fingers. She stood and reached for her clutch bag.

'I will just be a moment.' He nodded, and stood to his feet as she rose.

In the lavish and opulent powder room, after she had used the facilities, and checked her stockings and dress, she touched up her makeup. Let him wait. After a final flick of the hair, and slipping her jacket back on, for it would be cold outside and she'd not thought to buy a suitable overcoat, she felt into the pocket lining in her clutch bag. There was the triple wired gold ring she had bought three weeks earlier. She slipped it on the middle finger of her left hand before going back to join him.

In the reception area, he had his own overcoat on, and when he realised she had none, he took it off and slipped it on her shoulders. Spotting the ring, he let out a great smile, a huge grin that would go with sweetie wrappers and birthday presents and all things good. He lifted her hand to his mouth, and bowed and kissed the finger, then slipped his arm through her waist and walked her out the door. Another diner, just leaving, smiled at such a lovely scene of love and attention for the marvellous young couple who were so obviously enthralled with each other.

They moved to the car park and she found Midge and Mary waiting by the Mercedes Benz. The Claridge's driver, Robert, was parked next to them, and he came out of the car when he saw her approaching. As Dreyfuss moved to speak, she took the initiative.

'Mary, go back with the driver from Claridge's and clear down my suite. I'll send Midge up to pick you up after we have been dropped off.' Not waiting for a reply, she turned to her driver.

'Thank you for waiting so long, Robert, I do appreciate it. I will be returning with my fiancé, and will not be requiring your services further. But I would ask that you take my maid back, for her to collect my things.'

The 'maid' shot Dreyfuss a look, which Helene presumed had been met with a positive response, for she promptly left her position by the Mercedes and moved to enter the limousine.

'Just a second Mary, come here.' Helene turned and handed her clutch bag to Midge, who automatically received it. Helene's hand went to her ears, and she took out the diamond studs and handed them to Mary.

'These are for Minette. Robert knows who she is. Robert, I'll trust you to make sure that they are handed over to her. Thank you.' She handed Robert a twenty pound note as tip. He nodded his thanks, and slipped the note into an inside pocket in his coat

She turned from them, and moved to Dreyfuss's side. Midge gave her back her clutch, which she took graciously. Midge then opened the Mercedes door for her, and she slipped Dreyfuss's coat from her shoulders, and seated herself.

Dreyfuss waited to check she was buckled up, then settled his coat across her knees. Midge held the opposite door open for him, and he settled beside her. Once buckled, he turned and spoke to her.

'Those were very expensive earrings.'

'You don't like diamonds.'

'Half my fortune is yours.'

'Then you only lost one earring.'

He actually smiled then. 'I have missed you.' Then he took her hand, and kissed the back of it.

'How did you find me, by the way?'

Midge had started the car up and was driving off.

'I did not look for you. I engaged Violette in the task. She has minions everywhere.'

'That doesn't tell me much.'

'Shall we just say there are an awful lot of vampires in Brazil.'

On the rest of the ride back, Helene contemplated the concept of a psychotic vampire with a sense of humour.

It did not compute.

CHAPTER TWENTY-SEVEN

The drive took little over an hour, and Midge deposited them at the front door before turning straight around to go and fetch Mary. Mungo opened the front door for them. She hesitated as she passed him, everything in her wanting to scream and rail at the man, and at the very least, slap him hard. She stood as Dreyfuss handed him his overcoat, scarf and gloves, and he melted away. Dreyfuss looked at her.

'Welcome home.'

The words made her feel sick, and he would know that, so she said nothing. He indicated the stairwell, and she went upstairs.

'Do you mind if I shower and change first?' she called back to him.

'No, not at all, I shall be up myself in a moment.'

When he did arrive, she was washed and freshened up, with her makeup stripped off and in a night gown and dressing gown. She was working cortisone cream into her wrist, as she sat on one the armchairs. He went straight to a shower, and returned a few moments later with a towel wrapped round his waist.

'Mungo will bring up some tea in a moment.'

'Thank you, that is very kind.'

She carried on creaming her body as he towel dried. There was a light knock, and Dreyfuss opened the door, taking the tray and excluding Mungo. He placed the tray on the table between the chairs, and poured her one, then himself.
She again thanked him, and wiping her hands on a hand towel, she sipped her tea.

'Will you be wanting sex this evening?'

'Yes, I will. I have waited a long time for your return.'

She nodded. 'I will find it very difficult.'

'Only if I will it to be that way. You will enjoy it if I will it. You will not, if I will it. You will be whatever I decide.'

With nothing more to say on the matter, she slipped her dressing gown off and got into her side of the bed. A few moments later, he turned off all the lights and joined her. She lay there, rolling her thumb around the base of the ring on her middle finger.

A talisman from harm.

She would survive: she would live.

When he was asleep, she rose and showered, and watched the blood and sperm rinse away down the drain. She'd also brushed out her mouth and gargled and spat him out. Then she sat and carefully examined what bite marks she could see. Often, there was a memory of the bite, either sharp and painful or luscious and addictive, and dried blood. But no puncture wounds. No sight of a wound at all. It had often been a source of her wondering about her own sanity, her own memory. Now, she combed her body to find evidence of bleeding. There was a blemish on the swell of her left breast, where he had taken blood to maintain his erection. She had a clear memory of it, difficult, as he'd used thrall on her. As she watched, the blemish faded to nothing. She looked at her wrist, and the ridges and creases. He was driven to tear, for pain... and for what else? To mark? There was no mark upon her now, of his blood taking. If he beat her, she bruised. If he tore her flesh, it split. But when he took blood... nothing remained unless he inflicted tearing. Also, his blood could heal. If he split her, and he used blood, she healed. The same must be true, in some way, about his saliva.

It made sense. Vampire bites, all Hammer horror and obvious, would be dangerous. Would be evidence of what had occurred. Evidence was the enemy of the Kin. Not existing was the safest cover. That must be why they would kill those who tortured for the sake of it: it was too dangerous. What had he said, he could kill her instantly for madness? Madness must be one of the unforgiven things. So how had he survived?

She returned to bed but lay awake for some time, pondering the issue of his blood and resolutely not thinking about being back under his physical control. The mental control was worse, anyway. He had brought her to orgasm several times during his assault, and she had to take those thoughts and feelings and lock them in a deep dark box.

She would survive, first and foremost, she would survive.

Mary brought her belongings from the hotel up in the morning, and Helene cast her out of the bedroom with the instructions that neither she, nor any of the Stooges, were ever to enter it if she was there. Dreyfuss was content to see her mark out her own territory. And appreciate that she was sensible enough to make it clear that they did still get to clean and tidy their quarters, just never to do it in her presence. Helene then cast out a great many possessions from the wardrobes, and the dressing room, that she decided she no longer required. Again, Dreyfuss was content, especially when her face fell into ashen ruins when he mentioned the clothing could not be taken into Marlborough, due the unfortunate death of the lady in the vintage clothing shop.

She continued with her task, however, and by late evening, one of the spare bedrooms was literally crammed with one of the finest and most expensive jumble sales to have ever graced Wiltshire.

'What are you going to do with it all?'

'I'll phone a clothes agent, later on in the week, and have them all collected. Can I have my own bank account with the proceeds?'

'You already have several. Just decide which one you want the money to go into. Go up to the office and arrange it all yourself. You have the passwords, after all.' There was no rankling tone... just that he knew that she knew, that access to cash was no longer an issue.

He was pleased she was thinking good sense with the money. It boded well.

After a week, when she was used to being back, and having enjoyed as much of her body as he could, to bolster him for what must come... he settled down to discuss it all with her. To explain it out. It would be easier, he felt, if she knew the thinking behind what must occur. The reasoning. It was a conversation he had never had before, so the words were new. She had been sitting in the window seat of the office, reading a book. He sat down and joined her. He wasn't sure how to begin.

'You look worried.'

'I am.'

'Well, I guess that makes me terrified.'

'It should.'

'Oh.' She put the book down. 'Have we reached it then, the Turning?'

'No, not as such. But we must start. Soon. Later on, today, perhaps tomorrow.'

No amount of pretence at lightness could be kept going, so she settled back into silence and listened. He reached over and lifted her left hand, and touched the ring on her middle finger.

'Now you have to earn this, and you will not want to. I know your plan Helene, you think you will start to feed from me, and then you will Turn, and then your clock starts. Tick, tock, tick tock, how many years until you are free of me. But it will not be so simple.'

Yeah, like she thought it would be.

He stood up, and took to pacing up and down the office, whilst she sat and listened, her skin crawling up her spine and all the heat and breath slowly leaving her body.

'I have told you before, how many Changelings die, in those first few years. There are many reasons. Some people, no matter how strong, when the Turning is upon them, they turn mad. It is not recoverable from: they regress. When they are newborn, they are like newborn humans – all they need is food and sleep. If left, they can kill and drain humans dry, one after the other, for decades. Their minds are gone, they have only need: a revenant. Many vampire newborns enter in this state, but most can be controlled and brought out of it, within a few days. Their reason returns, and they can function. Others, a few, stay in that primal level of birth, where there is only need for food. What was once a need for mother's milk, is now a need to rip out veins and suckle down all. To devour all, continually.'

He left time for his words to sink in.

'Very few, does this happen to. But it is a risk. Often, our kind take lovers, and decide to transform them. And in doing so, turn them into monsters. Which must then be killed quickly. That could happen to you.'

That his voice held genuine regret, and softness; that he was telling her this with a catch in his throat, and a sense of sorrow... did not make it any easier.

'Also, there is an even rarer madness. Sometimes, they go into a Turning as one person, and emerge another. The other is always a dark force, and utterly, completely insane. There are those amongst us, and the Council approve this... those amongst us who say that a demon has invaded the mind and body, at the moment of Turn. Demons must also be killed, instantly.'

Council, what frigging Council...? A COUNCIL?

'It's a very bad thing, to have a demon born in front of you. Sometimes, you do not notice it. We have specialist people, vampires trained to assess the mind, using a special type of thrall. If they suspect you are demon, they can penetrate your mind, and see into you...' There was pain, and fear in his voice. She put all thoughts of this council aside, to try and catch every nuance of what he was saying. 'It is a terrible invasion. It cannot be done gently. The entire point is to tear away concealment. Some do not even know they carry the demonic inside them. Even those who are clean of this stain... some do not recover from the finding out of it. They collapse under the assault. Go mad from the invasion. If a demon is found, the vampire is killed, instantly. If they go mad from the inspection, they are killed, instantly.'

He had to have had this test. He spoke of it with such... emotion. It scared him, of what he spoke. She filed that away, deep down.

'And, of course, some simply die. Their heart ruptures, their brain seizes, their blood congeals in their veins. Not everyone is strong enough, in body, to survive the moment of the Turn. It is intensely painful, and bodies will sometimes simply fail.'

How nice of him to have kept this all to himself until now. Although, really, what difference did it make. It's not like she had a choice, was it? Although it made sense to her about other things. Why the Three Stooges were still human, for instance. They liked pain and domination and they were paid killers. Why not be vampires? Well, dying for your wish is not a risk many would undertake... that made sense to her. There would be more vampires and fewer servants, if it was easier to do.

'I appreciate this is not comfortable information for you. But it is by no means the most important thing I have to explain to you today.'

He sat back down by her side, turning his body to face hers, the circular window above their heads, like an unblinking eye, witnessing the horror unfold.

'The state your body is in, when you Turn, is the state you will return to in times of famine and hardship. Turned the old way, as you will be, you will be able to gain weight above that, and look normal.'

The old way...? There is another way...? Fucking hell, what was going on!

'But if you are Turned looking healthy, looking well fed... you will always look well fed. In famine and war, this is a death sentence. In famine and war, you must be able to hide. Otherwise, you will never be able to feed without notice. You will either starve from lack of feed, or be revealed from suspicion of it.'

The weight of the words was heavy, and the meaning of them unbearable to her. He left her the time to come to her own conclusion, and smart as she was, she got there in one.

'So you must starve me.'

'So I must starve you.'

She already knew hunger. She knew how bad it was. She knew how every waking thought devoured you whole. How every moment of lack, was to be swamped with the desperate need to be full. She had gone hungry at his hands many times, and since his blood had gone into hers, she had always felt an edge of what he must feel. Already, she must eat slowly and continually through the day, or feel that edge of panic and fear pushing into her. She shut it all out of her mind to concentrate on him. She would not panic and lose a precious clue, one scrap of useful information.

'That is easier than it might sound. For it is also true, that the more physically adept you are, the stronger your muscles and heart and sinews are, when you go into the Turn, the stronger you will be on the other side. You are far from being fit enough, so we must work you. We must work you hard.'

We? She didn't like where that was going.

She let a deep sigh out, there was too much air in her lungs. He absently patted her on the leg, as one would a dog. Then he rose up, and began his pacing again.

'Of course, the Turning itself is not the cause of most Changeling deaths...' His tone had changed, utterly. He had moved into pontificating school ma'am mode. He was utterly divorced from what he was saying to her now, unlike the previous bit, which he had emotional connection to.

He really was worried she'd die in the Turning, or go mad. *Shit.*

'The most common cause of death amongst Changelings is...'

He was doing the dramatic pause thing. This was him in rote learning. This was him going through a sequence in his mind, trying to make sure he ticked all the boxes, and then got to the dramatic reveal.

'... suicide.'

Well that sure got her attention.

'Perhaps not always obvious as such, of course. It is rare that New Blood display such reason and thinking, that enables them to destroy themselves with one act. But it is self-destruction, their path. Faced with the reality of their life, especially the females... they slowly fall to despair, and death. That is why you have a Master for a century. Because it takes a long time, sometimes, for the melancholy to take over. Many a newborn Kin has revelled and adored their new life, their power. Their Master has to do little than prevent them killing too often, and too obviously.'

The Three Stooges came to mind again. Oh yes, that would be *such* a bad idea.

'However, ultimately... they cannot cope. They fail.'

Once, long ago, before a certain April evening in central London, she would have asked... 'Why the females especially?' Goodness, was she ever that young, that naïve... that stupid? She supposed she had been. Violence had never bruised her. Deprivation had never eaten into her. Rape had never penetrated her. Despair had never darkened her mind and desperation had never driven her to scream even when she knew that to scream was to be hurt more.

She'd known *of* such things... she'd known female babies are killed more than male ones. She'd known that slavery existed, she'd known that abuse existed. She'd never been touched by it. She'd never stood on a crowded street in a filthy gutter and watched young girls being sold for sex by their guardians. She'd never seen dead bodies, male and female, covered in bullet holes, abandoned in ditches. She'd never watched from afar, whilst a man had whipped a young girl, and then kicked her back into their hovel, with several other young men and older women watching silently. She'd never lived in a world where you had to always sit by the Mamas with the fat babies. She'd never lived in a world where once, the Mama with the fat baby had a back covered in bruises and a missing front tooth.

She'd seen many dead bodies as she'd travelled on past Mexico City. Most of them were male. She'd seen workers in the field, beaten by their bosses. She'd walked dusty roads and took the cheapest of buses. In many places she'd been, life was so cheap that the bodies were only moved out of the ditches if someone complained of flies. Men were of no note in many places she had been. A man was just as quick to be hit, abused, shot... as any woman. Crime on the streets made the men die. But crime in the home killed the women. Everywhere she had been... being female was less than being male, even when being male was being less than nothing.

She had thought she'd escape Dreyfuss, when she ran. She had, however, just found how many of him there were. And how many Helenes.

He had noticed her reverie, and had respected it. He was not sure what had caught her, and moved her to memory, but something had. The silence stretched, and she noticed, and came back to the room.

'I'm listening.'

He nodded and carried on.

'You will not fail Helene, I will not allow it. You will not Turn
to discover life is empty and devoid of solace. You will not discover
after the event, that you do not have the stomach for it. You will not get
half way through to your freedom, and discover you have no means
inside you to continue. This, I promise. I will not lose you.'

There really wasn't anything to say to him. He wasn't going to
say more, she could tell, and really, she wasn't sure she could say more.
What he was saying now didn't really make sense to her. She just
nodded.

'Tomorrow we will start off your training. Tonight, you can eat
well, and rest, and we can watch a movie together, and we can relish the
peace whilst we may.'

Yes, because she always so *enjoyed* his company.

'But before we do that, there is something I need you to do.'

'Yes?'

'I need you to sign your will.'

It was 26 pages long, and required several signatures. She
wondered if it was a bluff, as she sat and methodically signed her name
where all the plastic tags had been put. But no, on balance, it was
obviously not. They had spent a long time before her escape, setting her
up to take possession of a lot of his estate. That had clearly been
continued in her absence. She legally owned a lot of stuff, including the
house they sat in. She knew that, as she'd just signed it back over to
him, in event of her death. And what would a death certificate matter to
a man who could produce a birth certificate for someone who had never
been born? Or signatures, for that matter.

No, she knew she was signing it all to make a point, but also...
because he wanted her to. There were no witnesses, but he would cover
that. But it was her signature, and that was what identity was about. It
was her real signature, it was real inheritance. Whilst he'd handed her

over all this stuff, for her Turning it made sense that he could claim it all back, if she died.

And who, in reality, would control her death? One hand gives, the other takes away. Although a shocking amount of wealth would have been wasted in the transfer, if he did end up with it all back.

'You've been paying taxes on all your properties and investments for a few months now. Everything will be lodged with your tax lawyer, and copies here and in No 1, and in your safe at a hotel I've purchased for you in Chelsea.'

Yes, she'd seen that as she'd signed.

'That way, should anything occur to me, you will be protected. My will is lodged in Switzerland, where my executors, the bank, will take charge of everything, should anything happen to me.'

Of course they will. You die all the time.

They ate in the kitchen, informally, as he'd sent the Stooges to their cottage. Then retired to the bedroom, with a large stack of snacks and drink, and watched movies. Judy Garland, of all things, and first she met them in St Louis, and then took them along on the yellow brick road.

Nothing about her life made the slightest sense.

CHAPTER TWENTY-EIGHT

In the morning, they went again to the kitchen, for breakfast. She couldn't get past the wrenching fear and panic in her gut, but she made good show if it. The warning shot was the look on Mungo's face. She hesitated on the threshold as they entered, but with Dreyfuss behind her, there was no choice. She went to sit for the meal, but none was set. So she concentrated on breathing instead.

Breathe in, breathe out, in out, that was it, wasn't it?

Dreyfuss came fully into the kitchen, and sat down where breakfast would have been. She sat beside him.

'I want to make things very clear to everyone.'

All four of them listened to him carefully.

'When Helene is in this house, she is to be accorded respect, and she is the mistress of the home.' The Stooges nodded.

He faced Helene directly.

'When she is outside this house, you three are in charge.'

Helene felt the panic rise, and the tears start to spill from her eyes. She could feel the blood drain from her face. He couldn't mean it, he just couldn't.

'Take her outside.'

Her hand shot to his, completely unwittingly. He moved his out of the way, and other hands grabbed her. She was pulled up backwards out of her seat, and dragged the length of the kitchen. She never stopped looking to him, pleading with her eyes. He waved them on. She screamed his name, but it was of no use. Dreyfuss turned from her, and left the kitchen.

She stumbled, and was kept upright by the savagery of the grip. That just so had to be Mungo. She was twisted round, and physically pushed out the kitchen doorway. It was a cold hard February morning, and she was wearing flimsy satin house pyjamas and her silk and leather house shoes. The cold immediately attacked her wrist and shoulder scar. She was pushed along, down the length of the garden, past the staff quarters, along past the stables, and on into the riding barn.

It was just what it said it was. A large tin roofed barn, modelled on some older structure, but now entirely given over to horse riding. It had double doors for the horses to enter, and a smaller door beside that, for humans. Inside was normally empty apart from a thick sawdust and sand floor and some jumps. On the wall by the entrance was space for tack and feed, although it was seldom used for either. There was a separate tack room in the stables. The centre of the space now contained several of the training machines from the gym room. She stared at them as she was pushed on past them, to the far wall. This contained a series of small interconnected pre-fabricated huts that housed hay and straw. Again, it was excess storage for the stable areas, and was rarely used. One of the little huts was the storage for the sawdust and sand mix that lined the floor, and was always full and had a wheelbarrow and pitchfork, for clearing up after a horse dropped dung. She was pushed towards the huts, and then pushed into one. She tried to run back out, when she saw what it contained, but she was literally thrown back through the door, to land on the hard packed sawdust floor. The tiny hut, not quite tall enough to allow her to stand, contained a bale of straw, a blanket, two buckets and a set of chains and manacles driven into the wall. The plaster boarding of the storage hut wall had been cut back, so you could see the chains went straight into the brick wall behind. The single bulb shone in the iron frame that protected it from accidentally being smashed by a swinging pitchfork.

A vicious kick to the leg announced that Mary had entered the hut. Helene turned quickly and tried to stand up. The other woman's boot sank into her stomach. As she doubled over and retched, some clothing was thrown onto the floor.

'Put them on, and come outside.'

It was a tracksuit, identical to the one she'd been told to put on the day he'd killed in front of her. Socks and training shoes were dropped on the pile. The thin plastic door was slammed shut.

She lay for a few moments as she tried to learn to breathe again, shaking and trying to get hold of her crying. She could not show them fear, she couldn't. She'd seen the look in Mungo's eyes, the dead look, and she knew fear would excite him. When she could stand, she stripped and dressed in the track suit, leaving her clothes and slippers on the straw bale. Then she went out, as no way they going to come in and get her.

She tried to school herself back, back to the apartment, back to showing no reaction. It was going to be so hard, closing everything down again. She had to force herself into vacuum... she had to. She'd managed it with them during the prior training, she could do it again.

The Stooges had rigged a rope around the ring of the barn, creating an oval track. She'd used it herself, in her riding lessons, to ride around in circuits. There was, of course, no horse. The stooges each held a baton, and had spread themselves around the circuit. Mary was closest to her. The baton she held in her hand turned blue at the end and crackled.

'Run,' she said.

She ran.

He left her for a week, before seeing her. The trolls gave him status reports, and he was very confident that they were not taking things too far. Extremely confident. That brand on Mungo's thigh had cemented his authority nicely. During the planning, Mary had asked what she should do to stop her screaming for help, when she was locked alone in the hut. Dreyfuss had explained that she wouldn't do that. Mary hadn't believed him. She believed him now, and she eyed him with a lot more respect. Similarly, when he'd said the cold may hurt her, but it wasn't going to kill her... they understood that now.

She'd been getting three cups of rice a day, with some olive oil mixed into the rice. As much water as she could swallow without throwing up. Getting weight off, with muscle being built on the legs, had been the priority, so they'd been running her round the track, 12 hours a day, in 4 X 3 hour sections. As she transitioned to more of her calories being his blood, they would increase the time of each section. Vampires were stronger and faster, but they only had a slight advantage over humans in endurance. She had to develop endurance before the Turning, just as he had.

He knew he'd have to join the training at some point, but was leaving it off for as long as he could. He didn't trust himself not to react too strongly. Either by attacking the trolls, for harming her, or wanting to harm her himself, just a little too hard. It had been very difficult for him not to lash into her that week she was resting from her return. Very hard. Not because she'd done anything to deserve it... but because he could. He'd not hit her all that time prior, and that seemed so unnatural to him now. Her escaping had lifted the fog he'd been in, he could see that now. He'd been too considerate of her, and had enjoyed the calm before the storm too much. Now the storm was here, he was waiting it out, in anticipation of taking part when he was really required. This is what the trolls were for; *why keep dogs and bark yourself?*

At the morning report, Mary had suggested that today was the day Helene's body would collapse. They were as familiar with people who were being worked hard, faking exhaustion to avoid more work, as he was. They had been taking careful note of her body's boundaries, and her pain thresholds, in order to gain a clear picture of what currently was, and wasn't, possible. So when she said it, Dreyfuss had paid attention. He had spent the morning dealing with the anticipation of being called in, and of seeing her. Her right hand was flexing unconsciously. Half way through the afternoon, Mary came in to report that she would either have to eat properly, or the punishment would have to stop.

'Do you not mean training?'

She corrected herself.

'My apologies, master, I mean her training will have to be interrupted, if she is not to receive more nutrition. She's been on the ground for three jolts, and there isn't enough strength in her to stand.'

He nodded. 'You are quite sure? There is no deception?'

It was Mary's turn to smile with that self-assured smile of absolute confidence in her abilities. 'Rest assured, there is no deception. If she was capable of crawling away, she would have.'

He returned with Mary to the barn. Had he been more honest with himself, he would have accepted that *anticipation* over what state she was in, was secondary to his fears of such. Throughout the week she had been in the barn, he had been fighting dreams, nightmares, memories and flashbacks. He'd repressed then as ruthlessly as he'd repressed his victims. He'd pummelled them down and silenced their voices. If he had attended to those voices within himself more, then he would not have been waking in the night, screaming, with his bed covered in his own blood. But if he'd been capable of listening more deeply to his own fears… he would not have been Dreyfuss.

As it was, he strolled over to the barn, with Mary by his side, affecting nonchalance.

The smell hit him first, as he stepped into the barn. Foetid human body, blood, fear, piss and excrement. A familiar tone. She had fouled herself where she lay on the ground. Ah, that was why Mary had been so sure. And yes, Mary indicated that Helene had received a massive electric shock to the back of her leg, in order to make her get up. Instead, her body had ejected all solid waste. It was a classic sign that the body was on the edge: it wanted all extra material away from it, to give that final burst of speed: anything to escape the tiger. Better to die running than be eaten. One of them had thrown water over her, but it did little more than move the shit around.

He stepped over the mess, to lie down on the sawdust beside her. Her eyes were locked and drifting, her lips cracked and bleeding, her face puffy. Her clothes were rank from sweat and blood. She smelled strongly of piss. Using a bucket was an art form, one she had not mastered... although the cattle prods may have caused her to let her bladder go involuntarily.

He lay down on the floor, his head lying alongside hers. His eye line matched with hers. He waited a few moments, then whispered 'Helene... Helene...'to her.

After a few moments, recognition dawned within her. Her eyes focussed, took in the sight of his. A cry escaped her lips. He leaned into her, whispering in her ear.

'You must choose now. You are nearly finished. You must choose to die... or to live.'

As he spoke he slit across his own right wrist, and held his wrist to her mouth. He smeared his blood across her lips. She would have to be quick, he healed so quick... she latched on. He felt her go from the weakest of caresses, her tongue running across the wound, to the tiniest closing of her lips. As his blood flowed into her parched and starving flesh, she gained strength. From the first swallow, she had enough energy to take more. Within five minutes she was latched onto him like a leech. He flexed his arm and wrist to pump more and more into her. Still she suckled, swallowed, her tongue moving over the wound in that incredible rhythm that pulled blood out of the veins, even if the heart had itself ceased. Her arms came up to her side and she raised herself to her knees, and then grasped his arm, pulling her weight up to pin his arm to her mouth. Midge made to move, to react, to protect Dreyfuss, but he raised the other arm to ward him off. She could have her fill; there was none living who could drain him.

Dreyfuss twisted his arm so she had to turn her face towards him. He so wanted to see her do this, and to gloat at his achievement, his triumph. The full view of her face, the bruising over one temple, the shot and hollow eyes, the cracked and broken lips... the pain of hunger in every cell of her, as she swallowed... swallowed... swallowed. He felt as though a death blow had been struck to his heart. Only the need to keep control with the others, kept him there, pinned by her need.

Midge noticed the draining of colour from Dreyfuss, the ashen colour that touched his lips. He mistook it for danger, and moved forward one more. Again, Dreyfuss raised his other hand to stop him. Mary had turned from the scene, and started to check equipment. Mungo stared at Helene with hungry eyes.

It was over suddenly. She went from active feeding to asleep in one movement. She pitched forward, and Dreyfuss caught her weight. Midge moved to catch her with him, and they gently laid her down and turned her over onto her back. With them all watching the miracle, his blood pumped around her body, healing her. The cracks in the lips closed, the grey colour left her tissue. The bruise on her temple disappeared, her lips and cheeks blushed with pink. Even the hollows filled slightly. Ever the problem, how to starve and transition at the same time. So much had to be taken out, and yet so little had to go in, to replace that which hunger had stolen.

'A job well done. You have all done well. Take her through to the cottage. Bathe her, and place her dry and naked on the bed. I shall be there presently.'

He went back through to the house to change his soiled clothing. Half way there, he threw up. Again, he ruthlessly repressed any hint that what he'd seen was hurting him.

He showered and changed and collected the prepared flasks of broth. She would need comfort when she woke: this was a familiar routine.

When she did wake, warm and cosy in a bed, with his arms snaked around her waist, she thought she was dreaming. She had actually dreamed this moment, many times on the floor of the hut, that she was warm and safe in bed. So she lay there and waited for the cold and terror to truly wake her up, out of the comfort of the dream. When it didn't, and she turned and sat up, and found she was in bed with him, and he was holding her, she burst out crying. He held her whilst she cried, and stroked her hair, and rocked her. Then, when she had stopped sobbing, he spooned warm broth into her mouth.

In break with the tradition, she wretched, as if to throw it up.

'I don't want it. It smells awful.'

'Swallow it, or I will call the trio, and hand you to them.'

She swallowed it down, spoon by spoon.

'I know you don't want it. I know the blood fulfils you. But it is also killing your stomach, bit by bit. If you don't eat food, real food, you will lose the ability to take in goodness from it. Food other than blood, will be poison to you. That is dangerous to your survival. Now swallow.'

When the broth was gone, and she'd kept it down, he held her again as she shook.

'It will feel bad, and it will give you pain, but I am here.'

She began to sweat, and moan, and shake. He held her until it passed and she fell asleep again. Then he lay down beside her, and slept with her. She was too far gone to hear him when he woke from his own nightmares, and found he had ripped open the wound she'd fed from, and they and the bed were covered in his blood. He called Mary and Midge over to clean up the mess, and lifted Helene into the other bedroom. They just assumed it was hers.

If she noticed that she'd woken up in a slightly different room, she didn't say so. But then, as she woke to spew violently, everywhere, there wasn't much time to react to the bedroom. He waited for a gap in the sprays, then carried her through to the bathroom. There, she spewed endlessly over the bath. When she was down to dry heaving, he handed her a glass of water.

'Rinse and spit. Don't swallow.'

She did as she was told. She then found she could stand. He switched on the shower and hosed them both down.

'Your body is getting rid of the waste from my blood. You have to eat now, and help it all move through, that which has been ingested.'

After they were both dried off and wearing robes, he took her down to the kitchen.

'Come and eat.' He got a small plate of cooked meat, and a larger one of sliced fruit, out of the fridge and placed them in front of her.

'Eat it all, or you go to the trio.'

She didn't argue, just picked up a slice of apple. She tried to get it into her mouth. Somehow, her mouth wouldn't go near it.

'Eat it, or I'll hurt you so badly, you'll wish for Mary to tuck you into bed with a lullaby.'

She ate it. And then some meat. And then more fruit. It took four hours.

Then he held her again, as she lay moaning, sweating, groaning and spasming in agony.

Then she fell asleep again.

There was no time, nor space, for her to try and react to what was happening. No moments where she could dwell on what had been happening, how she felt, what horrors had been visited upon her, again. There was just the waking, being sick, being forced to eat, and then passing out. It seemed to be endless, but in reality, it could not have been more than a day. He held back from her, that he was waiting out the transitioning of blood she had ingested. Every trace of his blood that made it through into her stomach out to her organs and sinews, would have to come back and be processed out through her kidneys. The waste that was not thrown up would have to be excreted. When she pissed red-black urine, and ejected oily slime from her backside, she was once more clear of him. Until then, she was made to eat and pass out, eat and pass out.

As he held her in her shakes and shivers, he reflected that it was harder on him, than her. She was asleep for much of it. He was awake for most of it, lost in his memories.

She began to piss clear again, after the red-black. He told her to shower, and climbed in with her. He made sure every inch of her skin was scrubbed: her sweat would have been corrosive to skin during the last few hours of the clearing out of his dead blood from her living body. He rubbed her down with salt and washed her off. As they were drying off, she smiled and said 'I feel really quite good.' Her voice signalled her amazement.

He nodded. 'You will now, with the dead blood gone. Your gut has taken what it needs from it, and got rid of the rest. Do you think you are well enough to walk back to the main house?'

She giggled. A sound he'd never heard from her.

'Oh yes, you're ready to go back to the main house, come on.'

Whilst she staggered around, giggling, and finding funny things to look at, he pulled a robe over her, and lifted her into his arms. She continued giggling. Half way to the house, she fell asleep in his arms, and he carried her through. He had hoped to get her in the main bed before she'd passed out, but, well, what matter did it make? He settled her into their bed, and closed the drapes. Leaving her, he went down to the kitchen, and let the trolls know they could have at least two days off, after they'd cleared up the cottage bedroom and bathroom.

When he returned to the bedroom, with flasks and trays of food, she was still in blood drugged sleep. In taking off her robe, he became aroused by the scent of her, and the feel of her skin. She smelled of life, and longing and needs met. He fed numerous times as he worked, sinking his teeth into her breasts, her thighs, her buttocks. Her Changeling blood intoxicated him, and he lost himself in pleasure, passing out in the strength of his orgasm, embedded deep within her flesh.

The scent of thyme was mingling with that of lemons ripening on the tree. Cool breezes played along his back and buttocks, teasing and licking his skin and sending shivers along his spine. He woke, cool flesh that smelled of cinnamon and cardamom, pinned beneath him. The moment of his awakening and the slightest shift of his weight, sent shivers across his testicles and penis, and they stirred, hardening into her. She moaned beneath him, matching his shivers. As she convulsed in orgasm, her legs opened wider, drawing him deeper down. He began to thrust, eager to bring her to more pleasure. Her back arched, her claws ripped across his back, he orgasmed into her, his head first rearing high then dropping down to fall sideways, snuggling her, neck to neck.. As the pleasure washed through him, throbbing waves of ecstasy, radiating out from his groin, she raised her head to his ear and whispered, 'More.'

Before he could understand what she'd said, apply it to himself and the molten world he was floating in, a sharp pain lanced his neck. He tried to scream, retreat, but his head was held fast by her hand, his shoulder pulled in a vice downwards by her other arm. Slashing, tearing pain devoured his neck, and whilst he tried to pull back, his erection hardened in response to the pain and threat. Her legs snaked around him, trapping him into her.

'More.'

He was caught in agony, unable to move.

'More.'

He was immobile from pain and fear, and whilst she worked herself upon him, her hips grinding into him, she moaned in pleasure. Terror began to wither him.
As soon as she sensed there was less to work with, she gave command.

'Begin!'

The lashes started to rain down on his back, his legs, his buttocks and soles of his feet. Fire exploded upon him, his screams echoing out through the gardens and vineyards. She latched onto his neck once more, blood pouring into her and spilling around the sides of her mouth. The whips drove the rhythm that pushed his body into hers, the pain keeping him erect at her bidding. He passed out as she screamed her own orgasm.

He awoke in the hut, naked, bleeding, and chained to the floor.

He crawled off her, sliding along until he fell sideways off the bed. There, he lay, for a few moments, before crawling the length of the room into the shower area. He half stood, switching on the jets, then crouched back down on the floor, the water spraying over him. He lay there, foetal, rocking slowly.

CHAPTER TWENTY-NINE

She woke with what felt like a hangover. Her head throbbed, her tongue was thick and dry, her body ached. *Where was she?* She sat up, and felt dizzy, slumped back down. What day was it? *OHMYGHODNOpleasedontletitbemonday...* she tried to sit up again, and her head felt as if it was going to split... was she going to throw up? She sat on the edge of the bed, eyes closed, grabbing the edge of the mattress. Something to secure her reality upon, and tell herself she was not going to throw up. How much had she had to drink? Where was she, what day was it? The room was dim and full of shadows, she couldn't make any sense of the shapes around her, or the feel of thick carpet under her feet. She tried to find a bedside lamp, but only knocked something over. As she tried to work out what, a light flicked on. Stabbing pain made her close her eyes, as if she'd been asleep for a thousand years and her eyes would never accept light again. She rubbed them hard, trying to remember where she'd been and... who with.

'Everything is okay, you shall be fine in a moment. It often takes a moment or so.'

The voice was soft and reassuring, and male. She was terrified of it, but didn't know why. She opened her eyes again, slowly, and tried to take in the room, and the figure standing on the other side of the bed. Her eyes where pained again, by the light. She blinked hard and rubbed.

'Your eyes will adjust, slowly. It will be fine.'

She tried to take a step back, to see better, but found she couldn't. Fear was rooting her to the spot. She really had to clear her vision, and see who was in the room with her, and where she was. She worked hard on opening her eyes.

She stared at him for a full minute, before her memory awoke. As understanding and awareness worked its way through her mind, the memories of who he was and where she was and who she was now had worked their way to the forefront of her mind: she screamed.

It was a scream of death and blood and terror. It hit him like a force of nature, and he took a step back, staggered by its power. When the air in her lungs died, so did the scream. She stood, swaying, tears flooding down her face.

'I'm sorry, I'm so sorry.'

Was she asking for forgiveness for screaming, or for forgetting him? He stayed silent, and still, listening.

'I don't know what happened, I don't know... oh god, I don't know.' She threatened to collapse into tears and wailing.

'Go have a shower, get yourself clean and dressed, we can talk over breakfast.'

She did as she was bid, instantly: her body had not forgotten. Under the jets of hot water, she lay foetal on the floor, rocking.

He'd laid out a breakfast of fruit, seeds, nuts and meat in the conservatory, and used information as a pathway for them to journey together once more, overcoming any reluctance from her treatment. She needed his information too much to reject him, of that, he was sure. He'd been planning on it, once this phase began. So he kept engaging her, with a steady trickle of snippets of new information, mixed with old. For her part, she sat in silence toying with food. How could she have been so hungry, and yet now not want any food? She pushed the thoughts of how hungry she had been in the barn, and then all thoughts of the barn, away from her.

Down, down down such thoughts would go, swallowed up like the tiny slivers of food she was forcing into her body.

'From now on, you must stay away from wheat, processed foods, all milks, butter and cheese, and alcohol. Those things will attack your stomach as you change. Avoid them now, and you will be fine afterwards.'

'Afterwards?'

'After your Turning is complete. We are the only ones who can eat real food afterwards, all the others cannot. But even we must be careful of some things, especially now.'

'The first time you made me... I drank your blood... you put it in milk?'

'Yes, to deaden it. Milk and blood mixed is as ancient as human hunger. Milk and blood together, does not begin a change. It was symbolic. You must avoid all milk now, until you are mature in your Turning. It will attack your gut, and your gut is what gives you life. You must feed it now, to protect yourself for eternity.'

She stayed quiet, nibbling on Brazil nuts, which tasted less foul than meat, hoping he would carry on speaking. He did.

'A few vampires are not real vampires. They are night turned... they have no Master, and no protection. They have been turned by an accident, or greed by another vampire. Some are taken for food, and the vampire feeding off them becomes lost in his own thrall, and he offers his own blood to continue the feed. They feed mutually off each other, and a Turning is started. Many are lovers or pets of masters, and the master Turns them on a whim. They are Turned without training, and once they feed off human blood, the Turning is complete. These Halflings are weak and feeble things. Kittens in the night. They cannot exist on real food, only blood. They have little strength. No survival skills, and are burned easily in even weak daylight. They are trash. Most die, painfully, very quickly. Eat more food.'

She crammed a piece of banana into her mouth, trying not to gag, and sat silently listening once more.

'Being Turned slowly, methodically, to accustom the body to stress and starvation, to allow the mind to break before the Turning, if it is weak, to slowly school the body in taking blood, and food... these are old skills, seldom used now. Now is the time of quick and wasted Turnings, followed by quicker and more wasteful deaths. That will not happen to you.'

She swallowed down the banana, and sipped some water.

'It is how you were Turned.' She said it quietly, matter of factly.

A statement, not a question.

'Yes, it is how I was Turned. It is how I know the strength of it, and the secret of it, and how I know you will be the best of them all, when I have finished with you.'

'It's hard to eat.'

'I know, I remember.' His voice held ghosts, and she shied from them.

'When I woke up... I didn't know who... where I was, who I was?'

He took the pathway she offered out of his own memories.

'Yes, you were so deeply asleep. With vampire blood in you, when you sleep, you sleep so far down, so far into the depths of your mind, you have to travel all the way back up again. It can take a few moments. It can be... disconcerting. You will learn to control it, like everything else. Time and practice. It is why many consider us to be dead, that we can sleep so soundly, and wake so disoriented. As if we have died.'

'Do we die?'

He turned to her, sharply.

'What a curious question.'

She fought to put into words, her thoughts and wonderings.

'I just wondered... if at the moment of Turning, we do die? Do we come back to life? You sometimes call us the undead. And that's what vampires are always called. I know about the healing. I know about the strength. But are we ever actually dead, really?'

He thought for a long time, slowly popping grapes into his mouth, as he pondered.

'I think we must do. It's a question I have wondered upon, for a very long time. However, the answers are only clear now, in this modern time. Only now, we would understand the... mechanics of death. Do we die? Our heart can stop beating, and we can stop breathing. Is that death?'

'I don't know. Can our hearts start again, do we breathe in air again?'

'Yes, we do. We heal. So have we come back to life…? I truly don't know. I have thought of it, often. None of us have not. If you do too much damage, we will not recover. Take a head off, or burn the body until there is nothing left… we will die. Damage major organs, and they will heal. Take out the liver, or the heart, or the lungs, we will die. Anything else, will regrow. The liver is the slowest to heal.

'Drowning, as I've told you before, is the biggest threat. Or rather, being lost in a large body of water. Like all humans, if we drown, we breathe in water, and it hurts very badly. It burns, and we are weaker. But we do not die. To be lost, alive, with burning lungs… in water… to drift and to be lost in water… that is a fate worse than death. Some have been found, days, weeks later. When the water is drained out of their lungs, they breathe… they recover and they heal. But their mind is usually gone, and they have to be killed. But do we ever die…? A drowned vampire can be eaten alive, in the sea, and thus die properly… but the drowning itself, it is not sufficient. Not for some time. Long enough to go mad first.'

'If you are human, and the heart stops and you no longer breathe… you are dead.'

'But you can be returned to life, can you not? Are you undead in the space between?'

She shook her head. 'I don't know. I know the brain dies without oxygen, so even if the heart…'

'Yes, even if the heart beats again… but the person is dead and gone, yes?'

She nodded.

'No, that does not occur with us. We can stop breathing for hours, and as long as there is fresh blood to feed upon, we will heal from it. Our brains do not die, we stay awake and know we have stopped breathing. You know you have stopped breathing if you are drowned. You feel the pain. Sometimes we stop breathing as a way to mimic death, and use that so everyone thinks we are dead, to wait until the right time, and… slip away. You can train your heart to stop beating, and then to start up again. I've told you this, many times.'

'I know, I was just wondering… do I have to die to Turn?'

He looked at her, really looked at her, and then smiled.

'You think if you refuse to feed, and choose death, you will Turn?'

She hid her eyes from his sight, trying to hide her answer.

He laughed. 'No little one, that is not an option. If you die out there, you will be dead. My blood is not what Turns you, not like that. You are not... undead... yet.'

His smile became obscene, one of possession and control and power. The idea that she had been thinking death was under her control, not his, and that he had fathomed her thoughts, aroused his sense of ownership.

'You cannot escape me early, you cannot leave when you desire it. Die if you wish, but it will be true death. Refuse my blood, and you will be killing yourself.'

His hand stroked her hair and cheek.

'You do not Turn until I say so, and then when I say so.'

His hand carried on down, to touch her neck, and then her chest, and then he slipped it into the top of her robe, and her breast, concentrating on the nipple. It hardened under his attentions, which was why he'd done it. She flinched, and he leaned into her neck, to whisper in her ear.

'You are mine, and I will choose the day, not you.'

She had no option but to sit and wait his pleasure. Which he took, with her on the table, spread beneath him. The table dug painfully into her hips and spine: there was no fat to cushion her against his thrusting weight. As she looked up to the sky through the glass roof, she closed her eyes against the cruelty she thought she could see, as the clouds mocked how powerless she was.

Her thumb stroked the base of the middle finger of her left hand: she would not be powerless forever.

He left her to shower again, and she went to the bathroom, and ran hot water and filled it with bubbles and scent. The heat held and comforted her, and she tried to breathe the perfume deep into her. To take the scents of jasmine and lavender and lilies, and lock them into her pores: anything to mask the stench of pee and shit in a bucket, and vomit and sour sweat on her clothes that was burned into her nostrils.

The Thought That Would Not Be Denied was large in her mind. She'd discovered that whilst she could not push it under, she could hold it as a line of words inside her, and look at it dispassionately. Just keep staring at the words, and not react to what they were at all.

...when will I be taken back to the barn...?...

She had two more days, of comfort and talking and information, and food being pushed at her, and sex taken everywhere and anywhere. She'd never seen him so aroused, or so passionate. She'd be walking through a room, and he'd grab her wrist, and pull her too him, and kiss her, and his hands would take her, and then she'd be pushed and pulled around like a doll, and taken in whatever position he fancied. She knew there was more to this than she could fathom, and the blood taking that enabled it to happen repeatedly, was affecting him somehow.

As she'd analyse what was going on, what he was doing, from a little box inside herself, where she could look out and examine, theorise... but not be touched by what was happening... she decided it was mostly about blood. Her blood. What was it he'd said about mutual thrall...? When he finished, he was always flushed red, and slightly tipsy. Not drunk... but merry.

During one very long and involved attack, she began to have flashbacks to the main bedroom at No 1, and had only managed to hold herself together by the skin of her teeth.

.. wouldn't the barn be easier...?

Halfway through the afternoon of the third day, she went into the kitchen and began to poke around the cupboards. She was hungry, she decided, and if she could just find what it was she fancied... he was looking at her across the counter tops.

'Hungry?'

She went to nod, but his stance warned her to stop. She froze.

'I thought so. Oh well.'

He shrugged his shoulders in that way of saying everything, and nothing. When had he become so... human, in his gestures? She took a step back, as if she was really thinking of fleeing. He was beside her, and had pinched both her wrists in an iron grip. She tried to struggle.

'Do not harm yourself. There is no help for it.'

His free hand was stroking her hair back, framing her face, all compassion and sadness.

She spat in his face.

He stared into her eyes, calmly, and then felled her with one blow. He then hoisted her over his shoulder, and walked her down to the barn, to her hut cell. He threw her onto the hard packed floor, and shackled her wrist and ankle. He'd been careful that she could be contained without rubbing, and without the left wrist being encumbered at all. The shackles were lined with a surgical moulding that breathed and kept her from rubbing her skin raw. No one had ever done that for him. As he checked she was breathing okay, he smoothed her hair off her forehead, and then bent to kiss her on the cheeks. Tears spilled from his eyes as he turned and left her. He had been angry with her until he'd entered the hut and spotted the shackles, then sorrow had flooded him. All the time he was cautioning himself not to go too far in his excitement at what was taking place... when the most common reaction so far had been pity and sadness.

The trio were resting in their cottage, where he knew the frenzy they'd gotten into after her first week's training had resulted in them releasing an orgy of sex and violence upon themselves that few would have been strong enough to endure. Yet they seemed to thrive on it.

It repulsed him, as pretend torture always had: amateurs. He was very careful to make sure they were emotionally removed from their own games, and back under his control, before he sent them back to her.

'She needs to lose more weight, and gain more muscle. As she now has ingested my blood, reduce her ration of rice to two cups a day. Lifting and weights for this section. Work on her arms, legs and abdomen.'

They moved from cattle prods to woven strip whips. Every time they did this the threat would have to be greater, the pain more sharp, or she would just stop in her tracks. It was all about escalation.

His heart and soul ached for what he was doing, as he watched them walk towards the barn, Mungo cracking out the leather whip as he went. Then he hardened himself with thoughts of how much better he was going to be to her, than Eléan had ever been to him. There were no blades in his conversion kit, and neither were there branding irons.

They moved through three escalations in quite a short time. As April came round, and the third anniversary of her capture, she was emaciated, raving and so strong that it was taking the four of them, at times, to keep her under control. Menses had stopped and her hair had begun to fall out. She was almost ready. Even beatings could not force her to eat when she was in the throes of his blood going through her, so they'd moved to using a feeding tube directly into her stomach. This was a very dangerous technique, and could go badly wrong, so it took immense precision and control to do, especially when she was struggling so hard it took three of them to hold her down. The agony it caused her also meant she was having to be chained down in the hut, rather than taken to the cottage. When she was pissing clear again, he no longer took her into the main house, but allowed her some rest in the cottage, and then returned her more and more quickly to the barn.

In the few short weeks in which this had all occurred, he'd had many answers delivered to him on puzzles that had haunted him for nearly two thousand years. To begin with, there was her blood. As each day passed, her blood became richer and more intoxicating. In turn, feeding from her fed his libido, and he was aroused by her even as her breasts shrank and her body withered in seeming old age. He'd always wondered why Eléan had tortured him so, to service her again and again and again, when he too was famine-starved to skin and bone. Especially when she owned so much more virile meat than he had become. He found the answer in her – it had nothing to do with her body, and everything to do with what the Turning was doing to her blood. Her blood, and his blood, for everything in her had now come from him. He was feeding off all three trolls regularly, to sustain Helene in his blood. But only Helene's blood brought him joy.

Of course, his sexual favours upon Helene, where much easier on her, than Eléan's had been on him. Eléan had him tortured until he had an involuntary erection, and then used thrall to keep him erect as she worked his body or had him beaten in a rhythm she liked to feel from underneath. Helene need only receive his attentions, passively, and he required nothing from her. Often, she was unconscious as he slipped into the hut and feasted, in all senses, upon her. He tried not to do this, as it left him with uneasy feelings and often there were nightmares of whispering voices in his ears, and ghostlike traces of hands and fingernails across his body. But when he was called down to help control her, or feed her... he could not resist. The scents from her body, when she struggled, excited him instantly. Again, it was something about what was going on with her blood, as the Transition came closer and closer. Blood called to blood, on all levels.

As she was started on what was her fifth and hopefully final journey through her Turning, and he sat in the office pretending he was doing something else, when all was about waiting to be called to be with her... Midge came up to him, and asked permission to speak.

Midge was an interesting character. He was far more experienced and disciplined in combat than Mungo, and had been a serving officer, twice. He was dominant to Mungo sexually, but apparently submissive to Mary. Dreyfuss knew that it took exceptional self-knowledge and understanding to be different things with different people. Especially when the people all knew each other. He and Midge had never had any occasion to inter-act, as Midge was exceptionally well found in all things asked of him. Dreyfuss suspected he was the real leader of the trio, but it was just that Mary wasn't intelligent enough to realise this. Midge got what Midge wanted, and Dreyfuss respected that. He therefore considered the request favourably.

'Certainly, would you like to sit?'

'No thank you Sir, I'll stand.'

He 'stood at ease'. 'Sir' was utterly acceptable when said by Midge.

'Please, continue.'

'Thank you, Sir. I have a concern I feel I need to bring to you. It is Mungo, Sir, and how this mission is affecting him. Mungo and your lady. I'm very afraid for your lady, in his hands. I thought it best to speak.'

'Please elaborate.'

'Mungo doesn't understand what we're doing, Sir. Neither does Mary, really, but she's learning. She watches, and she absorbs. Mungo stopped doing that when your lady escaped. He's still angry, I reckon, that she fooled him. He doesn't process emotion properly, sir. He thinks you don't care for her. He doesn't understand that that there is real purpose here.'

'Yes, I had noticed that. Please continue.'

'So far, it's been easy to make sure your lady is never left alone with him. But these past few days, as she's been so much stronger since she fed off you... he's been stepping out of line a little. Not too much, but I have worries. Mary seems oblivious, and she controls him. So I am worried. I know you'd want to know.'

He nodded him on.

'I have especial worries if you were planning to have us... carry out, eh... intimate training... on your young lady, sir. I know you tested us for control during the interviews, Sir, but that was so different to what's been going on here. For Mungo, I mean. I think it would be a very bad thing indeed, even if you were there, to have him touch her, even once.'

Dreyfuss absorbed the information, and looked at Midge afresh.

'I see. There are no such plans. The threat is all that is required, but it may not have panned out that way, which is why you were tested. What was needed occurred on the Chase.'

Dreyfuss rewarded Midge's integrity to his employer by sharing the information with him. 'Why have you brought this to my attention now?'

'That's more difficult, Sir. I need to talk personally to you, to have that discussion.'

He considered the options. Finally, he gave assent.

'Thank you, Sir, I appreciate the confidence. How she's going now, your lady, it is to plan. I can see we can carry on, without much problem. If she was going to crack, she'd have done so before now.'

Midge let his respect for Dreyfuss show through clearly. Dreyfuss accepted the gift with a nod of his head, encouraging the solider, which is what he was at core, to continue.

'However Sir, if you'll excuse me, I think you're in danger of making a mistake. Leaving something out.'

He left it there. Totally alone. Dreyfuss would either accept his thoughts, or blow up. Dreyfuss considered.

'Please continue.'

'She needs a carrot as well as a stick, Sir. I've seen how well trained she is, and I've never seen anyone as well trained as she, I can assure you. She still has spirit, and that's very rare. My worry, Sir, is if you carry on with her Turning, without you being part of the worst of it, she won't make it. I think her body will break.'

Dreyfuss was genuinely perplexed. Midge continued.

'My particular worry is the ropes. We'll be getting there this time, as I understand it. But if we go into the ropes, without you...' he sought the right word. '...encouraging her... she may break. I don't think either Mary or Mungo should be allowed to do the ropes, Sir. I think it has to be me, and you. She doesn't care anything about me Sir, I don't annoy her. She hates the other two. If she's to survive the ropes it has to be you on the other side of her. You, and me.'

Midge had said what needed to be said. Dreyfuss sat and pondered, for a long time.

'Thank you Midge, I appreciate your honesty. But before you go, I believe you have something else to say to me?'

'Yes, Sir, I do. Just to let you know that when you get to the end game, with the other two, I'll be heading on out.'

Dreyfuss looked directly into the other man's eyes, something he was usually careful not to do, in case it spooked the staff. Midge looked straight back at him, with neither defiance, nor discomfort. Dreyfuss accepted the look without challenge.

'That's fine, Midge, I understand. I take it your time in my employ has been useful to you?'

'Exceptionally, Sir, and you'll appreciate I have made plans for my future. I was unsure, and needed to understand fully, before I could proceed. I can proceed with confidence, now.'

'I am glad to have helped. You may go.'

Midge nodded, and left the office, leaving Dreyfuss with much to consider. One thing was clear to him, however, and that was that Midge was going to make an excellent vampire.

It should have galled him, that a human would be taking his knowledge and using it for them self. He despised the others, and their weak understanding of their own kind. Another minion to join them should have annoyed him... but Midge had absorbed much from him. On one level, he should ensure that knowledge stayed put, and continue with his plans for all three of them. On another... he respected the man's ability to see, and to drive forward, and so he put it to one side, and considered instead, the problems that had been raised. It didn't even bother him that Midge had got what he wanted from him partially from flattery. After all, the flattery had been genuine.

He was still musing about it all, a couple of days later, when Mary came up to the office to tell him that they had reached the need for moving to the ropes. As was his habit, he questioned her first.

'You are quite sure?'

'Yes, Master, very sure. She has strength still left in her, quite remarkable strength. But her legs simply won't move. The muscles are completely spent, just as you said they would be.'

'You have made her stand, and seen what happens?'

'Yes, the legs themselves cave under her. There are muscle spasms and it is painful, as she screams. She has said she is trying to move her legs, but they will not work.'

He nodded. 'Yes, she is on the edge. The muscles are dying. Very well.'

He moved down to the barn, with Mary trotting beside him.

Helene was slumped over on the running track. Her latest training suit, 4 sizes smaller than her first, hung off her. All she was taking in was his blood, so although she looked emaciated, there was a wiry strength that sustained her. She was covered in old sweat, dried sweat, new sweat. They'd been having to hose her down and oil her skin, twice daily, to stop her skin chafing and cracking from the sweat and toxin load. He'd made sure that only Mary or Midge touched her at those times, with Mungo on the hose. She was crumpled over, foetal, and grasping her stomach. Her legs twitched and spasmed as he watched. Mary hung back at the door as they entered, and Midge was standing over her, keeping guard. Mungo was prowling the empty spaces of the barn, the short chain whips they'd been using to spur her on clinking angrily as he moved.

Dreyfuss pulled his attention back from the others, and centred upon Helene, drinking in all the messages her body was sending him, by scent and movement. She was far from driven under with the work, as she had angry and distrustful eyes. But her body was dying under her.

He knelt beside her. She looked at him out of the sea of pain and rejection that was all that she really was, at this moment, and saw the hate for him, and what he was doing to her. That was a good sign. He opened his wrist and offered it to her. This was the first time he'd done so, when she was so aware of what was going on.

She latched on without hesitation. Such an important victory, with no one really aware of it. Although on that thought... he glanced at Midge. Yes, in Midge's eyes, he saw the reflected glory he required: the soldier understood what had just occurred.

He pulled his wrist clear of her, before she could be sated. She protested a little, but he was businesslike and brusque.

'Get up and run one more circuit.'

'I can't, my bloody legs don't work.' Her voice was thick with anger and defiance.

He leaned closer into her, just to be sure, and whispered in her ear. 'If you do not get up right now, I will have both men rape you where you lie.'

The outrage in her eyes hit him like a force.

He smiled. 'I mean, it... Midge!'

Midge took one step forward, and started to pull down his track suit, freeing himself. She screamed, and her body convulsed as she tried to make it move away from him. Nothing happened. Midge moved forward to grab her ankle, and pull her splayed onto her back, as he knelt down between her legs and began manipulating his penis to bring him to an erection. She screamed again, but still nothing happened. Her arms beat down on to the sand and sawdust, and she tried to get leverage to pull back, but it wasn't happening, with her legs refusing to do anything she told them too. Satisfied that she was completely unable to move, even after the feed, Dreyfuss tapped Midge on the shoulder. Midge tucked himself back in, stood up and backed away.

'Go get the ropes.'

Midge nodded, as Dreyfuss spotted Mungo moving backwards out of his eyeline. The man turned round, to face the barn wall, trying not be noticed, but the hand holding the chain length was so firmly clenched, it was bone white. The chain jangled against his leg. Dreyfuss decided he would have to attend to Mungo sooner, rather than later, which was a pity as it spoiled his plans.

Midge brought the ropes from one of the storage huts. With Mary's help, they got Helene to her feet, and tied her ankles, knees, thighs and waist to both himself, and Midge, matching each point on their own body... ankle to ankle, knee to knee. Midge was on her left side, Dreyfuss her right. They hooked their arms over and under her shoulders, and slowly began to walk forward, in step unison, with her puppet-like between them.

She began to scream.

'Try not to scream, it uses energy. Concentrate past the pain. Nothing will make us stop, and so you must just deal with it.'

As they moved on and on, relentlessly lifting up her legs and putting them back down, Dreyfuss observed that Midge had been right. The more Dreyfuss talked to her, the less she cried, and the more focussed she was. He began to talk her through it.

'The cells in your legs are dying, and they will atrophy slightly, until the blood you have just taken in fires them back to life. If we keep them moving, pumping, shifting what's now your blood and mine around your legs, moving your muscles and sinews and tendons... getting oxygen into your cells, they will be stronger, better, come the change. Every step you take now, will protect you, all of you, for the Turn. Your heart will beat stronger, your lungs will breathe deeper and better, your muscles will carry more load. Everything you do now, pays out a thousand times, the moment you finish Turning.'

They had a good rhythm going, and she was listening hard. Some of her weight was going onto her legs, for all her pain and confusion. Both he and Midge felt the slight shift as she started to regain some control over legs.

'And now we run.'

This time, nothing could prevent her screaming.

They ran, and she screamed and then she whimpered and once she passed out, and still they ran. Her heart was strong, her will was intact, there was just the pain, and they ran for her, carrying her through it. Both of them had been foot soldiers, both of them knew how to set a pace and keep to it, and both of them were used to packing weight. They kept her body moving like one enormous muscle, with his blood pumping through her body, and on and round and back and on and on they ran. Slowly, each part of her ceased and died, and slowly, they kept the blood pumping through her, healing, changing, reforming the very cells of her body. After several hours, when both were near their own point of exhaustion, her pace picked up. She was once more pushing herself, and their rhythm began to falter, as she had no skill in keeping with the pace they were matching each other in. They stopped, and cut her free. Spent and exhausted, they lay on the floor, catching their breath, whilst she carried on. There was a smile on her face as she ran on. The pain was gone, and once more she was in charge of her own body: it felt marvellous.

Dreyfuss waited quietly, patiently, until she slowed, then faltered, then dropped like a stone, unconscious. Then he directed them in various tasks, making sure that Midge went to shower, eat, and rest, that Mary washed Helene clean and oiled her skin well, and that Mungo set the equipment to rights and raked the floor level, obliterating the track they kept running into the floor.

Then he went and slept, and dreamed of ropes and pain and torture, and woke once more screaming, and covered in blood. Which he ignored utterly, concentrating only on how close they were to the end, now that Transition was on her.

Or so he had thought. He was extremely disconcerted to find her awake when he returned to check on her, in the early morning light. Awake and normal. As normal as you can be when that hungry, and chained to the floor. She sensed there was something amiss in how he reacted to her, but waited for him to speak, or act. There was, after all, nothing she could do anyway.

'How do you feel?'

'Hungry, cold.'

'Tired?'

'Not really, I've been awake an hour or so.'

'How much water have you drunk?'

She pointed to the bucket, it was half empty. He nodded.

'That's good.'

He unshackled her, then examined her body, touching her skin, poking her muscles, and asked her to stand and stretch. She did all he asked, without any problem.
He was confused, but decided to ignore it. She sensed his confusion, and decided there was nothing she could do about it.

'Are you hungry for food, or blood?'

'Blood. Can I have some?'

He smiled, and bowed a courtly bow. 'Of course, anything for my lady.'

She took a fair amount, before stopping, sated. She did not fall asleep. Curiouser and curiouser. He doubted himself, and his own memories. It had, after all, been two thousand years. Had this happened to him? He was sure not, but then... so much of that time was lost.

With his blood running through her veins, there was a faint blush of pink to her cheeks. Even in the hollows of the starved out face, there was a thrill of life and delicacy. Her eyes... her eyes were so beautiful, in fact...

He brought himself out of it sharply. That was thrall... he'd started to slip under her thrall! She seemed oblivious to what had happened, and he quickly pulled them both out of it, by re-establishing the routine.

'Out on the track please, and work on the machines. Muscles for the next section.'

He opened the door and sent her out to the trolls, well, to Mungo and Mary. Midge had been sent into town, to a sports physio, for treatment for his legs. He may have matched Dreyfuss in the run but he had not, could not, recover so seamlessly. A day of ice baths and massage was required, before he could be employed fully again. Dreyfuss has been aware, as had Midge, that really he was sending him out for the end game... it was going to be interesting when he returned, to find they were not yet finished.

It took another four days, of heavy work with practically no sleep and no solid food, for her to start to wear down. He fed her his blood, each time expecting her to collapse into sleep, and each time she stopped of her own accord, and carried on with the exercise. He was dumb founded and had to work hard at not showing it. She should have woken from the ropes, ravenous and feral. She should have fed then, on fresh blood and Turned. That she was feeding to full on his blood, and not falling into a blood coma... the feeling of not being in control grew, as did his nightmares. She just kept going, on and on, through the pain and fatigue. He drove them all, to keep driving her.

Eventually, the exhaustion pressed in and she faltered, and they had to push her on further and harder than ever before. They did not use blades, but he could see now, why they were such a good idea. They brought you down quicker than anything else, and bled you out at the same time, increasing hunger. Part of him itched to move to them, with her, to accelerate the process, but the darkness in him baulked. The memories were too strong.

He carried on the routine. All four of her keepers tired out before she did. By the time she had started to fail, they had been sleeping and working her in shifts. He had wanted her to have endurance. Part of him was a little apprehensive by how much he had gifted her. Slowly, however, she was pulled down. She started to snarl, and to snap. Dreyfuss watched her as Mary and Mungo harried at her with the chain whips, using the threat of them on her legs to keep her moving. Her eyes never left their throats, their wrists, their veins. She was licking her lips, and watching them from behind ravenous eyes... she was almost there.

Finally: he was to witness a Turning.

Midge was also watching with keen eyes. Dreyfuss enjoyed that, enjoyed a witness to his triumph.

As she slowly descended into the exhaustion, stumbling and falling, needing the chain whips to actually meet her flesh to keep going, Dreyfuss allowed her a break, in order to set the scene better for rest of the day's events. He had all but the multi-weight machine cleared out of the arena, and fastened a set of her chains to the heavy base of the machine. In case containment was needed at the moment of Turn. He also had a solid set of ropes on hand, and had new sawdust put down. He and Midge conferred, and felt that she had a few hours left to go before she was driven under totally, and they agreed between them that Mary & Mungo should drive her on for a little longer, whilst they retired to rest. Midge no longer intended to leave just prior, and was happy to remain until full Transition fuelled her to feed on her own for the first time and start the Turning. And, of course, to help Dreyfuss clean up the subsequent mess. Dreyfuss was not sure of why he was allowing this, but he was, and he was not going to look at why. That it had been a lonely journey for him, from the moment of his own Turning, to hers, and that he was enjoying the companionship of Midge, did not occur to him.

So much that never occurred to him.

Midge went to the cottage to sleep and prepare, whilst Dreyfuss retired to the house to do the same. He reckoned there were about 5, maybe 6 hours left in her before she keeled over this final time. Sleep, however, would not come, and he prowled the house, awaiting the call to return and finish the job.

He was in the office, reading financial reports, when Mary ran into the house, and up the stairs. Her speed had alerted him to a problem, and he met her on the landing outside the office. She was grey, and bloody, and a large bruise was swollen along her left eye bone. Blood, dead blood, blood that was old and dried, stained her face and neck.

'Mungo... Mungo... he knocked me out...' She could barely stand, and breathing was difficult.

Dreyfuss understood instantly, and shouted to her, 'Get Midge!' and then, he ran.

Mungo was still raping her as Dreyfuss entered the barn, at such speed that the door broke from the hinges. Mungo had just tried to move away, when Dreyfuss reached him. He cannoned into him as he started to rise, and they both went over in a tumble of limbs. Dreyfuss reached his feet first, as the man tried to crawl away and stand. Dreyfuss stomped down on the back of his left leg, snapping a bone in two. Mungo let out a mewling cry, like a kitten stood on by mistake. He slammed his foot down on the other leg, and the second snap tore a scream that shook the roof. Dreyfuss ignored him to turn to Helene, as she was more important than vengeance at this exact moment.

Dreyfuss's heart seized at the sight of her, a torn and bloodied ruin. He lifted her up into his arms, and beneath was so wet, she was too slippery to hold. He slowly turned her over, to see what lay underneath. Her heart was faltering. She was failing as she'd almost been bled dry by the slashes in her flesh from lashing with the chain whip. Her back and the backs of her legs were slashed open runnels of blood and torn flesh. She was barely conscious. Of course, he would have wanted her conscious. He slashed his wrist and put it straight to her mouth, smearing it across her lips until she latched automatically. She fed. It was slow, too slow, but it was feed.

A red film descended over his vision. He stilled himself to stay with her, to keep feeding her. Mungo continued to scream and moan, as he tried to drag himself away from the scene by his arms. Keeping her alive was more important than killing Mungo. That's what he told himself.

Midge ran into the barn, through the now open space of the door.

'Get a scalpel!' Midge turned on his heels and ran back out. Dreyfuss shouted to Mary, who had appeared in the doorway. 'Get out of my sight if you want to keep your head. But if you leave the estate, you will beg me to kill you!'

She looked over to the crawling Mungo, then bolted out of the barn.

Still Helene latched and suckled, but it was slow, so terribly slow. Her heart was no longer faltering, but neither was it recovering. Dreyfuss was truly fearful: emotions he had long denied were his, were threatening to emerge. The thought of her dying... leaving him... leaving him alone with his memories. He screamed his rage and frustration, but kept his wrist locked to her mouth.

Midge returned with a packet of scalpels. Dreyfuss directed him to cut all the clothing off Helene's back and legs, what was left of it. He did so quickly. Dreyfuss was now kneeling beside her, so that his left wrist was at her mouth, with her face down. He raised his other arm and directed Midge to slash along its length. He did so without hesitation.

Blood poured out of Dreyfuss, and fell along her back. The cut healed, and he again directed Midge to slash. They repeated this three times. As the final curtain of blood poured out of him onto her, Midge caught some of it in his cupped hands, and poured it over an open wound on her leg. At his wrist, Helene was drawing in more blood. Dreyfuss was starting to pale.

'Fetch me that filth behind.'

Mungo has almost made it to the back of the barn; in his panic, he was crawling the wrong way. Midge grabbed him and dragged him backwards, ignoring the screams of agony from his erstwhile companion and lover. Midge lifted Mungo's neck to Dreyfuss, who sank his teeth in and gorged. Mungo screamed even more. Helene suckled upon Dreyfuss, as Dreyfuss drank the life blood of Mungo.

Thus, her life was saved.

When her heart was strong and in steady rhythm, Dreyfuss pulled his own wrist free from her. Midge was holding her upright, cradling her in his arms. She was confused and disoriented, but she would survive.

Dreyfuss turned to the garbage that was Mungo. He was already dead, Dreyfuss had stopped feeding as his heart had died. That was of no matter. Just as he had done once before, Dreyfuss applied his rage to the body's head, and pulled it clear away from its home.

It was not an easy thing to do, and neither was it silent. The sounds of sinews, muscles and bone being torn from each other, were appalling and disgusting and vile. Midge averted his gaze, a privilege Helene was denied in her shocked state. Dreyfuss stood with the head in his arms, and the gore and blood and liquids from the brain cavity flooded down onto his clothes. He screamed, a primitive sound of fear and anger and defiance, and threw the head as far as he could. It hit the barn wall with a sickening, wet and splattered thump. Midge felt his gorge rise, and swallowed it down quickly.

In his arms, Helene began crying softly, before finally passing out into blood coma.

Dreyfuss tore off his clothing, from the waist up, and then leaned down to pick Helene up in his arms.

'Serge, I would appreciate it if you cleaned up this mess. My lady and I will be in the main house.'

'Certainly, Dreyfuss.'

The exchanging of names cemented their new relationship. Vampire and human working together, mutually, at least for the time being. Serge Alois Federspiel had not intended to become involved with his employer, but was exceptionally pleased to have been given the opportunity. The Vampire Maker had much to teach him.

Dreyfuss has intended to take her straight to the house, but common sense prevailed, and he went via the cottage. He stripped them both naked, washed her off and them himself, and still naked and dripping water, carried her up into the house, and their bedroom. He laid her down on one side, before fetching towels and placing them on the other side of the bed, then he gently turned her over onto her front to examine her back. He was worried that sand and dirt from the arena floor would have been driven into her wounds as Mungo had raped her, and the dirt would be sealed into the healing scars. But the feed had been deep enough that she'd bled out any foreign matter. Whilst all the wounds had closed and were healing, the sight of so many wounds that had been gaping mouths in her flesh... chilled his soul. He could remember how that felt, and could feel each slice of the blade as he'd been cut up as badly as this.

He could hear the laughter. *The whispering...*

Dreyfuss realised Mungo had to have worked on human flesh a great deal to have such clean and even cuts from the whip that had been in the kit he'd supplied. Chain whips were for terror, not actual use, and he wondered at how clean and deeply the flesh had been sliced. He must have used something else. It looked for all the world like a normal bullwhip had been used, with a metal ending, deliberately designed to slash. As her back was clearing through, as his blood pulsed through her veins, the skin re-knitting seamlessly, he turned her gently onto her back to thoroughly examine her front. There had been a few wrapping injuries, as the tail of a whip had snaked round her back and impacted on her front. A deep gouge in the right breast required he smooth his blood over her again, but mostly, it was all healing. The problem was... this was too much damage. His blood should be making her stronger, right now, not healing her from damage. How would this... savagery... affect her change?

There was also what had happened in her mind, as Mungo had beaten her down when she was both alone, and helpless, and not capable of fighting back. How long had he had her to himself? At least an hour, maybe more, to inflict this much damage, and then there was the rape... how often had he taken her...? The animal within him wanted to take her there and then, to flush out the stench of the human who had usurped him, replace his scent on her body. The man who loved her wanted no part of it. He'd not heard that voice clearly before, and sat in stunned silence, arguing with himself. His eyes drifted to her wrist, and the mounds of scar tissue, which had not healed at all, as he'd hoped they would when she began to Turn. As he'd prayed they would. He thought of the crater on her back.

He tried to put the thoughts to one side, tried to shy away from the reality of her broken shoulder, and what Mungo had done to her back, as being mirror images of each other, but such avoidance was impossible, even for a master in self-deception such as he. She was completely unaware of it, but he did heavy penance for that broken shoulder as he watched over her healing sleep. Tears slid from his eyes as he sat and watched her breathe, sat and watched her broken body heal.

Finally, in the small dark hours before dawn, he pushed everything to one side and away: he would have no more if it. No more of worry, of feeling vulnerable, of being anxious or unsure. It was done. It could not be undone. Mungo was dead, and she would be what she was. It would be fine. He knew he should shackle her, she might rise mad... but he could not bear to move her from her sleep, or his bed. He lay down beside her, arms seeking her body as benediction, and he fell into sleep, holding her to him.

As Helene emerged from sleep, he woke with her. She was groggy, and tired, and disoriented. That was normal given the amount of damage she had had to heal. She was not seemingly mad, or out of control. There was the usual deadness to her eyes... that always followed when she had been... disciplined. There seemed to be no difference, given Mungo's treatment of her, than that of many mornings when she had woken from his own embraces. He ruthlessly rejected any thoughts on that subject at all. If she could move on ahead, without reference to anything, so could he. He was not about to admit that anything Mungo had done had been either the equal, or more savage, than anything he had done. Neither would he consider that he had needs of his own to take care of, in respect to the situation. Therefore, there was nothing to think about, or to be done, other than carrying on as normal. She had been on the verge of Transition, and then been fed full, so she would need to work out the blood feed once more. He suspected Hunger would show her true state.

She appeared to know who she was, and where she was. She was terribly weak, and not inclined to movement. She lay in the bed, drifting in and out of sleep for some hours. Finally, she tried to rise, and he helped her to the bathroom, where she pissed dark black fluid, and then helped her back to bed. She fell asleep again quickly.

That she did not vomit dead blood was extremely telling. She had absorbed the entire blood load she'd taken in from him, which had been most of his own blood flow. The end was here: her body was fully primed. Transition had occurred. It had been two days since Mungo's death, and he and Serge had prepared for all eventualities. Whatever path this Turning took, they were prepared. He sat in the armchair and pretended to read as she slept on.

Another twelve hours sleep, and she gave signs she was starting to emerge into Hunger. Her head began to bob around, sniffing the air, looking for feed. Primal instincts were taking over. He laid down in the bed beside her, and folded her into his arms. She moved closer to him, her nose buried into his arm, as she breathed his scent. Her nose was following the veins on his arm, her head bobbing up and down faster and faster. As her mouth found his wrist, she made a soft moan, and turned her entire body towards him. He was up and out of her reach by the time she had begun to lick her lips. As her eyes opened, so did her mouth: she was unconsciously moving to bite and suckle.

Excellent.

'Good afternoon.'

She said nothing to him as she sat up. She was grace and beauty, even with her withered flesh, as she stretched and pulled her body this way, and then that. She looked refreshed, if shrunken. Snow White, emerging from the coffin after years of wasting. Or perhaps Sleeping Beauty... but he was not going to be foolish enough to give her a kiss, not now.

The look was in her eyes. The look of need; the need of blood. He smiled. Again, it had not been what he expected, but there was blood lust in there, if somewhat abated and under control. He was comforted. She did not speak much, and resumed her silent and withdrawn persona. Having had to deal with how he truly felt for her, so recently, the distance pained him. He put it aside, for that could be dealt with easily. There was plenty of time for Restoration, afterwards.

Hunger was the dominant issue: hunger was driving her to wake fully, and to act. To hunt, did she but know it. She rose out of the bed and approached him, with that gleam of need in her eye. He deflected her to wash, to dress, to carry on routine. She was not happy, anger and frustration pulsing out from under her skin as she huffed past. He danced around her, keeping her moving, watching her control weaken as the Hunger took hold fully. She paced around the house several times, before simply asking for some of his blood. He refused. She stormed into the kitchen, in silent, manic temper, to find something to eat. She could not tolerate the slightest morsel of food. Nothing would force her mouth to open, her hand to carry food into it. She threw the food she had tried to eat across the floor, and stormed out. She retreated to the bathroom, to lie once more in scented water.

The clock started to tick down.

It had started as a dull ache in her jaw. Once, after she had had a wisdom tooth removed, she had developed a jaw infection. The pain was similar, like a throb that dived so deep into the flesh of her mouth, it drove into the bones of her jaw. When it was so insistent, so powerful that it was beating a rhythm out in her mind, a pulse beat of agony, she left the bath: nothing was distracting her from this. None of her usual tricks or deceits worked. Whenever she tried to fly from this pain, it grabbed her by the ankle, and pulled her back down again, pulled her slowly under its grip.

She returned to the bedroom to dress, and finding him there, had asked him about it. He talked her through it, being careful to keep his distance as he once more denied her a feed from him.

'It is the need for human blood. Real blood. Fresh blood. Vampire blood is already partially dead, changed, if you prefer. Our blood will not do: it is not sufficient. When this pain starts, you have to feed. You don't have to kill, of course, but you have to feed. Just a few mouthfuls, at first, as you are about to be Newborn. Just let your body have a first taste. You should not have need to kill for at least a year. Showing a sign of ageing is the prompt for killing. This is just for food, not death.'

She ignored what he was saying, it sounded wrong. There could be nothing more of need, in her, that this pain did not announce. This was surely the worst pain there could ever be. She carried it with her, stalking about the house, furious he would not feed her. He was content to offer only the voice of calm, directed, required, information.

'You have started the Turn. You must now complete it. There is no choice.'

She did not want to look at what he was saying: this had been avoided for a very long time, and she wished to continue to avoid it. She could not see the temper, *the rage*, that was underlying everything she said or did, at that moment, but when she did speak, it was harsh and sharp: far more aggressive than he would have allowed normally. As he took her through it again, calmly, when they were both in the kitchen as she once again failed to eat anything, she spat a question at him.

'What you mean, is that you want me to drink from someone, now, isn't that it?'

His silence was his assent.

She shook her head. 'Never!'

She stormed off again. He followed quietly, finding her sitting on the hall stairs.

'It cannot be stopped. Neither the pain, nor the process. You are too far gone. Your gut is now completely primed for blood. The pain will just build, until it consumes you. When it takes you, you will devour anything, anyone. You will do less damage, if you feed for the first time in control of yourself.'

She sat sullen, silent, pouting.

'The pain will overwhelm you. There is no need to fight this. Just accept it, upfront, and we can move on.'

He didn't mention that she was controlling the pain, and the need, remarkably. He didn't think she needed to know how atypical her behaviour was. How they had prepared for preventing her from feeding too much... were not prepared at all for a *refusal* to feed. But then, was she not so much more, as he had crafted her? A smug smile slipped out, as he looked on her with pride.

His Changeling....

She jumped to her feet and flew at him, beating him with her fists, which he easily captured and held still.

'You could always bring me some, bring me a drink in a glass!'

He remained calm, non-committal, and she burst out crying, sobbing into his chest. Aggressive and petulant all at once: another good sign.

'When you can stand it no longer, come to me, and we can fix everything easily. It will just be a few mouthfuls, and then you can rest. I shall be in the office.'

He walked past her, up the stairs, removing himself as a distraction.

She screamed in frustration, throwing a massive china vase onto the floor to smash into a thousand pieces. He carried on up, ignoring her. She fell to the floor, crying, and beating her fists down on the marble. Eventually, as all crying storms must do, the sobbing faded and she was left hot, sweaty and feeling faint. She lay on the cool floor, ignoring the shards of pottery that were digging into her bones, as she lay. When the adrenaline left her, she was shaky and weak. After she'd pulled herself up to her feet, she climbed the stairs and went back to bed.

After a few hours, pain was spreading round her whole mouth, the agony in her front teeth the worse, like the gums were being slashed with a razor. Every bone in her body ached worse than flu, although she'd never had flu, she was sure. But it was worse than that, surely? She was so thin, with such little fat to cushion her bones, nothing was comfortable. No bed, no seat, no couch. She retreated to the only place of comfort: floating in a tub of hot scented water. Every thought she had, was of blood, and swallowing blood. But those thoughts brought sounds, obscene sounds of ripping and tearing and popping... she had to think of nothing.

Nothing.

She poured more hot water, steam curling up from the water's surface, trying to cover her own heat with the benediction of the water. She felt faint, dizzy and unreal. She felt she was no longer human, and was now a creature of fairy. Water soothed her as she floated, feeling translucent, empty of substance. She tried to slip away from her body of flesh, of blood, to that of the elements, unfettered and primal. She was now of water, not land. Like the enchanted tales of her childhood, she was a mermaid who had been half way transformed. She walked on legs of pain. To walk at all, was to walk upon the flashing blades of hunger. Her only respite was to float in water. She had given everything she could, to this change: she had even given up her voice.

Surely it shouldn't hurt so much? Surely there was no pain she could not slip from? She always had before.... Eventually the pain grew so much the water ceased to be a comfort.

She drained the bath, tears flowing over her face at the pain standing up had caused. She was, she knew, profoundly confused and in shock. She wasn't quite sure of where she was, and her senses were playing havoc with her. Colours were not quite right, light was strange and shadowy, sounds were too loud... everything that touched her skin, hurt. She found herself drawn to morbid thoughts of sunlight and danger. He had talked her through all this a dozen times. Explained that she would be going through a psychological adjustment more than a physical one and that no, the daylight was not going to harm her, burn her, and yes, she could touch a crucifix without bursting into flames. But she found herself avoiding the windows, and the sunlight, longing for the dark. Surely it would all hurt less in the night?

Surely it could be over soon?

She hadn't reckoned on... well, on a lot of things. She certainly hadn't reckoned on being left like this, alone in the house. Left to call him when she needed him?

...he hadn't come when she called him when... had that been part of his plan....?

That thought was repressed.

The problem was... there was so much to be repressed, there was nothing left to think about. Nothing to distract her from the Hunger. Nothing to stop her dwelling on that, and what it meant. To try and think of anything else was to think of what had occurred in the barn... all of it, in total, not just the finale. So there was nowhere to go, but to keep looking in front of her. The final frontier loomed, and there was no humour in the thought. Was she going to die... could she die...? Should she? All this time, she'd thought of herself, and him. It had never really hit her, that there would have to be a third person, a... victim. Until she'd seen Mungo... she closed her eyes to block out the knowledge of the last thing she'd seen of Mungo... but could not block out the sound... the sound of his head hitting the wall. She tried to work round the sound, the awareness, as she'd worked round so much in the past, just tiptoe past it in the night, not awaken it in her fully... she'd been aware there would have to be blood. Blood taking. A human, a human for her to drink from. A living donor. But she'd never looked at it. She'd never truly believed...

...was that true, that she still hadn't believed...?

No, she had believed. She'd believed since the moment that boy's throat had been torn out. She had believed. But she had not *understood*. She'd not held the information inside her, knowing it whole. She'd never *understood* what it would be she'd have to do. Somewhere, it had all been silenced under the blanket thought that she herself, Helene, wouldn't care. That the Turning would change how she thought about such things. That the Turning would be a change inside her head, her mind. That she wouldn't mind what she had to do.

That her human feelings would be gone. *It would be easy...*

She'd looked forward to that. To no longer be powerless, either with him, or with her sense of self.

Her left thumb caressed the base of her middle finger. Just a few mouthfuls, and she would Turn, and she could put the ring back on. Well, not that ring. She looked down at her shrunken hand. She'd need a child's ring now, for a while, until she put the weight back on.

Just a few mouthfuls.

Just a few.

Could she do it? She didn't think so, and returned to prowling the house.

The hours stretched endlessly in front of her and behind her. There was just the pain in her mouth the aching in her bones, the *need*. She was raw, unconscious *need*. Every emotional ache she had ever endured, from a skinned knee, to her father's death, rose up inside her. Her throat developed a pain, like a knife stabbed through the centre of her voicebox. She found it difficult to breathe past the rawness. She would sit at the window, looking out at the night, and sob with loneliness and the aching hollow inside her. *She must feed.* Why had he left her alone? She needed him, she wanted comfort. To be left alone like this, left alone in a void of emptiness... it was inhuman.

She was inhuman.

She started to run another bath, and lost the strength to get into it. Thirst had started to drive into her, on top of the hunger, the need for more than she had. She could force water down into herself, it felt like liquid glass, cutting and slashing her, but she could do it. It sat inside her, molten lava, going nowhere. It didn't satisfy the thirst. It didn't sate her.

Nothing would satisfy her, nothing except... the thought collapsed into her. There was, after all, nothing to be done. He was always right.

She climbed up the stairs to the office. He was sitting in the window seat, waiting for her. She staggered over, and fell into his arms, which he'd raised to accept her. Tears spilled out of her, tears and sobs. He stroked her hair, her face, her back. Worn rhythms of comfort exchanged between them once more. She could smell the blood in him, hear his heart beat. The skin on her arms goose bumped at the thought of his blood, she nuzzled into him, her mouth reaching for his neck. It wasn't what she really wanted, but it would suffice...

He fastened his arms around her wrists, and pushed her back, gently.

'No darling, not now. Later, but not now. Now is not the time. Later.'

She sobbed and cried and begged, but he kept refusing, and pulled her to her feet, and walked her down the long walk to the barn. All she could hold within her was the smell of his blood, and the memory of how it would taste as it gushed into her, hot and heavy and salty and...

...the scent of fresh blood, human blood hit her.

She was not even at the building, still was on the night strewn pathway, and the heat and warmth of the blood signalled to her. It called to her, opened her up like sunlight on a flower, pulled her to its embrace, like pollen to the bee. She would taste of it, and drown in honey. Sweet, salty, hot honey, blood red and vital.

There were other scents mingled with the blood; sweat and fear. Sweat and piss. The notes played along her senses, totally subordinate to the blood, to the heady, heavy scent of pulsating life. Her brain ordered the scents, and processed them whilst her mind utterly ignored everything but the siren call of the heart beating somewhere in the barn. Could she hear it, from outside, from here? Or was her mind supplying that rhythm, to accompany the scent? Her own heart started to race, as she drew in the scent of all that delectable blood. She salivated, oblivious that she was licking her lips.

Dreyfuss pushed open the door, and went in first.

CHAPTER THIRTY-ONE

She was outside the barn, looking at his back, as he entered. His body hid the source of the blood, the life. Then he moved, and she saw it. Saw the blood beating and pulsating in front of her, contained in a covering of skin. She moved forward, slowly, gently, as if to savour every second of the smell, the sight, the loveliness of what was in front of her. She sensed Dreyfuss standing back, and signalling to someone to move. The hunter instinct kept her aware of everything, but the desire for filling, for satiating, for drinking and swallowing, moved her on to her goal. She could hear the heart beating... *pitter patter pitter patter tiny bird...* she could see the glow as the blood pulsed through the skin... she could taste the hot rush that would fill her... fill the need, make the pain go away.

She licked along the line of the neck, tasting salt and hot skin, and sourness and... a hint of metal. The skin tasted of copper... of blood, of heat... she drew back, flaring her mouth, her nostrils and her eyes, she would strike just once... as she moved in, her gaze met that of her victim.

Mary stared back at her, with fear and terror written on her face. Helene's head carried on down, her mouth fastening on the woman's throat. She found the stream of blood that had been slowly dripping out of her, from the cut that Midge had made in her neck. Her tongue played over the cut, licking up the blood, her mouth tingled. She moved her tongue over the hot flesh, seeking where to bite and tear and pull. Finding the spot where the skin was thinnest, the blood-flow under it strongest, she bit down and twisted savagely.

As Mary screamed, hot blood flooded into her mouth. She held it for a second, allowing the wonder to play upon her tongue. As she prepared to swallow... she heard a far distant sound. A clanging, a clattering, a frantic pealing of metal on metal. She hesitated, listening to the sound get louder, more frantic. What was it?

It was that damn bell, again.

Again!

The bell sounded louder and louder, drowning out the sound of the heart beating under her. Mary, on feeling the action upon her neck cease, started to struggle. This was nearly her undoing, as instincts deep

inside Helene awoke, and responded swiftly. Prey struggling was so…
enticing.

It was the word *prey* that caused her to stop. To stand back, and
to spit out the blood in her mouth.

Prey.

Food.

Feed.

Even now, as she stood staring at the woman, her mind saw…
feed. But it also saw two other things, now she was looking. It saw the
bruises, and the stained clothing, and the fear. It saw the look of fear,
and it smelled the fear, and it remembered the fear. Staring into Mary's
face, a face she'd hated, and cursed, a face she'd promised herself she'd
obliterate, one day… her world view changed. For a moment, her
eyesight fooled her, and she was looking not at Mary, but at Joanne.
Joanne, lost, alone, terrified. Beaten, bruised, bullied. Joanne stared
back at her, pleading. The look of fear, fear of what she was going to do,
to… *herself.*

Fear.

Feed.

Two visions of the world fought for dominance. One, where she
was looking at lovely soft meat, and feed. Another, where she was
looking at a woman, lost in terror and pain, covered in fear. The taste of
the blood in her mouth, drove her forward again, one step closer to
herself. Just one bite, she'd have just one bite….

Her mouth fastened once more over the wound in the woman's
neck. She twisted and pulled at it, with her teeth, and blood flooded into
her once more. Warmth and heat and light and… life. She began to
swallow, pushing down the vision of fear, and replacing it with feed.
She picked up the woman's heart beat, as she swallowed, feeling it
pulse… knowing it would soon end.

…it would all soon end… it would all end soon…

What ended was the warm salt in her mouth. She opened her
eyes. She was standing back, apart from the woman. How had that

happened? Somehow, she'd moved back; how? The voice in her head finally came through, finally was heard.

...you will kill her... you will kill her... you will kill her...

The sound of a throat being ripped out, of a head being torn from the spine that held it, roared through her.

She paled as the blood, her blood, drained out of her face. She could taste the woman's blood on her, smell it. She could smell the pulse beat of her heart. She knew, utterly, that it was true. If she fed of this woman, *this human being...* she would kill her. Her blood was already inside her, already moving down into her, filling her. She glanced at Dreyfuss. The look on his face was obscene. Gloating, pleased, proud. Triumphant.

...his Changeling was his pride and joy...

His erection pressed tightly on his trouser front.

Mary's blood was in her mouth and her body sang with the joy of it. The pain was gone, and in its place was happiness. Her body was not just sated, but equally aroused. The sight of his erection had made her body tighten with anticipation. She could feel the light that was Mary's blood open her up from within as she swallowed it down.

Helene fell to her knees, her head dropping forward. Before Dreyfuss, or the startled Serge could react, she'd stuck her fingers down her throat and vomited up the little blood she'd taken from Mary. Dreyfuss recoiled. This didn't prevent Helene from standing up, leaning forward and punching him hard on the face, hard enough that he had to take a step back.

'Liar! LIAR! You are all lies!'

She slapped and punched him as he stepped back, and back, her blows never stopping. Finally, he bumped into the horse jump that they had strung Mary up on. Mary screamed.

Her attention caught, Helene stopped hitting Dreyfuss, and turned to face Midge.

'CUT HER DOWN!'

Midge moved to do as she said, and Helene turned and stormed out the barn, only stopping briefly at the door to shout back at them:

'You are all mad! And I will have none of it... *none of it*!'

She stalked out into the night.

Her bravado was short lived. She slumped onto the pathway as the adrenaline that had fuelled her outburst, waned. Despair crashed her down, hard, and she lay on the cold pathway, crushed. Hunger was eating her, no matter her fury, no matter her rage. No matter her despair and defeat. Hunger that had thought it was to be fed, and was screaming that it needed blood, now, forever, and in all ways. Blades of hunger sliced her bones, her flesh, her mind. Every sense in her had woken on the tasting of Mary's blood, and all screamed at her now, to get up, to go back, and to finish what she'd started. Her soul, that inner voice of comfort that had always spoken the words she needed to hear, kept up its litany:

...you will kill her... you will kill her... you will kill her...

She crawled, literally, up the pathway to the house. Dragging herself upright, she all but fell into the kitchen, and staggered to a fridge. She would eat, she must eat, but it would not be... human.

Never.

Everything she looked at, made her feel sick. There was nothing she could eat here, nothing. She slammed the door closed and turned to the cooker. There, hanging in a suspended rack, were eggs. She picked one up, cracked it against the unit, and dropped it into her mouth. It tasted vile: foul and dead. She forced herself to swallow it down. Her body screamed *no!*: this was not possible, and she began to retch. She quelled the sensation with her mind: this was *so* happening, she was not losing to her body, not now. It would comply. *It would. Her body was not having a human life. She was not him.*

She pushed the egg shell down into the sink disposal unit, and moved away, quickly.

The pain as the egg flooded her shrunken stomach dropped her again on the floor. Her legs cramped up as her stomach lit fire.

He found her there, curled foetal, forcing her body to hold onto the food, although that escaped his notice. He lifted her gently up, and carried her, crying and sobbing and hitting him with her fists, to the bedroom. He soothed and hushed her, and lay on the bed, and let her cry it out. She fell asleep, eventually, the bed a ruin of crumpled sheets from the tossing and turmoil. He lay in the dark, trying to work out what to do: she would have to drink.

How to get her to drink?

She would have to drink. It simply *was*.

He replayed the scene in the barn, over and over again, trying to find a way to ascertain what she had been thinking, what had happened. Unable to comprehend any impulse that was not selfish, or based on power and control, he was at a loss to understand. That she was squeamish about death, injury, to another... yes, that was logical, to a certain extent. She'd grown in a very cosy world. However, it should not have over ridden what had happened within her, how her senses would have woken when the blood first entered her mouth. Nothing about what had happened made any sense to him. But then, what ever had, with her? He reconciled himself to yet another lesson in how the world was somehow different when applied to her. He wrapped the thought in his usual conceit that the difference was himself: it was not as if Eléan had truly been stronger than he, in the end. As *he* was Master, *his* Changeling was bound to be different. He spent many hours wrangling it all through, as she slept.

Lost, with no map or understanding of what was occurring, he decided to try replacing one hunger, one need, with another. His own need to have her was pulling at him. He'd seen her reaction to his body as she'd tasted the blood. He'd seen how she'd looked at him, and had needed him. He had scented her musk in the air. It had been a moment he would never forget, to see that look in her eyes. He took the hope that the look had given him, and used it as the light to show the pathway out of this puzzle.

She began to snuffle and root, and to signal that she was waking up into the Hunger. He acted swiftly, taking charge of her body and her awakening. He used all he had, both in terms of knowledge of her body, and her mind, to pull him to her. He caressed and wooed her, even as she was still locked in dreaming. It worked to some extent, as her body was moving with sexual need, not the Hunger, as she rose through the layers. She moaned, and her legs opened willingly to him. He shied away from his own pleasure, and brought her to her own with his hands and tongue. She tipped over into wakening, as she orgasmed, and he felt her tense as she had realised this was not some erotic dream, but a physical reality. Her eyes opened and he locked her into his thrall. Needy for comfort, love and acceptance, slashed to shreds by the Hunger... she fell into his gaze without a murmur. He held her mind, and whispered softly into her ear...

'Drink for me... drink for me...'

He thought of the blood himself, used his memories of how it was to feed. As his mind pushed into hers, his body responded to the power of the invasion, and, inevitably, he mounted her and began to ride her body simultaneously as he pushed further and further down into her mind. She held all of him in her, in all senses, and her gaze met his. He carried on whispering into her ear as he moved himself in pleasure upon her, driving his thoughts down, down down into her psyche.

'Drink for me... drink for me... drink for me...'

On the surface, his cry was strong, powerful and aware of all things. He offered her knowledge of the marvellous freedom her body would have, once she was fully Turned. Through him, she knew power, strength; immortality. She could feel what it was like to Master all, and to haunt the dark. To be the thing the darkness was afraid of. Through his memories, she could feel the great surge in power as veins opened and hearts began to slurry, as life moved from the feed, to the fed. The power was so attractive. With that sort of power, she could be safe... *safe...* safe from him. *Safe from everyone... anyone.* Her thumb stroked her middle finger.

It would be worth it, wouldn't it?

'Drink for me... drink for me... drink for me...'

As he orgasmed, the thrall pulled her into the swell of power with him, firing an orgasm across her own body. As she lit up underneath him, her mind blossomed out, and her thrall caught him. He was locked into her gaze, as he had been, briefly, for a split second, on that fateful day in No 1. She slipped into his mind, and this time, she was aware of what she was doing.

Like a thief, hurrying through the house after dark, trying to find the safe before the lights flicked on... she searched. Searched though his memories, and his thoughts, trying to find something, anything, that would help her. She didn't know what it was, didn't know if it existed, but she sensed how little time she had, and how much opportunity must be grasped. Shapes, images, people, flooded past her, as if she was standing motionless at a train platform, and everyone hurried past her on their way to somewhere else. Although it was Dreyfuss that stood there, not her. She was inside his mind, looking out through his eyes.

An old man, of great height and stature, looked directly at her, at Dreyfuss. He had grey hair and beard, tired blue eyes, and wore what looked like Roman robes. He had tears in his eyes, and when she looked down, at her own hands, the hands of Dreyfuss, they were covered in blood. The blood dripped from her hands, to those of the old man, and he stood, the front of his white robes splattered in blood, sobbing. The blue eyes were stained with pain, grief and loss, as the tears fell to mingle with the blood. Dreyfuss reacted to the tears, and she almost lost control. She blinked the old man away, and moved on... that memory had been too painful. On she moved, searching. Another man emerged from the crowds, not as tall, thinner, and younger. He had black hair and navy blue eyes, clean shaven fair skin and a snide smile. He was dressed in a costume of pale trousers, skin tight, and a short black jacket. A mound of lace at his throat. He leered at she who was Dreyfuss, and at the same time, he bowed, giving show of politeness and respect. Behind him, a waif of a girl stood, short and skinny with straggly dark brown hair and startling violet eyes. Barefoot and ragged, she looked starved. Seeing the stark need on her face, made the hunger inside her, and Dreyfuss, jump.

She blinked again, moving on, searching, moving. As the people moved through what had become the image of a real railway station, she saw London buildings rise and fall, and rise again all around her. A huge dome was begun, and slowly finished, and she looked at St Paul's as it had looked, when it was huge and shining and dominated the entire City. Then it fell back, to nothing, and wooden buildings tumbled everywhere. The river Thames was on the far right somewhere, growing fatter and thinner and fatter, and then freezing over in ice, then melting into spring floods. Wooden boats docked on raw rock, the sails creaking in the wind. She turned away, to her left, this was all too mixed up, and moving too fast. Over on the far left of the nightmarish scene, the people faded as the edges of the buildings gave way to soft green bushes, and trees. Warm sunlight bathed fragrant green fields. She walked towards them, smelling herbs on the breeze, and the scent of lemon in the trees. Under her feet, soft grass cushioned her as she moved. She could hear water trickling along.

She pushed some bushes out of her way, gently, and found them, laughing, by the stream's edge. He was young, so handsome, so very human. His skin was sun tanned dark brown, his face, arms and legs ten times darker than the pale torso revealed above the cloth tied around his hips. Discarded beside him, leather armour, a sword and shield. Discarded, as they had stripped to sport together. His hair had bleached blonde streaks over the matting curls of brown, his black beard scraped back almost to bare skin. His teeth were white and even, and his limbs lithe and glorious. He was heavily muscled and a soft sheen of sweat decorated his flesh. The human Dreyfuss was a wonderful sight.

She lay beside him, under the shadows of the olive grove. She was entrancingly beautiful, and Helene knew she was seeing her through the eyes of her lover. Her skin was warm chocolate brown, her eyes black, glittering with starlight. Her bone structure was finely chiselled and delicate, her limbs long and graceful. She was his height, a matched pair, but delicate like a bird. He was brawn and she brain. Her hair was braided into tight rows, with gold flashing in the weaves. She had been wearing long robes of fine pale linen, which had slipped and spilled away. Her skin colour was even throughout her entire length, and her tiny delicate feet had rings on several toes. Her ears had heavy drops of turquoise and gold, with a matching necklace of beaten gold shapes adorned with turquoise beads. Her eyes were lined with kohl and gold leaf. To Helene, she looked like an Egyptian queen, or a super model on a catwalk. Dreyfuss viewed her simply as *Goddess*.

She raised her left hand and used it to feed a morsel of food to the laughing male at her feet, mad drunk on her beauty and power. Her left hand was contained in a casement of leather straps woven around it, centred upon the middle finger, fastened to a gold ring. The straps wove back up her whole hand, and finished at the wrist in a woven band. As she moved her hand, the gold of the ring flashed in Helene's eyes, and she looked down, dazzled. When she looked back up, a third figure had appeared in the scene, ghostly and unseen, hidden in the far trees. He looked down at the pair, tears falling from his eyes. It was the old man from earlier, but he was younger here, middle aged. His hair and beard were black, edged with grey, and his eyes a brighter blue than they had been, flecked with the green notes of the sea. He wore leather armour, Roman, with a short leather skirt over a pale tunic. She realised this too was the armour that the human Dreyfuss has discarded. In his hands, the older man held a sword, held it so tightly his hand was bone white. Tears were still flooding down his face, staining the dusty armour as they fell. The breeze gently played the leaves, and the scents of summer played around them. Spiced scents of cinnamon and cardamom rose in the air as the breeze played over the couple.

The older man stood, silent, staring, his gaze was only for Eléan, she who gleamed like a polished gemstone. Tears coursed down his cheeks as he turned away and walked out of the scene. Oblivious, the human Dreyfuss was still playing the lover, whilst Eléan, who had lifted her elegant head and looked straight at where the older man had been, only smiled to herself, a secret smile of the cat that had got the cream, and returned to play with Dreyfuss. She leaned forward and whispered something into his ear. He smiled, and leaned forward and whispered...

'Eléan.'

The name crossed the millennia, and voiced in Helene's ear. One small word, to contain such longing, such loss, such pain. She reacted to his whispering the name, and turned away. The thrall was broken, and she returned to the bedroom and found the shaking quivering wreck of him, as he lay upon her, sobbing, broken.

So startling was the transition that she found the strength to roll her hips up and round, pushing him off her onto his side of the bed, before she'd caught herself in not reacting. He curled into a tight ball, shaking. Instinct warned her to get out of bed quickly, and leave him to it. She didn't trust any outbursts of emotion from him, and wanted to be far away from him. However, there could be danger in moving too fast, just as there could be danger in staying. His sobs were pitiful. She could hear them for what they were, without necessarily being touched by them. That he could cry real tears was somehow fitting.

May he cry them for a thousand years.

As soon as she thought it, she felt regret. The image of the vital young man who'd sat in the sun's shade, laughing, was superimposed on the hollow wreck of the crying, sobbing mad vampire in front of her. It was shocking, the waste and pain and... sorrow. Her hand reached over and touched his shoulder, gently. His left hand, his dark ring gleaming on the middle finger, reached up to hold hers. It was a soft and pathetic touch. Feeling awkward, she moved forward a bit, and patted his shoulder. He moved to anchor himself around her waist, sobbing continually. She found it loathsome, but could not reject him. Her hand stroked down his back, although she could not force herself to do more. He clung to her as if she were the rock, and his feelings the tide, crashing him to his doom. The problem was that he was so close, and she was so hungry... the feel of his heart beating against her, skin to her skin, the scent of his blood, rising in his distress. She groaned, and tried to push him away. He grabbed her tighter.

'Magnus, please... if you cannot let me feed, please let me go.'

He looked up at her, his eyes bloodshot, and she realised that blood had tinged his tears. He looked a thousand years old in his pain, and yet his skin was still so clear, so perfect. She could see a reflection of herself in his face, and she didn't like the vision that rested there. She was not, and never could be, a goddess, and this could only end very badly for her. She reached forward and touched his hair.

'Please, let me go from you, right now. All I want is...' she lifted up his right hand, and stroked his wrist across, sniffing the skin. '...your blood. You said it would harm me, to have more of you...?'

She put the right amount of pleading, of asking him for help in understanding, into her voice. He responded to the flattery.

'Yes, it would harm you now.' His voice was hoarse and shaky. 'Go, leave me alone for a little while. I will wash and dress.'

He moved back from her, releasing his grip on her body. She slipped away, working hard on putting one foot in front of the other. As she moved away from him, the Hunger woke up and roared through her.

She must eat, she had to eat, she had to have *something*.

CHAPTER THIRTY-TWO

Fighting the pain and the nausea, she staggered down the stairs, holding herself upright by any means. Stairwell, furniture, walls. She dragged herself into the kitchen, all thoughts but the Hunger driven from her bones. She stood in front of the egg basket. She would have to be careful... rummaging round the drawers, she found a chopstick. Picking up an egg, she poked through the shell, and sucked out the gross, disgusting and totally evil liquid it contained. She felt it burn all the way down and grasped hold of the unit edge to stop from falling when it slammed into her stomach. When the worst of the agony had passed, she carefully put the empty egg back onto the basket, and drew out the contents of two more. The pain was terrible... but the Hunger, the Hunger was knocked back. The roaring died, for a time. She was no longer being slashed by knives. She was no longer the mermaid, staggering upon the unfamiliar shore, pierced by blades of self-sacrifice.

As soon as she could force her body to move again, she went back upstairs and got into the shower in one of the guest suites. She would be clean of his stench. Part of her felt mean for thinking so badly of him after what she'd seen. It was a small part of her, and she ruthlessly pushed it down with all the other pains. Standing under the warm jets of water, she moved to the next part of her plan. The part she thought was going to hurt real bad, but it would have to be done. She opened her mouth, and let it fill up with the warm water. She then forced it down, into her, even though she knew how bad it would burn. Like acid, it fell into her stomach, and she once more fell to the floor. It was unbelievable how much pain that could be held in the human body, and yet it could still function. Air could still be drawn into lungs, the heart could keeping beating blood around the veins. How much more pain could be contained? How much more could anything hurt?

...killing someone would hurt more...

He entered at that moment, misconstruing her position, thinking she had collapsed from exhaustion. She let him lift her up and take her through to his bed, giving no sign of anything. Goodness knows what mood he'd decided to take with her. She'd just lie here, all passive, and see where he led her.

...that's a good way to end up back in the barn...

She pushed the thought aside. All this pushing she did, did this mean her mind was really strong? Could she compete in the Olympics for pushing thoughts, feelings, fears and reactions constantly away from her? He settled her down on the sheets, which still smelled of rape. His hand slowly traced down her left cheek, and she turned to look into his face, and see what she could see there. He looked sad, and lost, and in pain. The look on his face was so tender, so loving. A tear slowly moved down his cheek.

...he would win the Gold, I'd be stuck on Silver...

'You must drink, little one, you must.'

His wrist was so close to her face, her mouth, her nose. She could smell the blood pumping round inside him... the salty smell of...

...NONONONONONONONONONONONONONONONO!...

She pushed her head away, burying it in the duvet. He was using thrall on her again, to bring the Hunger back to life. She realised then where thrall came from, the power in the blood, the power to call to you, and seek out your most secret desires. Blood called to blood, always. She could taste blood on her tongue, feel it slide down inside her, feel it warm her body and her mind, uplifting her soul. She flew the nights on wings of blood. She was him again, this time his lips wrapped around a pulsating fountain of life. She bit down on the covers, and screamed.

'You cannot resist. It is not possible. You will have to drink... or die.'

He kept up the litany, ceaseless, gentle, murmurings and whispers.

...drink for me... drink for me... drink for me... you must drink, or die... drink for me...

There was not enough strength in the Universe to resist. Not with every cell in her body aching for blood, every nerve within her raw with need. He slowly, gently, pulled her under to his will with his voice. He kept bringing the Hunger *up... up...up...* by the power of his memory and thoughts, by the endless sensations in him, about taking blood. She slowly entered the dance with him.

What he was doing was so transparent, so obvious... by constantly talking about the blood, the taste of the blood, the need for the blood... he was hoping to wear her down. As the hunger rose up again, he was trying to slowly push her will away. The problem was... she could hear his lies. Every time he lied, no matter how much she'd been enjoying the sound of his voice, how soothing it had been, how she'd been thinking that yes, he was right, a little drink of blood would be nice... she'd hit, hard and fast, upon his lies. It all warred within her mind, as her body writhed in agony and her mouth felt it would split her open into fragments of bone and flesh.

The primal lie, that she'd only need to drink a little blood, was the heaviest. When he spoke those words, the lie's weight bent and buckled the air that held it. She knew, as she knew that breathing brought air into her lungs, that starting to drink... *anyone*... would result in that *anyone*'s death. It was too hard to think of it being Mary. She hated Mary. She loathed Mary. She had thought, many times, she would like to kill Mary. Now, faced with the reality that not only could she, but it was his plan... she couldn't bear to think of her name, her face, the smell of her fear. She knew he was going to kill her anyway, if he hadn't already. She knew that Mary was, to all intents and purposes... dead.

...so why did it matter...?

She didn't know why it mattered. She just knew that it did. She was not going to kill anyone. She was not going to drink anyone. She was not going to become... *him.*

So the battle wore on. Him, tearing into her with all the thoughts and feelings he could bring out of her with his thrall, the sweet seduction on his memories, his voice, driving into her, clawing out her need and longing, until it hung in the air, raw and bleeding. She, fighting both his assault, and her own hunger. Fighting hard to hold the thought of being human, of not eating humans, of not devouring their life. Fighting to not see that as glorious and deserved, after all, she was of a superior race... on and on, the whisperings into her soul. As hard as she fought, he matched, wearing her down, down, down. He'd had two thousand years to practice, and she was so very very hungry.

One rock held her fast, a truth, to grasp with her broken and torn hands, as the ocean of blood raged into her, trying to claw her into its never ending depths. No matter how hard, or how softly, he worried at her mind... his lies kept her anchored. How she couldn't trust one single thing he said. Particularly all that guff about how she was going to starve to death as nothing... *nothing* ... could be taken in by her body now she'd reached Transition.

Nothing.

...not even water...

Lies, all lies, he is all lies....

It was relentless, however; his strength and desperation, his access to her thoughts and feelings. He knew blood, intimately. Blood lust, blood strength, blood fire, blood power. Blood greed. He could devour all that blood could give him, he was a god of the greed that was blood life. He could eat her whole. On and on... the description, the discussion, the dissection... of blood, blood, blood. She tried to get away, physically crawl from the bed. He grasped her wrists, pushed his body upon her, and weighted her down. Whispering in her ear, her mind, endlessly.... *drink for me.* She could feel his own pulse beat of blood, impressed upon the length of her body, as she lay trapped under him.

...drink for me...

She had to walk away in her mind, and try and think of other things.

But there were no other things to think of, apart for the pain, the Hunger, *the need.* There was no refuge inside herself to be found. The rock slipped from her grasp. She was cast upon the waters, as the storm raged over her. She should be in this ocean of blood, swimming freely... *she should.* As she sobbed and shook, he lifted himself off her. She rose, tried to flee, but her limbs were not designed for land. She folded down onto the floor, crying and shaking and rocking. He was there, inside her, owning her, as he always had.

'Just one little sip, one small drink. The pain will go so quickly, so completely... you will be whole again, and I'll let her go... she will be safe. *All you have to do is drink a little...*'

...whisper... whisper...whisper...why was the whispering so much worse... how could he get inside her skull like that...

She tried to keep her head up, above the waves: why had she given up her tail, for useless, broken feet that pained on walking? Why? She was pulled under, submerged, again and again. She fought back up, one, twice, thrice... it was no good. She was lost. Through her tears, she found herself nodding.

'Yes ... yes... let's get it over with... yes.! Take me to her!'

Giving in made it easier, didn't it? The pain would go and she wouldn't mind the price?

She was becoming him, after all: there would be no more pain?

She was lifted up, and carried, light as air. Shouldn't she weigh more? The pain she carried, must weigh something. Shouldn't she be too heavy to carry? She floated in his arms, the world spinning around her, and there were dark flashes of green. This time it was the trees of the forest, as he took her outside and carried her down the path, to the cottages. In giving in, there was time to think, at least.

She was carried, bride like, over the doorway of the staff cottage. Mary was in the living room, all clean and fresh and quite calm. Some of the bruises had faded, and she even looked... well, not terrified. Her scent, however, her scent told another story. As Dreyfuss settled her down on the couch, beside the other woman, all Helene could think of was how easy it had been for him to read her, all that time ago. She could hear the heart beating so fast, smell the fear in her breath. Her senses, tuned to the hunt, could read the scents and sounds of a body, completely. Nothing was hidden.

All of this was pushed to one side, as the blood lust inside rose up, and reacted to the smell of fresh blood, human blood, flooding her pores.

Again, a nick had been made on Mary's neck, and blood was dripping out. Her body writhed with need. The last conscious act she had was locking Mary in her gaze, taking her mind in thrall as her mouth snaked forward to clamp on the wound.

At least she could make it enjoyable...

As the blood poured into her mouth, Helene's mind tore into Mary's.

... Angela... my name is Angela...

In her fear and terror, in knowing she had reached the moment of her death, all she wanted was... her name.

Angela.

In the second of hesitation that occurred, in the shock of that first active invasion of another's mind, Helene saw who Angela was. She saw the pain she had inflicted, the suffering she had meted out, and the death she had brought people. Death she had enjoyed. She deserved what was about to happen to her: her hands were stained with blood, innocent blood. *She had killed so many people!*

...my name is Angela... my Mum calls me her Angel... my name is Angela...

It was the sound that broke into her. The sound of Dreyfuss shrieking. The world had warped around her again, she had moved through space, and not noticed. She was standing back, upright, having retreated from Angela's neck, somehow.

Angela was still on the couch, still with that look of fear of dying on her face. Her own mouth was red and streaked with the woman's blood. It dribbled down onto her clothing. Her front was stained red with blood. She raised her hands and tried to brush it off. Her hands stained red with the blood. She looked at them, confused.

Dreyfuss grabbed her upper arms, a banshee of rage and impotence, screaming and shaking her. Midge had somehow disappeared. How much time had she lost? Helene looked at Dreyfuss, dazed. It was as if someone had used the mute button. She couldn't hear anything, wasn't touched by anything. His mouth moved, his eyes leaked tears, her ears said she was hearing some horrible noise... they rang with the assault...but there was nothing.

She stared, aware she was in a maelstrom, but not touched by it. Dreyfuss turned aside, and grabbed hold of Angela's wrist. He pulled her upright and his hand slashed across her throat. He caught her as the blood poured out, spurting upwards. He held her up as sacrifice to his goddess, his kali.

'Drink!'

The scent of blood pulled her into the centre of the storm. As the warm liquid hit her clothes, soaking into her, touching her skin, laying upon it a warm fire of loving touch... she locked gaze with Dreyfuss, all the need she ever had, and the hungers she had ever endured, crashed into her. The crimson tide rushing to the shore to swallow her. He was the tide, and he was dragging her into the undertow of his thrall. She tried to break free. He lifted Angela's body up higher, pushing the pulsating throat, slashed open by a scalpel, up to Helene's lips.

She could not break free. He had two thousand years of practice and discipline. The roaring increased as his images of a tide of blood crashed over her. She tried to resist, her temper flaring. The scent of the blood rose up between them, locked them in place within each other's minds.

'Drink for me... drink for me...'

She resisted again, and pushed back with all the defiance she had:

NO!

Lost in self-deception and ignorance, too arrogant to understand how much he'd given her of himself, how over extended his blocks had become... he surged onwards, using all that he had.

All that he had, based on fear and deception, power and cruelty, was little. She, based on warmth and heart and humanity, had much. He poured hatred and rage into her, trying to call out her beast. She rejected all he offered, looking past his anger, and his violence, to what lay deeper down: his pain. On touching it, it erupted, completely, gushing up through both of them. She broke gaze for a moment... shocked... *no one should ever be left in that much pain...* and she instinctively reached for him, in her mind.

He looked eager, relieved, that she was coming for him, to rescue him, and he reached his blooded hands out, once more, to catch hold of hers. The longing, the neediness, the lack of loving in his life, the vulnerability of his loneliness, reached up out of him, to meet her warmth and humanity. She reached back, for a heart's beat, wondering if it was possible...

...could he be healed..?

He felt her reach into him, into the void, searching. He needed her to drink so desperately, to end his loneliness. In the dark corridors of night, they stood, facing each other. The air shimmered between them, his hand moving up to touch her face. Tears welled up from his eyes, falling freely down his face. The pain within him writhed as a living creature, trapped in his flesh. There was a moment of acceptance, salvation, between them, a move to benediction. She made to take one step forward, her hand outstretched... as soon as she had done so, his eyes flared with greed. She would be his! His true self, his core self, his greed, rose up, pushing all else aside. The hand he had raised to touch, entreat, turned to a fist, to snatch and grab. Sorrow flooded through her. For a moment, a long moment of searching for Truth, she considered his ruin.

Should she...?   Could she...?   He was such a pitiful creature... perhaps...?

No! Her own true self spoke. She was not responsible for him... she would not have it! Her anger lit out to meet his greed: she was not a *possession!* She turned her back to him.

She pulled shut the connections between their minds, and cast him out, utterly. So close to what he'd wanted, desired, needed, all these long years... he saw her retreat from him at what he had thought was the moment of his own release. He'd seen the doors of his prison open, and for one moment, she'd looked to step into his cell, and comfort him. Now, she stood back, and swung shut the door once more. As ever, his own part in the dance, was completely overlooked, ignored; repressed.

He roared his defiance, his body instinctively reacting to his anger. He dropped Mary's body and swung his right hand up in a vicious back slap, slamming into Helene's right cheek from underneath. The back of her head slammed into the wall behind her, as his hands raised to encircle her throat. The scent of the blood on his hands lifted up through her senses, opening her Hunger up again. Her need for blood blossomed out, calling to him. He responded, trying once more to take her for his, with no thought other than control.

SHE WAS HIS!

The pain lost her a second's edge, and he pushed into her mind. Again, his brokenness could not hope to compete with her wholeness, and he was cast back into himself, like a stone dropping into a well. She was still pushing him back, when his control shattered; his mind fell open to hers. As his hands let loose her throat, and he fell to his knees, she walked straight into his most deeply protected memories, the memories that defined him. A desperate cry revealed he understood what was happening. He raised his arms to block her from his sight. It was too late. He had collapsed. The more he tried to defend himself, the more firmly she was rooted in his mind: witness to his darkest memories. She stared down at him, again seeing two visions of the world, one present, one past.

CHAPTER THIRTY-THREE

He was kneeling upright on a stone floor, naked. Around him, a sea of blood. Blood covered him, blood and gore. His hair was flattened to his scalp, by blood. Limbs were scattered in the blood, female limbs. Long hair, hair that could have been any colour, as it was coated in thick dark blood, was lost in the swirling patterns of blood. Bodies were in that gore: women he had killed. He was looking at his hands, the blood on his hands, and then looking around at the bodies scattered in pieces everywhere. He looked at the blood, and started to scream, terrible, piteous cries of horror. In his mind, he retreated from her, could not bear that she could see what he had done. As she watched, he turned and fled, slipping in the blood and gore, falling into it more, and he slithered over the smooth stones with its red lake of pain, and he whimpered as he curled into a ball, his hands hiding his head in shame. As he cowered down, she moved to him, instincts of care once more fired by the sight of a being in so much despair. His lifted his head up, and through the tears, his tears, his gaze sought hers, and locked her down again. Even as he was pleading for his soul, he tried to bend her to his will:

...drink for me...

He was sorrow. He was weak, and in pain, and needy. She had to drink. She had to end this loneliness, this agony. She had to give him hope, and care, and love. She had to take him out of this hell hole, and let him wash himself clean. Help me, please. Only you can help me... only you can end this torment. He raised his bloodied hands to her, begging for her aid.

.. drink for me... drink for me...

He was a lost soul, and she was love, and she must grant him release. As Angela's life blood flowed out of her, and cooled, pooling between their bodies, to flow onto the floor and drown her feet... evoking the blood and scents in his memories... Helene could see and feel, understand and smell, *know*, only one thing.

He needed her.

He. Needed. Her.

Not just anyone, or anything. Not Eléan, not some nameless mate to hold fast to him. *Her.* Helene. Something in her, was what he needed, to make himself whole. In that realisation, there was power. In the dreamscape, wind began to move around the stone room that held them both. In the cottage, the hairs on the back of her neck stood straight up. Both versions of Dreyfuss were weeping, sobbing, rent with fear and pain.

She *understood.*

Understood that she was stronger than he.

That he wanted her for her strength. He was the weak one, and *he needed her...*

Her mind closed down against him. Once more, she cast him out. He saw the moment of her rejection, and in both the room, and the dream space, his eyes closed. He collapsed inside, flinging her rejection away as he closed down. The dreamscape collapsed, and she was once more outside his mind, standing in the cottage. His blood was in her veins, however, and she could still sense his pain.

He collapsed down onto the body, sobbing. His physical body again kneeling upright, covered in blood, over the body of a mutilated female. Broken tearing sobs erupted from him. He had been so close, so near absolution... and now he was back, back with the despair, and the pain, and the betrayal. He moaned, and in the sound... she sensed his mind snapping.

Heard the surface cracking, insanity and inconsistency erupting up through the fissures.

Chaos was flooding in, driving out any pretence of order. The beast in him was being let slip. Her survival instincts snapped into place: to hell with the Hunger. Hunting could wait until she was sure she was not to be the Hunted.

...she had to get out of here, NOW!

She tried to take a step back, and found the wall pinned her. In the last throes of his sanity, he raised his face up to her, tears streaming down his face.

'Please, please my love...'

He raised his blood stained hands, begging her. She must do this, she must end his pain. She knew it was too late; he was lost so very long ago. She began to move to the side. His hand reached up for her, tried to grab her. The blood made him slippery, and she pulled free. He dropped over Mary's body, prone, crying and mewling. She could sense the final shreds of reason tearing... *she had to get out of here!*

She slipped as she moved aside, slipped on the blood. Her mouth, her nose, all her senses of taste and smell... wanted the blood: the Hunger blossomed up. She ordered it back, the chemicals and hormones of fear driving under the need. As she scrambled for her feet, she used the image of Dreyfuss, naked and alone, cowering in a torn tumble of limbs, to drive her on. The image of Dreyfuss, begging her to help him. The image of Dreyfuss, needful and alone.

She was stronger than he.

She made it to the door, as he crawled over the blood, again, reaching for her hand, begging for her aid. He was crying, softly. His hand rose up once more...

'...help me... help me... *you BITCH!'*

She stumbled out of the cottage.
She staggered up the path, chucking off the blood soaked pumps, stripping herself out of her clothing. She had to get rid of the blood, had to escape the blood... she was only so strong.
She entered the kitchen, naked, and stood by the sink, pouring cold water over herself. She had to get this blood away from her, before she gave in. The Hunger smashed into her.
She grabbed the basket of eggs, and ran up the stairs.

Wasn't adrenaline a wonderful thing?

In the shower stall, scrubbing the blood off her as fast as she could, she forced herself to swallow. Egg after egg, mouthful of water after mouthful of water. Every time her body threatened to eject what tasted and felt like poison, she thought of Dreyfuss, kneeling in the blood. The sound of Mungo's head hitting the wall. How it felt to hear Angela scream inside her mind.

She kept the liquids down.

Haste was not going to be her friend right now, something she schooled her mind to accept as the rolling agony in her stomach poured out to all her limbs, leaving her exhausted and spent, as she fought to keep moving.

Slow down, keep steady, don't push it too far.

She dressed clumsily in trousers and a top, pushing shoes onto her feet: everything was way too big and she needed a belt to keep the trousers up. She made her way up to the office via the spiral staircase in the bedroom.

The safe was in the attic space above the main bedroom, sunk into a chimney stack. It took moments to empty into a box she'd dumped books out of. She took the inner stairwell down to the dressing room, and hastily emptied what jewellery she could from her side of the room. She got a small suitcase out, and dumped everything in that, before piling in the purse she kept her documents in. She walked through to the opposite bedroom, which faced the front of the house, opened a window and threw the case down into the drive. She had to keep her hands free, she just had too. No idea why, but it felt important. The keys to the vehicles were kept in the kitchen, in a wall safe. It was never locked now, but it was where all the car keys were. Which way to go?

She took the quickest route, down the back stairs, and slipped into the kitchen as quietly as she could. Faced with the strips of hanging keys, she was frozen with indecision for the first time. Forcing herself to act, *now*, she took the Range Rover keys, just in case she needed to go off track. It made as little sense to her as throwing the case out the window, but she did it. As she checked her route out of the kitchen, she had a thought, and returned to take all the other keys off the hooks. She stuffed the keys she wanted in her trouser pocket, and then put all the others in the bin by the door. It wasn't exactly imaginative... but the intent was there. As she stood there, swaying, feeling dizzy and sick with both the Hunger and exhaustion, her hand automatically locked shut the kitchen door. Then she thought of all the horror films she'd ever seen, when locking the door meant to be locked in with the madman. Indecision caught her again. She wasn't sure how long she'd stood there looking at the door, but she flicked it back open.

...caught between the devil and the deep red sea...

She had to get out of the house, before her strength gave. She turned back to the main areas, to walk through to the main door. The house was in shadow. Had all the lights been off? She had no idea.

One step out of the kitchen, and the smell hit her. In her weakened, blood starved state, her senses heightened for the hunt, it was like a blow to the face. As if a slab of concrete had smashed into her nose. The chemical odour was burning, harsh, and tore into her lungs, as if to rip them from her chest. She bowled over, coughing and spluttering. The voice took charge again.

...get up... get out...NOW!

She had to get out of here. She would never withstand another throat being offered to her. Even if he didn't kill her... if he caught her now, with Midge, and offered him... she had to get away. She straightened back up and staggered through the Dining Room. The fumes were so powerful, it was as if she was moving through liquid. Should she go the other way, out the kitchen? That way took a long time, and whilst this terrible smell told her that he was in the house... Angela's body was back there. The blood was back there. She didn't trust herself, and moved on. As she staggered into the main hall, and reached for the door, hardness slammed into her head, and she fell into darkness.

She came too, coughing. Heat and smoke were all around her, and fire was lighting up her vision. She was seated, in one of the Dining Room chairs, in the middle of the Living Room. He was seated across from her, in another chair. His gaze was searching her face, desperate for her to wake up. Had he slapped her awake? Around them, was an ocean of fire. His face was illuminated by the flames, and it suited his madness well. As she looked at him, he tried once more to take her mind. She batted him away with barely a thought. She tried to stand, and found her hands were tied to the chair. He laughed.

'Don't worry my love, my darling *little one*, we shall be together, in a moment. Just you and I, for eternity. As I promised.'

She could see through his eyes, into his thoughts. *Cleansed.* That was the word emboldened there, *cleansed.* He was going to be cleansed by fire, and she with him. The pain would stop, the darkness would be lifted. Flames would heal him of his stain.

'We shall be together. Always.'

The drama was somewhat lost as he coughed and spluttered for breath. There was so little oxygen left in this room. She could feel her eyes drying in the heat, her lungs baking as she drew in the air. She pulled against the ties, nothing, it was futile. He tried again to catch her under thrall. Again, she batted him away, as she tried to think of something to do. He followed her thoughts.

'There is no escape, little one. There never has been.'

His smile was up there with Jack Nicholson at his best. For all the heat, her blood ran cold.

'You arrogant shit.'

She could have hoped for something more, but it was all she could think of. She stood up. As she thought, the chair went with her, bowing her over. He stood up, too, surprised. Without the slightest hesitation, she slammed her head forward into his stomach. All around her, glass shattered, as the windows and mirrors exploded from the heat. She hit him squarely, winding him, and he dropped back into his chair. She turned behind her, to the loudest of where the broken glass sounds had been, watching the trajectory of the flames as they flared with the increase in oxygen. They died back, were lessened, and there was darkness amongst the light on the far wall. With her hands holding onto the chair arms, she hunched over and ran, straight into the flames.
She felt the heat swell up around her, burning... *please God, please let me have got this right...* she turned sideways as the burning crosses became clearer, hitting the window frames with the chair as much as with anything else.

The jarring pain of impact was immense, but she carried on pushing... and fell out the window, down onto the drive. She hit a potted plant on the way down, and the chair smashed as she rolled sideways. Landing hard, she felt glass and gravel bite into her arms and face. Behind her, the furnace was sucked out in her wake, trying to claw her back. She lay winded, for a heart's beat, then crawled away, dragging broken bits of chair tied to her. After about ten feet, the heat receded slightly, although the pain from the landing and the drive way scouring her, broke through.

Coughing and spluttering, she smashed off the remains of the chair, leaving the ropes still tied to her. She turned round to look, still lying on the ground. Arden Coombe was lost. The blaze had broken through the roof, and as she watched, the central eye of the round window exploded outwards.

She stood up, and realised her right trouser leg was on fire. She'd not noticed. She beat out the flames, with no feeling of pain, in either the leg, or her hands. She had to get away, before she could feel what was happening to her....

She patted her pocket, and found the Range Rover keys were still there. She grabbed them, and moved across the front of the house, to the garages on the drive side. She fell over her own case, and landed heavily. She was unsure if the scream was hers, or his. Fearful he had launched out the gaping hole to follow her, she looked up. There was only a sheet of flames, devouring the entire front of the house. Adrenaline pushed her back to her feet, and common sense made her grab the handle of the case. She staggered, limping, to the garage doors. She only had one shoe on, and she kicked the other off, to make it easier to run. She beeped the electronic fob on the key ring, and the garage doors rose. For one awful moment, she realised she was stuffed if the Rover was parked behind anything else: why hadn't she thought to bring more than one set of keys? God was in his heaven, as the black Rover with the tinted windows was in the front row of vehicles.

His meticulous training came to the fore, and she was inside, with her case, and started up within moments. She drove out onto the drive as the left wing of the house exploded, rocking the car. Had it reached the kitchen and the ovens? The car stalled, and she swore as she made herself calm long enough to restart without flooding the engine. It turned over, once, twice, then caught. She revved the engine, dropped the clutch, and shot out down the drive. As she crested the rise and curved out of sight, she looked back in the mirror, and saw the flames shoot into the sky, the dark giving way to their spite.

She gunned down the drive, dangerously close to crashing. As she reached the main road through the forest, her training again took over, and she slowed and started to pay attention. What way should she go? Across the forest, in the Marlborough direction, red and blue flashing lights were bearing down on her. The fire brigade were arriving. She calmly turned the car East, and headed to Hungerford, and thence to London.

She pulled over before leaving the forest. She was a wreck, barely managing to stay awake. Her clothes were in tatters, blood splattered her arms and legs. A burn on her right leg was starting to fire into life. Her hair was burnt on one side of her face, and she looked like death, literally. A skull barely covered by parchment skin. She did what she could to make herself look more normal, which was little, and thanked the universe for the darkened window glass in the Rover. She had a full tank of petrol, and a great deal of cash in the case. Setting back off for the M4, the Hunger rose back up again, adding to the pain of everything else. She ignored it: she was good at ignoring things.

Dawn was breaking in the East as she turned onto the M4, and schooled herself to drive carefully, sedately, but not too slowly. A plan started to formulate, the only thing she could think to do.

She would find the others.

35

Lightning Source UK Ltd.
Milton Keynes UK
UKOW050608011011

179568UK00002B/34/P